Esther Verhoef was born in 1968 and gained recognition for her critically acclaimed action thrillers *Restless* and *Under Pressure*. She is also the author of *Close-Up*, which was shortlisted for the 2007 Golden Noose for best thriller of the year.

Alexander Smith was born in 1984 and graduated from Cambridge University in Modern and Medieval Languages in 2006. He has lived and worked in the Netherlands, Japan and South Korea.

Praise for *Rendezvous*

'This tense psychological thriller from Holland's answer to Nicci French utilises a classic trouble-in-paradise set-up . . . what makes *Rendezvous* so effective is the broader picture Verhoef paints of dislocated dreamers out of their depth, obliged to cede control over their lives'   *Guardian*

'*Rendezvous* is splendidly modern . . . Verhoef is terrific at building menace and brilliantly conveys Simone's growing desperation as she falls into the hands of the blackmailer'
Sunday Times

'Tales of idyllic years in Provence or some equivalent foreign Eden have become a publishing cliché. *Rendezvous* is an antidote to all those glorified memories . . . The plot is well signalled, so emotion rather than action drives the story, and it is the seeming reality of the personalities involved on which it stands'   *Literary Review*

Also by Esther Verhoef

Close-Up

RENDEZVOUS

Esther Verhoef

Translated from the Dutch by Alexander Smith

Quercus

First published in Great Britain in 2010 by Quercus
This paperback edition published in 2011 by

Quercus
21 Bloomsbury Square
London
WC1A 2NS

A CIP catalogue record for this book is available
from the British Library

ISBN 978 0 85738 134 7

10 9 8 7 6 5 4 3 2 1

Typeset by Ellipsis Books Limited, Glasgow
Printed and bound in Great Britain by Clays Ltd, St Ives plc

Welcome to the other side

Part I

I place my forearms on the steel toilet bowl. My stomach contracts and the pain this causes is indescribable. No respite ensues. Only more pain, briefly pushing the nausea and total desperation into the background.

My insides all feel raw, as if my body is one big biological alarm gone haywire. As if I'm dying.

I push myself away from the toilet and sit down on the bed. Vacantly I stare at the wall, institutional green-painted concrete, covered in illegible scratches and slogans. Carved cries, last messages, doodles, silent witnesses to people who came before me.

The nerves are racing through me. I gasp. Suck in air, but it's not enough. A panic attack. I've had them before, over the last few months. But never this extreme.

Don't hyperventilate, Simone, don't hyperventilate.

I fold my hands over my mouth and try to concentrate, to breathe as steadily as possible. Count, count to three. Breathe out. Breathe in. One, two, three. Breathe out. And again.

Banging on the door. It barely penetrates as far as my overstrained senses. The hatch opens. '*Madame?*'

'*J'arrive,*' I say, as was my custom over the past year, when the baker or the postman, or whoever, came to deliver something and I couldn't get to the door quickly enough. 'I'm coming.'

At the same time it strikes me how inappropriate my cry is. I still have just enough presence of mind to tuck a damp lock of hair behind my ear. My hands are shaking uncontrollably.

The door is unlocked and a policeman – dark hair, twenty-five or so – appears in the opening. He's chewing something. Hanging from his leather belt is a holster containing a pistol, handcuffs and a two-way radio.

He looks at me with an expression somewhere between disapproval and pleasure.

I stand up, still shivering with nausea. Keep myself on my feet by leaning against the wall with one hand.

The policeman enters. It's as if he's floating, as if he's not human, unreal, just like my role in this scene. A bad dream from which I can't wake up.

This can't be real, this would never happen to me. Not *me*.

I look up and read in his eyes what he sees. Not a mother of two, one-time school volunteer, owner of prestigious *chambres d'hôtes*. He sees a woman with tangled, greasy hair and a blotchy face, wearing a T-shirt that clings to her body. He can smell my panic.

4

I'd like to crawl away in shame. I've thrown my life away, I realise all of a sudden. Completely. It's all over. I'm thirty-four, I had everything, and I've thrown it all away. My life, Eric's and the children's. And for what?

Or rather: for who?

I

I have a thing about old buildings. Crumbling walls, collapsed roofs, skeletons of wood and stone, without windows and doors. They move me. Bare and naked, without pretensions.

As I walk around, the atmosphere washes over me. I feel like lying down, flat on my back, arms spread wide. Like a child making a butterfly in the warm summer sand. Breathe in. Drink in.

I don't.

Why do we never do what we really *want?*

The plaster on the outer walls was the same colour as the clouds resting, leaden and heavy, on the hilltops. The cement, swollen with damp and algae, was showing cracks. In some places the cement had been knocked away, exposing the underlying yellow-red fieldstone. Dark rectangles, blow-holes without glass or frames, marked where windows and doors had once been. Stems of wild ivy and morning glory wound themselves unobstructed from the outside in and back again.

I walked via the stone staircases to a hole in the façade,

through nettles and weeds that had taken root in the joints and came up to my shoulders in places. My pumps were wet through.

It was colder inside than out. The first thing that hit me was the smell of wet stone and rotting wood. There were wooden boards on the floor. The wall was covered with peeling olive-green paint and mouldy brown wallpaper that had come away here and there.

The large hall was dark, with a wide wooden staircase leading to a balustrade on the first floor. The house had clearly been grand. There had probably once been a chandelier hanging overhead, giving out a soft, sparkling light. With a little imagination I could hear, faintly, the voices of the people who'd lived here long ago. Piano music, the clink of glasses.

I shivered and wrapped my coat tighter around me, gripped the lapel with one hand and looked up. On the ridge, two storeys above me, there was a slate roof. Raindrops were slipping through the gaps. They fell over the edge of the roof and landed at my feet.

This wasn't how I remembered this house.

Perhaps I'd made it prettier in my mind since we'd seen it for the first – and last – time in May, almost four months ago, and bought it on impulse from an English estate agent.

CHARMING, STYLISH 18TH-CENTURY ENSEMBLE
FOR RENOVATION, SITUATED ON RIDGE. TOTAL

POSSIBLE LIVING AREA: 5,000 SQ FT. MAIN HOUSE
(APPROX 3,000 SQ FT) WITH ORIGINAL FEATURES
(FIREPLACE, OAK FLOORS), WINE CELLAR AND
TOWER. OWN SPRING, WELL AND VARIOUS
OUTBUILDINGS INCLUDING A PIGEON HOUSE,
GRANARY AND 600 SQ FT STONE HOUSE FOR
RENOVATION. 20 ACRES OF LAND ATTACHED,
INCLUDING 8 ACRES OF WOODLAND AND SMALL
FISHPOND, PANORAMIC VIEWS OVER HILLS.
SECLUDED LOCATION (NEAREST NEIGHBOURS 1/2
MILE), VERY PRIVATE, 20 MINUTES' DRIVE FROM
ALL AMENITIES AND FRIENDLY TOWN. ENSEMBLE
FULL OF POSSIBILITIES! VERY SUITABLE AS
RETREAT OR FOR CONVERSION TO GÎTES,
CHAMBRES D'HÔTES OR HOTEL.

In May the trees and fields had still been in bloom. White
pear blossoms, lush purple of wild lilac and fields full of
yellow rapeseed. The sun in a clear blue sky. Not a cloud
in sight. You could see, as far as the horizon, an ocean of
hilltops in all shades of soft purple and blue. Flocks of swallows swooped past the house and shot up again, in search
of insects or a place to nest. Crickets chirped in the grass.
The scent of herbs and flowers, sweet and overpowering,
carried by the gentle breeze and accompanied by the
croaking of frogs in the lower-lying lake, in the dale near
the woods.

Eric had opened a bottle of Bordeaux, which we finished to the last drop on the overgrown courtyard.

We behaved like people are supposed to behave in that kind of situation. We were drunk with joy, on a high. This was paradise, a place where fairy tales were born. And this spot was to become our new life.

'I know what you're thinking,' I heard Eric say beside me. He ran his fingers over the wall and rubbed his thumb over the greenish-brown substance that stuck to his fingertips. 'But it'll turn out OK, honestly. It'll be fantastic, Simone. Really great.'

I wasn't sure what to say. There were so many thoughts swirling in my head.

Without a word we walked through the hall. Our footsteps on the oak boards were drowned out by the rumbling of thunder in the distance. Eric went into the left wing. I stood there till he disappeared from sight.

Directly beneath the balustrade, to the right of the staircase, was a yellow-tiled room. There was an old, white kitchen unit below a water heater, and a jumble of lead pipes, oxidised white by the damp, had been fixed higgledy-piggledy to the mouldy brown walls. The tiled floor was covered with puddles of water. I sank to my knees and played with my fingers in the shallow liquid. Cold and slippery.

I tried to suppress one of the many thoughts that sprang to mind, but to no avail. I saw my mother standing beside me. Her unfathomable gaze focused on the mouldy walls, then on the holes in the roof, and the messy water pipes. With her high heels she meticulously avoided the puddles, gripping her skirt with one hand for fear that the delicate fabric would get stained by the countless sources of dirt in this house. She said nothing, my mother. Nothing at all. She never said anything when she disagreed with me. And that happened all too often. I listened to her holding her tongue and learned to interpret the various forms of silence.

I saw her standing beside me, totting up all the faults in this house, the answer written all over her face.

She liked her home comforts, my mother. Comforts she'd had to go without and wanted so badly for her only daughter. She hoisted me into dresses that made me feel awkward, and dragged me to tennis clubs and hockey pitches, where she expected to find important people with sons of my age. Quiet sulking, a silent disapproval, which grew in frequency and length as my adolescence progressed; long, silent days in my teenage years before my marriage to Eric, who was no doctor, prince or property investor, but a business-school student living in digs, with an old bike, an earring and a student loan. Only a year before we got married did she realise that I was doing exactly what she wanted me to do. Just in time. Just before she died.

My fingers were still splashing in the shallow water. 'You'd hate it, Mum,' I whispered. 'You wouldn't understand.'

Did I really understand it myself?

Eric was on his way to the kitchen. I could hear his footsteps on the floorboards in the hall and quickly stood up, stuffed my wet hands into the pockets of my trench coat.

I turned to face him.

'I'm wondering,' he said, 'if we wouldn't be better off asking Ellen to keep the children for another few weeks.'

Ellen was Eric's eldest sister. Our children were staying with her and her husband Ben this week, leaving our hands free to make the initial arrangements.

'Even in a few months' time this house still won't be habitable,' I heard myself answer. 'So there's no point in keeping them away any longer. Besides, the school year starts in only a week and a half . . . You know, I think they'll love it here. The long corridors, all those rooms, a scary cellar, the tower room and the lake with the frogs . . . To them, this is bound to look like a castle, an adventure. They can go exploring every day.'

'But then we'll have to sort out a caravan first. I don't think I've come across a single dry room here. The entire roof needs replacing.'

'We could stay in a hotel.'

'Do me a favour, Simone: it's going to take at least six months. I'll buy a caravan so big you won't even notice it's a caravan.'

2

Twenty feet long, eight feet wide. Cream-coloured with green stripes along the sides, forming a rising line at a slight angle beyond the last window. Inside, a U-shaped settee with a small table, a midget shower with marbled lino on the walls and floor. A chemical toilet with a broken lock, a sink, two gas rings and four berths. The satellite dish on a pole at the side was the finishing touch.

Hi-de-Hi!

It stood smirking at me from its smoke-coloured plastic windows. Ugly, right down to the chassis. It was laughing at me, with its fiddly taps and narrow beds. Roaring with delight, it stood on top of the crushed weeds, behind the main house. It was temporary, reason told me, and above all, I didn't want to *make a fuss*. Certainly not now that the sun was taking a break and the constant rain was trying to drum into me that the path we'd taken was long and completely unpaved, and that we'd need any kind of positive stimulus, however small, to get through this intact as a family.

Eric unrolled a long power cable and connected it to our temporary home. Electricity at last. A branch of the central overground cable network led to the remotest corner of our house, closest to the road, and disappeared into a mysterious-looking oblong grey plastic cabinet. When I flicked the light switches in the hall and in the kitchen, the light came on. Our house was insured and we had a phone line. On the road out the front, at the end of the four-hundred-yard long cart track that was our driveway, there was a letterbox bearing our name. And we'd arranged it all ourselves.

'It's raining,' said Eric, looking on in surprise, with his upturned face cocked to one side, as if it had only just dawned on him.

'Yes, it's raining. Again. Or still.'

Eric looked at his watch. 'What time did they say they'd be arriving exactly?'

'Between five and six, Ellen reckoned.'

'What time did they set off?'

'About eight.'

'You might as well add another two hours to that then.'

Ben was sixty, fifteen years older than my sister-in-law Ellen. He had worked his whole life with and among all kinds of machines. Ben had a quirk, one of many that characterised him: my brother-in-law didn't need to look at dials to know when a machine was working optimally. He had developed an ear for it. The optimal speed of Ben and

Ellen's Toyota was fifty-five miles per hour. Everywhere.

'That gives us time to go for a bite to eat in the village in a minute,' I heard Eric say. 'And have another ask around for workmen. There's no way I'm starting this by myself. That'd be hopeless. And I think some of the roof beams are rotten, by the way.'

I straightened up. 'Wouldn't we be better off bringing a team of workmen over from Holland? Those two Polish brothers might be available, the ones who put in the dormer window for Henk and Margo last year. They did a decent job. They might have—'

He shook his head. 'Not Poles. Things work differently here. Different measurements, different materials. Local workmen know what's available and what they need, so it just works out better that way. Besides, it fosters goodwill if you work with French people. If you bring foreigners over to do their job they're not going to be very happy about it. I was planning to build something, not demolish it.'

'Eric, you can't even see the house from the road; nobody comes here.' My voice betrayed my despair. 'It'll be winter in three months. I can't bear the thought of still being in that caravan by then.'

'Well, get used to the idea, because even if we work with ten men day and night it still won't be finished before February. I didn't expect the house to be so bad. The roof, the rafters, the beams, the floors, all the wiring, the pipes . . . It's very old, and it's been standing empty for thirty years now. You can't just do it up in a few months. Loosen up, darling. We'll see how it goes.'

'But,' I said, a little less forcefully, 'if you bring people over, then at least something will *happen*. We've been here a week now and all we have is a caravan, a satellite dish and electricity. I'm fully aware that it might take longer than we first thought, and I don't want to make a fuss, either, but if we could just make a start, then that'd be something at least. Even if they just did the roof for now, and installed windows in the right wing, and a front door, then at least we could move in . . . And unpack our stuff.'

I was referring to the white shipping container standing to the right of the driveway in the rain. The contents of our house were stored in it. I was slightly worried about mould in the Persian rugs and our winter clothes, and wondered whether the computer or the stereo was starting to rust. I didn't even dare check if the metal colossus really was waterproof.

Eric's expression left no doubt that this was non-negotiable as far as he was concerned. 'Simone, we've only been here a week. What do you expect?'

I rubbed my hands over my face. 'Sorry. It's the stress. I'm tired. So many new experiences, saying goodbye . . . It'll pass.'

Eric threw his arms around me. 'Can you hear the frogs?' he whispered. 'Look, there in the distance, that white steeple. Isn't this wonderful? What difference do the extra months make, in the grand scheme of things? This is a fantastic place, Simone. Have a little patience. It'll turn out all right, honestly.'

Over the past few days Eric had made frantic efforts to find a builder, or put together a team of workmen somehow. Because our house, our rural estate that was going to be converted into luxury *chambres d'hôtes*, was only the beginning. The renovation of this paradise in the making needed to become a breeding ground for talent that would stick with Eric's future business in the years to come. Eric wasn't here to enjoy the nature, the Bordeaux wines and the mild climate. He was here to build a holiday park. That was his goal in our paradise. The *chambres d'hôtes* were to be my area of responsibility, and back in May this had still seemed like a dream come true.

Despite Eric's enthusiasm and language skills, things weren't exactly going smoothly so far. We travelled hundreds of miles along windy asphalt lanes through the hills to isolated hamlets with unpronounceable names (where nobody ever went, apart from the residents themselves and the postman), in search of Monsieur Deneuville's nephew, who still lived with his mother and installed septic tanks. From there on to a friend of the mayor's son, who ran a firm of contractors from an old vineyard. Woods, fields, meadows, grassland with drenched Limousin cattle, yet more woods and piles of tree trunks. From hamlet to hamlet. To no avail.

'What do you think,' I heard Eric say, chuckling. 'Shall we let off a bit of steam? Christen that truly splendid caravan before lunch?'

'Don't you think that's happened already? About . . . a zillion times.'

'Shush. It can be the last time, for now. Once the kids are here the party's over.'

It had never occurred to me. Caravan. The children.

No more privacy.

Eric was sitting across from me at a table in the local restaurant. The bottle of rosé between us was almost empty already and the food had yet to arrive.

Eric's mobile lay beside a well-thumbed copy of last year's *Pages Jaunes* given to him by the waitress. He phoned six builders and handymen. Yes, they wanted work, but no, it was too late this year for a project on that scale. June next year was the earliest they could fit us in.

'Mistake number one,' I thought, aloud. 'We could have seen this coming; we should have sorted it out when we were still in Hol—'

'Nonsense. You know as well as I do that over in Holland you have absolutely no power over what happens here; it would have made no difference. And we simply didn't have time.' For a moment it seemed as if cracks were also starting to appear in Eric's armour of enthusiasm.

I was the first to admit that we hadn't exactly planned

our move very carefully. That there'd been no mention of an emigration plan. Or any plan at all. There was a reason for this, of course. There was a reason for everything.

We'd had just four months. And four months, it turned out, was simply not long enough to wrap things up properly and prepare thoroughly for what was the biggest step we'd ever taken. Not practically, let alone mentally.

Before we left for France Eric had been so busy winding up his current projects and training his successor that he rarely came home before ten o'clock. And in the last few months nearly all my time was taken up with packing. Unbelievable how many things you could accumulate in your life and above all how many you still turned out to need every day. I lost count of how often I'd tackled, yet again, the wall of neatly stacked boxes in the utility room with glassware and winter clothes, in search of the one Mickey Mouse cup that Isabelle insisted on taking on her school trip, or Bastian's jacket because it was surprisingly cold for the beginning of July. Subscriptions had to be cancelled, moving cards sent out, the mail redirection service set up. In between times there were emails and phone calls from Dutch and French estate agents and notaries, and viewings for our old house, which we managed to sell at the last minute, despite the stacks of boxes in all the rooms. Friends and acquaintances who wanted to say goodbye, and were constantly beating a path to our door unannounced because they realised we would soon be disappearing from their lives. Eric's brothers and his sister, their spouses and children, our parents, uncles and aunts, they all attended the surprise party organised by Miranda. Bastian's and Isabelle's teachers had held a French Day at school with a goodbye party afterwards. The pupils had secretly drawn pictures and written letters; Isabelle's teacher had pasted them into two separate scrapbooks with a copy of Bastian's and Isabelle's class photos on the cover.

The neighbours, the postman, the checkout girl at the local supermarket, even people we barely knew, literally everybody stopped me in the street. Only during our final weeks in Holland did I begin to realise how many people we were leaving behind; so many friends, family members and acquaintances we'd always been able to fall back on.

In our new life we were going to have to do everything by ourselves. We didn't know a single soul, not even super-ficially, within a five-hundred-mile radius of our new home. I'd tried not to dwell on it too much. It seemed best to focus on what lay ahead, our new life. Our *better* life.

In the period between the purchase and the actual move I hadn't even had time to think properly. Everything just went too fast. We'd done what was humanly possible, then left.

Eric poured the last drop of rosé into my glass. A skinny girl with a pale complexion and spiky hair brought our slices of smoked duck rimmed with fat, warm goat's cheese and crunchy lettuce.

I picked at it listlessly and looked outside. Rain. 'Welcome to the South of France,' I couldn't resist saying.

'There's a reason why it's so green here. In the Gers last year everything was yellow, remember? You found it so barren then.'

'Yes, I remember. But I hate rain. It can stop right now as far as I'm concerned.' I looked up to gauge Eric's reaction, but he was engrossed in the *Pages Jaunes* again, making notes on the back of a leaflet.

I pushed the last shred of duck on to my fork and ate it while looking outside, at the *boulangerie* across the road. An old woman with a poodle was leaving the baker's. A baguette was sticking out of her shopping bag. She shuffled across the pavement and the dog followed her on its stiff little legs.

'Lighten up, Simone.' Eric's voice interrupted my daydream. 'We're in *France*, for heaven's sake. *Laissez-faire*. Why do you have so little faith in me? Haven't I always been a good judge of things?'

I just nodded and finished off the last drop of rosé.

He was serious. Eric believed in this: I had to give him that. He wasn't chasing a dream; he truly believed in it.

And I completely went along with it. Why? I don't know. Friends called me brave for *daring* to take this step. Those were the words they used: guts, courage, daring. I didn't feel so heroic myself. In fact I'd barely given it a moment's thought. A rash decision made on the dizzying basis of a warm *maison*, served on a bed of grass and flowers, and washed down with half a bottle of good Bordeaux.

Considered? No. Brave? Anything but. I followed out of cowardice, perhaps even laziness. Marriage could be extremely practical for women like me.

Eric was the brains, a role he'd grown into. Besides, he had the gift of the gab. He spoke four languages fluently. Most of all he was loving. Sociable, friendly and optimistic. And those were by no means the only positive traits that applied to him. Eric had them by the dozen.

I couldn't remember ever contributing anything active to this relationship, anything essential, that came from me and made a difference. Stability perhaps. Monotony.

Eric deserved all the credit.

3

Isabelle's shoulder-length hair was tied in two limp pony-tails. Bastian needed a haircut. His dark hair was sticking out over his ears, I noticed now.

I'd expected them to cling to me, to be awed by our new house, perhaps, by the location and the space, but I'd misjudged them. Once released from their seatbelts, they dashed whooping through the corridors. Bastian made ghost sounds and Isabelle squeaked. They went completely bonkers.

'We're in France!' I heard Isabelle shouting. 'France, France, France!'

'Awesome.'

'This is my room.'

'No, it's mine!'

'Where's the pool?'

'We don't have one, dumbo. Daddy hasn't built it yet.'

Ben, my hero of a brother-in-law who looks like a retired concierge, stood scratching his balding crown and couldn't resist saying for the thirtieth time: 'Well, well, you'll have your work cut out here, Eric.' He turned to face me. 'And you too, Simone. You're brave! I wouldn't have touched it with a bargepole.'

Ellen was standing beside him. She looked exhausted. The journey had taken almost thirteen hours instead of ten, because Ben had taken the wrong exit back in Belgium and only owned up after another sixty miles. After that they'd found themselves in Paris itself rather than on the ring road, which had been partly closed off due to roadworks. The traffic in the city centre had been gridlocked. It had been a less than successful trip, in a word.

'It's lovely here, isn't it?' Ellen remarked. 'With all the nature and stuff. But it was so hard to find. All the roads look the same here. They don't put signs anywhere either.'

'Are you sure you don't want any more coffee?' I asked.

'Oh, no, Simone, really,' Ben answered. 'We'll leave you in peace. I saw a little hotel on the way here, near the town, and that's where we're heading now. We're driving home early tomorrow morning and I want to be properly refreshed behind the wheel.'

We walked with them to the courtyard. Light raindrops were falling around us on the weeds and beige gravel.

'But *what* a gorgeous house,' Ellen couldn't help saying, taking one more perfunctory look at the house. 'Really beautiful, with all the stone and that staircase, and things like that. And that tower, absolutely beautiful. We promise we'll come back next year when it's finished, but—'

'—You'll have your work cut out,' Ben chimed in.

I forced a smile.

Barely an hour after they'd arrived we were already waving goodbye to Ben and Ellen and their green Toyota, until they turned on to the cart track that led to the main road and disappeared from sight.

Dusk had fallen. The sky was turning orangey-red and the sound of chirping crickets was coming from all directions. Overwhelming.

Children's voices rang out from the house, squeaks of joy. Bastian and Isabelle came running outside, boisterous and full of energy.

'Come here,' I said, crouching down and hugging one child tightly on either side. 'Did you have a nice time with Uncle Ben and Aunty Ellen?'

'Yeah!' answered Bastian. 'We were allowed to choose what time we ate.'

'And what time we went to bed!'

'And what did you two eat?' I asked.

'Pancakes with jam, chips . . .'

'Chocolate!' Isabelle chimed in.

'Are you glad to be back with us?'

'Yes, of course,' said Bastian, suddenly serious. He looked at the house and I followed his gaze. The building, with its high tower on the right, formed an enormous, dark silhouette against the now purple sky.

The crickets seemed to have fallen silent for a moment.

'Is this where we're going to live, Mummy?' asked Isabelle timidly.

'Yes, darling. This is where we're going to live. This is our new house. Do you like it? It's like a castle, isn't it?'

Isabelle wasn't listening. 'Do we have to start speaking French now? Like *fleur* and stuff, and *so-leil*?'

'French is dumb,' said Bastian.

'Yes, sweetheart, we're going to speak French. But not at home: here we can carry on speaking Dutch, as usual. Daddy's also put up a satellite dish so you can watch Dutch TV. *Rugrats*, and *SpongeBob*.'

'When do we start school?'

'Thursday: five sleeps to go.'

'*That* soon?' cried Bastian.

'And at school don't they all speak . . . like we do?' asked Isabelle.

'They all speak French. The other children and the teacher too. But you'll pick it up in no time, and by Christmas you'll already be speaking better French than Mummy and Daddy. It won't take long at all, believe me.' I listened to myself speak. Wisdom gleaned from internet forums.

Isabelle reached for my hand and pressed herself against me.

I felt a lump in my throat.

'*Madame?*' says the policeman once more, as if he doubts whether I can really see him, really hear him speak.

I look into his eyes in confusion, in the hope of finding warmth, solidarity perhaps, or humanity at least. He stares back impassively. His private joke, or whatever it was, has completely vanished from his face. No sympathy, no warmth.

'I want to phone my husband,' I say. 'Please let me phone my husband.'

Eric must be worried sick. He saw me being taken away this morning. Cuffed, across the courtyard, flanked by two armed officers. As the police car juddered towards the path and I shot a desperate look at Eric, who remained behind alone in the courtyard, I saw the dismay break out on his face.

Thank goodness Isabelle and Bastian were still in bed.

'That's not possible,' he replies. 'You are not allowed any contact with the outside world for three days. These are the rules.'

I squeeze my eyes shut. Open them again. Try to stay calm.

'But my husband . . .'

'*Je suis désolé* – I'm sorry. There's nothing I can do.'

I have a brainwave: a lawyer. A confidant, who I can talk to and who's free to come and go. Someone I can ask to put Eric's mind at rest, let him know I love him, and the children.

I look up. 'I want a lawyer.' It sounds desperate, exactly how I feel.

The policeman shakes his head. 'Not until after the questioning, *madame*.'

4

I often gaze at the sky. By day, when aeroplanes crisscross overhead and the clouds race along. But preferably by night, when the countless specks of light twinkle above, out of range, out of reach. I imagine I'm one of them. Rise, embrace, absorb and disappear into millions of pieces. It's a pipe dream, a wish.

Everything disappoints if you set your hopes too high.

The one ray of hope was that the goodbye on the first day of school didn't degenerate into a crying fit from the children. They waved to me bravely as they entered the school where the grown-ups and children spoke a language they couldn't understand.

The absolute low point of the day was my own crying fit in the car on the way back home. I wasn't sure exactly why I was crying. Was I proud of them? Did I feel sorry for them? Or was it a combination of both?

During the first week of school I couldn't relax. I thought about them nearly every minute of the day. Isabelle and Bastian, in a strange class, with an unfamiliar teacher and children who regarded them as curiosities. They couldn't understand a word of what was being said, and were bound to be feeling anxious and insecure. That thought stuck in my mind, and I couldn't rest, not for a moment. I wanted to stay near the telephone in case the headmaster rang. But the call never came. Bastian and Isabelle were coping well. Bastian *had* said, when I tucked him in yesterday, that he missed his friends a lot and that he thought he'd never learn to speak like the children at school. They'd played football in the playground at breaktime, something that had never been allowed at his old school in Holland, and he saw this as a good thing. He'd also joined in with catching lizards, which abounded on the school walls.

It was scary how well Isabelle seemed to be dealing with the new situation. They had exactly the right sort of coloured pencils at school, she said, and worksheets that involved circling things. There was even a computer. And she understood more or less what the teacher wanted her to do. She just did what the other children did.

The school dinners were disgusting, they both agreed. Warm, pureed vegetables were very strange, like a kind of baby food, and the spaghetti was all stuck together, without ketchup. Mummy was a better cook than the one at school.

The main problem was the long French school day, from nine to half past four, with only Wednesday afternoon off.

Eric was now working on the house every day. I saw him messing around with cables and wood. He hadn't the faintest idea what to do with them. I'd done my best to give him ideas, give him a helping hand, even, but just like Eric I didn't have a clue how to measure up a window frame or how to replace the beams so high up near the ridge, running from one side of the house to the other. And neither of us dared go on to the roof to straighten out the tiles.

We couldn't do this on our own. We were doing our very best, but it just wasn't working.

I did what I could. I'd tried to brighten up the caravan a little, make it feel like home. We'd lugged the freezer and the fridge from the shipping container to the dry half of the kitchen on the ground floor. Eric had bought a four-ring gas burner with a metal lid, which was now on an old table we'd found in the basement. On the floor next to it was a green gas bottle with a pipe leading to the gas burner. Diagonally opposite was the washing machine, next to the drier. For water, which had a strong smell of chlorine here and was so rich in lime that the warning light on the coffee machine flashed every couple of days, I had to use the tap on the other side of the room. Here there was a deep sink the size of a hip bath, where I did the washing-up.

We rarely went into the bathroom, which was on the first floor. There was no hot water yet. The basement housed a boiler, but Eric didn't dare switch it on. A man he'd spoken to at the baker's this morning knew a serviceman who was a dab hand with central heating boilers. He said he'd send the man over to see whether our boiler was a ticking time bomb – as we suspected – or a serviceable appliance.

I was dying for a bath, or a shower at any rate. It was warm, the first week of September, and I felt sticky and sweaty.

And I was increasingly starting to wonder what I was doing here, whether I wasn't beginning to develop a masochistic streak.

5

The atmosphere in the house had changed. Yesterday Eric had bumped into a man in a big supermarket in town. A Belgian, Peter, who'd said goodbye to his homeland seven years ago and come to live in this area. Just like us he'd been drawn by the nature, the space, the affordable country houses and the climate, and just like us he'd run up against a wall of disinterest or overfull work schedules.

Peter had spotted the gap in the market and had been filling it for around five years now. Not without success, according to Eric. Peter employed forty people, whose sole occupation was doing up farms, country houses and castles for foreigners like us. Belgians, the odd German and an awful lot of British and Dutch who had a dream, but were all fingers and thumbs.

He now drove a nearly new Land Rover and lived in a wonderful place, so he said, twelve miles away, with his girlfriend.

Peter said he'd come over tomorrow. He reckoned he'd soon be in a position to free up a few people to make a start on our house, meaning that, whatever happened, it wouldn't be long before we could move in.

It was a nice feeling to know that something was going to happen, that our house would soon no longer be our problem alone, but a problem shared. I was looking forward to meeting this Peter.

Since the boiler still wasn't working we'd gone for a shower yesterday evening at a service station on the motorway. For a few euros you could stand beneath the hot spray for minutes on end.

It cheered us all up.

On our return the acquaintance of the customer Eric had met at the baker's had arrived. A blue Peugeot 407 was parked in front of the archway. After fiddling for an hour the man had got our boiler working. It didn't explode. The thing made a lot of noise. It rumbled, and there was an empty soup tin beside it to catch overflowing water. But we no longer had to go to the service station, at any rate. We could start showering in the old bathroom on the first floor.

Thanks to these strokes of luck, things were looking up.

I walked through the hall, then went outside and stretched. The September sun had broken through and was warming the damp land. Eric had mown the weeds in the courtyard and fresh blades of grass were seizing their chance here and there. I could hear nothing but the birds and the crickets. Otherwise it was quiet. Peaceful.

I walked towards the gateway, an arch of large, beige blocks of limestone at the entrance to the courtyard. Lizards were clinging to the rough surface, warming themselves in the sun with upturned heads. They darted into the cracks in the wall when I passed under the gateway.

The prettiest part of our house wasn't even the house itself. It was what they advertise in estate agents' brochures as *une vue panoramique*. There were more hilltops than I could count. They stretched out in front of me the moment I started walking from the courtyard towards the lake. Like hushed waves, one after the other, they made me feel like I was standing on the roof of the world. Somewhere in the distance a white church tower rose up out of the green. Even further away I could see the vague outlines of a castle. High above me large birds of prey were soaring through the sky.

I turned round to face the house. It looked more welcoming like this, in the sun. I tried to imagine how it might look if it had windows with bright blue shutters. Window boxes underneath, full of ivy geraniums in pink and red. The courtyard, not bumpy and covered with grass and weeds, like now, but flattened, with several levels and wide steps, beige gravel, varnished blue pots with flowers, and a fountain or watering place. A stone bench for guests to sit on, so they could look out over the hills and let their stress ebb away here in the tranquillity.

For the first time since May I was able to picture it again.

The house was starting to come alive.

6

It is said of the inhabitants of Corsica that when they want to make a path, they get a donkey to walk in front. The farmer saunters behind his pack animal with his hands in his pockets. The route the donkey takes becomes the path. No, more than that: has become the path. It's a rather uncomplimentary story, illustrating the alleged laziness and passivity of the Corsicans.

His name was Peter Vandamme, he was articulate, and at first glance he looked about forty, but much older on closer inspection. He had brown eyes, the same as Eric's, and light, curly, greying, close-cropped hair. An oval face with strong features. Peter peppered his monologues with French expressions, winked and gestured a lot, and gave the impression of being at ease wherever he went and pretty well settled into French life.

Peter was my ministering angel, the Hercules I'd been waiting for. Someone with an understanding of wood, bricks and mortar.

Our house turned out to be in fine condition.

'A charming house,' he kept saying. 'Really charming. It was a good buy. These kinds of houses are scarce and are getting scarcer all the time.'

He followed us through the house, scribbling all kinds of things on a folded-back notepad. A shopping list for the local builders' merchants and the sand supplier. Peter left Eric to order it all. He said he'd bring scaffolding himself and other tools to work with. And labourers: about six or seven men, he reckoned.

'We start Monday,' said Peter. 'We'll be working until eight o'clock. Between twelve and two is breaktime.' He turned to me. 'Can you cook?'

I stammered something in the affirmative.

'My lads are used to good food. I insist on it. Varied, healthy, with protein and especially carbohydrates. They work hard. They need it and they deserve it.'

For a moment I was lost for words. This had come as a surprise. I'd never fully transformed into Simone the domestic goddess; this was something I still aspired to, later, when I had all the time in the world. And a luxury kitchen.

I felt a slight panic coming on. Started counting. Eight hungry men, ten adults, including Eric and me. One four-ring gas burner, one table-top fridge and a freezer.

I had to stock up. Make a plan. Collect recipes.

In time for Monday.

'The house will be weathertight by the winter,' said Peter,

turning back to Eric. 'Two months, three, tops. Then you can move in.'

'What about the hotel part?' I heard Eric ask.

'That's the least of our worries. First we need to sort out the roof, the beams, floors, wiring and water pipes. The rest is plain sailing. The windows and the inside walls are nothing really.'

The way Peter spoke, it sounded so easy. Peter said things people wanted to hear, it struck me. This was probably his strength. And perhaps he was right, and it really was all so simple.

We waved goodbye as he drove off in his dark-green Land Rover. Eric was by my side, his hand on my shoulder. 'See,' he said. 'Didn't I say it would turn out all right? Weird, isn't it? Simply bumping into someone like that at the supermarket checkout.'

As Eric walked back to the house, I looked up. The sky was blue and cloudless. An aeroplane was crossing the airspace. I couldn't hear it, only see it. A silver, gleaming dot leaving a straight, white trail in its wake, which slowly broke up and dissolved into nothingness as the aeroplane progressed on its journey. I felt like lying down. On the ground, flat on my back in the grass. Simply staring at the white trail in the air, spreading my arms and making a butterfly in the weeds.

Instead I followed Eric.

In fact I did exactly what I'd been doing for the past

thirteen years. Taking the safe course mapped out for me by Eric.

Eric was my donkey.

7

Monday morning, half nine. I'd taken the children to school and was getting out of the car. Just beyond the gateway there were three white vans parked in the courtyard. They were covered with scratches and dents. The sliding doors were open at the side, revealing the contents: tools, rope and boxes of materials. There were people walking all over the place. They were wearing work clothes: T-shirts with advertising slogans, faded jeans and tracksuit bottoms full of holes. Leather belts were slung around their hips, with hammers, screwdrivers and tape measures attached. A radio was playing, doing its best to be heard above the noise and racket. Scaffolding was being erected, inside and out, almost level with the roof.

Peter was giving instructions. It made me feel good to see something actually being done, and the energy with which Peter directed his men, the speed with which they responded to his instructions, inspired confidence. I saw Eric consulting with Peter and pointing to the roof.

I decided there was nothing else I could do, and I could

make myself more useful by fetching fresh baguettes and salad. I got into the Volvo, checked whether I had my wallet with me and fastened my seatbelt.

As I was about to start the car I jumped at the sound of a loud knock. Eric. He was standing beside the car and had banged on the roof with his hand.

I opened the car window.

'Simone, this is not on.'

'What?'

'Sneaking off without introducing yourself.'

Sneaking off?

'I'm not sneaking off; I'm going food shopping.'

'Those lads were asking me just now where my wife was. I said I'd introduce you to them when you got back from the village. Out of the corner of my eye I saw you driving up and then leaving again straight away. Be sociable; introduce yourself like a normal person.'

I looked past Eric in the direction of the courtyard. A few men were watching us with curiosity.

'Oh. Sorry.'

I got out and followed Eric to the courtyard. The men approached us from all directions. They were a mixture of ages. The oldest had already started greying slightly; others were young, around twenty, twenty-five. They smiled amiably.

I shook their hands, introduced myself, feeling ridiculous because I kept saying the same thing over and over, and ill at ease as the only woman among so many men.

I worked my way down the line. A man with only three fingers on one hand, and a lined face, who was called Louis. A blond boy of around twenty with a pierced eyebrow and a tattoo on his right shoulder, Bruno. Antoine, about thirty-five, with dark, twinkling eyes and feminine features and mannerisms. Arnaud, who looked the oldest, balding, with greying hair, a moustache and callused hands. I'd never been very good at remembering names, it was going too fast and I just hoped I'd learn them by heart in due course. Pierre-Antoine was number five. He was very dark, with a deep tan and jet-black hair, like a Spaniard.

The last one was slightly taller than me and was wearing shabby tracksuit bottoms that had slipped down, revealing the top of his briefs. Flat stomach, taut young skin, broad shoulders. The moment I shook his hand and laid eyes on him, I was overwhelmed by a sultry look that seemed to pierce straight through me. Suddenly I became aware of his body, so close to mine, unabashed in all its manliness, stripped to the waist. He introduced himself as Michel.

There was silence, a vacuum.

One of the men broke the tension by laughing out loud and giving Michel a friendly poke. He let go of my hand and gave a quick-witted response I couldn't understand, which went down well with his friends. A few of them chuckled.

Peter came running up to me. Before I realised what was

happening he bent forward and kissed me on both cheeks. Squeezed my shoulder, then made a gesture that sent the men back to work. For a second he looked like an animal tamer in the circus; the men were at his beck and call. They were clearly a good team, Peter and his men. A close-knit group.

'These are your diners,' said Peter, smiling broadly, but with a pedantic undertone I couldn't help noticing. 'Simone, love, don't forget: everybody's on the lookout for workmen here and we tend to go and work where the food and atmosphere are best.'

I tried to smile and mumbled: 'Can you . . . I mean, is the food really so important?'

Peter gave a toothy grin. 'This is France, not Holland. People work hard, but they also enjoy life. An elaborate meal, making time for good conversation, that's not just a bonus, it's essential.' Peter nodded in the direction of his men. 'Don't forget to shake hands with them every day, in the morning, but also when they go home again in the evening. They set great store by courtesy here. Show an interest; give them decent food. They appreciate that. So do I, for that matter. Everybody does here. As a Dutch woman your nationality is already a disadvantage. Awkward, rude, tactless, loud, culturally and culinarily handicapped. If you can prove them wrong, you'll get along fine here. They'll be idolising you before the week is out.'

I gazed at him and it dawned on me that it was time for

me to say something. Something intelligent. Nothing sprang to mind.

Peter nodded once more in parting and went inside.

I looked around but couldn't see Eric anywhere. All I wanted to do now was get away, to the car.

As I was passing I saw Michel standing on the scaffolding. His body was naturally muscular and lightly tanned by the sun. A poster boy for male sexuality.

Extraordinarily beautiful.

He was looking straight at me. I nodded briefly, forced a smile and quickly walked on, in the hope that my inner thoughts hadn't surfaced all too visibly.

8

Humans learn in exactly the same way as animals. The basic principle is straightforward, very simple, in fact. Any action that makes you feel good is repeated, continued or even increased. It works the same the other way round: anything that makes you feel bad, you will avoid, stop, reduce.

There's no faulting my theoretical knowledge.

'Do you like it there?' Miranda had a husband with a pot belly, two children and a permanently tidy home.

I could hear her voice as if she was standing right next to me.

'It'll take some getting used to,' I said, stirring pasta in the pan, the receiver clamped between my ear and shoulder. 'We can't move into the house yet. But the area is really beautiful.'

'I have a piece of news for you,' she quickly interrupted. 'Hannah's decided to leave her husband. She's traded him in for a bloke with a sock shop. Els told me this morning, at school. She's left the kids with Fred and now he's got a problem, because he can't take time off work. Honestly, everybody's talking about it.'

I tried to lift a string of spaghetti out of the boiling water. It kept slipping off the fork.

'. . . and he came home at three o'clock in the morning. Well, you can imagine what she did then . . .'

Shouting in the background. It sounded urgent: Miranda's children, a boy of five and a girl of seven, were waging a mini-war. For a brief moment I could picture Miranda's living room. A house with a through lounge in a new-build development with immature trees, on a wide street with driveways left and right. Catalogue furniture, because you could pay in instalments. Children's drawings stuck to the fridge with magnets. A fresh bunch of flowers on the coffee table, a supermarket flyer with the week's special offers.

Not long ago my world looked more or less like that too.

From the kitchen, I looked through the hall and outside, where the sun was beating down and the workmen were walking back and forth, and realised how different my daily life had become, simply by moving to another country. Deafening hammering and drilling were coming from the left wing of the house. I could hear the radio blaring. French pop songs, soul ballads, rock. Someone was singing along at the top of his voice.

'. . . so then I told her to ring Tom, which she did. And guess what he said then? Be careful, he said . . .'

Success! I wound a string of spaghetti around the fork. Blew on the end and tasted it. Perfect. Just slightly softer than *al dente*.

'I have to go,' I said, interrupting Miranda's monologue. 'Speak to you soon.'

Cooking for a large group of people was a lot harder than I thought.

I drained the pasta in a colander in the oversized sink, added some coarse sea salt and gave the colander another shake to distribute the salt. A dish of salad – oak-leaf lettuce, lamb's lettuce, cherry tomatoes and sliced shallots, with a dressing of olive oil, vinegar and basil – was ready in the fridge. I slid the slippery strings of pasta into a couple of earthenware bowls and sprinkled them with olive oil. Then scattered a pound of fried, diced bacon, some chopped basil leaves and toasted pine nuts on top.

On the tabletop next to the gas burner there were baguettes I'd bought at the local bakery. I took a Port Salut, a Camembert and a pack of butter with sea salt out of the fridge, and put them on a separate tray.

Pasta, healthy salad, cheese and bread. It looked like a good spread. Hopefully it would pass muster.

The lads, as Eric had started calling them, had been at work for four days now and mountains had already been moved. Michel had been away for the past two days. Oddly enough I had mixed feelings about this. Disappointment and relief at the same time. His absence gave me room to breathe, as it had become painfully clear to me over the last few days that it would be a huge struggle to act naturally around him.

Michel always seemed to be looking straight at you. The implicit sensuality in his eyes, that beautiful head of his and the sculpted body which carried that head so proudly and effortlessly were getting under my skin. Thirteen years ago, before I married Eric, this would have been very pleasant and welcome, a field of tension inviting me to go deeper, explore. But now, in this situation, it was troubling. Too confrontational. So it was a good thing he was away today, and it would be better for everyone if he never showed up again.

I put the plates on to a tray, added some knives and forks and went outside.

The sun was blazing in the sky and the heat fell on me like a blanket. Just beyond the gateway, far from the war zone our house had become – a place where bricks could fall without warning and huge clouds of dust swirled round – Eric and Peter had put up a table. The lads had made it out of wood from the house, eight feet long and five feet wide. It was surrounded by our garden chairs, six teak folding chairs and simple stacking chairs in dark-green plastic.

I arranged the plates, laid the cutlery and went back to the kitchen to fetch the bread, the cheese and the glasses.

I was still struggling with the routine, or lack of one. When Peter told me last Monday that they needed good food, everything in me protested, but now that the house was coming along nicely and everyone was so friendly, I was taking increasing pleasure in spoiling them a little. Not for Peter, but for the good feeling it gave me; the lads had been very complimentary over the past few days. What's more, it was a good test for next year, when we would have guests.

As I was bringing the cheese, the bread and the glasses over to the dining table, the phone call with Miranda flashed through my mind. I'd hung up mid-sentence. Not on purpose, but nevertheless I was worried Miranda wouldn't ring again for a while.

Or perhaps, on the contrary, I wasn't worried at all; it was probably what I really wanted. Her not to ring me any more.

'What do you want to eat?' asks the policeman.

Eat. I can feel bile rising; it's creeping up my sore gullet and burning in my throat. I lift my chin and pull a pained face. All of a sudden I can't help yawning. I put my hands over my mouth and retch at the rancid smell that escapes from my mouth. Bile, gastric juice.

'I'm not hungry,' I say finally, and try to swallow. 'I really don't want anything. I just want to talk to my husband.'

The policeman carries on looking at me, unperturbed. He's seen it all before, that look tells me, the hundreds of detainees who came before me. And he knows that many more will follow. It will never end: an unbroken line of people who, sucked in by criminality, end up on this judicial scrapheap. In this cell, on this bed where I'm sitting now. Men, women, old and young, guilty and innocent, wailing and silent. Some of them have carved their grievances and thoughts into the wall of this cell. The shallow grooves whisper that I'm not unique. Even though I've always thought I was.

'You must decide for yourself,' he insists. 'You have a right to food.'

I look up at him. This is not sympathy. Not genuine concern for my health or eating habits. It's simply routine. This is his job; I am his work. Nothing more, nothing less. No, I'm not unique. I'm not even a person, but a defective cog in the machine, a faulty product.

'We will fetch it for you. You can choose from pizza, spaghetti, McDonald's . . . or any other takeaway meal. Whatever you want.'

I wave him away. 'No, *merci* . . . I . . . I really want to phone my husband.'

'*Je suis désolé, madame.*'

With a nod he leaves the cell and shuts the door behind him. I shudder at the grinding of the lock. I crawl up against the wall on the bed, pull my knees up and shut myself off.

9

Nine o'clock at night. I'd put the children to 'bed' in the caravan, but not before spending well over half an hour looking for Isabelle's Bunny (it was under the caravan, among the weeds) and having a good talk with Bastian; it had dawned on him that this adventure was permanent. He missed his old room, his PlayStation 2 – there was no room for it in the caravan – and his old school, where he didn't have to rack his brains over every remark he wanted to make. But more than anything he missed his friends, particularly the boy next door, who was the same age as him and hung out with him nearly every day.

There were no children to play with here.

Just a whole lot of space, and that, too, was becoming ever more restricted. Eric had declared the house off-limits because there was too much scaffolding, too many cables and too many tools lying around. It was, in short, too dangerous to let children of eight and five run around un-supervised.

I decided to take them to the small ruin near the lake

tomorrow after school, which I'd forbidden them from visiting on their own. I went there every day, usually in the morning for a while, after taking the children to school, and sometimes in the evening as well, when I'd put the children to bed and Eric was still busy preparing for the following day and had no time for anything but his notepad and calculator.

He was miles away. Unapproachable.

And that stung. Especially now. Because I was filled with doubts, about everything. Bastian's tears tonight had hit me hard. And the woman behind the counter at the Préfecture in town, who snapped at me this morning because I didn't have the right forms to transfer our car over to French number plates, had affected my mood more than I was willing to admit.

And strangely enough, I missed Michel. He'd been away for a week now.

This afternoon over lunch Peter had told me why Michel wasn't there: he needed him on another job, for a Dutch couple living on the other side of town. Peter had lost two men on that job who were now at home with back pains. Michel was strong, young, more resilient than the over-thirties. So Michel was now working for a pair of fellow countrymen I didn't know.

Somehow I was jealous of these people. And to be honest, I wanted to know all about it, down to the smallest details. But I pretended I wasn't interested. Too scared my interest would appear too obvious.

Eric failed to notice. He was so busy with the house, with the progress of the building work, the plans, the conversations with Peter – they were getting on like a house on fire – that I sometimes got the impression he'd only notice my absence the moment he sat down to lunch and his food wasn't shoved under his nose.

And perhaps it was no worse than usual, the fact that Eric had no idea what was going on in my life. Even in Holland I never went over my whole day with him when he came home from work. For the most part it wasn't worth talking about, and I simply kept certain things to myself. Eric knew part of my inner self. Not every part, just a small part. Only what he wanted to know and what I wanted to reveal. Not everything. That would make it harder for him to feel a connection with me, and that feeling is particularly important in a marriage.

That's why I'd never done anything about it.

But now I was prepared to have a deep conversation with him and really lay myself bare if it meant he'd put his arm round me for a moment. A reassuring word. A kiss. Or more. Attention. Love.

I walked round the outside of the house, then diagonally across the courtyard to the steps near the door. The house had changed inside. Apart from the stuff lying around all over the place (tools, crushed beer cans and empty water bottles, chunks of brick) it also smelled different from when we arrived here. Fresher. There was the smell of newly sawn wood.

I found Eric in the left wing. He was up a ladder, drawing vertical stripes on the wall with a thick pencil.

'Eric?'

'Hmm?'

'What are you doing?'

'I'm marking out where the roof beams are going to go, so Arnaud and Pierre-Antoine can get straight to work here tomorrow.'

'Don't you think it's time to call it a day? It's gone nine.'

Without looking up or round, Eric came down the ladder, shifted it and then climbed straight back up. He used a flexible ruler to measure the distance and marked something on the wall again.

'I want to get this done,' he said curtly.

'Will it take much longer?'

'Quarter of an hour or so . . . I also need to nip to the builders' merchants in a minute.'

The builders' merchants was on the outskirts of town and a twenty-minute drive from our house. I went there regularly to fetch things and it was always swarming with people, as if they were giving everything away. It was the cheapest builders' merchants for miles around, and the opening times were flexible: from seven in the morning till ten at night. Every day, except Sunday.

'At this hour? You're going into town at nine o'clock?'

He looked down in annoyance. 'Simone, what do you want? Do you want to be living in your house or still in that caravan next year? I have to keep the lads busy, otherwise they'll be standing around twiddling their thumbs tomorrow morning because we don't have any materials.'

'Can't you just spend an evening with me?'

'I *am* here.'

'I mean, *together* . . . I feel like opening a bottle of wine.'

'Go ahead. I'll be back about half ten, and then we'll finish it off together. OK?'

'It's dark already,' I said.

'I really need to do this, Simone. Work is going to have to come first for a while.'

Once night fell it cooled down very quickly outside. As a result, it would turn damp all of a sudden; everything you touched felt moist and slippery. What's more, I was rather ill at ease in the dark. The idea of sitting by the caravan, with only a few tea lights on the camping table and the total, all-encompassing darkness around me, wasn't particularly appealing. As soon as the sun had gone down I wanted to be inside, in the caravan. And I couldn't turn the light on in there, because that would wake the children.

'I just want to talk to you for a minute,' I persisted. 'Bastian was crying just now. He's missing Niels.'

'That's to be expected.' Eric shifted the ladder slightly once again. 'But that will fade when he makes friends here.'

'But that's precisely the point: he can't understand anyone, and the children at school don't understand him, so how on earth is he supposed to make friends?'

Eric drew another line. The tip of the pencil broke off and he took a knife from his belt to sharpen it. He was starting to look more and more like the workmen. A metamorphosis, considering he'd barely touched a tool of any kind before we arrived here. The skin on his hands had become rough and was full of little cuts.

'That'll happen once he can speak French,' he muttered. 'Another few months, and things will be looking up for him . . . It's difficult for us all at the moment, for you, for me and for the children too. Maybe you should run through those French lessons with him again, so he'll learn faster.'

The end of the wall was now in sight. Another two lines.

'I went to the Préfecture today,' I said to the back of Eric's head. 'They weren't exactly helpful there. I'd taken the papers I applied for from the DVLA, but they wouldn't accept them. They said I'd have to get hold of papers from the Volvo importer in France.'

'You've got no choice, then. The sooner that car gets French number plates, the sooner we can stop paying the road tax. Maybe you could give them a quick ring tomorrow.'

Eric came down the ladder. He put his arm round me and gave me a quick kiss on the cheek. 'Darling, I'm just nipping out. Open a bottle of wine ready for me and get some Camembert out of the fridge. I fancy a bit of that later as well . . . I'll be back in an hour and a half.'

'All right,' I heard myself say.

When I heard the Volvo drive off I went into the kitchen to get a bottle of wine and a Camembert. My hand hovered over the pack of cheese. I hesitated. There was no way I was going to sit outside for an hour and a half waiting for Eric. Besides, by the time he came home he'd probably already have forgotten his promise. He'd fall asleep the moment his head hit the pillow.

I closed the fridge door, turned out the light in the kitchen and went back to the caravan. Perhaps I'd be better off trying to get some sleep.

10

It would appear that in wild rabbit colonies there are periods when the scrotums of the established males shrivel up. And then sometimes, by chance, a strange male rabbit comes along. A young male, in the prime of life, who has yet to find a place of his own. Since the males in the colony are no longer reproducing, they don't even notice this new male. In this way a strange male can, at exactly the right moment, enter the colony unnoticed.

And reproduce.

It was still early in the morning. I'd taken the children to school, exchanged pleasantries with the mayor and a few people from the town hall I bumped into on my way back to the car, and then gone to the baker's for the regular daily order of four baguettes. At home I'd gathered up Isabelle and Bastian's dirty clothes in the caravan, beaten the dust out of Eric's T-shirts and trousers and put them all in the washing machine. And that was that. My new, exciting, stimulating life in the deep South of France.

There was little else to do until eleven o'clock. With

seventy-five degrees in October, glorious sunshine and beautiful white woolpacks in the sky, all I wanted to do was lie down somewhere in the grass, read a book, take a break and recharge my batteries.

The men were at work. A radio was blaring, the lads were singing along to a rap song at the top of their voices, but were drowned out by the decibels of hammering and sawing.

I took a book from the cupboard in the caravan and strolled down the hill, through the tall grass where a vague path was gradually taking shape, formed by my daily trip to our lake.

It lay behind the ruin, which had probably been holding out along the fringe of the wood for over two hundred years now. It had been a house, narrow and tall, with two storeys. You could still make this out if you looked carefully. Nothing remained but the walls, which had crumbled away partly on two sides. The windows and the doors, like the roof, had simply vanished. Disappeared into nothingness, swept away by time. Rotted away, or much more likely, reabsorbed by nature, by countless wood-eating insects. Isabelle and Bastian called this the 'witch's house', and I had to admit that if witches, fairies and elves existed, they'd probably want to live in this precise spot.

Further on I passed the remains of a *pigeonnier*. It had originally been a round tower with a peaked roof and entry holes, but all that was left now was a circle of large boulders, only slightly taller than my hips at its highest point, over-grown in places with climbers: ivy that wound its way round the stones, and a variety of light-green stems with purple, cup-shaped flowers sprouting from them.

The water was crystal clear. Small insects were hovering in tight groups over the still water surface, like grey, scattered little clouds, forever changing shape. A bumblebee came buzzing past. The crickets chirped nonstop.

I took a deep breath. The whole atmosphere was sweet this morning, thick and sweet with the countless wonderful scents, as though it was summer, or even spring, rather than the beginning of autumn.

The building work was audible even here, very faintly, and the sound was reassuring.

I couldn't help thinking about yesterday's conversation with Eric. I wondered what had happened, why he was so preoccupied with the house and couldn't or wouldn't under-stand that now especially, in this confusing new situation, I needed someone to support me. I was the one who took care of Isabelle and Bastian, made the trips to the Préfecture, built up social contacts in the village, cooked for the workmen. I had taken on the paperwork. I read the totally incomprehensible letters we received, written in compli-cated French, and answered them with the help of a dictionary. The family allowance, health insurance, phone bill, electricity, banking, mobile-phone contracts. I had a lot thrown at me, day after day, without anyone looking over my shoulder to check if I was making mistakes, or helping me avoid them.

And there wasn't a moment's rest. Not in the morning, when I got up at seven o'clock to dress the children, take them into the house and give them a wash and do their hair; not when I took them to school, four miles away, and met dozens of people there who already had a long-standing bond with each other, wondering all the while whose hand I should shake to avoid appearing rude and surly. And there was certainly no rest around noon, my rush hour, when I was expected to provide a full, nutritious, lovingly prepared meal for the workmen, lay the table, serve the food and for the next two hours take part in conversations conducted in such rapid French – presumably partly in dialect – that I could only catch the gist of them. After lunch I had to clear up and do the dishes, do the paperwork, make phone calls and sometimes fetch simple items Eric and Peter needed from the builders' merchants. The next task presented itself in the form of picking up and then entertaining the children: helping Bastian with his homework, teaching them both new words or taking them for walks, making sure they stayed away from the house. As soon as the workmen left at eight o'clock I could start making dinner and we ate together at the large table outside. Then I washed the children, put them to bed and laid out their clothes ready for the next day. After such a packed day I was simply worn out. I could keep my eyes open for another hour or so, but after that I fell straight asleep from exhaustion, despite the total lack of comfort in our caravan.

All this without exchanging a single word of consequence with Eric. There was barely a pause anywhere in that packed schedule, which loomed like a runaway train the moment I opened my eyes in the morning.

Except here. That single hour in the morning, and sometimes that half hour in the evening, which I needed so badly to recover. I claimed it for myself; I stole those moments, without a hint of guilt, because I knew that if I didn't, I'd burn out within a couple of weeks.

I couldn't concentrate on my book. I put it down beside me and lay flat on my back. Took a deep breath, spread my arms. Savoured the sweet scent of herbs and flowers around me. I gazed at the white trails of the aeroplanes high in the sky above me. At the birds of prey, circling silently at a lower altitude, at the clouds, in all shapes and sizes, forever forming new familiar figures.

People sometimes say that you quickly grow used to things, and there comes a time when you no longer notice certain nice or less nice things in your environment.

That wasn't true for me.

Day after day I continued to be amazed that I now lived here, hundreds of miles from 'home', and that this surprising, breathtaking nature all around me was *our* garden. Perhaps I'd get used to it eventually. That point was still a long way off.

I made a wide butterfly motion with my arms, just like I used to do on the beach, when I was still a child and such movements were still considered acceptable. I smiled and kept on smiling. Blissful, as I slowly swept my arms through the grass and felt the soft stalks tickling my skin. I closed my eyes.

Some people think that you can feel a person's presence. It's said to be detected by a sense, which has nothing to do with sight, hearing or smell. This completely immeasurable and still unknown sense signals the proximity of a person, and alerts you if someone is watching you. On the bus, when you're at home alone, and outside. Everywhere.

Scientists have studied this phenomenon and in their infinite wisdom they have come to the conclusion that it cannot be possible.

I opened my eyes. Raised myself a little, still in disbelief, doubting myself.

Michel was standing there watching me. His hands in the pockets of his worn-out tracksuit bottoms, with the top of his grey boxer shorts sticking out. No T-shirt, no shirt. Only skin. He appeared to have been standing there for a while and made no attempt to hide this. An amused smile slowly faded from his face. He devoured me with his eyes.

'It's beautiful here,' he said.

'Er . . . yes,' I answered.

Then he said something, very softly, that I couldn't quite make out. I *thought* he said: 'So are you. You're beautiful too.' But I wasn't sure and I didn't want to ask him to repeat it, because I was feeling awkward enough as it was, embarrassed that he'd seen me during a rather personal moment of relaxation, which even Eric didn't know that I had sometimes.

The next moment he turned round, without acknowledging me or saying another word, and walked back, up the hill, towards the house. Lithely, without the slightest visible effort. I kept following him with my eyes, until, a faint dot, he disappeared behind the hill.

Michel was back.

11

'Mummy, I'm hot.' Bastian looked at me unhappily, his cheeks turning slightly red.

Isabelle and Bastian had the day off from school: the teachers had gone on strike and were now protesting somewhere in town. The specific reason had escaped me: more time off, a pay rise, or both.

I'd given the children paper and felt-tips and was now drawing the fifth bunny rabbit for Isabelle and the third car for Bastian. Their colouring was becoming increasingly sloppy and I knew I couldn't keep them quiet for much longer. They wanted to go outside, do something; they were growing restless, but half the men were now on the roof and pieces of brick or roof tiles regularly fell to the ground without warning. It was too dangerous near the house. Perhaps I was better off taking Bastian and Isabelle into town to do some shopping.

I looked at my watch. Too late for that now. It was eleven o'clock, almost rush hour, meaning we wouldn't be able to get away until after lunch. For a moment I was overcome with a slight feeling of panic. How on earth was I going to manage to keep the children away from the house while also getting a full meal on the table?

'I want to go to the lake,' said Isabelle.

'Yes,' said Bastian. 'Swimming!'

'It's too cold for swimming now,' I answered.

'It's not cold at all!'

'No, but it isn't summer any more, and we can't swim today.'

Bastian scratched a green felt-tip over the drawing. 'When are we going to Holland again?'

'When the house is finished.'

Two pairs of eyes looked at me in shock. 'That'll be a hundred years!'

I smiled and tucked a lock of Isabelle's hair behind her ear. 'No, much sooner. I think we'll be going to Holland as early as Christmas. We can stay with Grandma and Granddad. That'll be nice, won't it?'

Bastian was silent for a moment. Isabelle kept looking straight at me. 'I really don't like it here, Mummy. I want to go back home.'

Her lament cut me up. I couldn't show it. To Eric this was one big, exciting French adventure; he was doing what he'd been dreaming about for years. My dream would come true eventually, when the house and the guest rooms were finished. But for Isabelle and Bastian this move was pure hell. I was fully aware of this, and at the same time I knew

I couldn't go along with it, because if I expressed my doubts, actually showed them the sympathy I felt so deeply, the floodgates would open. I had to stay positive in front of the children, regardless of what I felt personally. Or thought.

'This is our home, darling. This is where we live. And it's going to be really nice, believe me. You two will get your own rooms again soon, and a huge playroom. With its own television and a DVD player, and a bookcase full of books.'

'Mummy,' said Bastian all of a sudden, in a tone of reproach, 'you and Daddy said there'd be a swimming pool, and that we'd get a dog and that the sun would always be shining here . . . And it's not *like* that at all!'

This wasn't going to plan. 'Mummy's got to go and make lunch for everybody now, and then we're going into town. We'll pop into Gifi and you can choose a little present.'

Yes, presents . . . bribing your children. How low can you go, Simone?

'How much can it cost?' came Bastian's reply.

'Four euros.'

'Can you buy a car for that?'

'You can at Gifi, I think.'

'And an Action Man?'

'No, I don't think so. But a car will be OK.'

That satisfied him. For now.

'Would you two please stay here, in the caravan, while Mummy's cooking?'

'But it's *hot* in here!' said Isabelle.

I opened one of the small cantilever windows wider, and then another, so the air could circulate better. It wasn't particularly easy and I had to push quite hard, supporting myself with one knee on Isabelle's bed. That caravan and me, we were never going to get along. I couldn't understand all those people who spent their holidays in a caravan for fun.

'It's not hot any more.' I looked at them both sharply. 'Can I count on you to stay in the caravan?'

They nodded meekly, but I wasn't convinced.

'You really mustn't come over to the house. It's too dangerous there now – bricks could fall down.'

'Daddy and his friends are there too,' protested Bastian.

'They're big; you two are still small. You really have to promise me.'

'Can I have an Action Man then?'

I sighed. 'We'll see when we're in town.'

I left the caravan and walked around the house, not overly confident that they really would stay in the caravan. This wasn't going to work; this wasn't going to work at all. I couldn't split myself in two. Three, even: the telephone was ringing in the kitchen and no one was answering it. I decided to let the thing ring and ask Eric this evening if it would be possible to extend a cable to the caravan.

In the courtyard I almost bumped into the scaffolding. Bruno, the lad with the piercing, raised his hand. '*Bonjour*, Simone.'

'*Bonjour*, Bruno.'

By now I'd mastered the lads' names. I'd got to know them better during the conversations between twelve and two. I talked to Antoine mainly, who made the effort to speak slowly, and leave out the dialect and the confusing *verlan* (whereby words are said back-to-front, hugely popular among our workmen), and frequently corrected me so that I started growing ever more familiar with the language, learning more words at the same time.

I threw my head back. Arnaud and Pierre-Antoine were up on the roof. Behind them – I could catch only a glimpse of his tangled blond hair – was Eric. It looked very dangerous, at that height. The rest of the workmen were nowhere to be seen.

I went over to the kitchen and opened the freezer. Picked out a large bag of frozen broccoli florets. Shook three-quarters of the contents into a pan, added water, some butter and salt, and put the pan on the stove with the lid on. Today there was something on the menu that went against all forms of culinary delight: meatballs. I'd already rolled and fried them yesterday afternoon when I found out the children were going to be off school today, and they only needed heating up for a few minutes. As I turned round to put the meat next to the gas burner, Michel appeared in the doorway.

I almost dropped the dish.

Isabelle was sitting on his shoulders. She was gripping

his forehead with both hands, looking no less guilty than Bastian, who was standing there bashfully, his fingers caught in Michel's tracksuit bottoms.

Michel grinned. 'They were running around in the court-yard.'

He raised his hands, reached for Isabelle and put her down on the ground in front of him. From this movement I caught a whiff of the washing powder he used, or what-ever it was; it was a smell that suited him and had a devas-tating effect on my biological system.

I tried to ignore Michel after that and turned my atten-tion to the children. This was only partially successful.

Bastian was bracing himself for a confrontation; he went and stood protectively in front of his sister. 'It's too hot in the caravan, and Isabelle keeps scribbling on my drawing.'

'I don't! You keep scribbling on mine!'

'You started it!'

'Children, that's enough.' I took Bastian by the arm to calm him down. 'We all agreed: you were going to stay in the caravan and you didn't do that.'

Bastian wrenched himself away. 'We really don't want to stay inside; we want to go *swimming*!'

I looked up, on impulse, for support, and this turned out to be a bad idea. Michel was leaning against the doorpost, one hand on his upper arm, an amused grin on his face. 'Anything I can do?'

I looked at the children, then at Michel and back again. 'Er . . . no, thank you. I can handle this.'

The broccoli was boiling. I moved the lid slightly to one side to let the steam escape.

'Will you two at least stay in the kitchen?' I asked.

'We're bored, Mummy.'

I looked past Isabelle at the doorway. Michel had disappeared.

'I'm fully aware that you're bored, but I have to cook now. And you two can't start running around in here, because it's very dangerous. Shall I go and put the TV on? With a biscuit and something to drink?'

That worked.

I turned down the gas, got a packet of biscuits out of one of the cupboards, took Isabelle by the hand and walked back to the caravan, going out of my way to avoid the house. I left my children in the care of Nickelodeon and a packet of biscuits, and at this point I already knew I'd be giving them a present this afternoon to buy off my guilt. Supernanny would have stepped in here, stood her ground. I knew all this, in theory. But theory and practice are two different things.

A conversation started up over lunch but I didn't join in. It was going too fast; I could only follow a few words, just enough to know what they were talking about. The progress of the building work, of course, then something about

President Chirac, a united Europe or the lack of one, and famous people I didn't know.

Michel was looking at me. Small laughter lines appeared when he caught my eye. I did my very best to fake a polite, distant smile. The keener I was to give the impression there really was nothing going on, the less I seemed to succeed. Agony.

Mechanically I served myself some food. A little broccoli and some chips, no meat and no sauce. I found it all bland; everything tasted the same and I struggled to finish it. My mouth was dry as dust and my stomach had contracted.

Eric was deep in conversation with Peter, in Dutch now. They were discussing things I knew nothing about (the pros and cons of certain types of metal and couplings). I decided to focus on Isabelle and Bastian, but was aware of Michel's presence with every movement I made and every word I spoke.

'Hey, Simone, listen to what Peter's got to say.'

I turned my head towards Eric and Peter.

Peter ran his hand through his curly hair. 'We're ahead of schedule. If everything goes to plan, you'll be sleeping in the house in three weeks or so.'

This was good news. Correction: this was fantastic news.

'You still wouldn't think so at the moment,' he continued, 'but the roof will be done by the end of this week. Then we'll start putting the beams in. The floors will be another couple of days' work and then we can begin finishing off upstairs.'

'The surfaces,' Eric clarified. 'Wallpapering, painting, plastering.'

'We've just agreed to start by getting three bedrooms ready for you.'

'Provisionally,' Eric chimed in. 'We'll sleep in the left wing for the time being and carry on with the ground floor. Then we can take our time over it and make it *really* nice. And when that's done, we'll start on our living quarters.'

The right-hand side of the house, with the tower, was going to be our home. So far it had barely been touched. The work had been concentrated on the left wing and the roof.

'Great,' I said. 'So we won't have to spend this winter in the caravan?'

'We still need to sort something out in the way of heating. According to Peter it can drop well below freezing here in the winter, so heating is no luxury.'

The sun shone on the laid table, warmed my back and cast elongated shadows of the workmen over the plates and dishes. Winter seemed like something abstract, like something from another world.

'Well below freezing?' I asked.

'Last year it was,' said Peter. 'We were pretty busy with cracked water pipes then; a lot of people ran into trouble. It's never been so cold in all the time I've lived here.'

'So, darling,' Eric recapped, 'grin and bear it for another three weeks or so and we'll be sleeping in our own bed again.'

'Fantastic.' I looked round at the house. Scaffolding against the façade, rubble everywhere, wood, tools, odd items of clothing that had been taken off and thrown on the floor as the day wore on and the sun started shining brighter.

'And windows and doors?' I remarked.

'That's a day's work,' Peter answered. 'We've already ordered them to size. It's a matter of putting them in. You're lucky: the house is structurally sound. With older houses you never know what you're going to find, so I was cautious when it came to the planning, but it went without a hitch.'

I start out of my lethargic state. For a moment I can't remember where I am, until I see the wall opposite me. Green. With slogans, scratches. *Fuck the police* has been carved above the steel toilet bowl.

I must have dozed off. What time it is, I don't know. I had to hand over my watch, this morning, on arrival. A policewoman searched me. My watch, receipts left in my coat pocket, the house key and coins for parking were immediately put in a separate bag and labelled. I had to take off my shoes. The policewoman picked out the laces, put them with the rest of my possessions and handed back the laceless pumps. I had to sign a form. Another policeman stamped it. I'd half expected them to give me overalls. Orange, like you sometimes see in American films. But I'm still wearing my own clothes: a T-shirt from Esprit, a long, wide cotton skirt. And laceless pumps.

The footsteps are approaching. Somewhere deep inside it flickers in my consciousness: the questioning. They're coming to get me for the interview. I start breathing faster.

What should I say? Or should I, on the contrary, say nothing at all? Everything I think I know about these kinds of situations comes from American TV series: 'You have the right to remain silent. Anything you say can and will be used against you in a court of law.'

Did they say something like that this morning, when I was arrested, in French? I can't remember; only Eric's face, his dismay, has stuck in my mind.

His wife, a suspected murderer.

12

A year before her death my great-aunt confided her greatest wish to me. She wanted to rollerskate, like a child. Outside, on the pavement past the houses, pirouetting, on one foot.

She told me, only me.

She never did it.

Instead, she donned her walking shoes and took the dog for a walk.

'Simone?'

I left the washing-up from breakfast untouched and went outside.

Eric, Peter, Antoine and Michel were in the courtyard. It was warm: it must have been at least eighty degrees, even though it was October. The advantages of emigrating to the south were now gradually starting to unfold.

'Yes?'

'Are you really busy?'

'Not particularly.'

'Then would you drive to Biganos and fetch those

couplings and pipes for the central-heating boiler and the wood-burning stove? Peter rang Gérard Millechamps this morning and they said the stuff is in stock.'

'Biganos? Where's that?'

'South-west of Bordeaux,' answered Peter, as if that meant something to me. 'Towards the coast,' he added. 'It's very easy: it's on the A66, and if you head for Arcachon on the motorway near Bordeaux, you'll come across a sign for Biganos on the way.'

I'd never gone beyond the Bordeaux ring road, and then only with Eric behind the wheel.

'It's an hour and a half by car,' said Eric. 'Perhaps a bit longer. I would have liked to fetch them myself, but I'd really rather carry on with the beams this morning, then we can put the new ones in tomorrow and maybe make a start on the floors. If you fetch the couplings now, we can continue with that this afternoon. Michel has just offered to go with you to check the stuff; they seem to be pretty careless there.'

I stood rooted to the spot.

Michel avoided eye contact and shifted his weight from foot to foot. Finally I managed to stutter something out. 'Doesn't . . . Michel have to work as usual?'

'He's got trouble with his knee, so he's not much use to us anyway,' answered Peter.

Antoine and Peter walked away, towards one of the vans.

'You won't forget your chequebook?' said Eric, following

them. 'Michel knows where it is; he's been there before.'

'Eric?'

He turned on one foot. 'Yes?'

'Can't Michel go by himself? I can phone the company to find out how much it is, and write a cheque before he sets off.'

Eric came walking back. He leaned towards me. 'I can't guarantee there won't be problems with some of the stuff. Michel can check for that. And in that case the lad will be stuck there with a cheque for too much money.' He examined me for a second. 'Now don't be difficult, Simone. You just follow the road, according to Peter, nearly all motorway, really easy.'

Eric thought I was reluctant to drive. Any other objections now would attract attention.

I nodded in spite of myself and walked away, around the outside of the house to the caravan.

To Biganos, an hour and a half by car (or longer), with Michel by my side, to fetch couplings and pipes. Of course. Nothing wrong with that. In the seclusion of the caravan I ducked into the tiny shower stall and looked in the mirror, checked if my mascara was smudged under my eyes and if my hair looked OK. Then I brushed my rebellious hair obsessively and wondered if this personal grooming in the middle of the day could be misinterpreted. I glanced at the toothbrushes and decided an extra brushing could do no harm.

My heart was in my mouth. Of all the men walking

around here, did it have to be Michel of all people who came with me to Biga . . . What was it called again?

I took the chequebook out of the drawer, grabbed my bag and walked to the car.

Michel was already standing next to it. I wondered what he was thinking. He glanced at me for a fraction of a second, and I knew enough.

Gérard Millechamps s.a.r.l. was situated on an industrial estate just outside Biganos and consisted of white corrugated walls surrounded by a large fence. The gate was closed and the car park was empty.

I stopped the car just in front of the gate. Michel got out and went over to the intercom, then looked at a plastic sign hanging beside it. I could see from his demeanour that he was annoyed. He came back and got in. 'Closed.'

'*Closed?*'

He shrugged his shoulder. 'It's five past twelve. They're at lunch till half two.'

'Oh no . . .'

'If we hadn't hit traffic near Bordeaux, we'd have made it easily. Rotten luck.'

'Is there no one who could spare a minute to help us? I mean . . . can't you ring somebody, or something? They really can't manage that? We've driven for two hours.'

'No point: there's no one there. Forget it.'

What now? Go back home? That was nearly two hours'

drive. And then we'd have to come back again. Pointless.

'Let's have lunch,' I heard Michel say. 'I'm peckish.'

When the doubt showed on my face, he added: 'Keep driving, towards Arcachon.'

Instinctively I reached for my mobile and dialled our landline number to let Eric know we'd been delayed. I let the phone ring ten times, eleven, twelve. Nothing. There was no point ringing Eric's mobile. I'd seen it charging in the caravan shortly before I left.

'Are you ringing the house?'

I nodded.

'They'll never hear that telephone; they're working upstairs on the beams.'

I tried again. No answer.

I started the car. 'I'll try again later.'

We found an empty table under a blue and white awning in a restaurant called Le Pirate, with a view over the promenade, the beach and the water. The menu was a mishmash. Pizza, steamed mussels, pancakes, hamburgers, salad with exotic fruits and mozzarella.

It was pretty full for October, mainly with *Bordelais*, according to Michel, judging by our fellow diners' accents: people from Bordeaux for whom Arcachon on the Atlantic coast was the equivalent of Deauville for the Parisians.

Michel was likely to know: he was born and brought up in this area. I was eager to know more but he steered the conversation towards things that barely interested me in normal life (French dialects, which apparently didn't differ as greatly as the dialects in Holland: French people could understand each other all over the country), but now fascinated me no end because the information was coming from his lips. Michel had a beautiful voice. A rolled 'r', a deep 'a' that invariably ended in a sort of groan. He spoke in a rather throaty voice, and also rather slowly, and he searched for simple words because he knew I wouldn't be able to follow him otherwise. I lapped up his words, just like the house sangria that the waitress had put on our table as a welcome drink.

'This is how you recognise the Marseille accent: they lengthen each word at the end of a sentence. So when a word ends in an "f", you get "effe", for example.'

'I still don't know the language well enough to be able to hear the difference.'

'Once you know, you'll hear it too, believe me.'

'I'll listen out for it from now on.' I took another sip of my sangria and chewed on a small chunk of apple that accompanied the sip.

The nice thing about this situation was that I could look at Michel openly; when you talk to people it's normal for you to look at them, or focus on their face at least. What's more, there was no one we knew here. No one who could pick up on the interest we were showing in each other.

I couldn't find anything about him that didn't appeal to

me. He was beautiful, manly, comfortable in his skin; his muscles weren't from a gym, and he didn't flaunt them either. I didn't get the impression he was vain. You couldn't expect workmen to wear their best clothes on a job, but they often wore things they'd liked at one time, and this way you could still find out more about them from their work clothes. Hence, when Eric was working, his outer clothes consisted of two washed-out pink Lacoste polo shirts and a Gaastra sweater with a broken zip, marking the time when he'd taken up golf so he could also socialise with his clients.

Michel was wearing a faded black shirt and grey track-suit bottoms, not exactly couture. Nor had I ever been able to spot him in special designer clothes that highlighted his body. The fact that his washed-out clothing did this never-theless was unintentional, and probably due to my skewed perception.

'Where you live,' he said, 'they turn everything ending in "ai" into a long "e". So *je sais* – I know – becomes *je séé*, not *je sè*. Arnaud does that very clearly; he comes from Bergerac.'

'Does that interest you, language?' I asked, somehow truly amazed that this seemed to appeal to him.

He shrugged his shoulder apologetically. 'Not particu-larly, it's just the way it is.'

The conversation was interrupted by the waitress coming to take our order. After a quick glance at the menu Michel chose a hamburger and chips. I went for a salad because I was worried my stomach couldn't cope with anything heavy.

'You get on well with Bruno, don't you?' I asked, when the waitress went back inside.

'Bruno is like a brother to me. We live in the same house.'

'Do you live together?'

'No, he lives on the ground floor and I'm on the first floor. It's an old hospital where they rent out rooms. Since the university arrived in the town, loads of old buildings have been done up like that and converted into accommodation.'

'So are there a lot of students living in your house?'

He laughed. 'Students, the unemployed, drug addicts, illegal immigrants, all sorts of people. The upside is that when you need something, no matter what it is, you can always knock on someone's door.'

Our conversation sounded unnatural. Anyone giving us a casual glance might not have noticed, but there was an unconscious nervousness, a tension, as if neither of us was truly interested in what we were talking about, but we were both afraid a silence would reveal the underlying motives.

My gaze passed from his face to his chest, his shoulders, upper arms, hands, which were skilfully rolling a cigarette, and back again.

Our knees bumped into each other under the table every now and then, eliciting an apologetic smile from Michel and nervous giggling on my part – which annoyed me no end because I felt like I was losing control.

'Are you happy with the work you're doing?'

He shrugged his shoulder and cocked his head to light the roll-up. 'It's OK. It's hard work, especially in the summer when it's hot. Last year we had two weeks when it was over a hundred degrees; when you're on the scaffolding hacking into a wall in that heat, it's tough. Oh well. I have a job, food to eat, a roof over my head, a few good friends. It's a great team, and Peter and his wife are really great people, so I can't complain.'

I wondered if he'd still be doing this work in twenty years' time, like Arnaud. Michel struck me as too intelligent for that. But I knew nothing about the French school system and even if I asked him about his education, I wouldn't be able to understand the answer.

Two plates were served, along with a basket of warm, crusty bread and a bottle of water.

'Can I bring you another two sangrias?' asked the waitress, clearing away the empty glasses. Before I could protest Michel had already nodded and she'd disappeared again.

'I'm driving,' I whispered.

He looked at his watch. 'Not for another hour and a half. If you eat something now, it'll soon be out of your system.'

I picked at the salad and decided to eat it all. Leave nothing. I hadn't eaten much this morning. Wolfed down a prepackaged roll, a sort of cupcake, in fact, with jam in it. Two coffees, an orange juice, that was it. Alcohol made me affectionate, slightly uninhibited, and the combination of Michel and drink was therefore tantamount to looking for trouble.

Normally the salad would have tasted great, but right now it wasn't very appealing. It felt like my stomach had been squeezed shut, like all my taste buds were numb. It had been like that for a while now. In the evening, when the lads had gone home, I had no trouble eating and could even enjoy it. With Michel around it was simply impossible. My scales were still packed up in a box in the container, but I felt like I'd lost a few pounds.

Michel had stopped talking. There was no problem with his appetite. He tore one of the pieces of bread in two and handed me one of the halves.

It was a small gesture, but it was typical of the intimacy that had been growing over the last half hour. Which had probably always been there, from the moment we first laid eyes on each other, a 'click' that had occurred on a lower, unconscious level.

I pushed that thought aside. The sangria was going to my head. Perhaps I should drink some water now.

Michel poured a glass of water and put it next to my plate.

Now he could even read my mind.

Our conversation fell silent. Michel's plate was empty, and so was mine, apart from a few lettuce leaves and hard olives.

He looked at me. 'Coffee?'

'OK.'

The waitress at Le Pirate, a woman of around fifty, was a natural. She appeared right away and cleared the glasses and plates at high speed, except for the water glasses. No doubt she was used to working under pressure, in the summer season when it was teeming with tourists and day trippers here, and the customers had to be served quickly to make way for the next sitting.

She brought two espressos and the bill. I put my credit card on top of it. Michel got out his wallet (canvas with a Velcro fastening) and added three euros. The waitress came back with a pen and a receipt. I signed.

The minuscule cup of coffee was gone in three sips and I left the accompanying little chocolate untouched.

Then I drank the rest of my glass of water to wash away the strong taste and saw Michel doing the same.

Somewhere deep inside, hidden away deep down, on what might be described as an animal level, I could feel the reason why. And on a slightly higher level, the part that makes a human being human, the part that was now losing ground, I knew I'd now reached a point where I had to make a choice. And whichever I made, they both had their consequences, with unforeseeable implications.

Michel stood up. I pushed my chair back and when I got back on my feet I noticed I was light-headed.

Michel crossed the promenade and made his way to the beach. I ran after him.

Arcachon was situated in a cove, and in the distance I

could see a dark strip of land. The sun was still shining, but a strong breeze was cooling the air. To our right, on the side where the water from the Atlantic Ocean flowed into this bay, far away from the coast, dark clouds were gathering.

Almost at the water's edge, I stopped to take off my shoes and socks. The white sand chafed. I put my socks inside my shoes and held them by the laces in one hand. Michel did the same.

Keeping the sea to our left we strolled on, right beside the water, leaving prints in the damp sand, cool and crunching under my bare feet. I was still feeling light-headed.

We walked on in silence, completely unhurried, in the direction of a pier. It ran from the promenade over the beach into the sea, supported by large, white pillars. Boats had been moored on the pillars, probably pleasure boats, with lots of glass and big aft decks with seating. The wind blew under my hair and pulled it in all directions. I turned round, held my hair away from my face with my hand and forearm, and looked at the footprints we'd left behind in the sand. They meandered along the coastline and led further back than my eyes could see.

I tilted my head. An immense, angry bank of clouds, dark and heavy, was slowly creeping from the Atlantic Ocean towards the coast, forming an unearthly contrast with the sweet pastel shades of the promenade, the grand white balustrade that separated the beach from the road, and the exotic-looking trees with their glistening leaves rustling on their branches in the freshening wind. The atmosphere here was totally different from the one I'd left behind this morning.

Breathtaking.

I broke into a smile. Walking here was like being on holiday, a day out. No hammering, drilling, dust and bricks, washing-up and cooking, but fresh sea air, beautiful houses in pastel shades, a wide sandy beach.

And Michel, who was standing right behind me.

When his arms slipped around me and I felt his chest against my back, I forgot to breathe. My legs were literally trembling under me. My shoes fell in the sand. He kissed my neck and I shuddered. My skin contracted under his hands – those beautiful, strong hands of his, marked by the hard work – which slipped under my shirt, over my stomach. Cautious, fumbling touches, triggering tingles in all the cells of my body that converged in my abdomen.

I turned round and looked at him.

'You're beautiful,' he said, moved. Solemn almost, brushing back my hair. 'Really beautiful.'

I was speechless. It was surreal. Like in a dream, a film, I wasn't me, but someone else.

I forgot everything around me.

I ran my fingers through his hair, over his neck, his face. I wanted to touch him, all over, and I wanted much more besides. The moment our lips met, the first raindrops fell.

Fat, heavy drops, which cooled my skin. I tasted his tongue, quick and slippery. The time for thinking was over; I was glad it was over. I clung to him. All that remained was to feel, submit, live for the moment. Exist, and simply enjoy that gorgeous, young, strong male form pressed against me, and the electrically charged chain reaction that shot through my body.

My hands slipped under his T-shirt and felt the powerful muscles under his skin, the deep groove of his spine, the curve of his back. The raindrops fell around us; they surrounded us, soaked into our clothes. His hand slipped under my skirt, grabbed hold of my buttocks. He pressed his stomach against me. I gasped for breath and moaned, unabashed. My legs turned to jelly; they could barely support me.

We were startled by a flash of lightning, then an enormous bang, a deafening, crashing explosion which echoed and reverberated and tore the heavens open. The ground trembled and shook beneath our feet.

The shock made me let him go. I looked around in panic. The downpour was almost totally blocking my view of the promenade; the air around us was radiating fluorescent green. A subsequent flash of lightning illuminated the coastline eerily. The promenade was deserted; the restaurants had rolled up their awnings. We were the only people on the beach, the only people still outside. Where was everybody? The trees lining the promenade were like faint shadows, swaying to and fro, bending under the downpour.

Hastily we groped for our shoes and ran towards the promenade. The pavement was covered with a thin layer of water, with millions of raindrops crashing into it. We ran barefoot past the terraces, the restaurants, the gardens and the cafés to a narrow side street where the Volvo was parked.

As a new thunderbolt shook the south-west coast of France, I fell on to the driver's seat, trembling and panting, and shut the heavy door beside me. Shut out the world. Michel dived in next to me. The rain drummed on the roof, streamed across the windscreen. The windows steamed up straight away.

It took me several minutes to recover. I closed my eyes and gasped for breath. Threw my head back to get more air. Michel leaned towards me and pushed his hand under my skirt, between my legs. An electric shock shot through me. My pelvis rose up, instinctively. He buried his face in my neck, moaned, his hand rubbing over the thin cotton of my knickers, massaging, stroking. Our breathing was fast, hasty, shallow. He smelled fantastic, intoxicating; he moved flawlessly, his mouth tasted divine.

I ran my hand over his stomach. The shirt was soaking wet and clung to his stomach like a second skin. My hand slid further down. The slippery, drenched fabric of his tracksuit bottoms left little to the imagination. My God, I wanted him, I wanted him so badly. In response to my touch he withdrew his hand and pulled his trousers down a little.

There were people walking on the pavement, right by the car. I could see them out of the corner of my eye. It was a couple with a buggy; they were hurrying along. The man looked me in the eye for a second, straight through the layer of condensation that had spread over the windscreen. I turned my head away in embarrassment. My eye fell on one of Bastian's toy cars on the back seat, a red metal scale model of a Ferrari with a missing wheel. Michel's still bare feet crumpled a drawing Isabelle had brought home from school last week that I'd forgotten to take out of the car.

I pulled my hand away, recoiled.

'No,' I said, breathlessly. 'No, not . . .'

Michel wasn't convinced and pressed on. I couldn't trust myself any more; if he carried on with this I could give no more guarantees, I would let him have me right here in a parked car in the middle of a town. Not just any car: our *family car*. On the driver's seat, where Eric always sat, surrounded by Isabelle and Bastian's things.

My heart was thumping in my chest. This had to stop, this had to stop right now. I was seized by panic. I grasped his hand. 'No,' I panted, 'forget it, forget it.'

'What?' He looked at me in disbelief. His eyes were now as dark as the thunderstorm; he was breathing quickly and looked irresistible.

'No,' I said once more, more forcefully this time. I was still panting. 'Don't. I mean it. We can't do this. Stop.'

He looked me in the eye and when he realised I was serious, he sank back on to the seat beside me. Pulled his tracksuit bottoms up, laid his head against the headrest and looked dejectedly at the rain-spattered windscreen. He pressed the ball of his thumb against his crotch and grimaced.

'*Bon*,' I heard him say, more to himself than to me. 'OK.'

I straightened my skirt, which clung around my legs. Everything was soaking wet and I shivered.

Ten minutes later we were leaving a rainy Arcachon.

In less than half an hour we had the couplings, pipes and other things in the back of the car. I'd written a cheque – nine hundred euros – while Michel loaded up.

The staff had commented on our soaking wet clothing and my dripping hair. On the weather, the downpour. Perhaps we were radiating something, something intangible, which others couldn't fail to pick up on, for the teasing innuendos came thick and fast. I kept smiling amiably throughout and acting as if nothing was wrong, as if my world hadn't been totally and utterly turned upside down. After that we got back in the car and joined the main road, towards Bordeaux. Michel hadn't said a word since we'd driven away from Arcachon, which was fine by me.

I was startled out of my thoughts by a noise and a vibration. It took a moment for it to dawn on me that the vibration in my coat pocket was my mobile.

I took it out of my pocket. 'Hello?'

'Simone?'

My God, of all the people who could ring me, it was the voice of my conscience.

Could he have *felt* something? Was that possible? Could people far away feel there was something wrong?

'Er . . . yes.' I glanced nervously at my watch. It was almost half three.

'Where are you?'

'We're on our way home. When we got there the place was closed, would you believe. And it didn't open again until half two, so we . . .' I looked at Michel in panic. He was rolling a cigarette, giving me a questioning look. '. . . had lunch while we were there.'

God, this feels bad.

Awful.

'Couldn't you have let me know?'

'I . . . I called you, but you didn't answer.'

'When was that?'

'Er . . . straight away. Just after twelve . . .'

'Where are you now?'

I looked around. Eventually asked Michel, because I had no clue whereabouts we were.

'Just past Bordeaux,' Michel answered.

'Near Bordeaux,' I copied.

'In that case you'll be another hour at least. I trust you'll be too late to pick up the children?'

That was a rhetorical question. School finished at half four. There was no chance I could reach the school in less than an hour.

'Can you borrow one of the lads' cars and pick up the children?' I asked.

The irritation grew in Eric's voice. 'OK. We can't go any further here without those couplings anyway.' I could almost hear him thinking on the other end of the line. Drilling and hammering in the background. 'Oh well, there are enough other things to be doing, so we'll get going with that tomorrow. Are you driving carefully?'

'Yes, no problem.'

'See you soon.'

Eric rang off.

I clasped the phone tightly in my hand, on my lap, and stared ahead.

'Was that Eric?' asked Michel.

I nodded.

It didn't seem to bother Michel one bit.

I started shivering. Suddenly I felt cold. The whole situation was now dawning on me, only now. Not only that: the panic was hitting home with full force. The thick cotton of my coat was soaked through with rainwater. My coat, my skirt, T-shirt, socks, everything was drenched. All I wanted to do now was get dry as soon as possible, cover all the tracks. All the tracks of what I'd done earlier today, allowed to happen. I couldn't let Eric see me, nor Isabelle, nor Bastian, *anybody*, with clothing that was still even slightly damp from the rain.

'We have to dry our clothes,' I said. 'We can't go back like this.'

'Why not?'

'*Why not?* How can you explain this?' I raised my arm by way of demonstration. The cotton stuck to my skin. 'We're wet through. You don't get this wet dashing from a restaurant to the car.'

That can only result from an intimate encounter on a deserted beach, in the pouring rain, and then only because in your intoxicated state you didn't even realise it was raining; that's the only way you can get so wet. Eric will see it; everyone will see it; they'll look at you, at your clothes, your wet hair, smell the sea air, on you, on Michel, and they'll know. The images that have lodged themselves in your brain will be played out like a film, clear and plain to see, to anyone who looks at you.

He shrugged his shoulder. A gesture that suited him so well: everyone else shrugged with both shoulders, he only one.

'We'll be dry by the time we get home.'

'No,' I said, sharply. 'I don't want to risk that. Suppose that's not the case? What then?'

As he lit his cigarette I heard him mumble: 'We could always stop off in Libourne. I know someone who lives there. She has a dryer.'

The idea of visiting a woman with a tumble-dryer,

together with Michel, soaked to the bone, having to apologise to someone I didn't know from Adam, having to undress in a strange house and wait until this woman had dried my clothes in her dryer, struck me as surreal.

The last few hours all struck me as surreal.

I brushed back my wet hair. 'Libourne, OK. Fine,' I heard myself say. 'Libourne is fine.'

The woman Michel knew was called Jeanette. She was the same age as me or slightly older, perhaps. A warm, friendly face, with thick, dark-brown, curly hair tucked under a wide headband. Jeanette had a lovely, voluptuous figure with swinging hips; she had a gypsy-like air. She was clearly a chain smoker. And perhaps a drinker as well. Underneath the coffee table there were three empty wine bottles. Her house opened directly on to the narrow pavement. Every lorry that passed by caused a vibration, making the cups on the coffee table dance.

Jeanette clearly had a hard life.

She acted as if it was the most normal thing in the world, as if she often found a drenched Michel on her doorstep with a strange woman, wanting to use her tumble-dryer.

My God, how relieved I felt, as I sat on her sofa drinking tea in an oversized housecoat and a pair of pink slippers.

I wondered how they knew each other. It was hard to tell.

Michel sat beside me, playing with Jeanette's dog. A young animal, lanky and mischievous; a husky-like appearance with one blue and one brown eye.

Jeanette liked the dog considerably less than Michel did. I listened to her complaining about the animal, which had far too much energy in her opinion. She'd made the wrong choice; she should have bought a *caniche*, a poodle, but this dog had sat there as a puppy, looking at her so sweetly from the pet-shop window, she'd been unable to resist.

'I'm always like that,' she said, smiling apologetically. 'Soft. I can't say no.' She stubbed out a butt in the ashtray and grabbed a packet of cigarettes from between a plant and a couple of photos of cats.

Bleu lay stretched out on his back on Michel's lap, with his hind legs sticking out, then rolled over, crawled up to his neck, placed two paws on his shoulders and started enthusiastically licking his face. His thick, grey tail was wagging excitedly.

'I wish I knew somebody who wanted him,' I heard Jeanette say. 'Because I don't want to take him to the shelter. They might put him to sleep. And he's a sweet animal. It's just that energy, you know? He doesn't belong in a town. He should go to someone who lives *à la campagne*, where he'll have space to run around. That'd be ideal.'

Michel looked at me. 'You hear that?'

I nodded.

★

The motorway sloped along with the valley where we were driving. Acre after acre of vineyards, as far as the eye could see. On the odd hilltop you could see a castle, or a country house. The rain had stopped, but the sky was overcast.

Bleu was whining on the back seat. He clearly wasn't used to travelling in cars. The whining became a soft howl.

'Maybe he needs to pee,' said Michel. His voice sounded tense.

There was a car park a short distance away. I drove to the middle and switched off the engine.

Michel got out. He opened the back door, called Bleu and walked a few yards across the grass, in the direction of a wood. I saw him talking to the dog. Bleu pricked up his ears, looked up at him, his head cocked, full of trust, his tongue sticking out. His tail, an almost closed ring of spiky hair, was swishing cheerfully to and fro over his back.

In the distance there was a car with a caravan at the rear. I could see a woman bent over the back seat of the car, occupied with her child. She passed a small white packet over her shoulder to her husband, who took it to a rubbish bin.

Michel and Bleu looked like they were having a great time. The dog was jumping up at him, challenging him; Michel was playing around with him and making feints. A warm feeling welled up inside me. As I watched the two of them I couldn't escape the terrifying realisation that what I was feeling wasn't just physical attraction. Not just lust.

It was more than that.

We drove for mile after mile, in a silence that was unbearable, painful, but I had no idea what to say. The suggestions that sprang to mind struck me as too emotionally charged, or simply very wrong. We had a language barrier that only made things harder because I didn't know whether he'd understand what I wanted to say. And I was becoming increasingly aware that I was the one who'd engineered this situation, or at least allowed it to happen, as if I was footloose and fancy-free.

'You need to turn off here,' said Michel.

I steered the Volvo behind a big lorry and indicated right. Almost five minutes later we were driving along the road leading to our driveway.

Almost home.

My stomach contracted.

'I want to see you again,' said Michel all of a sudden.

I shook my head. 'As long as you're working for us you'll see me every day.'

'You know what I mean.'

Another five hundred yards.

On impulse I parked the car on the verge, turned the ignition key and started talking, without looking at him. 'I have children, Michel. I love them a lot. I'm married.

What happened this afternoon, that . . .'

He leaned over to me, faster than I could react, placed his hand on my neck, behind my head, and kissed me full on the lips.

'I want to see you again,' he repeated, letting go.

I closed my eyes for a moment and waited until I'd calmed down a little before starting the engine.

13

The composition and cultivation of the outer person require constant maintenance, essential in avoiding social rejection.

Artistic expression, such as literature, is supposed to satisfy the hunger of the inner person, but after reading it becomes clear that there is no second, identical inner person: which strengthens me in my belief that every person is alone in the depths of his or her being and that the semblance that this isn't the case is based on a culti-vated veneer and superficial character traits.

Pigeonholes and categories, index cards, distinguishing features. Skin colour, sex, hairstyle, job, children, age, musical taste, class, faith – not in that order.

Which would mean that almost all types of relationship are based on appearances. Sad, but maybe a lot safer that way.

Reassuring.

Guilt.

Terrible guilt.

Eric had no idea.

I'd been away from home for seven, eight hours, and it seemed more like seven months.

Michel went straight over to Peter and then disappeared somewhere in the left wing of the house. Peter and Bruno unloaded the things from the car and sorted them. After a short pause the work carried on as before.

Isabelle and Bastian welcomed Bleu so enthusiastically they almost squeezed him to death. Isabelle pressed her little face in his thick, soft fur and beamed. Bastian called him 'gangsta'.

Eric had frowned. I'd explained it as follows: in Arcachon we'd bumped into one of Michel's friends who was with Bleu, and I'd fallen in love with the animal there and then. I left the rest of the story unchanged, although I did embellish it slightly.

'What could I do?' I'd said. 'She was about to take him to the shelter. They might have put him to sleep there.'

'I don't think it's a good idea,' came Eric's reply, with an intonation in his voice he usually reserved for when Isabelle or Bastian was being unreasonable. 'We're incredibly busy; you could at least have waited until the building work was out of the way. These things should be a joint decision, Simone; by doing this you're putting me on the spot.'

'Don't just think about yourself for once,' had been my response, astonishingly sharp and clear, as I pointed to the children. 'We've dragged them to another country, taken them away from their friends, their family, everything they know, and made them start all over again here, made them sleep in a caravan, stuck them in a school where they can't understand anybody and nobody understands them. *They* didn't ask for that.' Then, softer: 'You know how much they've always wanted a dog. Just look at them, Eric.'

It has to be said: the children and Bleu made a splendid picture, like in a film, or a television commercial. Bleu behaved as if he'd never lived anywhere else. He ran in circles with Isabelle and Bastian, let them cuddle him, made several attempts to fetch a stick that Bastian had thrown for him. The children were evidently overjoyed with their new dog, their new pet, and Eric had a change of heart – and rightly so.

Eventually everything carried on as normal, as if nothing was wrong, nothing had happened, as if I wasn't radiating and glowing with the events of the previous day. I pushed the gnawing guilt firmly aside.

At around eight o'clock the workmen went home, but not before shaking my hand one by one, in the courtyard in front of the steps. Michel was the last to approach me. I avoided his gaze. Out of sight of the others he wiggled his middle finger playfully in the palm of my hand and fortunately left it at that, for I could sense that my body was about to betray me. When I was younger, at school, I blushed very easily. This got better in time, but I still recognised the feeling that preceded a red face and it wasn't far off.

I escaped inside to make dinner. Out of habit I started by filling a pan with water and began peeling potatoes. Eric came into the kitchen and opened a bottle of wine. Poured two glasses and leaned against the table with the gas burner on it. He handed me a glass.

He's going to say something now, I thought. He'd been waiting for the right moment. Now it was quiet, everyone had gone, the children were watching TV. Now he was going to confront me with his suspicions. Or perhaps he didn't only suspect it, perhaps he could feel it, *smell* it.

'I spent a lot of time working with Peter today,' he said. 'And talking to him. He really is one of a kind.' He took a sip of the wine and gazed towards the courtyard through the hole that was going to contain our front door. 'He told me about Michel's background today.'

Any moment now. I carried on peeling. One potato after another. Turned off the tap. Took a new potato.

'That lad had a pretty bad start in life. Peter and his wife more or less took him in; he'd nearly gone off the rails. Did you know that?'

I shook my head. 'No.'

'His mother was a swimmer.'

That explained his build.

Don't think about it, don't think about his body, don't think about anything.

Peel, peel.

'A competitive swimmer, at a pretty high level. She moved to America to swim for the American team and she met a married guy there who got her pregnant. This bloke didn't want anything to do with it. So this woman, or girl in fact, came back to France. She was still terribly young, only twenty. Her parents wanted her to get rid of it, but she didn't want to. This all led to a huge argument and she moved in with a cousin, in Les Landes, just outside Arcachon.'

I couldn't hear that place name, that beautiful place name, without images immediately flashing through my mind. Images, colours, scents. Emotions.

'Apparently, in the last few months of her pregnancy she had trouble walking. She ended up in a wheelchair and Michel was eventually born by Caesarean section. His mother was in a wheelchair for a long time after the birth with terrible postnatal depression. By the time she got back on her feet, she couldn't swim any more and she was on medication. Then she met a new boyfriend and he was a drug addict. Heroin, according to Peter: that was apparently the in thing at the time.'

I mumbled something and carried on peeling potatoes. Diced them.

'Michel once confided to Peter that he knew his mother just wanted to *die*. She even said so on a regular basis, to anyone who would listen, even to the lad himself . . . Awful, isn't it? Having to go through something like that when you're still so young? A father who doesn't want to know you and a suicidal mother?'

I nodded again. 'Terrible.'

Eric looked straight at me. I wanted to hear a lot more about Michel; I was burning with curiosity. But at the same time it felt so incredibly wrong. Somehow I found it totally inappropriate for me to know these things and tactless of Peter to tell Eric, or anyone at all, such intimate details about someone else's life.

But curiosity got the better of me. 'Did Peter say anything else?'

'Yes. The lad was taken away from his mother and put in a children's home when he was thirteen or so. A few years ago Peter got to know him through Bruno. Peter set himself up as a kind of father figure and is now encouraging him to go back to school. It's great, what Peter's doing, really exceptional.'

I sensed I should ask another question at this point, or at least show an interest. But I simply didn't know what to ask, or rather what I would have asked if Michel had been just any of the workmen, and not someone I'd been kissing like a love-struck teenager in a downpour on the beach in Arcachon that very afternoon. And down whose trousers I'd stuck my hand.

'Are you all there?' asked Eric.

I looked up in surprise. 'Sorry, I was only half listening.' Then I lied: 'I'm tired. It's been a long day; I'm not used to driving long distances and . . . and then speaking French all day as well. I think I've just had enough for one day.'

The door opens and I press myself against the wall. It's too early, it strikes me, far too early.

If they start questioning me now I'll talk, tell them everything.

No way. They musn't know anything. Anything at all.

What do they know already?

The same policeman is standing in front of the bed. He puts a soft plastic cup down on the floor in front of me. '*Voici, madame.*'

I stare at the cup. The first drink of the day. I notice I'm thirsty, want to wash away the disgusting taste in my mouth. My throat feels sore.

'It's not too late for me to get you some food,' he says. 'It's half past one.'

I look up. 'When is the . . . questioning?'

The policeman shrugs. 'I can't talk about that, madam.'

'What's normal?' I ask, clearing my throat. The insides of my cheeks are swollen and rub painfully against my back teeth when I speak.

'In the afternoon, I expect.'

There's a commotion in the corridor. Someone is knocking on a cell door and shouting. The policeman looks up.

'So you don't want anything to eat?'

I shake my head.

Without acknowledging me he turns round and closes the cell door behind him.

I'm alone again.

14

'Keep next Saturday evening free,' said Peter.

'What's happening?'

'Our business has been going five years, so we're having a party, at my house. A *real* party, with a live band, food, drink, the works. About fifty people are coming. It'd be great if you could join us. Claudia's eager to meet you as well. Anyway, if I'm not mistaken we're expecting another four Dutch couples from the area. This way at least you can get to know a few more people.'

'A party, sounds good,' I said. And I meant it. We hadn't had a single night out since we'd moved here. Our world had really shrunk. Meeting new people, live music and dancing sounded great to me, healthy at any rate.

Eric, who was sitting next to me at the table, hummed in agreement with a mouth full of spaghetti bolognese.

'Oh, wait, we can't,' I thought aloud. 'The children. We don't have a babysitter.'

'No problem at all. There are other people with children coming. I have a television room, with computer games and things like that. The children will have a great time. Wonderful sauce, by the way.'

I smiled and took some more salad, as the spaghetti was literally flying out of the pan and possibly I hadn't made enough for us all.

I'd thrown the sauce together at the last minute, with olive oil, chopped onions, fresh garlic, peeled pomodori tomatoes, fresh basil, salt and sugar. A personal revolution had taken place in the kitchen, a serious achievement for someone who'd not long ago scoured the shelves of the biggest supermarket in town in vain for packets of spaghetti mix, and come home disappointed, thinking it was impossible to make tasty spaghetti without the help of fluorescent-orange instant powder.

I started to enjoy it more and more, cooking, particularly combining less obvious flavours and avoiding ready-made products. The fact that I had this in me, that I proved to have a talent for it, was a revelation to me, and I took pleasure in every little triumph within the confines of the old kitchen. The guests who were going to come here next year could rest easy. They'd want for nothing.

Bleu was sitting near the men, between Bruno and Peter, looking expectantly with his one blue and one brown eye. His soft ears were pricked up. Naturally, you never knew when someone might drop something from the table. Or simply slip it to you.

Michel was sitting directly opposite me. He broke off a

chunk of baguette and dragged it through the leftover sauce on his plate. Every now and then he cast me a subtle glance when the others were deep in conversation and nobody was paying either of us any attention. I sensed I was answering his glances. Since our escapade in Arcachon the tension hadn't eased, but increased, because we hadn't had another chance to talk things over. In the morning he got out of Bruno's car, an old bashed-up Peugeot, or – when it had broken down again – one of Peter's white vans, and set to work. At eight o'clock in the evening he got back in, and off he went.

I tried to convince myself that this was a good thing, that I'd been completely reckless, that on that day on the Atlantic coast I'd boarded an express train bound straight for Hell, on a one-way ticket to Purgatory, and managed to jump off at the penultimate stop just in time. Everything I could muster in the way of common sense, reason, grey matter, told me not to pay him any more attention, but the traitor that was my body reacted so violently to the very idea that he was nearby it was impossible to ignore.

That wasn't all.

This morning the lads had started kissing.

No more shaking hands, now that they were here every day. A handshake was for strangers, neighbours, people you knew superficially and ran into regularly. I cooked for the workmen and Eric worked with them as best he could. He listened to their stories, told them about our life, what we'd been doing in Holland.

We were *presque famille*, Peter had said. Practically family. So now we kissed.

As a result, the *bonjour* and *au revoir* had taken on very different overtones. I was scared everyone would notice that Michel and I had kissed each other before, that I kissed him too eagerly. Or conversely, that I adopted an unnaturally distant demeanour, to avoid any suspicion, while everyone knew this was precisely how to spot lovers in company. In short, this kissing business was a total nightmare.

The telephone was ringing inside.

'Leave it,' was Eric's response. 'We're eating. If it's important they'll ring back later.'

I couldn't do that: the children were on a school trip today. Something could have happened.

I rushed indoors.

'Hello.'

'Hello, Simone, this is Eric's dad. Could you possibly call him over for me? I need to speak to him for a moment.'

My father-in-law had never been so abrupt. He was one of the most sociable chatterboxes I knew; he was always making jokes and could get on with literally anybody. When he was still working as a fluorescent-lamp salesman these qualities had proved a blessing. It was obvious where Eric got his social skills from.

'I'll go and get him.' I went back outside, where, if I wasn't mistaken, a conversation was going on about dogs and what breeds Bleu's parents must have been.

'Eric, your father's on the phone.'

Eric stood up and went inside. I sat down again and scraped a bit of food on to my fork. I hoped it was nothing serious. My in-laws were both in their seventies, and still very active. Eric's mother was in a drama society and was often cast in the role of the know-it-all, which she played with verve and relish. My father-in-law was the treasurer of the athletics club and played cards at the local café every week. They often cooked together. Their house was a home where everyone, at any time of day or night, was welcomed with coffee and attention.

These two people held a special place in my heart; they were a classic example of a married couple growing old together in a wonderful, harmonious way. A rare thing.

The lads had finished eating. The packets of loose tobacco and cigarettes appeared. As if preprogrammed, I started clearing the table and went inside to make coffee.

Eric was still in the kitchen. He looked serious, shaken.

I put the tray with glasses and plates down. 'What's wrong?'

'My mother . . . She's in hospital. She's had a stroke.'

I put my hands over my mouth. 'Oh God.'

'She's having trouble speaking; in fact Dad said she can barely speak at all. She's still very confused. Her left side is completely paralysed. One moment they were playing cards together, the next moment Dad saw the left side of her face fall and that was it.'

I put my arms round Eric and felt tears welling up. 'Oh, Eric, how awful.'

He placed his chin on my head. 'I need to be there. Tomorrow.'

I bit my bottom lip. At this moment I shouldn't have been thinking of anything but my mother-in-law – why her, the poor woman? – and my father-in-law; he was bound to be completely shaken up right now. Completely at a loss without his lifelong companion. But the idea of having to sleep in the caravan without Eric, with the dark night around us, and the rustling and creaking of the trees, filled me with terror. We had Bleu, of course, but he was so playful, so affectionate, that I was under no illusions about his qualities as a guard dog. There was *no way* I could say this right now. There was no point. I couldn't take the children out of school; they were only just starting to settle in and they were already such outsiders. And I couldn't burden Eric with anything else.

We'd cope. Don't make a fuss now.

'The work must go on,' I heard Eric say, as he let go of me and rubbed his face. 'We've got no choice . . . I'll discuss it with Peter in a minute.'

'No problem, Eric: we know what we're doing here,' was Peter's response. 'Needs must.'

He then spoke to the workmen in rapid French, who all, without exception, looked serious and expressed their sympathy.

'When do you think you'll be back?' I asked Eric.

'I don't know. It's two days there and back whatever happens; I'm thinking three, four days or so. In which case I'll be home on Sunday evening. If nothing else comes up . . . If it's really bad, then . . .'

'Don't think about it, Eric,' I said. 'I'll manage; don't worry about us.'

Peter was listening carefully. 'Perhaps we could bring our own food. We don't want to make things any harder for you than they already are.'

'No need,' I replied. 'The children are at school all day tomorrow and Friday, and you're not here at the weekend. It's absolutely no problem to cook lunch on those two days.'

'But then you'll be without a car here,' said Eric. 'If something happens to the children, you're stuck.'

'Then . . . how am I supposed to take them to school?'

Eric looked at me in surprise. 'Damn . . . Either way, you need the car. It never occurred to me.'

He jumped up from his chair and went inside. I refilled everyone's coffee cup.

'This is one of the annoying things about emigrating,' said Peter, when silence had fallen. 'Family. There's no problem as long as everyone's healthy, but they're not immortal, and then it hits you that hundreds of miles is a pretty long way.'

I nodded. Silence fell once again. Bruno pushed an

earphone into his ear and switched his MP3 player on. Bleu was nowhere to be seen.

Finally Arnaud and Pierre-Antoine struck up a conversation with Louis and the others joined in. I didn't listen. My eyes sought Michel, who answered my gaze from under his eyelashes. It was difficult to tell what he was thinking. He sniffed and reached for his tobacco.

I played with the spoon in my mug. If I was honest, I had to admit I was worn out now. Tired. Beyond tired. And instead of slowing down, things were, on the contrary, becoming more chaotic all the time. Eric hadn't been much help, but he'd been there at least, and the idea of spending three nights alone with the children in the caravan, bearing the responsibility for them alone, without Eric, made me nervous. What if something happened, meaning he had to stay longer? Then I'd be stuck here with no one to help me. All I had was Peter's phone number. They might be *presque famille*, but I didn't have an address for anyone at the table. The sum total of our social contacts so far. It brought home to me how important Peter's party was going to be for us. We'd have the chance to get to know new people there; it could be a starting point to build a social safety net.

Everyone was friendly at school, to be sure, but nobody had invited us over yet, and nor could I ask them round to our house, because we didn't have any accommodation to put up guests properly.

In Holland we'd had a choice of at least ten people who were happy to babysit, who were willing to drive us anywhere if there was a problem, anything at all. So far we hadn't had the chance to spend a single day or night together; worse still, I hadn't had a day to myself. On weekdays my day was broken up by the cooking and at weekends the children were at home.

'All sorted,' I heard someone say behind me.

Eric returned to the table. 'If you take me to Mérignac Airport, Gerard will pick me up in Amsterdam. Then you'll have the car here. Gerard and Erica are going to drive here on Friday, so you won't be alone.'

I looked at him. 'Gerard and Erica?'

Erica was a good friend of mine. I'd had an awful lot of fun with her at secondary school and we'd stayed in touch ever since. She was one of the few women I knew who could be almost painfully honest. She said exactly what she thought, regardless of whom she was speaking to, and I found this trait enormously attractive in her. Only now did I realise that I hadn't rung her in all the time we'd been here.

Great friend I was. Out of sight, out of mind.

'You know Gerard and Erica have a caravan in Saint-Hilaire, in that new holiday park, don't you?' Eric replied. 'Erica immediately offered to come here. Of her own accord. They were actually planning to come down south next week, but seeing as they're almost flooded out in Holland at the moment it was no trouble to come earlier. Problem solved. You can go with them to the campsite, if you want, so you won't be here on your own at the weekend. They arrive Friday evening.'

15

All morning I'd been on the go. I'd not stopped for a moment. I'd phoned Eric a few times, both yesterday and today, and he told me his mother was lying between the hospital sheets like a bundle of misery, barely able to speak. Her eyes were clear, he'd said, but she was talking nonsense and seemed to be aware of this, because she was angry and bad-tempered. According to the nurse he'd spoken to, this was a good thing; she had a lot of fight in her, and now it was a matter of waiting to see how well her body could recover from the damage it had sustained.

The potatoes were on the stove. I washed lamb's lettuce and sliced cherry tomatoes in two. Cooking, concentrating on cutting, chopping and peeling, calmed me down a little. The nice thing about cooking elaborate meals is that you have to stay focused all the time. You can't take your mind off it or nip off to do something else. Cooking suited me fine. I hadn't used butter for frying in weeks, only olive oil. According to Antoine, who was very knowledgeable about French cuisine and encouraged me enormously and gave constructive criticism, you could draw a line through Europe level with Bourgogne. This, he said, was the butter boundary. Above it, hence in northern France, Belgium and Holland, people fried with butter. Below it, with oil.

The two days without Eric had been pretty dull. The telephone had hardly rung. The lads got on with their work and left me in peace as much as possible. Michel seemed to be sparing my blushes; he presented his cheek in the morning and evening and that was it. Nevertheless, the kissing was still awkward. My pent-up emotions didn't subside; they were simply masked by a numb feeling that I was alone now, in a foreign country, and that the mother-in-law I loved so much was lying in a hospital bed hundreds of miles away, fighting to get better.

The children were worried. Grandma was ill, and this was a scary thought for them.

'Is she going to *die*?' Bastian had asked.

'No,' I'd replied, 'she's not going to die, but she's very poorly. She won't be able to walk for a while or speak very well, but she could get better.'

The children had both drawn pictures for her at the last minute on Wednesday evening, which Eric had packed in his case, and which were now hanging above my mother-in-law's hospital bed.

Peter had tried to look out for me. Now there was no man about the house, he seemed keen to take on this role. He regularly asked me if I needed any help, paid me compliments, involved me in the building work. I was growing increasingly fond of him.

I drained the potatoes and left them to cool. Put some lemon-infused olive oil in the frying pan with chopped onions and garlic. Then spread some pieces of chicken breast around the pan and stirred it all until the meat was the same light colour all over. Quickly squeezed the water out of some raisins and dried apricots, which had been soaking, and added them to the pan. Stirred everything once again, sprinkled it with a little sea salt and added some orange juice. It sizzled. I turned down the heat slightly and started to slice the steaming potatoes.

This evening, perhaps even earlier, Gerard and Erica would be arriving. This was a relief. I was worn out. A little support would be more than welcome. I wondered how it would all work out, practically speaking, because one thing that had stuck in my mind from Erica's lively tales about their caravan in Saint-Hilaire was that it had only two bedrooms. One double and one single. Of course, I could always make Isabelle and Bastian sleep in the single bed and lie down on the sofa myself. Or an airbed. That left what to do with Bleu. Dogs were completely unwelcome on some campsites.

For the past few nights I'd had trouble getting to sleep. I'd lain there listening to the sounds outside, but Bleu's presence had put my mind at rest. If a strange sound didn't disturb him, then it had to fit in with the surroundings. During the day Bleu roamed the grounds. I'd gone looking for him several times, and more than once I'd been worried he'd run off, but he kept reappearing, tail wagging, tongue sticking out, with a twinkle in his eyes. At lunchtime he could invariably be found near the dining table, because people were always slipping him bits of food. In the afternoon he knew I went to pick up the children and was already waiting for us at the end of the driveway. Bleu was in his element here.

'Dogs are not allowed on the campsite,' said Erica. 'God, what a pain . . .'

We were sitting at the large table outside; the sun was shining and we were drinking coffee.

Gerard stroked Bleu's head. 'Can't you just leave the dog here?'

'No,' I said. 'The house has no doors yet and the caravan is far too small.'

'Wow,' said Erica, putting her cup back down on the table. 'I really can't believe you've got a dog.'

'We haven't had him for very long.' I couldn't help remembering Jeanette's hugely oversized housecoat in Libourne. The very thought of it made me blush a little; I could feel it, but nobody noticed.

'And don't you have any extra berths here, in your own caravan? So we can sleep here?'

'We have a three-quarter bed and bunk beds,' I replied. 'I could possibly sleep in the top bunk, with you in our bed and Isabelle and Bastian in the bottom bunk.'

Bastian heard this. He was playing with his toy car under the table. 'There's no way I'm sleeping in the same bed as Isabelle,' he protested.

A deafening racket was coming from the house. The radio was crackling at full volume.

Erica looked past me at the house. 'Is it like this every day?'

I nodded. 'From the crack of dawn till around eight in the evening.'

'Including weekends?'

'No, Monday to Friday.'

'Have you and Eric ever actually had a night out? I mean, without the children?'

'No. Never. We can't, anyway: we don't have a babysitter. Not yet. But we will eventually.'

'I have another idea, Simone.' Erica glanced at the house again and exchanged a knowing look with Gerard. He nodded in agreement. 'If we take the children to Saint-Hilaire, you can have a few days off as well. Recharge your batteries a bit.'

'No, don't be silly. There's no need. It's fine.'

'Come on, Simone, you don't need to put a brave face on things. Look at yourself. You look like death warmed up, for God's sake. We'll take Bastian and Isabelle to the campsite; we'll keep them entertained there. They can have fun in the pool and make crêpes, giving you a few days of peace and quiet as well.'

Bastian emerged from under the table, looking at me expectantly. 'Oh, Mum, *can* we? Erica and Gerard have a swimming pool. Did you know that? And we want to go swimming! You never let us!'

Bastian looked to Isabelle for support. 'Isabelle, do you want to go swimming as well?'

She nodded in delight; her eyes lit up. Then her little face fell. 'But Mum won't let us.'

Finally, I said yes. What else could I do?

I went to the caravan to get two bags and grabbed their swimming things, extra clothes, Bunny and a few toy cars. When I returned to the courtyard Isabelle and Bastian were already in the back of the Opel. Gerard was fastening their seatbelts.

'You've got our mobile number, haven't you?' asked Erica, taking the bags.

'Yes, I have.'

She kissed me goodbye and squeezed my shoulder. 'If you feel like coming over tomorrow then you're very welcome, you know, but I think you're better off taking it easy for a while. Take some time for yourself, girl.' She looked around. 'Christ, if you're surrounded by this all day, this racket and commotion, till eight o'clock in the evening, then it's about time you had a few days of total peace and quiet. Have you got any books?'

'Yes, enough.'

'We'll bring the children back sometime on Sunday.

Don't worry about a thing; we'll keep them amused. And if you want to see them before then, just call us and I'll give you directions.'

'OK,' I heard myself say.

As the Opel headed towards the path, hooting loudly, and I waved goodbye, I saw Michel. He was sitting against the wall of the barn, rolling a cigarette, looking straight at me.

'Got the place all to yourself?' he asked. 'Are the children staying over?'

I nodded, not moving. He looked me up and down. I forgot to breathe. The way he looked at me, I could physically feel his gaze; it pierced right through me.

Yes, I was alone this evening. The first evening since we'd moved to France.

And Michel knew this.

I gulped. Stood there for a moment, wasn't sure what to say.

Michel cocked his head to light the roll-up. Took a puff and laid his head against the wall, not taking his eyes off me for a second. 'Shall I come over?' he asked, finally.

My heart went into freefall and was now beating in my abdomen. Did I want him to *come over* this evening? He was asking me. It was a choice. Now all of a sudden it was a choice. Not something that happened to you, in the flow of events, now it was a question of yes or no.

Alarm bells rang in my head. I thought of Isabelle, of Bastian.

Of my in-laws, of all the hard-won certainties and support networks we'd built up over the past few years, the thirteen years Eric and I had been married, which were so dear to me. I truly loved Eric, despite his quirks, his distant phases, despite our already waning sex life, which had never quite recovered since Bastian was born. But fundamentally, sex wasn't the most important part of a relationship. It only *seemed* that way, because that's what you were led to believe. The fact was, passion cooled, and what remained – if you were lucky – was a solid foundation, a close bond, like Eric's parents had.

I looked at Michel. Perhaps there'd never be a better moment: tonight was *the* moment to put things straight. To get real. Michel, and everything he stood for, had begun to dominate my days, my life. And that wasn't good. It wasn't going to lead anywhere but trouble.

I was alone this evening. I didn't have to be on my guard. We could talk in peace; I'd be able to hold his hand, make myself understood.

There and then, as Michel continued looking at me impassively, awaiting my answer, I made the decision. Yes, Michel could come over this evening. But not for what he had in mind. I'd tell him how much I cared for my family, and that I wasn't going to jeopardise that by doing something foolish, something fleeting, with no future. The events of the past few days had really brought me down to earth.

'Yes,' I said. 'Come on over.'

★

Through the thick wired-glass window, high up near the ceiling and not much bigger than a shoebox, orange light from the setting sun is filtering into my cell. I'm grateful for the small window. It's my only point of reference as time passes and I doze off and wake up again, the thoughts racing through my mind.

Unbelievable how I was able to lie to everyone, how naturally and easily it came to me. All my life I've hated that so intensely, that scheming, lying and deceit. Women who cheat on their husbands with their best friends, men who say they have to work late and are actually carrying on with their secretaries – there's a reason those kinds of clichés are clichés; they're far too commonplace, they seem to make the world go round. In our old village, these things, these amorous excesses, never stayed secret for long. I listened to the stories, annoyed at the lack of depth and the ease with which people who were supposed to share everything with each other messed one other around time after time. People who were married, who were supposed to love each other, raise children together, grow old together.

Things like that don't just happen to you; you actively seek them out, *consciously*, because there's something missing in your marriage, something essential, such as appreciation, affirmation; for example, because you're sick of always hearing that you need to lose weight, your hair's too short, or too long, or that you're getting wrinkles and not performing in bed. Or perhaps all these things at once, disguised by your hubby as 'jokes', which he usually cracks at birthdays and family parties, in public, when he's had too much to drink. Or perhaps it's the precise opposite: because your husband is no longer the dazzling, virile demigod you once saw him as, and once the spell was broken by the daily grind, he turned out to be just an average Joe, who, just like you, puts on weight, sits on the sofa flicking through the TV channels, who can be moody and unreasonable, so human and so *ordinary*, that you spend the rest of your life longingly recalling that feeling, that intense, overpowering, blissful, exciting, near-drunken feeling of being in love.

Something like that. That's what I always thought.

Until Michel.

16

'Are you coping there?'

'Everything's under control. Bastian and Isabelle are staying with Erica and Gerard in Saint-Hilaire.'

'What about you?'

'Not without Bleu: dogs are not allowed on the campsite. To be honest, Eric, I don't really mind. It's nice to have some peace and quiet for once. How is your mother?'

'She's improving. Very slowly, but they have every hope she'll make a fairly full recovery. So do I, for that matter. She lies there swearing like a trooper. That seems to be a good sign.' He coughed. 'It's chaos in Holland, Simone, *manic* . . . I got another parking ticket yesterday, because the meter was out of order. And it's pouring with rain, terrible. I'll be happy to be home again. What's the weather like there?'

'The usual. The sun's shining at least.'

'Great. Now that Mum's getting better I'll probably come straight back tomorrow, a day early. I'll give you a ring as soon as I know what time I'll be arriving, OK?'

'All right.'

'Love you.'

'Love you too.' I put the phone down and looked at my watch. Nine o'clock. The workmen had left at eight o'clock. I reckoned Michel would need half an hour to get home. He'd take a shower, change and drive back here. I wasn't expecting him before ten o'clock.

I went to the bathroom, on the first floor. It had been a filthy place, encrusted with limescale and dirt, that I'd scrubbed clean on my hands and knees. Now the tiles and fittings were covered in a thick layer of dust and debris, just like in the rest of the house. The dust hung in the air, glittering in the empty space when the sun shone in. I turned on the tap in the shower and heard rattling and squeaking somewhere on the other side of the house. The boiler, but at least it was working. Warm water gushed over my hand. I looked towards the corridor. There was still no door. When I showered, usually very early in the morning or in the evening after dinner, I knew that Eric and the children were nearby. Now I was on my own, in an unfinished house without doors, with the knowledge that the nearest neighbours were half a mile away. I'd never been particularly brave and probably never would be. I took my clothes off and put them on the washbasin. Stepped under the shower and let the water wash over me. I shampooed my hair, lathered myself up with shower gel. As my hands passed over my hips, I looked at my skin. It had gone saggy after Bastian and Isabelle were born. It would never be the same again; no lotion or potion could put it right. My belly stored more fat; I could squeeze it.

I opened the shower door and rummaged in my toiletry bag with an outstretched arm for a razor. Shaved my legs, my armpits and my bikini line, scrubbed my face and neck and watched it all wash down the plughole. Then stepped out of the shower and reached for a towel, which I wrapped around my head. I began to dry myself off and looked at myself in the mirror above the washbasin. It was old and flecked with black, but displayed my reflection with sadistic accuracy.

'Look around you,' Eric always said to me, when I felt insecure and voiced this in the private intimacy of the bedroom, 'at women of your age. You've got a great body.'

But that was Eric, a unique characterological fusion of charm, intellect and forgetfulness – which strangers often mistook for naivety. Half my life I'd had the opportunity to study Eric close up. I was there, long before his life was taken over by monster contracts with buyers for hospitals, research stations and clinics, and meetings with the Ministry of Health about waste disposal in the social-service sector. I'd witnessed how happy he was with an old Citroën 2CV with a broken clutch, the first covered and motorised vehicle we ever owned, in which we'd travelled thousands of miles. How he later fell head over heels for a red Fiat which, on closer inspection, used up more oil per day than the average

Sicilian in a week, and finally gave up the ghost between Paris and Lille in a long traffic jam during the hottest summer for decades. I stood waiting for him in front of our house when – many years, applications and experiences later – with a smile that looked like it could light up the whole town, he drove home in his first company car: shiny and reliable, with a strong smell of new plastic.

That was then.

Eric's attitude and outlook kept pace with the cars he drove. As with his four-wheeled vehicles, the basic principle remained the same; only the mode of expression changed. Very gradually, over the years.

With the difference that our belongings became ever newer, more expensive, shinier, and our bodies went in exactly the opposite direction, at exactly the same rate. As if owning nice things was to compensate for this deterioration, like a plaster on a wound called mortality.

Was that why I was so attracted to Michel? Was he also something shiny and new, a kind of compensation?

I really had to stop running myself down, driving myself crazy. I took another look in the mirror, turned round, and back again, and ran my hands over my ribs, waist and hips, forced myself to view my body as a man would. I pushed my breasts forward. Of course, this wasn't the body of an eighteen-year-old; it had produced two children. But my skin was glowing, and my breasts were nothing to complain about. There were curves; everything felt soft and full.

Talk, Simone, you were going to talk to him.

Finally a smile appeared in the mirror, warming me. I slipped on a thong, put on a lacy bra and twirled on tiptoe in front of the mirror once again. I took a long frilly skirt of thin cotton, a tight vest, and threw a blouse loosely over the top. Then went downstairs to the kitchen. I took a packet of tortellini (cooks in just 1 minute, made with fresh spinach and mozzarella) out of the fridge, glanced at it briefly and put it back. Somehow I couldn't stomach any food. I drank a whole glass of orange juice, took an apple from the vegetable drawer and went outside.

Bleu came towards me, wagging his tail, and pressed his hairy body against mine. I tickled him behind his ears and stood still in the courtyard for a moment. It was dark now, quarter to ten. What should I do? Stay here, so I could 'receive' Michel the moment he arrived? I wasn't particularly keen on the idea of sitting down here on the steps and waiting in the dark, listening to the sounds of the night.

Was he really coming?

The only emotion I felt now was uncertainty. A gnawing doubt.

An owl hooted in the distance. Leaves rustled on the trees. Bleu pricked up his ears, jerked his head to the left and whined softly. He focused on something in the distance and then lost interest.

Now I knew for sure. I wasn't going to sit here and wait,

not outside. With Bleu panting by my side I went over to the caravan.

What on earth had I let myself in for? This afternoon, as I waved goodbye to Gerard, Erica and the children and the sun was shining, everything seemed so obvious, crystal clear. Not any more. Anything but.

Michel was one of the most beautiful men I'd ever seen, including the actors and singers who made the top-twenty-five-most-beautiful-men lists. He was flawless; everything about him was in balance. Yes, his teeth were slightly crooked. But they were white, well looked after. In fact, his facial features paled into insignificance beside his gaze, which was so unbelievably stunning it took my breath away. From the very first moment we locked eyes, logical thinking became impossible.

So who was I kidding?

A soft light from the windows highlighted the caravan, giving it a bluish glow in the moonlight.

I cleared away shoes belonging to Isabelle and Bastian, gathered a few drawings and put them in a pile with bills and newspapers, adjusted Eric's shaver stand. Collected Isabelle's and Bastian's toys, and put them under blankets, out of sight. I spent ten minutes running back and forth with things, just so I wouldn't have to think. Bleu kept getting in the way. It was impossible for him not to get in the way in those few square feet of free space.

I opened the door. '*Où sont les souris?* – Go and play outside, boy; catch some mice.'

Bleu went outside, wagging his tail, turned round, looked at me cheerfully and then disappeared into the night with his nose to the ground.

I turned the main light off, leaving only a 15-watt bulb on above the sink. The towel turban was still wrapped around my head. I pulled it loose, bent over and ran my hand through my hair. It was still damp.

He's not coming. Perhaps that's only for the best.

I took a deep breath. My eye fell on the red cover with Chinese characters. The bed was impossible to ignore. It was, without doubt, too dominant in this confined space.

I folded up the duvet and opened a cupboard, only to discover that it was crammed full of clothes. The same as all the other cupboards. I opened them one after the other; all were full to bursting. Suddenly I could feel myself growing rebellious. Whose idea had this been, this forced stay in this tiny, claustrophobic midget caravan, which was staring me in the face whichever way I turned? This whole French adventure? And in all the years preceding it, what had been my role other than agreeing, following and conforming? Shit. Did I want to carry on with this, this complete and utter disregard for what I felt so passionately, wanted so badly, with all my heart, simply because it didn't fit into the *picture*? Was it fear?

I stood there trembling, with the blankets in my arms,

until I heard the droning of an engine approaching in fits and starts. A beam of light shone in through the windows, flashed over me and then died out.

My stomach contracted. I had no desire to talk. Not any more. My whole body was shaking. Damn.

I dropped the blankets and opened the door. When Michel came inside he was followed by an intoxicating smell, a mixture of Michel and freshly washed cotton and country air. No *bonsoir*, no ceremony, no tense words and nervous fumbling. We almost jumped on each other, kissed, ravenously. My hands reached instinctively for his back, under his T-shirt. Muscles moving beneath supple skin. His mouth held mine captive as he threw off his jacket, prised his trainers impatiently from his feet, then grasped me, half lifting me up, half pushing me towards the bed, until we fell over each other on to the bed and he ended up on top of me, lodged his hips between my legs, pulled up my skirt with the same movement, hastily pulled down my thong, put his hand between my legs, rubbed, leaned over me, buried his face in my neck, moaned, trembled all over.

With hurried movements he took off his T-shirt. I wanted to see him, feel him: his chest, the ribcage that narrowed to his waist. My fingertips felt for his stomach, where the quivering muscles contracted under my touch. I fiddled with the zip on his jeans, got it open; he pulled them further down. Impatiently he pulled up my top and bra. Skin against skin. Michel tried to make eye contact, we kissed, slowly, his nose brushed past mine, lovingly, gently. I was shaking uncontrollably, I'd lost control of my muscles, I'd lost control of everything, thrust my pelvis up, whispered, urged him on. The next moment he entered me, overwhelmingly, completely. I closed my eyes and forgot where I was, who I was, surrendered myself to the rhythm, a tempo that made my head swim, made me gasp for breath. His lips against mine, his slippery tongue, his breath, my breath. He whispered things in my ear that I couldn't understand, slowed down, sped up again, until the whole room was spinning like a fairground ride, nothing above, nothing below, just feeling, being, a balloon expanding in my belly, swelling up, strangling me, until I started moaning uncontrollably, harder, started growling. He planted his hands on both my shoulders, half raised himself up, looked at me darkly, intently, kept looking at me, sharply, opened his mouth, gulped, moved rhythmically with that beautiful symmetrical body, damp with exertion, in a steady cadence, until, to my dismay, I started digging my hands wildly and uncontrollably into the mattress and an explosion ensued in my abdomen, sending shockwaves throughout my body. He raised his head with a jerk, a dazed look filled his eyes, then he shut them and the muscles and tendons stood out in his neck. He let out a long moan. Lowered his head on to the pillow next to me with a growl.

We lay there for a moment, panting. I put my arms round him, pulled him towards me. Clung to him. His skin was slippery with perspiration and his heart was beating against my chest.

'Fantastic,' he whispered.

My tears made their way to the pillow beneath me but I couldn't understand why. I started shaking, shivering, without stopping, and I couldn't hold back my tears, they kept on coming, flowing over my cheeks. My surroundings became blurred.

Michel noticed this, sat up on one elbow in shock and looked at me, slightly astonished. Brushed my hair out of my face.

'Are you hurt? Have I hurt you?'

'No,' said a voice that seemed to belong to someone else. 'I'm not hurt . . . I'm not hurt.'

There's a pizza box in front of the cell door. Red and green stripes on the white cardboard. The policeman fetched it for me about an hour ago, in town. His shift was over, he told me at the time; his colleague would be taking over.

I stare at the packaging, with half a pizza still inside. That was all I could eat.

I wonder what time it is. Half nine? Would they question me this late?

Or not until tomorrow? The day after tomorrow? *Tonight?*

I fight off an impending panic attack. To introduce some structure, to try to concentrate on something else, I start counting. The length of the cell, ten feet. The width, seven feet, maybe less. The height. At least eight feet. The length of the metal bed, riveted to the ground and with a thin mattress on top made of thick fabric that reminds me of the gym mats at primary school. French length. No more than six feet.

Only now do I begin to understand how animals in old-fashioned zoos must feel. The tiger constantly walking round in circles, wrenched from its environment and reduced to an object in a peep-show, safely stored away. I glance at the pizza box. Here, too, they throw food inside. I have enough to eat, drink, a bed. But at the same time I have nothing at all.

How long do they want to keep me here in uncertainty? Is this the intention? To frighten me, isolate me, leave me alone here with my thoughts, hour after hour, so that I'll be grateful when somebody wants to talk to me, and pour out everything I know and everything I've done?

17

I opened my eyes. Soft light was shining in through the smoky-brown windows of the caravan. I had my arm over Michel, who was lying diagonally on the bed, taking up almost the entire width of the mattress, breathing deeply and steadily. I kept looking at him, close up, in the filtered morning light. His closed eyes, his eyelashes, his nose, which, I now noticed, was slightly too big. He had a faint shadow of stubble across his chin and cheeks. My hand automatically ran over his chest, to the little hairs around his navel that formed a trail towards his now soft penis. My lips pressed against his skin. I curled up against him, sighed. He murmured something in his sleep, threw his leg over me. I couldn't remember ever feeling so relaxed.

My hand felt for his neck; my mouth sought his instinctively. I became aroused again. The corner of his mouth curled in a drowsy smile, and he ran his fingers absently through my hair without waking up.

Scratching at the door. Squeaking, whimpering. Bleu.

Carefully I wriggled out from under Michel and stood

up to open the door. The poor dog had been outside all night. As Bleu ran in circles around my feet, his tail wagging furiously, and pushed his head against my hand, I looked at Michel, to burn that image, worthy of a poster, permanently in my mind. I quickly put on a T-shirt and skirt and walked barefoot towards the house. It was chilly outside, colder than yesterday. The grass and weeds tickled the bottom of my feet. The sun was hidden behind a thick layer of cloud.

A perfect day to stay in bed.

The telephone rang. I hurried inside, with Bleu on my heels.

'Hello?'

'*Christ*, Simone, where have you been? I've been trying to ring you all morning.'

It was Eric; he sounded worried and annoyed, and the creepy thing was, it was as if I was hearing his voice for the first time. As if I had a stranger on the phone.

I jumped.

'What . . . what time is it exactly?' I asked.

'Quarter to twelve.'

Quarter to twelve. Overslept. Just how long were we at it last night?

'I slept late,' I said quickly, and this was no lie. 'You can't hear the phone in the caravan.' This was true as well.

'No, I know that. I kept ringing the landline, then your mobile, but it was switched off.'

I pulled nervously at the telephone cord. 'Sorry. I forgot to charge it up; the battery's probably dead.'

'What's wrong with you, Simone? Oh well, never mind. Anyway, I'm at Schiphol, and the plane leaves in half an hour. Would you please jump into the car and drive to Mérignac?'

'And . . . and what time are you arriving?'

'In about two hours, so you'd better set out straight away. I really hate waiting around at that airport.'

'I'll be there.'

'OK, see you soon.'

Eric rang off.

Bleu looked at me expectantly, his head cocked to one side. I opened a cupboard, took out a bag of dog food and filled his bowl. My movements weren't particularly coordinated and half the food missed the bowl.

I rushed to the caravan.

Michel has to go, I have to change the bed, put the covers in the washing machine, and take a shower. In that order. And all in a quarter of an hour. No, faster.

I wasn't going to make it, never; I was going to be late, I knew that even now.

I opened the door of the caravan. Michel was sitting up in bed, running his fingers through his hair. He looked at me languidly from under his eyelashes. His gaze completely blew me away. The corner of his mouth curled, a wry smile.

I was lost for words.

'Come here,' he said. 'I hadn't finished with you.'

Panic started gaining ground again. 'We can't. Eric called: I have to go and pick him up. From the airport. Right now.'

He stretched. The covers fell down, revealing his chest. Broad and athletic, a mass of moving muscles. 'No breakfast?'

'No. You have to go, you really have to go.'

He threw off the covers. I tried my very best not to look at him; he looked too good. Too inviting. My heart was bouncing uncontrollably behind my ribs, my abdomen was turning to warm jelly. In an attempt to tear my eyes away from him I nervously picked his clothes up off the floor and thrust the bundle in his direction. If I looked at him, I was lost. 'You really have to go.'

He put his clothes down beside him and stood up. Two arms around me, hands caressing my back, my buttocks.

'You . . .' I repeated.

His lips on mine. He pushed his belly against me, his erection sprang up against my stomach.

'. . . have to . . .'

An intense look, impossible to ignore. The last word died away in a moan.

'Traffic,' he whispered, brushing his nose along mine and pushing me backwards towards the bed. 'Tell him you got stuck in traffic. It's chaos, that A630 . . .'

Bastian and Isabelle weren't about to come back with us. We were sitting by the campsite's covered swimming pool, drinking wine, and this was the third time I'd called them. Each time, Bastian dived away and swam underwater to the other side of the pool. Isabelle stayed in the middle, beyond my reach, looking at me triumphantly. She was being kept afloat by two Mickey Mouse armbands and a big Barbie rubber ring. You could barely make out her little face among all that colourful plastic.

'Why don't you just leave them?' Erica suggested.

'They've got school on Monday.'

'In that case come and get them tomorrow evening. They're no trouble; they're good company, those two.'

'Yes, let us play happy families for once,' said Gerard. His legs were resting on a white stacking chair. A plastic cup of red wine was balancing perilously between two fingers and his thumb on his hairy belly. 'I've laughed myself silly with those two. They came and jumped on our bed at seven o'clock this morning.'

'Isabelle can already speak quite good French,' Erica remarked. Her dark, curly hair had dried in a ponytail on the back of her head. 'Last night they ordered a *jus de fraise* at the bar without batting an eyelid.'

'Very clever,' Gerard chimed in. 'You can just transplant them to a different country with a completely different language. Children are pretty flexible, that's for sure.'

'Yes, they're quick on the uptake,' said Eric. 'Give it six months, they'll be teaching us French.'

I didn't say much. My thoughts were miles away.

I played with the cup of wine in my hand and cast a perfunctory glance at Isabelle and Bastian, who were now chatting with two other children. Nobody noticed anything different about me. Including Eric. I'd arrived at Mérignac late, by well over half an hour, but the flight had been delayed, meaning I didn't have to make up an excuse. After Michel had left, I'd put the covers in the washing machine, changed the bed, had a quick shower and flushed away all traces of our encounter down the plughole with gallons of water. What I couldn't wash away was the raw feeling between my legs; it was burning slightly.

'You're already looking a lot better than yesterday,' Erica said to me. She briefly touched my arm. I looked up in confusion. 'Why don't you take some time off, the two of you, take advantage of us? We're here anyway now and it's our idea.'

Eric looked at me, raised his eyebrows. His eyes twinkled. 'Sounds tempting . . . The caravan all to ourselves: what a treat.'

I forced a smile.

It was two o'clock in the morning. The screen of the clock radio glowed green in the dark. I'd watched it turn twelve o'clock, one minute past twelve, two minutes past twelve. Watched every minute go by, wide awake.

I couldn't sleep. Not in this bed. Never again.

Eric had his arm over me, which was pressing on my

ribs. His breath brushed past my cheek. I tried to move away from him a little, wrenched myself from under his arm. This didn't work very well. The bed was too small.

What had I *done*? What had I got myself into?

This was hopeless. Totally hopeless.

Last night with Michel had been the most complete, fantastic, intense encounter I'd ever had with a man. I'd never experienced that before, not like that. Not with Eric, not with anyone before Eric. Never. I didn't even know it was possible, that sex could be so amazing. As I lay next to Eric in the darkness, the very thought of Michel, the way he looked at me, his smell and his voice, the feeling of his rough hands between my legs, was enough to send my heart racing and quicken my breathing. I squeezed my eyes shut and felt something contract in my stomach.

I was almost being torn apart with desire.

A crazy thought popped into my head. Leave. Start a new life, leave everything behind. On the back of the motorbike, my arms around Michel's waist, my body pressed tightly against his, the tyres racing over the tarmac. On our way to the sea, the mountains, anywhere, somewhere we could wake up beside each other every day.

Bastian coughed. A dry, deep cough that lingered for a moment. I raised my head from the pillow in alarm. Until two years ago Bastian had suffered regular asthma attacks. He'd grown out of them, and I'd almost forgotten about the nights when I'd barely been able to sleep, listening anxiously in bed to Bastian's coughing, hoping he'd sleep through it, that it would pass. The caravan was stuffy and old, a far from healthy atmosphere for children sensitive to asthma.

The coughing stopped. I laid my head back on the pillow and stared at the dark ceiling.

Was I crazy?

A moment ago had I really been considering running off with a twenty-year-old boy, on his clapped-out, rusty motorbike, making for the horizon until the thing broke down or we ran out of petrol or money and then, penniless but happy on the roadside, hitching the rest of the way to . . . *where* exactly?

I hardly knew Michel, but everyone could see he was a young pup, with his whole life ahead of him. The world was his oyster. He was probably too young to take this seriously. I had a family, a settled life, with material and social assets. Baggage. He had nothing to lose; I on the other hand had pretty much everything I'd accumulated with a great deal of pain and effort. What the hell was I doing? Eric, Isabelle, Bastian . . . I loved them. Thinking about Isabelle's sweet face, with her permanently lopsided pigtails, and Bastian's tough talk, in such sharp contrast with his sensitive, vulnerable character, I fought back fresh tears. I couldn't abandon them. No way. They needed me.

I had to get Michel out of my head, for good, so that

my memories of him could slowly fade to make way for reality.

This had never been my forte.

18

The cheese slicer glided through the lump of parmesan cheese, Parmigiano Reggiano. A world away from the soap-like powder from a bag that I'd considered as such in a previous life in Holland. The real thing, bought whole, is frightfully expensive, but you can turn it into beautiful, inch-wide curls, which you still sometimes see scattered over carpaccio in posh restaurants, so thin they melt on your tongue. Every so often I took a wooden spoon and stirred the pine nuts that were roasting in a non-stick pan on a high heat. The chopped bacon had been fried and was draining on three layers of kitchen paper, and the dressing was ready.

It was raining and it was getting cooler by the day, so alfresco dining was no longer possible. The wooden dining table was no more than fifteen feet away from me in the large hall. Today there was one plate missing from the laid table. Michel was away. He had been for four days now. I wondered where he'd got to. Was it because of me? Had Peter needed him on another job? Was he ill?

I didn't dare ask Peter, for fear that my interest in one of the workmen would attract his attention. Ridiculous, because if Pierre-Antoine or Louis didn't turn up I'd probably ask why without a second thought.

I took two large bottles of water and the salad out of the fridge and put them on the table. The hall was exposed to the wind. The rain was getting in, on to the oak floor. The doors were due for collection tomorrow, as were the windows. So it was only a matter of days before the house would be 'weathertight', as Peter and Eric called it. I couldn't wait.

Next week I'd be able to make myself a bit more useful, because then I could decorate the temporary bedrooms on the first floor of the left wing. This week I'd been hunting for carpet and curtains and placed my order. I'd plumped for royal blue for the children's rooms and dark red and ivory for the room where Eric and I were going to sleep in the coming months. I had no intention of giving them a personal touch; next year these same rooms would be occupied by our guests.

I'd been feeling a little out of place over the last few days and couldn't relax. Now it rained so much going to the lake was no longer an option when I wanted to take a breather, have a brief moment to myself. I had no choice but to withdraw into the caravan, which strongly reminded me of Michel and where I'd sat staring into space more than once over the past few days, in bed, one arm round a pillow and a book open on my lap.

I needed someone to talk to. Someone I could trust. But I didn't dare pick up the phone for anything other than superficial chitchat, for fear that Erica, or anyone else whose number I might dial, would pass on the gossip, which would eventually find its way indirectly back to Eric. We might have been living hundreds of miles away from our old village, but the lines of communication were fast. It was too risky.

If my mother had still been alive, I couldn't even have called her about this. She wanted a financially secure husband for me, a safe future. Comfort. The boyfriends I brought home who failed to convince her that they were interested in or destined for a glorious career were given the cold shoulder. She'd turn in her grave if she knew what I'd done. What I'd risked and above all for whom. All she'd see was a boy of twenty or so with an old motorbike. An unskilled labourer, illiterate, without money or possessions. Yes, she really would turn in her grave. I was now certain that ghosts didn't exist, because if they were aware of the deeds of the living, and could actually observe us from their transparent world, my mother would have haunted me.

I went back to the kitchen to get the glasses. Took the butter and cheese out of the fridge and put them on the table beside the baguettes. The kitchen timer rang. I drained the tagliatelle. As I mixed the ingredients together, I thought back to the time when I introduced Eric to my mother. It took a long time, a very long time, before she was willing to accept him. Eric didn't come from old money, from a wealthy family; he was just a boy like any other, and in her view that wasn't good enough for me. I was her only daughter. The only child she'd borne, the product of blind love, passion perhaps, for a man who abandoned her a few years after the birth because he wasn't ready to commit — and probably never would be. This is what she'd told me from time to time in those very rare, always far too brief moments when she opened up to me, and I could get an insight into her inner world. Into what lay behind that confident, domineering mask she'd assumed over the course of her life. Love, she told me then, wasn't important. Love was just a dead weight, and it was overrated. Love wouldn't make the pot boil. My mother had had a hard life, a very hard life. She wanted to spare me the same.

She succeeded in the end; that headstrong attitude had stemmed from the same love she'd opposed her whole life. This didn't begin to dawn on me until long after she passed away. Sometimes people have to die before we can understand their motives. Sad, but true.

The lads came downstairs. Some of them squeezed past me and washed their hands in the sink. They carried the smell of freshly sawn wood and their clothing was full of little splinters and dust. Bruno leaned against the fridge and rolled a cigarette. His bleached hair was covered in dust and stuck out in all directions. He was wearing a faded orange T-shirt, creased and stained. I nodded at him, smiled briefly. Should I ask him where Michel was?

I put the two dishes of steaming tagliatelle on the table and drew up my chair.

During the meal I didn't speak much. I did listen, in the hope that someone might say something about Michel, or ask a question. Bruno was bound to know what was going on; he lived in the same house and they were friends, as Michel had told me in Arcachon. So I tuned in mostly to what Bruno was saying, but right now he only seemed interested in technical details regarding the work on the first floor of the left wing.

'Next week we can finally sleep in our own bed,' Eric said to me. 'Probably towards the end of the week. Great, isn't it?'

I smiled.

'Do you think the curtains will arrive in time?' he added.

'They promised me they'd be ready on Monday. They said they'd ring to let us know when they were going to deliver them.'

Eric muttered something and turned back to Peter. He'd grown enormously fond of Peter, and this appeared to be mutual. The beginning of a friendship. Partly because Eric and Peter spent so much time together, I was feeling increasingly lonely. I had no female friends yet. But there was no point, at this early stage, in drawing conclusions. I had to think more positively. At Peter's party next weekend I was bound to bump into women of my age with whom I could strike up a conversation. I was really starting to miss that now: someone to talk to, face to face rather than on the phone, and in my own language, even if it was just small talk. A simple conversation with someone who would understand what it's like to emigrate, who knew that out-of-place feeling from experience and could reassure me that everything would turn out all right.

There was nobody I could turn to about that, either. Friends I spoke to on the phone had no idea what our life was like now, no clue. From their responses, I noticed they thought that all the men here in the deep South of France went about in berets, drove round in horrible Citroën 2CVs and gorged their geese on maize porridge.

It turned out that no one in my old circle of friends was aware that France was a modern, Western country with political disturbances, its own car industry, broadband internet and a lively youth culture, including drug problems, only with so much more space and a rather different culture. As for me, I was feeling more and more like an outsider in their lives. The change of country and routine had changed me. I could no longer genuinely empathise with the stress, the parking problems, the traffic and the nightmare of childcare. All in all, I was feeling increasingly rootless. Like I was floating somewhere in a vacuum, in no man's land, completely thrown upon my own resources.

In reality, of course, this empty feeling inside had everything to do with Michel, with his absence and the gnawing, almost unbearable uncertainty this entailed. I knew this in my head. But it had no effect on the dark clouds in my mind. The rain beating down outside, which showed no sign of stopping, did little to improve my mood either.

I took one last bite of my tagliatelle and looked at Eric, who, without so much as thinking, was wiping his plate clean with a carelessly torn-off piece of baguette, like a true Frenchman. I hardly had any contact with him these days; he could only think in terms of building materials, calculations, figures and inches.

It was high time I put a stop to this pessimism, this self-pity. Eric would probably come round once the building work was out of the way.

Things could only get better.

I'm lying on my back. Patterns in black and white and blurred lines are dancing in front of my eyes. A moment ago the light flickered out, all of a sudden, without warning. I'm about to look at my watch, but remember it's been taken off me. I have no idea what time it is.

They haven't taken me out of my cell all day. Not once. Why are they keeping me here without asking me any questions? I wonder whether it's routine, a standard procedure: keep people guessing and leave them alone with their thoughts, within these seventy square feet, without any distractions other than their own, churning thoughts. So that you're forced to think about what you've done, slowly going crazy – and are grateful in the end for any human contact to drown out that suffocating internal dialogue.

I turn towards the wall and stare into space, my eyes wide open, vacant. There are other people in this cell block. I can hear faint murmuring. Someone tapping on a pipe. A moment ago I heard a shout, a man's voice. I couldn't understand what he was saying.

My fingertips feel their way through the darkness and scrape across the wall. I think about Eric, about Isabelle, Bastian.

Don't think about them, don't.

I wonder if they're sleeping. I wonder what Eric's told them.

Stop it!

I fold my hands behind my head and close my eyes. I try to imagine I'm not here, but by the lake. If I just try hard enough, I might be able to feel the sun on my skin, the wind through my hair, hear the sound of the swallows and the frogs, the rustling of the grass . . .

No such luck.

I stare at the outlines of the cell that confines me. I don't want to be here. I want to be the one who decides what I do: turn the light on and off, listen to music, watch TV, read a book, go outside, go shopping, read to Bastian and Isabelle. Be *free*. I was free, but I didn't realise it. I only realise it now, now that I'm literally imprisoned; the bars of my cage, the walls around my marriage, my limited sphere of influence, it certainly wasn't my mother who created them. Nor Eric.

But myself.

I didn't just allow this to happen; I deliberately handed a brick to anybody who wanted one, and showed them where to put the walls that restricted me.

But those weren't real walls, unlike in here.

They existed only in my head.

19

Peter and Claudia's house was situated, like ours, a long way from the main road. The long driveway wound through an old chestnut wood and ended in a large circle with a fountain in the middle. Peter's house looked more like a small castle than a country house. Two dark towers stood out against the deep blue sky, where long trails of orange were visible from the setting sun. A soft, warm light was coming from the sash windows, lighting up the driveway. Most of the cars parked near the house had French number plates.

Bastian and Isabelle went absolutely wild. They almost tumbled over each other to get out of the car. I'd dressed them in their smartest clothes for the occasion: Isabelle in a pink cotton dress with a white ribbon in her blond hair; Bastian in a pair of three-quarter-length trousers with a white cotton shirt and his hair gelled in a parting. Muffled music was coming from the house – 'Give Me the Night' by George Benson – along with the sound of voices.

'Our house is going to turn out like this too,' said Eric,

walking beside me in his dark-blue suit, surveying the house
with approval. 'Just you wait. Living the life of Riley! Ha!'

'Will there really be Dutch children here?' asked Isabelle.
She was skipping along beside me over the beige gravel to
the double front door.

'Yes,' I said, taking her hand. 'Peter said so. He has a
room with a TV and sweets, especially for you.'

As I entered, I looked round for Michel. The past week
had been dull, dreary, restless and empty. I hoped he'd be
here, and — if this proved to be the case — that we could
perhaps take a moment to talk to each other, that I could
touch him for a moment. And if this wasn't possible, that
we could at least exchange a knowing glance which would
put me at ease.

People everywhere in warm yellow light, party outfits,
sparkling jewellery, old, young, whispering and laughing
out loud, blond and dark, but nowhere in that jumble could
I pick out Michel's striking face.

'Claudia, here come Simone and Eric!'

Peter walked towards us, grinning. His blue and white
striped shirt was open at the collar. A woman with short,
red hair, well built, with an energetic appearance, held out
her hand. She was wearing a white ensemble with black
piping, which looked like it came from the latest Chanel
collection.

I introduced myself to her, and out of the corner of my
eye I could see Peter ruffling Bastian's hair affectionately

with his big hands, messing up my son's meticulously styled side parting.

'I'll help you with the children first,' said Claudia. She held her hand out to Isabelle, who took it shyly. 'Come with me.'

I followed Claudia through the house. It was beautiful, really authentic with fieldstone walls, full of rough stucco and dark wood, and beautiful stone archways. I overheard conversations in French, Dutch, Flemish, English and German. Music from the live band echoed throughout the house. I hadn't located the musicians yet, but I'd already established that they were masters of seventies disco music. The singer had a warm, soothing voice. The atmosphere was wonderful.

No sign of Michel.

'Here we are,' said Claudia. She opened a heavy oak door. 'This is our television room. Peter spends a lot of time in here: he loves films.'

It was a luxurious room with an oak floor and two big, black leather sofas. A couple of oil paintings depicting horses were hanging on the walls. I counted five children, aged from four to ten. I recognised the Nickelodeon logo on the television screen. The children were lounging on the sofas, and one of them was lying on the rug in front of the television.

They looked at us with curiosity. Isabelle and Bastian shuffled along timidly and listened meekly to Claudia's instructions.

'Mummy and Daddy will be somewhere here in the house.' I squeezed their shoulders in parting. 'Do you think you'll be OK here?'

They nodded. One of the children passed Isabelle a plate of sweets.

Bastian made himself comfortable and glanced briefly at a boy the same age. 'Are you from Holland too?'

The boy nodded shyly.

'Do they have Coke here as well?'

The boy pointed to a sideboard with bottles of soft drinks and fruit juice next to stacked plastic cups.

'Let's go,' said Claudia. 'The children will have a great time. I'd like to introduce you to a few people.'

With one last look at the children I followed her through the corridors and past the rooms; most of the doors were open. Lots of rugs, cosily decorated, with stone, leather and wood. It was an enormous house, bigger than ours.

'It's a shame summer's over,' said Claudia. Her high heels clicked on the floor. 'Or we could have held this outside. Sometimes it's warm enough to have barbecues here until well into December, but sadly that was never on the cards this week.'

'At least it's stopped raining,' I replied.

'Yes, thankfully.'

Claudia took me to a large, central space. The living room, probably; at least three times the size of our old living room in Holland. Low ceilings with dark-brown beams. There were groups of people everywhere. I estimated there to be more than a hundred guests.

I kept looking round, hoping to catch a glimpse of Michel.

'Here's the bar.' Claudia pointed nonchalantly to a small bar in the corner. There was a young man standing behind it, small and thin, with dark, close-cropped hair. 'What would you like to drink?' she asked.

'Red wine, please.'

The barman poured me a glass and handed it to me.

Claudia was already beckoning. 'Come on, you have people to meet.'

She headed for a group of people and took a woman affectionately by the arm, who immediately turned to face me and looked at me with interest.

'Lucy, may I introduce you to Simone? She and her husband moved here a few months ago. They have two children at primary school and Simone is going to open a *chambres d'hôtes*.'

Lucy had fair hair and a deep tan. She was wearing a short skirt and a black blouse with a plunging neckline. I guessed her to be in her late forties. We shook hands.

'Lucy comes from Amsterdam,' said Claudia. 'She settled here four years ago, and runs a market stall selling Dutch cheese.'

I gave Lucy a friendly nod, but wasn't really sure what to say. In social situations, especially in groups, I'd never really felt at ease. Besides, at first glance Lucy didn't appear to be my type. But beggars couldn't be choosers.

Claudia cooed, threw herself on a new couple who appeared in the living room, and disappeared from view.

'A *chambres d'hôtes*, that was also my first idea, when I came here,' Lucy confided. 'I'd bought a house, well, *I* . . . together with *him* –' she pointed to an older man who squeezed his eyes shut reassuringly when our eyes met – '—with enough space, a separate staircase for the guests and a swimming pool. I spent a whole year fixing it all up, as well as the garden. But I'm not cut out to be a hostess. People can't half *moan*, awful. They want a holiday *à la campagne* but complain when the water pressure's too low, or when there are lizards running around in their bedrooms. And then they don't like fish, or they're vegetarian; I spent the whole day cooking, practically to order, and even then it wasn't good enough for some of them. The majority did enjoy themselves, but then the moaners are the ones you remember. They sap all your energy. In the end I'd had enough.'

'Then you set up a market stall?'

'They only sell Gouda here, and Amsterdammer if you're lucky. My brother-in-law is a cheese merchant so I thought: oh well, why not try selling a wider selection of Dutch cheese here? And I still do that now.'

'Can you make a living from that?' I asked, grateful she'd got the conversation going. I wondered if I should revise my first impression, as she seemed very friendly.

'Jack retired four years ago. We can live well on his pension, but I'm still a young woman, and I don't want to spend all day on a lounger by the pool. Amsterdam mentality, you know: I need something to do, otherwise I'll go crazy.'

Behind Lucy was the band, surrounded by sound equipment and a mass of cables. Three Spanish-looking men in yellow Hawaiian shirts and shiny black trousers. The singer announced a break. A CD of Spanish guitar music came on. I recognised the tune; it was by Los . . . Los something.

'Do you like Spanish music?' asked Lucy. She took a sip of a red concoction with ice.

'Yes, it's easy to dance to, but I don't know the first thing about it.'

'But then, you don't need to know everything . . . What did you do in Holland?'

The question took me by surprise. I lacked an exciting background to brag about at parties. 'I did a secretarial course and worked as an executive secretary for a few years.'

'Where did you work?'

'Capgemini.'

She pulled a face. 'One of those American conglomerates.'

'It's not so bad.'

'But you came here to escape the rat race?'

Lucy rescued me once again, without realising it. Now I didn't have to tell her I'd given up work after Bastian was born, because I couldn't face leaving my baby in a crèche all day. And then taken countless correspondence courses in psychology and studied philosophy. I gave it up in the end, because it was too confrontational, and I couldn't discuss it with Eric, who usually came home shattered. Besides, he had a more down-to-earth and practical nature and his knowledge of psychology was geared towards marketing.

'It was actually more my husband,' I replied, 'who wanted to come here.'

She frowned. 'What about you? A step like that should be a joint decision! Especially when you've got children. Your relationship needs to be rock solid or you'll soon end up in the danger zone. You don't want to know how many marriages I've seen hit the rocks here. Different country and different language, the ups and downs of building work, lack of comfort: there's no better breeding ground for a marriage crisis, take it from me.'

'It's not that bad,' I replied, taking a sip of wine. I noticed my hand was shaking. 'I'm just saying it wasn't my idea to move here. Opening a *chambres d'hôtes* was like a dream for me. I never thought it possible I'd be doing it for real one day, and living in France.'

'Well then, you should think yourself lucky your husband took the initiative; you only live once.'

Suddenly I saw Michel. He was standing diagonally under a spotlight, beneath the archway leading to the hall, scanning the smoky room. It took enormous self-control not to run towards him. Instead I quickly looked round, as if trying to spot Eric somewhere.

Michel had already seen me. He grinned, winked and the next moment he was gone again. I held my breath.

It was a wonder a boy like Michel was still working on scaffolding for the minimum wage, and hadn't yet been discovered by some modelling agency. They probably looked for their young talent in big cities and not in sleepy provincial towns.

Lucy was still talking to me. Her monologue faded into the background.

'Sorry,' I interrupted her. 'Please excuse me for a moment.'

I hurried over to where I'd seen Michel. He was standing a few feet away in the corridor. Bruno was beside him, with his back turned to me.

I hesitated.

The problem solved itself. Bruno turned his head towards me, exchanged a knowing glance with Michel and walked past me towards the bar. As he went by I saw that he was smiling. Bruno knew. And if Bruno . . .

The corner of Michel's mouth curled; he eyed me up. 'Looking good.'

I forgot everything instantly, I just wanted to hold him, run my hands over his stomach, press myself up against him.

There were too many people. I stayed at a safe distance.

'Where were you?' I said, quickly. I glanced briefly in the direction of the living room. There was nobody I knew.

'I'm working for a Belgian couple. On their roof. I've missed you.'

He was wearing a white cotton shirt, oversized, with three-quarter-length trousers in a green pastel colour, and a pair of loafers. It looked stunning on him. But even if he'd been wearing a diving suit, it probably wouldn't have made much difference to the innumerable chemical reactions taking place in my body.

'I've missed you too,' I said, firmly suppressing the impulse to drag him outside. Someone bumped into me and apologised in English.

'Why don't you come over sometime?' he said. His eyes were scanning the room. Just like me, he was on his guard.

'I don't know where you live.'

The band started up again. Very loudly. It gave me the opportunity to lean in closer to him. I took one step, then another, and he leaned over me. He whispered the most detailed set of directions I'd ever heard, or perhaps it was the only one that lodged itself straight in my long-term memory. The route to Rue Charles de Gaulle was stamped in my memory to the end of time.

'Maybe I'll drop by,' I said.

'You must. I've missed you.' He didn't take his eyes off the people coming into the corridor from the living room, on their way to the toilet and back to the living room.

'You're Simone, aren't you?'

I turned round with a start. Behind me was a balding man of around forty. He was wearing a bright-red shirt over a white T-shirt.

'That's my name,' I said, not overly friendly.

'Then I'm not mistaken.' He held out his hand. Fleshy and hairy, an expensive watch around his wrist. Light-blue eyes beneath bushy eyebrows. 'I'm Theo. My wife Betty and I moved here two years ago.'

Theo told me exactly where they lived, but it went in one ear and out the other. I couldn't remember any French place names of more than two syllables; they just wouldn't stick.

'We also have two children, just like you,' he continued. 'And we also renovated our house ourselves, with Peter's help, of course. I started on it myself, but it got too much for me. Peter told me you're making good progress with the work, in which case, you're lucky. You often find all sorts of things in those old houses. It never goes according to plan.'

'I've heard that before.'

I looked at the spot where Michel had been standing a moment ago. He was gone.

'I was chatting with your husband just now. My wife has invited you all over for dinner next week. We also rent out *chambres d'hôtes*; perhaps we could start exchanging guests. Every year during the season we have to turn people away: you know, people who try to book at the last minute. Maybe we could send them to you . . . People should cooperate more round here.'

'Yes, good idea,' I answered vacantly.

Eric came towards us. I could see in his eyes and his whole demeanour that he'd already had too much to drink. I couldn't help looking at the wine in my glass. I'd barely touched it.

Eric put a possessive arm round me. 'I lost you. Where were you? Ha, Theo, I see you've already found Simone.'

Theo slapped Eric on the shoulder as if he'd known him for years. I took a big gulp of wine.

'We've exchanged addresses,' Eric explained. 'We're going to dinner at their house next week. Betty and Theo had a restaurant in Holland, a fantastic place according to Peter, so we won't go hungry. Has Theo already told you they have two children? Two boys, about the same age as Isabelle and Bastian.'

I looked at Theo. 'That'll be nice for our children. They miss speaking Dutch and they haven't managed to make any proper friends here yet.'

'That'll happen in due course,' Theo replied. 'It took about a year before ours felt at home, but the eldest is now "dating" a girl in his class. The last time we were planning to go back to Holland, to visit family, he didn't want to come because he'd miss Juliette too much.'

'So there's still hope,' I remarked.

'Oh, definitely, don't worry. At first Betty was just worried the children wouldn't be able to settle, precisely because we love it so much here. But that's no longer an issue. The *chambres d'hôtes* are doing good business, the kids are already integrating well, and you meet more and more people as you go along. Right now, you're at the most difficult stage: the renovation, the caravan, the red tape . . . Your husband's told me all about it.'

The band struck up a new tune. One that reminded me of Cuba, proper dance music.

Theo was buttonholed by an Englishman, who took him away from us in order to introduce him to someone else.

'Are you having fun?' asked Eric.

I nodded. 'It was a good idea of Peter's, this party. You really do get the chance to meet people. That Theo seems like a nice guy. Have you met his wife, that . . .'

'Betty. Yes, I've already spoken to her briefly. I think you'll like her too. Anyway, we'll find out next week. This evening is perfect for networking, don't you think? So let's make the most of it. I'm talking myself hoarse. Where exactly are the children?'

I gave him directions to the television room.

'I'll go and check if everything's OK.'

'All right.' I took a few steps in the direction of the living room, following Eric. Michel was at the bar talking to Bruno and two girls. I stood watching them from under the archway, with a half-full glass of wine in my hand. As if hypnotised. He was so scarily beautiful. Frightening. Completely balanced. He radiated strength, in everything: his mannerisms, the way he spoke, laughed. A handsome face. Energy. Manliness.

I took a big sip of wine. And another.

'Beautiful boy, eh?'

Beside me was a woman of around forty-five. She was a lot smaller than me and had short black hair with red highlights and bright-green eyes. Gold jewellery sparkled against her tanned skin.

'Sorry?' I said.

She raised her glass towards Michel. 'I saw you staring. You were, weren't you? *That* . . . *that* over there, that gorgeous thing. Michel. The biggest charmer in the South of France.' She grinned and fluttered her heavily made-up eyelids.

I realised she'd had too much to drink. 'That boy is just . . . How shall I put it . . . Can you see the neon sign on his forehead?' She looked me in the eye and ran her index finger over her forehead, from left to right. 'S-E-X. That's what it says.'

I almost choked on my wine and looked the other way. I tried my best to think of a response, to no avail.

'And besides . . . He's working for you, isn't he? Peter told me earlier this evening, that Michel's in the team, with Bruno and the two Antoines. Last year Peter did our studio with the same men . . . That was a good time.' She smiled again and swung her upper body in time with the music.

Once again I didn't answer.

'Sorry, my fault: I haven't introduced myself yet. Rita Stevens.' She held out her hand. Yet more gold jingled around her thin wrists.

'Simone Jansen.'

'I've already met your husband, I believe. Eric, isn't it?'

I nodded.

'Peter introduced us to each other. You have a nice husband. He said it's been a real education. Only last year he'd ring a plumber when the tap was leaking, and now he's on the scaffolding himself. The things a change of country can do to people . . . Strange, isn't it? Don't you find it strange, the way people act differently here than in the place where they were born and bred? And discover new sides to themselves?'

Rita wasn't beating about the bush, but I had absolutely no desire to follow suit. It was really nobody's business, the most remarkable new side I'd discovered to myself.

'You're opening a *chambres d'hôtes*, aren't you?' she said, changing the subject when I didn't answer.

'That's the idea.'

'Good choice. If I were you I'd do something extra. Painting or cookery courses or something like that. You can charge three times as much that way . . . Ben and I run workshops: stressed-out managers come to us for courses, four days of pottery, good food and then back up north like new men. Then within a couple of days they're back to square one, but oh well . . . We moved here last year. Any regrets?'

I looked at her. She had lots of freckles, I could see now. She was probably a nice person, but I didn't like her. And to be honest, in all likelihood this aversion had everything to do with how she was looking at Michel and the way she talked about him.

'Regrets?' I repeated.

'Yes, regrets. About coming here?'

'No, no regrets. It's wonderful here.'

'*So* it is: wonderful,' she said, once again casting a knowing glance in Michel's direction, who was dancing with a girl of about twenty, talking to her and smiling at her at the same time. His dance partner had a cascade of dark curls and an hourglass figure in a short floral dress made of very thin fabric. She did a kind of pirouette, very elegantly, with a beaming smile. I felt a twinge of jealousy. Was she . . . his girlfriend, perhaps? I'd never asked him if he had a girlfriend. Or was he trying to pick her up, and later tonight . . .

Still looking in Michel's direction, Rita said: 'Ben has never set foot on the dance floor. He was sitting at the bar when I met him and that's where you can still find him. Dutch men don't know how to move their bodies. They're born rigid. That couple trying to dance, they're stomping around like dry sticks, as if they've pooped their pants. And then just look at that . . . that body . . .'

What did Rita want from me? Why did she keep going on about Michel?

Rita bumped into me and spilled some wine on the floor. 'Hey, Simone, tell me, woman to woman, do you sometimes think . . . I mean, with that boy around the house all day, with that divine body, do you sometimes consider—'

'Sorry, I need the toilet,' I interrupted, fleeing into the corridor.

In the privacy of the toilet I leaned against the cool marble, my back against the wall. I closed my eyes. That Rita, with her pottery courses and her studio built by Michel. All the common sense I could still muster was telling me there was no reason to let her upset me. Rita had just had too much to drink, like everyone else this evening, and found Michel attractive, just like me.

I wiped away small streaks of smudged eyeliner, washed my hands, took a deep breath and walked back into the festivities.

20

'I'd like to try cocaine one day,' I heard myself say.

Peter was the only one to respond. 'Why?'

He had a strange glint in his eyes, but it could have been the alcohol, or the late hour.

It was half past four in the morning and a joint was being passed round. There were nine of us left in Peter's television room, chatting after the party. The television was still on, cartoons, but the volume was muted. Apart from me and Eric, and Peter and Claudia, Peter's accountant, Julien, was still there, along with his wife, Annie, who were both Belgian, like Peter. They lived a couple of villages away. There was also a Dutch man in his early forties called Frank, who turned out to be one of Peter's business associates. He was a dark man with a rather glum face, a moustache and a mass of curly hair. Bruno was still there, as was Michel.

'Cocaine, why cocaine?' Peter asked once more.

'Because,' I said.

Eric grumbled. I felt the need to restrain myself a little in his presence, choose my words slightly more carefully.

'I've never tried it. But I have read a lot about it. It seems like the whole world's tried cocaine, except for me. It feels like . . . a lack of general knowledge.'

Bastian and Isabelle were asleep in the guest quarters. Much earlier in the evening Claudia had taken me to the television room to show me Bastian and Isabelle, who'd fallen asleep on the sofa. This had given me the chance to see the rooms behind the living quarters, separate guest accommodation, because we'd carried the children there and tucked them in. They'd been dead to the world, and remained fast asleep, murmuring occasionally. The room next to Bastian and Isabelle's contained a double bed and a small bathroom.

'You can sleep here,' she'd said. 'I always hate it when people drink and drive. There are a lot of fatal road accidents at the weekends, especially with the bends here.'

'You're not missing anything, when it comes to cocaine,' I heard Peter say.

The television room was blue with smoke. I'd taken a couple of puffs, not wanting to be rude, but it wasn't my thing.

'For the first ten minutes you feel like you could lift a billiard table, like you have the most wonderful ideas in the world,' he continued. 'And then it's over.'

Silence fell.

I took another sip of water. Perhaps it was time for bed. Eric had stopped actively contributing to the conversation a while ago. The marihuana had really gone to his head; it was making him sleepy. Claudia, too, had fallen asleep. She was lying against Peter with one arm across his chest. Frank had laid his head back against the sofa and didn't seem very alert either. Bruno whispered something unintelligible every so often and giggled, with a blissful smile on his face. Michel was rolling a beer glass between his fingers and appeared to be the most wide awake of us all. He hadn't touched any drugs, not that I'd noticed. He was sitting on the edge of the stool near the coffee table, trying to follow my conversation with Peter. I couldn't tell how much he understood.

Outside it was already starting to get light. I didn't feel particularly tired or drowsy, as I usually did after staying up all night. In all likelihood I was simply beyond sleep.

'In a moment I'm going to show you to your rooms,' said Peter. 'I think it's time.'

Eric suddenly woke with a start, leaned forward and poured himself another glass of wine. He was rather uncoordinated now and spilled some on the coffee table. 'One more,' he murmured. 'Then bed.'

Suddenly I felt sick. 'I'm just nipping to the toilet.'

As I walked down the long corridor towards the toilet, past the living room and the olive-green plastered walls with illuminated oil paintings, the nausea was already beginning to subside. There was less smoke in the air here than in the television room. I hadn't touched another drop of wine since two o'clock this morning, only water, but the alcohol was still clearly in my system. I was feeling rather light-headed. I couldn't bear the thought of having to return to the television room, into the thick smoke, with that sweet, overpowering smell that made my nose and eyes sting. I opened a side door and went outside.

A fresh morning breeze hit me in the face. I took a deep breath, and another. Birds were singing all around me. The sky had a light pastel tint, greyish-pink. I walked across the gravel to the corner of the house, in the direction of the guest quarters. The last time Eric had checked on Bastian and Isabelle was at around twelve o'clock. I opened the door and turned on the light in the small living room. Tiptoed up the spiral staircase and stood listening at the door. Steady breathing. Nothing to worry about. Deep sleep.

I left the guest quarters and noticed that the nausea had completely vanished. Birdsong rang out from all directions. It was a fantastic morning in a lovely garden, full of low hedges, shrubs and ponds. Claudia had told me it was one of her hobbies. A few years ago she'd made this plot of land her project. Back then it had still been a neglected vegetable garden, but she'd watched it grow in beauty year after year. It struck me as a wonderful hobby, and I resolved to take up gardening as soon as the building work on our house was out of the way.

Halfway along the path I stopped.

Michel came strolling towards me. The very picture he

formed, with the shirt hanging open, that gorgeous body of his . . . I couldn't think any more, didn't want to think any more. I tried as hard as I could to stop myself from running up to him and jumping on him.

Near the corner of the house he put his arms round my waist and kissed me. He pulled me along, out of sight of the house, against a blank side wall, and pushed me against the fieldstone bricks.

My hands slipped over his waist, which was narrow and firm. I closed my eyes for a moment. It felt fantastic to have him completely to myself. Wonderful, intoxicating, euphoric almost. No other women slobbering over him, just him and me.

'*Tu m'as manqué*,' he whispered. 'I've missed you.'

'Who was that girl?'

He kissed me on the neck.

'I want to know,' I persisted.

'Which girl?'

'The one you were dancing with, in the floral dress.'

'Jealous?' He curled the corner of his mouth, with laughter in his eyes. He found this really funny. 'Were you jealous?'

'Yes.'

'No need.' He bent forward to kiss me once more, one hand stroking my back, the other loosening my blouse and finding its way hastily under my bra, which he pushed up. He knew what he was doing. The speed of his movements made my head spin.

A morning breeze caressed my bare skin.

This was Russian roulette. 'Not here,' I whispered.

He bit my neck. 'I want you.'

'No, we can't: someone could come any minute.'

'Everyone's asleep, blind drunk or stoned. No one's going to come.' His mouth slipped down to my breast, with one hand cupping the other. I closed my eyes, laid my head against the wall. Then he came back up again. He brushed his nose along mine and pressed his pelvis against me, so that I could feel his erection. The blood was rushing through my veins, it was pounding, singing, I was leaning heavily against the outer wall. My hands felt automatically for the zip of his trousers. 'I've missed you so much,' he whispered, followed by something I couldn't understand. He pulled up my skirt, pushed my thong to the side. My breathing was shallow, I could no longer speak.

Eric would come looking for me. More people could come outside. Peter had already said he was going to turf us out a quarter of an hour ago.

'We . . . can't.'

'Relax.'

'No, no,' I spluttered. If I didn't act now, if I didn't call a halt to this, I'd have to answer for the consequences. I'd already gone too far.

To slow Michel down, but mainly to protect myself, I took his head in my hands, forced him to look at me.

'Look at me,' I hissed. I didn't know the French expression for 'get caught', so I added: 'I'm scared, OK? I'm really scared.'

This seemed to work. He let go of me.

I pulled down my bra, quickly fastened my blouse and tucked it back into my belt where it had come loose. Ran my fingers through his hair and ruffled it slightly. Michel looked at me gloomily; he followed my every movement. Then zipped up his trousers and rearranged the contents. 'You really must come and see me sometime.'

'And what about Bruno?' I heard myself say. I was still far from composed. I felt my cheeks flushing and my breathing was shallow. 'He knows me. And our car.'

My God, was this really happening? Was I now secretly making a date – intentionally?

Is this how these things work?

'He's never there on Friday evenings; he goes to see his girlfriend. Come on Friday.'

'What exactly does Bru—'

Michel backed away. I saw him looking, startled, at something behind me, and the next moment he was gone and I was alone.

I turned round. Peter.

I reacted more violently than someone with a clear conscience would have done. My face blushed even deeper; my mouth fell open. My body betrayed me; it always betrayed me. I managed to force a smile, but it was shaky, unnatural. I reached for the hook of my blouse, to check if it was fastened.

I had to say something now, something to break the tension, something to explain this rendezvous with Michel, one of his workmen, in the early morning light, against the outer wall, and ultimately make it pale into something trivial, something completely innocent.

Every second of silence would only make me look guiltier, *make* me guiltier, make too big a deal out of . . . Out of what? What had Peter seen exactly? Did he just *think* he'd seen something? No. He *knew* it.

I could see in his whole demeanour and in his eyes that he knew what was going on.

Oddly enough, he said nothing. He stood there for a moment, as if he wanted to enjoy my panic, prolong this moment. Then he simply smiled enigmatically and walked towards the back door, sniggering almost, shaking his head.

21

Bastian waved a papier-mâché sword like a madman and gave a battle cry. Isabelle was dressed as an elf, with little wings made from wire and tulle. An army of light-blue and pink elves was taking on evil dwarves and knights. The logic escaped me partly, the fast, unintelligible dialogue, completely.

I was surrounded by at least two hundred people sitting squashed together in the *salle de fête*. The proud parents and family of the Amandines, Lauras, Thomases and Lucs who were putting on the show this evening after weeks of rehearsals. The community centre was shrouded in darkness, with spotlights pointed at the stage. Only the no-smoking signs on the wall glowed softly. I felt proud, like everyone else here, but perhaps just a little more than the average parent.

The elves ran gracefully in a figure of eight on the stage, waving their arms. The music was blaring and the sound equipment crackled slightly. The teachers — the female teachers were called *maîtresses* here — were standing at the side of the stage, clapping their hands, spurring the children on.

I thought back over the past week. We were now sleeping in the bedrooms in the left wing. The caravan was abandoned. It was now only used by the children to watch television, and even that would soon be unnecessary, seeing as the guest room next to Isabelle's bedroom was nearly ready, and would be able to function as a temporary living room. I had mixed feelings about this. It felt like a victory, not having to sleep in that wretched thing any more. On the other hand, over the last few weeks the caravan had become a symbol. I'd experienced the most intense moments of my life within its metal and plastic frame. Now it was going to rack and ruin among the overgrown weeds, like a dubious monument.

Sleeping indoors wasn't the only change. Peter had told Eric he'd taken on a few new jobs that he wanted to oversee in person as much as possible, especially at the beginning. His supervision was no longer required for the finishing touches to our left wing. According to Peter, we could finish the job just fine with two workmen, three at most. So since last Tuesday all the workmen were gone apart from Louis, Pierre-Antoine and Antoine. Peter had only dropped by on Monday to inform us of this development and instruct the three lads who were staying on the job for the time being. As of next week, Peter told us to expect him every Monday morning, as he wanted to keep an eye on the progress of the work. And, of course, he wanted to collect the money for the previous week. He handed Eric an invoice every week, stating the number of hours worked. Eric paid him in cash. Peter signed the invoices, thus ensuring we never 'fell behind', as he called it. I was pleased that Peter rarely darkened our door now, as it was hard to look him in the eye, especially when Eric or the children were around.

The new situation was better for everyone.

Nevertheless I missed the lads. I'd got used to cooking for a large group, and having so much life in and around the house, their singing. And now, on the third day of the new arrangement, I still hadn't managed to adjust the amount of food at lunchtime to the smaller group.

Eric nudged me. 'Wow, Simone, just look at that little fellow. He's got talent, see? He's lapping up all the attention.'

I was startled out of my thoughts. 'Yes,' I said softly, repressing the impulse not to answer with '*Oui*', in order to blend in with all the French people. A man sitting diagonally in front of us turned round. I recognised him, but I couldn't remember whose father he was. He smiled back at me and looked ahead again.

Eric leaned over to me. 'You see Isabelle, with those plaits? That *maîtresse* must have had her work cut out with all those girls.'

'Yes, how sweet.'

'You should do that sometime, too.'

'Me? *Plaits?*'

'Yes, on Isabelle. They look nice on her.'

My response was lost in the applause. The hall was now brightly lit by strip lights on the ceiling. Everyone shuffled past the wooden chairs to the foyer. People were talking to each other, shaking each other's hands. Some of them immediately went outside for a cigarette. I would have preferred to go straight home at this point, but we still had to wait for the children before we could escape.

A few tables had been pushed together in the foyer. Two brusque women in their fifties, with short jackets and white blouses, were standing behind them, filling plastic cups with fruit juice, water and red wine. I reached absently for a cup of dark-red liquid. A little alcohol was welcome. Eric also took a cup from the table and stood silently by my side. People were walking past us, giving us friendly nods, some of them shaking my hand. I introduced them to Eric, but it went no further than the standard '*ça va?*' and a friendly smile.

'We're integrating well, don't you think?' I couldn't resist saying. I could have kicked myself.

Eric looked round. 'Do you remember those Iraqis, in Holland?'

I nodded. An Iraqi family had moved to our area a couple of years ago. They had two daughters, who entered the same school as Bastian and Isabelle. They were said to be well educated: he'd been an engineer, or a professor at a university, something like that. They'd fled their homeland to build a new life in Holland. Right now I could understand better than ever how unbelievably difficult it must have been for them. I couldn't help it, but I immediately thought of Michel. Certain forms of integration knew no language barrier.

'Those Iraqis always used to wander around like lost souls at these kinds of evenings too,' I replied flatly.

'Language barrier,' said Eric. 'People don't feel like having laborious conversations at social events. But it will get better in time, the longer we live here.'

I hoped so. But I wasn't sure. I wasn't sure about anything any more. In fact, right now I doubted everything, the whole project, the *chambres d'hôtes*, how much I really wanted this, and my decision to follow Eric. Even the decision I made thirteen years ago to marry him. I dug deeper and deeper in my memory. All our nice moments seemed to pale into insignificance beside what I'd experienced with Michel. Had it really been love, the reason I married Eric? Or had I just said 'yes' because I'd been brought up to believe that an economically attractive spouse had to be my goal in life – and therefore Eric's proposal at that time meant my mission was accomplished?

I couldn't remember a moment when I'd felt as torn as I did now, in that *salle de fête* in the deep South of France, when all the outlines of my life were wound together like a tangled ball.

'Do you know everyone here?' asked Eric.

'The majority, by sight. Most of them are parents.'

'It's weird to think,' he said, pointedly looking around. 'I really don't know anyone here, not a soul. And for you these are familiar faces . . . Somehow I think we've been living parallel lives recently.'

'That . . . that was to be expected, of course.'

Even in Holland it wasn't so very different. There it was the company, here the house.

'We're going to do things differently next year. It's still hectic now, but I've been thinking about it over the last few days. Maybe when the house is finished, I could take the children to school in the morning, for example, or something like that, and you could pick them up in the evening.'

'We could do that.'

I took a big sip of wine; it tasted bad. As I looked round uneasily, my thoughts wandered to last Monday.

I'd been extremely nervous to see Peter again. He'd cast me glances every so often, but left it at that. This had reassured me somewhat, as much as that was possible. I'd come to the conclusion that it would reflect badly on him too, if this got out. Michel was after all an employee of his company, and Peter would gain nothing from a crisis between me and Eric. The work would come to a halt. People skills weren't my forte, but I had the impression I'd got to know Peter a little by now; however friendly and amiable he might be, he was strict when it came to money. As soon as the lads had gone home and Peter produced his invoice, I was always struck by his distant, business-like attitude. It quickly changed again as soon as he'd put the bundle of banknotes Eric slipped him into his wallet. Peter had probably considered the constant flow of money from Eric's wallet to be more important than his burgeoning friendship with him. Or maybe that was just wishful thinking. Later, once the house was finished, if by any chance it fell within my sphere of influence, I intended to discourage the friendship between Peter and Eric. I'd do everything in my power.

Peter knew too much. After this I wanted him out of our life. But for the time being I could only hope that last Sunday morning would have no consequences.

I was startled out of my thoughts by a man approaching us. Sixty or so, with white hair and a balding head. The mayor of our village.

He nodded sympathetically, shook our hands and exchanged the customary niceties. 'I must say, your children were excellent.'

I smiled politely. 'Thank you.'

'Is the building work coming along OK?' he asked Eric.

'Absolutely, it's going fine. Another six months or so, I think, and the majority of the work will be complete.'

'Your house belonged to very influential people. Did you know that?'

Like two small children we shook our heads, simultaneously.

'It belonged to the Sagot family,' he continued. 'Wine growers. Forty years ago the last two sons of the family left for the city. After that the house was only used for holidays, and later not at all.'

I thought about the rolling fields surrounding our house. I hadn't come across a vineyard. Not so much as a single vine.

'What happened to the vineyards?' I asked.

The mayor – his name had escaped me – frowned. 'They were neglected; there was no one to maintain them. In the end they were all dug up in the sixties. Such a shame. Oh well, progress, eh? People left for the cities; they didn't want to live here any more . . . Shame about the house too. Everyone is pleased it's now being restored to its former glory.' With a friendly nod and another handshake he bade us farewell.

'That would be unthinkable in Holland,' said Eric. 'The mayor attending a school show and striking up a conversation with everyone.'

'I don't even know who our mayor was,' I thought aloud.

The first few children began to trickle into the foyer. I recognised a couple of them, two little boys in Isabelle's class.

Eventually I spotted Bastian and Isabelle's little faces. They came running up to us in delight. The teacher hadn't fully wiped away the make-up: Isabelle's nose and eyes were rimmed with blue.

'Mummy, did you see us?'

'Yes, darling.' I stroked her plaits. 'You were great, absolutely fantastic! I'm proud of you.'

I squeezed Eric's arm. 'Shall we go?'

He threw the last few drops of wine down his throat. 'Good idea. Blimey, it's half eleven. You and the kids have got the day off tomorrow, but the lads will be at the door again at eight.'

On the way home Isabelle and Bastian lay dozing on the back seat of the car. Eric had to make an emergency stop for two wild boar trotting diagonally across the road with their tails in the air. Their eyes lit up in the glow of our headlights.

'What do you think,' said Eric, 'shall we start planting some vines? It might foster goodwill.'

'No thanks. I don't know anything about wine. Neither do you.'

'Can't you learn? I might do that one day, grow grapes. The soil seems to be suitable.'

I said nothing and looked at the lane in front of me. The headlights of the Volvo illuminated the bushes and trees, and the odd solitary letterbox at the start of a cart track or path that disappeared into the woods. There were no street lights anywhere.

My thoughts wandered involuntarily to Michel. I hadn't seen him since the party. Somehow I was slightly disappointed in him. He'd left me on my own, that morning outside. Without a word or a warning he'd run away, avoided the confrontation.

And yet not an hour went by when I didn't think of Michel.

'Simone! *Ne dis rien!*'

I shoot up in bed. A shout, echoing in my head. I raise my chin and listen. Silence.

It takes me a while to realise where I am. Yes, I remember. The hard mattress, the all-encompassing darkness. The smell of fear, despair, sweat and bleach.

Don't say anything.

I pull the blanket against my stomach and clasp my arms tightly around my body. Was it a dream? Was I sleeping? My whole body pulsates in time with my heartbeat, as I keep on listening intently.

Only more silence.

I must have been dreaming. There's no other explanation. It's probably the middle of the night, and I can hear nothing but the beating of my own heart. The blood is ringing in my ears.

'*Ne dis rien!*'

My eyes light up in the darkness.

It sounds muffled, not like a shout, but it's as real as can be. I'm not mistaken.

I know that voice. Oh yes, don't I know it. I smile.

I'm not alone here.

Footsteps in the corridor, passing my cell. Someone calls for silence. I hear keys jingling.

With warm tears flowing through my eyelashes down my face, I make a silent promise.

I won't say anything. Anything at all.

22

'I'm going shopping.'

'Oh, Mum, can I come?'

'No, darling, it'll be too late; I want you to be in bed by nine o'clock.'

'What difference does it make?' muttered Eric. 'It's the weekend; tomorrow's Saturday.'

Bastian looked up at me expectantly. For him every trip into town was like a chance card: a ticket to a present or a bag of sweets. I was spoiling them.

'No, sweetheart, Mummy wants to nip out on her own, without children.'

Eric raised his eyebrows.

'I just don't feel like it,' I said sharply. 'I just want to . . . do nothing for a while, go shopping in peace by myself. Besides, I need a new skirt, not just groceries.'

Eric shrugged. 'Kids, Mummy doesn't want you to go with her. Maybe next time.'

'But I'll bring back some chocolate,' I said, to soften the blow.

'A Kinder Egg?' ventured Bastian.

'OK, but I'm not giving it to you till tomorrow. When I get home, I want you two to be in bed.' This was a veiled instruction to Eric. Not that it had the slightest effect, but I kept trying.

The supermarket in our village in Holland bore no comparison with the one here in town. Not by any stretch of the imagination. Our old supermarket paled into a stall on a Wednesday-morning market compared with this French Leclerc. It was almost an amusement park, something the lads referred to as a '*grande surface*' – which literally means 'large area', and that was putting it mildly. The supermarket was disproportionately large. Enormous in terms of dimensions, and above all in terms of choice. Dizzying. Aisles full of desserts, oils, meat, fish, shellfish, cheese, bread, chocolate, tropical fruit, soft drinks, underwear, crockery, electronics, books. Thousands of feet. You could completely lose yourself in there, spend days in there. Isabelle and Bastian's jaws always dropped in the meat section, at the whole beef tongues, sheep hearts, and various other, no less spectacular anatomical parts of hoofed animals that we in Holland only knew from pictures. The fish section was sometimes decorated between the salmon steaks with shark heads with expressionless, staring eyes, which the children examined from all angles, full of awe and visible excitement. The aquarium with live lobsters was also guaranteed their morbid attention.

Sticking to my list, I hastily pushed the trolley along. I avoided the freezer section. After paying at one of the thirty-seven tills I slunk into a clothes shop housed under the same roof, and left my trolley unattended near the entrance. I often did this; it never caused any problems.

On a rack of evening wear I found a black skirt, in a cotton-stretch blend. I grabbed a couple of bras from a nearby rack. Black lace, three-quarter cups. I tried on the skirt and twirled in front of the mirror. Put my hands on my hips. Twirled again. It really was very short. *Too* short? Could I carry it off? My confidence took a slight knock under the unforgiving light, which clearly revealed every lump and bump on my bare legs. I decided to hold on to the skirt anyway; nowhere was the light as unflattering as in changing rooms – inexplicably enough.

One of the bras fitted. A style I hadn't worn for years. I looked at my reflection and couldn't help grinning at myself.

With two full bags of shopping on the back seat I turned into the Rue Charles de Gaulle. A wide street with a great many old houses, tall buildings, lots of traffic lights and not a tree in sight. Nor parking spaces. It was dark now, and the road was lit by street lights giving out an orange light. I crossed narrow lanes of run-down houses, with cars parked left and right. The old hospital where Michel lived looked gloomy. Big, impersonal, built from large concrete slabs, with a main entrance in the middle. I left the Volvo in one of the side streets. A chilly autumn wind circled round my bare legs. I looked around. There was no one on the street. Faint lamplight shone on to the parked cars from the main road.

Generally speaking, I would never come to an area like this.

Yet here I was. My high heels clicked purposefully on the tarmac pavement. For the first time in my life I wasn't doing what people expected of me, but something *I* wanted with my whole being. I didn't know what had set this in motion: the emigration, my stage of life, the spartan lifestyle, the hot weather, or all of these things at once. What I did know was that I made my own choices now, and I didn't want to give that up. It felt fantastic.

It felt like a liberation.

I stopped in front of the entrance. Three steps up to the wired-glass double doors. I pushed the right-hand door. It gave way. The floor was covered with trampled cans and leaflets. I climbed the stairs: depressing grey concrete bathed in greenish light. The walls were tiled in dull yellow with grey pointing.

This was where Michel lived. This was where he walked at least twice a day, on these stairs.

On the first floor I was panting a little. My heart was pounding. Doors everywhere, not a window in sight. Off-white walls covered with smudges, caged ceiling lights. My liberation was manifesting itself as a prison.

I knocked on the door at number thirty-eight, but not before pulling my skirt down a little, shaking my hair loose and psyching myself up. I tried to swallow. My mouth was too dry.

Michel opened the door. He was wearing a tight, apple-green printed T-shirt and close-fitting black boxer shorts. He examined me, with an inscrutable look in his eyes. Then he opened the door invitingly wider and I entered.

I stopped in the middle of the room. The space wasn't much bigger than Bastian's bedroom. To my left there was a plain beige kitchen unit, clean and tidy. A small, square window opposite me looked out on to the multi-storey building across the way. A two-seater sofa of an indefinable colour and a metal three-quarter-sized bed with a plain grey-striped duvet. Grey carpet, a small TV and a CD player. A poster for a Tarantino film dominated the wall above his bed. A clock radio, a pile of magazines, CDs and two scale models of cars.

That was it. Nothing more. This was his house. His home.

A greater contrast with our affluence, the space, the countless rooms and the acres of land, was virtually impossible.

I hadn't spoken yet; nor had Michel. And yet there was a continuous stream of communication. A feverish tingling that vibrated through the room.

When his hand found its way purposefully under my skirt, and he nestled his face in my neck, I remembered why I was here. Everything else fell away. I would have travelled to the other side of the world to be able to feel this body against mine.

'I have something for you,' said Michel, when I returned from the toilet in the corridor. Michel shared his bathroom with eight other tenants. There was no sign of any of them. Apart from their dirty underwear, towels and a multi-coloured collection of cups with toothbrushes.

When I saw what he'd put in front of me, I stopped dead. It was the first time I'd seen it for real.

Cocaine.

I stared at the mirror, the handful of white powder on top of it. All kinds of thoughts and feelings were racing through me.

'Isn't this what you wanted?' Michel lay stretched out on the bed, two pillows behind his head. I didn't recognise the CD he'd put on while I was away. French rap.

So he *had* understood quite a lot of the conversation I'd had with Peter in Dutch, that night after the party. But that had been the drink talking, theoretical drivel.

Really?

I didn't take my eyes off the powder. Mesmerised. I bit my bottom lip. One line. Could it do any harm?

I cast a calculating look at the clock radio. It was nine o'clock. I had to be home at ten; it would look suspicious if I came home any later. This meant I had to leave in a little over half an hour.

Would it have worn off by then? Or would this choice, which lay before me now, result in me coming face to face with my family later with enlarged pupils, jumping up and down with energy and exuberance?

I'd seen it so often on TV. Read about it so often.

The whole world was at it. My own brother-in-law, a close female friend, whole tribes. Everyone. So why not me?

Why not gain a new experience? I noticed I was shaking and my breathing had quickened. Freud, Edison and Jules Verne were on record as cocaine users. If they'd done it . . .

I was breathing rapidly. Looked at Michel, then at the white stuff. Back at the clock.

'I can't,' I said, all of a sudden, more out loud to myself than to Michel.

Michel lay there watching me. Languidly. 'It can't do any harm. A tenth of a gram. It'll be out of your system in an hour.'

I shook my head. 'No, I really can't. Sorry.'

'Scared?'

I nodded.

'Too bad.'

I got into bed next to him and curled up against him. Kissed him on his nose. 'It's *very* sweet of you.'

The corner of his mouth curled; he played with my hair. 'You don't know what you're missing.'

'Perhaps that's for the best.'

He looked over my shoulder at the thin layer of white powder. Put his chin in the hollow of my neck. Stroked my stomach absently. I shuddered.

'Shall I keep it?' he asked. 'For next time?'

I hesitated. Perhaps a moment too long.

'Forget it,' he said. 'We don't have to.'

Strangely enough, I felt guilty now. I had no idea what this must have cost and how much trouble he'd gone to in order to buy it for me, but I could imagine. He didn't have a lot of money and the French anti-drug laws were terribly strict.

Michel had stuck his neck out for me, and Simone Jansen, the narrow-minded bitch, had chickened out.

'You didn't have to do this,' I said. 'It's too expensive. Too risky.'

'I wanted to give you something you really wanted . . . Something Eric didn't need to know about.'

'You're doing that already,' I said. I ran my hand over his stomach and downwards. 'More than enough. Believe me.'

23

Action, in any form, inevitably leads to a reaction. What you say, how you look, a forgotten handshake or a prolonged silence. The thousands of seemingly insignificant everyday decisions you make, consciously or unconsciously; all these things, imagine them as boomerangs you casually hurl into space on your journey through time. Step after step, decision after decision, encounter after encounter.

Many are washed up not far from you in the sand, and are forgotten. At other times they come back to you.

Not infrequently, you yourself have determined what comes your way. Without realising it.

Monday morning, half eleven. The large front door in the hall – brand new, still in its undercoat – was wide open. In the last few months I'd grown used to an open house. The dilapidated sheds on the other side of the courtyard looked grim. It was drizzling a little. I hadn't heard the chirping of the crickets for a while. The frogs had probably sought shelter in the thick, insulating layers of mud at the bottom of our lake, and the swallows had migrated. Early November in the South of France.

The lads were doing their very best to compensate for the silence. They were at work upstairs, making a huge racket. Dust blew about through the hall. The old tiles in the bathroom must have been bearing the brunt. To the right of the stairs there was a bathtub, a shower door and a sink, still packed in bubble wrap and cardboard.

This week we were going to get a proper bathroom.

Mindlessly I put a frying pan on the stove, waited until it was hot and poured in a substantial amount of lemon-infused olive oil. I dug a jar of frozen parsley out of the freezer, and sprinkled some over the lukewarm potatoes. Then a little more coarse sea salt, after which I slid the contents of the colander into the hot oil. It sizzled for a second. I broke the potatoes into small pieces with a spatula, waited a moment until the mass was lightly browned on one side, and turned it all over.

It was a wonder I hadn't ballooned by now, with all this food.

In one of the Dutch newspapers Erica had left behind I'd seen a cover story about French women. The fact that they stayed so slim, while still eating a full cooked meal twice daily and drinking wine nearly every day, was, according to the authors of the article, all to do with the food culture. French people didn't count the pennies when it came to honest ingredients, simple foods with a known and trusted provenance. They took plenty of time to cook meals and even more time to savour them. Day after day.

Perhaps that was traditionally the case, but all around me I saw quite a lot of women who'd evidently been missed out of this romanticised study. Besides, the magazine probably hadn't discovered the tempting varieties of crisps and sweets that were taking up ever more space on the supermarket shelves. Haribo was rapidly gaining ground in the deep South of France. These bags of German bribes were dished out unthinkingly at birthday parties and on countless long car journeys.

With the obvious results.

I was startled out of my thoughts. Bleu, who'd been dozing in the hall, jumped up and approached Peter, wagging his tail. Peter went into the hall, absently stroked Bleu's back and headed towards me.

My heart skipped a beat. I started compulsively doing all kinds of absurd things in an attempt to put off greeting him. I turned my back to him to rinse my hands under the tap and dried them on a tea towel. I gave off signals in the hope that he'd carry on straight upstairs.

He didn't. Right behind me I heard dust crunching beneath his feet. I turned round. It was still difficult to look him straight in the eye, so I looked past him a little. He kissed me three times, very emphatically, gripping my upper arms so I couldn't move. It was a pushy, rather macho sort of greeting, so typical of him. In the confined space of the kitchen, in the absence of Eric and the lads and combined with the underlying tension, it felt almost like an assault. I submitted resignedly and backed away as soon as he let me go. He gazed at me intently for a long time, giving the impression he was about to say something. Suddenly he turned ninety degrees and lifted the lid off one of the pans. 'Looks good. I'll join you for lunch.'

Then he disappeared into the hall, leaving me behind in confusion.

Over lunch everything seemed normal at first. Just six people having a conversation and enjoying a good meal.

I knew better.

Peter hadn't deigned to look at me once in the past hour. He'd talked to everyone at the table, except for me. My half-hearted attempts at engaging him in conversation proved fruitless. I started clearing the table.

When I put a full pot of coffee on the table I heard that a different topic of conversation had come up. The conversation was in rapid French and the subject was women. If I understood correctly, they were arguing that French men preferred foreign wives. It wasn't clear exactly what was wrong with French women. They were speaking too fast, and partly in argot – French dialect.

I played with the spoon in my coffee. Feeling the way I did now, I'd have been better off drinking tea. That would have had a calming effect. I comforted myself with the thought that it was already nearly half one. The lads would be going back to work soon. Another half an hour, three-quarters of an hour at the most, and Peter Vandamme would be out of the picture for another week.

All of a sudden Peter looked straight at me and switched to Dutch. 'It's France's best-kept secret, but most French women are pretty sly. Outwardly, they're very polite, respectable women, proper mothers to their children and devoted wives. But oh dear . . .'

I looked at him in amazement. My fingers remained clasped around the spoon as if frozen.

He smiled cynically. 'Did you know most of them take a lover? Some of them even have more than one. Especially here, *à la campagne*. The women are up to their necks in it.'

I tried to stay calm. As calm as possible, which didn't come particularly easily to me, and quickly glanced at Eric, who was listening with interest.

'By the way, you're starting to feel quite at home here, aren't you, Simone?' Peter continued. '*Presque Française . . .*' He cast me a triumphant look and sipped his coffee.

My heart was beating in my mouth and I felt like I was starting to blush.

'Peter's right in a way,' Eric chimed in. 'You *are* starting to feel quite at home. With the cooking and things. You never used to cook such elaborate food. The change of scene has done you good in that respect.'

Eric had completely missed the undertone, and I couldn't understand it, as it was staggeringly obvious what Peter was really trying to say. Not only that: the word 'guilty' must have been written all over my face in four languages, followed by thick, bold exclamation marks. I gasped and realised I had to respond. I looked round, and for a brief moment it seemed as if everyone was staring at me. I felt a panic attack coming on.

With all the willpower I could muster I forced a smile. 'I never thought I'd enjoy cooking so much . . .'

Leave it at that, please.

Peter sat there watching me. He didn't take his brown eyes off me for a single second, as if trying to pin me down, dissect me almost.

I picked a non-existent speck of dirt off my jeans and concentrated on this, scraping even further across the diagonally woven fabric to avoid having to look up.

'It must be great,' I heard Peter say, 'if you can simply do as you please.'

He has to stop now, he really has to stop now.

'Can I have some more coffee?'

It was Pierre-Antoine, the Spanish-looking lad.

I stood up and poured him some coffee. I only just managed this: I was still shaking. Automatically I filled the rest of the cups, including Peter's, in a last-ditch, in Peter's view probably rather desperate, attempt to make everything appear as normal as possible.

The conversation waned after this and the silence seized me by the throat. Suddenly half an hour, or three-quarters of an hour, seemed like an eternity. This was torture.

'Please excuse me.' I pushed my chair back. 'There's something I really have to do.'

A cold wind, bringing light drizzle in its wake, hit me in the face as I walked down the hill, towards the lake. Tough grass stalks rubbed against my trousers, which were slowly but surely soaking up the rainwater. It started raining harder, but there could be thunder, lightning, wind, hail, and I still wouldn't return to the house until I'd heard Peter's Land Rover pulling away.

I sat down in the damp grass by the lake and stared at the thousands of circles in the water. They flowed into each other; they kept multiplying.

I wrapped my arms around my knees. It was impossible to calm down; my heart was still pounding in my throat. I was almost exploding with frustration and powerlessness.

And I was afraid. Terribly afraid.

The whole situation was starting to get out of hand.

24

Theo and Betty came from the heart of Utrecht, where they'd lived above their restaurant on a canal. They'd sold it in order to open a *chambres d'hôtes* here. They made an odd couple. He was tall and stocky, with bushy eyebrows and a rugged air, despite being very friendly and entertaining. She, on the other hand, was slight, at least a foot shorter than her husband, with fine, mid-length brown hair and eyebrows so thin they looked like they'd been tattooed on. The most striking thing about her was her glasses with garish blue frames.

Theo and Betty had shown us the guest rooms with increasing enthusiasm – there were six, with antique-looking furniture, whitewashed wood-beamed roofs and untreated oak floors. The *chambres d'hôtes* were, unlike ours, separate from the house, situated on the far side of a square with ponds, fountains, rose bushes and sculptures. It would no doubt look attractive in a sun-drenched photo on their website. Now the rain was pattering incessantly on the grey gravel.

I prodded a piece of fish. Deep-fried catfish. Theo was a chef – he'd won his spurs, if he was to be believed – but his cookery was wasted on me this evening.

'Were you able to sell your house easily in Holland?' asked Betty. 'Like us?'

'We had all the luck in the world,' Eric replied. 'We bought our house in the nineties for a little over two hundred thousand – guilders, wasn't it? About ninety thousand euros. Nobody wanted to live in that village at the time, apart from the villagers themselves. Our friends said we were crazy for moving to the sticks. But now they've all left the city as well.'

'You see that happening all over Holland nowadays, don't you?' said Theo. 'Twenty years ago everyone wanted to live in the big cities and now they're moving away again en masse. It's all hype. They head to Friesland, Groningen, Drenthe . . . to the country, where there's still space.'

'And affordable houses,' Betty chimed in.

I took a sip of wine. I was drinking too much, but it was calming me down, and helping me make it through the evening.

'That's also a thing of the past now,' Eric remarked. 'The same house in our village worth two hundred thousand guilders fifteen years ago went for nearly five hundred thousand last year. Euros, I mean. Unbelievable, really, how quickly that happened. It's gone completely mad.'

Betty spread home-made tapenade on a piece of toasted

baguette. 'That's possibly the main reason why you see more and more foreigners here. The house prices combined with the space. Distances are getting shorter, you can get internet everywhere, the telephone, so you start looking further than your own backyard. Besides, you only live once, don't you . . . And those Brits are leaving in droves; have you seen the prices there? Last year we looked in the window of an estate agent near Brighton. Absolutely un-believable! And here you can buy a detached farmhouse with several acres of land for the price of a two-bedroom flat in Holland or England.'

'And better weather.' Theo scraped the remains of his catfish on to his fork. 'That was the main reason for me, actually. I could never get used to that cold and rain.'

Betty and Theo were kind, entertaining people, it went without saying, but we didn't click. Back in Holland we'd probably never even have met; we moved in different social circles. That was one of the hallmarks of living abroad: language was the common denominator, and any positive personality traits your conversation partners happened to possess on top of that were just a bonus. There simply weren't that many Dutch people to choose from. And there certainly weren't many Dutch people with children in Bastian and Isabelle's age group.

'We haven't half been getting a lot of rain since we came here,' Eric remarked. 'And we still are.' He prodded me. 'Do you remember: our first week here?'

'Yes, of course I remember. Rain, rain, rain.'

Betty leaned over to me. 'That rain you had, everyone here was crying out for it. In July we had extremely dry weather. With suffocating temperatures. Over ninety-five degrees. Never in my life had I thought I'd wish for rain and cooler weather, but last summer I was literally begging for it. It was unbearable. If you left a block of butter on the table it would melt within an hour.'

Theo tapped a cigarette out of a pack of Marlboro. 'You weren't missing anything with that heatwave. Some of the guests went back to Holland because they couldn't stand it here any longer. And besides, it was swarming with mosquitoes.'

In the room next door I could hear Isabelle and Bastian laughing out loud. It was impossible not to notice them. They were rolling over the floor with Thomas and Max, glancing at the television, grabbing a crab stick or a piece of French bread with cheese every now and then from the coffee table. The television was blaring. Betty had already gone to have words with them a few times and turn the volume down.

'More Bordeaux?' asked Theo. He didn't wait for the answer and refilled all the glasses until they were three-quarters full.

I put the glass to my lips and took two big gulps, in the knowledge that I'd now entered the danger zone.

Theo put his knife and fork down on his plate and lit a cigarette.

Betty started clearing the table and I stood up to help her. I felt the alcohol in my legs. She immediately waved me back to the table. 'Oh, no, don't get up. Relax. Things are hard enough for you as it is right now.'

Eric passed me a piece of French bread with tapenade.

'When are you planning to open?' asked Betty. Suddenly she was standing beside me again, putting a friendly hand on my shoulder.

'Open?'

'The *chambres d'hôtes*.'

'As soon as possible. In spring, I hope. Three of the guest rooms are already finished; we're sleeping in them ourselves at the moment. And they're working on the bathroom.'

'One?'

'Er . . . for the time being, I'm afraid.'

'That won't do! People like to have their own bathroom. Have you made allowances for that in the plans?'

I couldn't help thinking about Michel, about his bathroom, which he shared with eight other people. The dirty washing on the floor, the cups with toothbrushes. The long brown scorch marks from lit cigarettes on the rim of the washbasin. I took another sip.

Eric cut in: 'The idea is to build in small units later, with a toilet, a shower and a washbasin. The walls are already in place, as are the pipes. All we have to do is plumb the stuff in.'

This seemed to put her mind at rest.

No one had said a word about Peter all evening and this was now precisely the one topic of conversation that interested me. They knew him better than I did, or for longer, at any rate. I decided to take the plunge.

'How did you meet Peter?' I asked Theo.

'At the builders' merchants. I needed some stain, but all the pots looked the same. He spoke to me when he saw me floundering, and we got talking. Two weeks later he was working here, with no less than seven men. He's one of a kind, that Peter; I don't know how I'd have coped without him. Nevertheless, he's an odd fish. On the one hand he's a nice guy, but he's two-faced, in my experience. There's a lot more to him than meets the eye.'

'That's to be expected,' cried Betty from the worktop. She'd started loading the dishwasher. 'You don't build up a company with forty employees with kindness alone.'

'I like him,' said Eric. 'I like his approach. No-nonsense, straight down to business.'

'What do you mean by two-faced?' I asked.

Theo waved his hand. 'Oh, nothing in particular.'

'That's not entirely true, Theo.' Betty sat down beside me again. 'There were quite a lot of problems.'

'What kind of problems?'

'It's . . .' Theo cast her an authoritative glance across the table. 'Oh well, it doesn't feel right to talk about him like this. He's done – and still does – a lot of good. But . . .

Did you know those lads who work for him all have criminal records?'

I knocked the wine over. The ivory-damask tablecloth soaked up the red Bordeaux. At least a quarter of the costly fabric turned purple. The liquid dripped on to the kitchen floor.

'Oh, damn, sorry,' I cried, jumping up. I used the back of the chair next to me to balance myself. The chair wobbled, but didn't fall over. Betty rushed over to the sink for a dishcloth.

'Sorry, sorry,' I stammered.

'Don't worry about it,' said Betty. Perhaps I was only imagining the irritated undertone in her voice.

Together we moved the glasses and the candlesticks to the other side of the table. She turned back the tablecloth and started nimbly dabbing the tabletop. I wanted to help her and was already on my way to the kitchen unit.

'No, don't get up, don't get up,' she cried. 'It'll only take a second.'

She walked away and came back with a bucket of soapy water.

No, I hadn't imagined it; I was now certain that she was annoyed. I'd had far too much to drink, and this was plain to see.

The children came into the kitchen and inspected the damage. 'Has something happened?'

'No, darling. Mummy knocked a glass of wine over.'

'Has she had too much to drink?'

'A little bit, I think,' said Eric.

Bastian shook his head. 'I'm never drinking wine when I'm older. It makes you do all kinds of crazy things.'

'And it's gross,' said Isabelle.

'*Oui, bèùrk*,' her new friend Max chimed in, in perfect French, pulling a disgusted face to match.

Eric looked at his watch. 'It's time we made a move anyway. It's nearly eleven o'clock already. The children have school in the morning.'

'I don't want to go home yet,' cried Isabelle. The children shrieked and dashed after each other into the living room. We'd probably have to go looking for them in a minute. Under the table, behind the sofa, in the toilet. When Bastian and Isabelle were having fun we always went through hell getting them home.

Eric stood up. 'Come on, we're going. Are you going to round up our offspring?'

I found Isabelle and Bastian in the toilet, shrieking as they ducked away from me.

'You two really have to come with me now,' I said, as sternly as I could. 'Otherwise we're never coming here again.'

Empty threats.

Almost half an hour later we were on our way home. The evening had raised a lot of questions in my mind. What had happened with Peter, to make Theo describe him as 'two-faced'? What did Betty mean by 'problems'? And what concerned me most was the term 'criminal record', which was echoing through my head.

It's morning. Pale, cold light filters through the small window into my cell.

I hardly slept last night, but the panic is gone. I've had time to reflect, in those dark hours with no light or sense of time. And I know what I'm going to say when they come to get me: nothing at all. I'll cope; I'll manage.

I'll listen, but not respond. To anything.

Three days without contact with the outside world, the policeman had said. Today is the second day. One more day. Tomorrow evening, or the morning after, I can consult a lawyer. I need to get my story off my chest, to someone I can trust, someone who'll listen to me patiently, without judging me, and figure out how to get me out of here scot-free.

If that's even possible.

I'm startled by the sound of footsteps in the corridor, which stop outside my cell door. The same officer as yesterday steps inside.

He says something I can't understand. I gather from his impatient gesture that I have to follow him.

25

'Peter knows,' I said.

It was nine o'clock, Friday evening. In the back of the Volvo, in the lane, two full bags of shopping were waiting to be driven home. Here, in Michel's room, the November rain was lashing against the window. Michel lay beside me in bed against a pile of pillows, smoking a roll-up. His arm was slung casually around my bare shoulders. My body was still glowing, my skin was tingling, but the clock radio on the shelf was ticking relentlessly away, and there was still so much I wanted to discuss with him.

'He's making life difficult for me,' I continued.

'Are you serious?'

'On Monday he made a comment about French women, who act like they're such good mothers and faithful wives, but then consistently have affairs.'

Michel shrugged his shoulder. 'So?'

'He . . . I got the impression he was saying it on purpose. Eric was there, as were the others.'

'It's all in your mind.' Michel squeezed his eyes shut for

a second to reassure me. 'Peter's not like that.'

I put my cheek on his chest. 'Maybe he *is* like that.'

'Peter's like a father to me, Simone. He's never written me off; he took me as I was. And I wasn't exactly an angel. I had a reputation, you know. Yet he had faith in me, in Bruno too, Pierre-Antoine, the others ... No, Simone, Peter isn't like you think he is. No way. If he was, he'd be implicating me too; have you ever considered that?'

Michel was making Peter out to be a saint. I wasn't convinced.

Far from it.

'Do you have a criminal record too, then?' I asked.

He took a deep breath. 'Me?'

I nodded.

'I'd rather not say.'

'I want to know.'

'*Tant pis* – too bad.'

I got a bit annoyed. All things considered, I was the one with everything to lose here, not him. I looked at him side-ways. He puffed at his cigarette and followed the smoke with his eyes, as if he was deep in thought, and was still considering whether to tell me.

As I watched him and studied every slight movement he made, it dawned on me that I couldn't quite believe that he had something serious on his conscience. He seemed too sensible, too calm and level-headed. If someone told me Bruno had done something bad, I'd take it as read. A couple of times I'd seen Bruno blowing up at Pierre-Antoine, who had a short fuse just like Bruno. It was always over something small, but at such moments the veins bulged on Bruno's forehead and his eyes were blazing. Both times Michel had dropped his tools to break them up. He then started to talk them round, firmly gripping them by the shoulders until he'd smoothed things over.

Michel had a calming influence on the workmen. For that reason alone, and also because he was so good with Bleu and with Bastian and Isabelle, I couldn't believe he'd done anything wrong.

He put out his cigarette and rolled on top of me, buried his face between my breasts. Started kissing them. 'Come here, with that beautiful, soft body of yours.'

I froze. 'I want to know.'

'Why?' he said, softly, and carried on caressing me. My body reacted violently. I shuddered under his touch, his tongue, his hands, that body moving against mine.

'Because I want to get to know you better,' I said, weakly.

His hands cupped both my breasts; he circled his thumbs, which felt rough against my skin.

'You know me.'

'No, I know your body,' I whispered. I could sense that I was starting to lose control, that I was slowly succumbing. 'That . . . that's not the same.'

He grinned. His head disappeared under the covers. I protested, tried to wriggle out from under him, but his hands were gripping my thighs, holding them in place. A moment later I was staring vacantly at the ceiling as slow, forceful waves surged through my body, and my mind went completely blank.

Half nine. It was already too late to get home by ten.

Mechanically, I started getting dressed. Michel did the same.

'I'll walk with you.' He grabbed a jacket hanging from the back of his door.

We walked down the stairs, passing a man with a craggy face and dreadlocks tied in a messy knot. He quickly shook Michel's hand as he went by. I could see tattoos on the inside of his arm, messy blue dots and symbols.

He didn't look at me.

It was chilly outside, not to say downright cold. Michel put his arm around me.

We stopped near the car. I searched in my bag for my keys.

'Will you come again next week?'

'Maybe.'

'*Maybe?*'

It was dark in the lane. I could barely see his face. But I could smell him. If a perfumery managed to bottle a whiff of Michel, it would be the market leader in no time.

'You're angry,' he said.

'I ask you something; it's important to me, and you simply won't answer.'

He shrugged his shoulder and looked away from me. 'I'm not proud of it; that's all.'

'Michel, I have an awful lot of questions. I've heard things about Peter. I want to know what you know about him . . . And I want to know what you did.'

A horn sounded a short distance away; the piercing noise echoed through the lane. We turned round, but the car had already passed.

'We'll talk about that next week,' he said.

Peter would be back on Monday.

Another three sleepless nights.

'No, I want to know sooner.'

'Come on Sunday, then.'

I hesitated. Could I just slip away on Sunday, on my own? 'I . . . I'm not sure. Isn't Bruno home on Sunday?'

Michel dug a packet of tobacco out of his inside pocket. 'A friend of mine has a caravan. He's not using it; the thing is standing empty. If I go there, and you do too, no one's forced to find out, including Bruno.'

'But I thought Bruno already knew,' I snapped.

'He doesn't know; he thinks he knows. I haven't said anything. I'm not stupid.' Michel started calmly rolling a cigarette.

I glanced frantically at my watch. Quarter to ten.

'I really have to go now.'

'Do you know that restaurant near the slip road?'

I nodded.

'If you pass behind it, you'll see a path, slightly to the right of the car park. Follow it and you'll end up in a kind of park. There are several caravans. I'll be there on Sunday. Two o'clock.' He licked the cigarette paper and picked at the tips of the roll-up. 'You can tell your family you've forgotten to buy some groceries.'

He put an arm around my waist and rubbed his lips over my cheek. With two fingers he brushed a few strands of hair out of my face. 'And you have to promise me something . . .'

I looked up at him, confused by the sudden seriousness in his voice.

'If he does it with you tonight, think of me.'

Eric kissed me on my forehead, slowly rolled off me and got out of bed. I heard his footsteps on the wood in the hall, and listened to him turning on the tap in the adjoining bathroom.

I stared into space. Turned over and pulled the cover over my shoulder. I couldn't go on like this.

The sound of pattering water was coming from the bathroom.

I stood up, went to the bathroom and sat on the toilet. Warm liquid trickled out.

I could feel myself growing nauseous.

Eric turned off the tap and crouched down in front of me. He kissed me on my forehead.

The light over the washbasin was shining brightly in my face.

'I'm going to nip downstairs and get something to drink. What would you like?'

'I'm tired; I'd rather sleep,' I said. Timidly.

Cowardly.

'Are you feeling OK? You look . . . pale.'

'A bit too much to drink,' I mumbled. 'I should have steered clear of the wine.'

'You barely drank anything this evening.'

'Two glasses, actually.'

'Next to nothing, then.'

'I'm probably coming down with something,' I whispered, nervously avoiding his gaze. 'It'll probably be gone by tomorrow . . . if I go to bed now.'

26

In 1210 Llewellyn, Prince of Wales, went out hunting. What Llewellyn didn't know was that the people in whose care he'd left his young son Owain left the child unattended in his cradle.

During the hunt Llewellyn's faithful Irish Wolfhound, Gelert, ran away. The dog had never done this before, and Llewellyn anxiously returned to the camp. There, Gelert came running up to him. His snout, chest and legs were covered in blood. There was no sign of the maidservants. Llewellyn ran anxiously through the camp to the tent containing Owain's cradle. The cradle was overturned and smeared with blood. In a fit of anger, and overcome with grief, Llewellyn killed his dog with his sword. Then he heard a baby crying. Owain was lying under a bed, unhurt. A short while later a dead wolf was found right by the tent. With deep sadness, Llewellyn buried his faithful dog, who'd saved his son's life. The village of Beddgelert ('Gelert's grave') in Snowdonia, Wales, owes its name to this Welsh myth.

Since Friday it had been terribly cold. Winter had closed in all of a sudden, without warning. The wood-burning stove still wasn't working properly; it was missing some parts. The bedrooms were being kept warm with electric heaters that Eric had rushed out to buy. They couldn't all be switched on at the same time, we soon discovered. The fuses had blown three times. Eric didn't want to bring someone in from the electricity board yet, because Peter had advised him not to. He said we'd be better off doing that when the building work was out of the way, otherwise they'd only start making life difficult. Apparently, there were strict rules you had to follow if you were in the middle of renovating. What's more, we hadn't officially applied for planning permission from the town hall, which could land us in hot water.

So now it was cold throughout the house, except in the room adjoining Isabelle's. An electric heater was switched on permanently in there. Yesterday we'd furnished it with the bare essentials as a temporary living room. Out of necessity I'd taped newspaper over the window, and we'd brought a few pieces of furniture in from the container and covered the wooden floor with a rug.

Eric was now installing the satellite dish. It wasn't going very smoothly. I could hear him swearing in frustration outside when I shouted 'No, nothing!' at him for the umpteenth time.

The screen was blue, then started breaking up and finally turned blue again.

It was nearly one o'clock and I could feel myself growing

increasingly nervous. Early this morning over breakfast, I'd said I wanted to go shopping this afternoon – one of the smaller supermarkets in town was open on Sundays – but Eric said there was no point. Tomorrow was Monday and the children would be at school, so I might as well do the rest of the shopping then. I'd responded by announcing I wanted to cook something special this evening, titbits we could eat from the coffee table in front of the television, sitting cosily beside the warm heater. I explained that this was my way of celebrating the fact that we were now completely free of the caravan, and that I wanted to give the children ice cream as an extra surprise.

Eric had looked at me strangely in the beginning. I was almost shaking when I told him this, but presumably my argument had been sufficiently persuasive as he'd taken my word for it without too much protest. First I had to help with the satellite dish. Then I could leave. Alone, since the ice cream was a surprise.

'Mummy,' Bastian complained, 'Isabelle keeps scribbling on my drawings!'

I looked round at the children, who were lying on their stomachs on the rug, surrounded by paper and felt-tip pens. Isabelle looked at me with tears in her eyes. 'He's touching my drawings too,' she said, in a quiet little voice.

'Kids, can't you just play nicely for a while, a *little* while longer. Mummy and Daddy are trying to fix the television, and when that's done we'll put Nickelodeon on. OK?'

Bastian nodded and pulled his drawing pointedly away from his sister. Isabelle turned on to her side and scribbled absently on her paper. I was slightly worried. She'd been listless and irritable all morning and she was complaining of stomach ache. I was afraid she was coming down with something.

Poorly children don't eat ice cream. And they need their mother.

'Yes, it's working,' I cried.

There was a programme about Hinduism on TV. I immediately switched over to the children's channel. 'Kids: *SpongeBob!*'

My work was done. I wanted to go. It was already half one. I rushed to the bedroom, pulled a clean thong out of the wardrobe, then dashed to the bathroom, brushed my teeth and quickly got changed.

I went downstairs, grabbed the car keys from the worktop and took two empty shopping bags outside with me.

'I'm off!' I called to Eric, who was putting his tools away. 'See you later.'

He raised his hand absently.

People with children were walking to and fro in the car park next to the restaurant. A number of children were playing in the adjacent playground, despite the miserable weather.

I drove round to the back of the restaurant, where there

were a few more parked cars – probably belonging to the staff – two lorry trailers and a few rubbish containers that were almost overflowing. It took me a moment to locate the path. It was practically hidden among the trees. I left the Volvo near the rubbish containers.

It was dusky in the woods, almost like night-time. About three hundred yards from the car park, just beyond a small hill, there were three caravans beside a wooden cottage. No cars, no bikes or motorcycles. There was a satellite dish on the ground next to one of the caravans. All the doors were closed, as were the curtains. There was no sign of life.

Over the past few months I'd realised that people in this part of France sometimes led rather unorthodox lives: drifting from one empty caravan or *gîte* to another, taking any seasonal work on offer in between times. Louis had told me this was how he lived. And, he'd assured me, he wasn't the only one.

In any case, these caravans weren't occupied, or their occupants had been away a long time.

I glanced nervously at my watch. Five past two. I turned round towards the path, which looked no less deserted than this place.

Near the wooden cottage I found a grimy garden chair and sat down.

Time ticked by. Quarter past two. Twenty past two. Half two.

I jumped up and ran to the path whenever I heard an engine, but it was a false alarm every time.

Quarter to three. I couldn't sit still any longer; I walked between the caravans. By now I knew them down to the tiniest detail. Twigs snapped under my shoes; autumn leaves rustled. It was getting colder, or perhaps it only seemed that way. I put my hands in my pockets and watched my breath clouding up in the air.

Where had he got to?

I was haunted by all kinds of thoughts. Something had happened; he'd had an accident. I'd seen near-misses with motorcyclists more than once, kamikaze pilots zigzagging across the winding two-lane roads, venturing across the white lines at high speed and responding to approaching lorries by speeding up rather than returning to their side of the road. Had Michel set off late, and . . .

Three o'clock.

I paced up and down the clearing, from the path to the caravans and back again. It started drizzling. My fingers turned red with the cold and I began to shiver uncontrollably.

I couldn't believe Michel and I had never exchanged mobile phone numbers. If we had, I could have called him, or sent him a text message. Then at least I'd have *known* something.

Perhaps with my coloured perception I'd overlooked something on Friday evening. I racked my brains and came to the realisation that the only proper conversation I'd ever had with him had been in Arcachon, on the covered terrace of Le Pirate. And that had been about things like dialects, nothing important. After that, everything had gained momentum. We'd barely said another word.

As I waited in vain for a sign of life, getting colder and colder, I started to wonder, among the deserted caravans, whether I wasn't idealising Michel too much. Whether I wasn't creating an idealised picture of Michel based solely on what I wanted to see. How well did I *really* know him? What did I know about him?

Betty had let slip that he had a criminal record. Not only him, everyone who was working for us. Her words had also made me realise that Peter was untrustworthy. I was becoming ever more aware of this now. Michel saw Peter as a father figure: he'd made that clear enough; he didn't want to hear a bad word said about Peter.

Maybe Michel was at home now after all, sitting in front of the television drinking a beer; maybe he simply didn't feel like talking to me, or being pinned down and ordered around by a woman and this was his way of getting through to me: by making me wait here like a total idiot, in the drizzle, in the most desolate spot I could imagine. I saw him vividly before me, a bottle of beer at his lips. Laughing, joking with Bruno.

I looked at my watch again. Quarter past three.

Michel wasn't coming.

I walked back to the car, overcome by countless emotions. Disappointment, anger, sadness.

Shame.

Only as I was getting into the car did I remember the shopping.

I'd promised my family an enjoyable evening.

27

Peter hadn't said much over lunch. Nothing to embarrass me at any rate. I scrubbed the burnt-on food off the frying pan with a scourer, listening with one ear to the business transactions in the hall. Peter and Eric were sitting at the large garden table; the lads were working. Out of the corner of my eye I saw Eric counting out hundred-euro notes. Another five minutes or so and Peter would be gone again. Then I could breathe easy for another week.

I'd worried for nothing, had a sleepless night for nothing.

I put the pan back under red-hot water, added extra detergent and left the pan on the worktop. It needed to soak; there was no way I was going to get it clean. The amount of washing-up that passed through my hands every day was astonishing. One of the first things we were going to plumb in when we had a proper kitchen was a dish-washer.

I heard Eric climbing the stairs. Someone started cutting tiles upstairs. The machine screeched and rattled, drowning out the radio.

Peter was suddenly standing behind me.

I jumped, but quickly composed myself. Out of habit I turned to face him, expecting to find two big hands clasped around my upper arms, followed by three forceful kisses and an '*Au revoir*'.

He had a strange glow in his eyes, which alarmed me. He said nothing; he just stood there, right in front of me. In an attempt to defuse the tension slightly, I took the initiative. I kept my arms by my side and offered him my cheek.

I froze when I felt his hand on my hip, his fingers groping their way upwards, to my waist. I flinched as if he'd punched me in the stomach.

Peter gave me a penetrating, almost sneering stare. 'You aren't always so reluctant, are you?' He said this very softly, but the menace in his voice was unmistakable. He took a step forwards, jamming me against the worktop.

Upstairs the sawing and singing continued unabated.

He smirked. 'Or perhaps you go for little boys barely out of nappies instead of real men? Do they frighten you, Simone? Real men?'

My heart was beating in my mouth. What should I do? Hit him? Knee him? Start screaming? Call Eric? Even if Eric heard me, Peter would tell him what he'd seen. If I did nothing, Peter might continue. He kept looking at me. His expression was bordering on madness. My God, he wasn't really going to . . .?

I was trapped. My stomach contracted and I started panting.

Peter gripped my jaw forcefully, unnecessarily hard, with one hand. He pulled me towards him and kissed me full on the lips.

'Bye bye, Mother Teresa, until the next opportunity.' He turned towards the hall, stopping in the doorway.

I wiped my mouth emphatically with my sleeve. He saw it.

'Oh, yes . . . I might come back tomorrow and spend the day working here.'

We were sitting next to each other in the temporary living room. The children were in bed. There was a series on television about two English friends, one of them an Indian Sikh, who'd bought a ruin in the French Ardèche. Eric supplied a running commentary on every step and mistake they made while drinking a bottle of Bordeaux. The electric heater glowed. It was dark outside and a strong wind was blowing.

Eric chuckled a lot, and started laughing out loud when the French workmen, summoned by the English friends, simply didn't turn up one morning.

'Top-class entertainment, Simone, this series. Fantastic! Well, we've got it made compared with those two dimwits . . .'

I felt no need to respond. Silently I ran the events of the past few days through my mind and tried to find a common denominator, as well as a solution, a way out.

There didn't seem to be one, or perhaps I was too confused to see it. I'd never felt so lonely, and so empty. The fact that I didn't have a shoulder to cry on was starting to get to me now more than ever.

I resolved to visit Michel next Friday, in any case, if only to ask him why he hadn't shown up on Sunday. I also wanted to confront him with Peter's behaviour today, tell him I felt more than a little threatened. If, after that, Michel still insisted that Peter was such a wonderful guy, then it would be clear how things stood. Or clearer, at any rate.

I looked up from the dictionary and saw the grey-haired Englishman on the TV screen, who was obviously no spring chicken, lugging bricks about, flushed with exertion. Then it cut to a commercial break.

Eric stood up. 'I'm going to get another bottle of wine.' He left the room.

I stood up to close the door behind him to keep in the heat. On my way to the door I changed my mind and followed him downstairs. I was suddenly dying for a cup of hot tea.

It was extremely cold in the house. I felt sorry for Isabelle and Bastian, who were now sleeping under two blankets, with their pyjamas on. We'd taken central heating for granted in Holland.

We didn't take anything for granted here yet.

Eric was fiddling with a corkscrew in the kitchen and

looked up when I grabbed the kettle and filled it with half a bottle of mineral water from the fridge.

Bleu was scurrying about beside him. Our four-legged friend wasn't bothered by the cold. He didn't even want to lie by the heater in the living room.

'Tea? Are you sure you're not ill, Simone?'

'I'm still not feeling very well,' I said wearily.

The telephone rang.

'At *this* time?' grumbled Eric. He grabbed the receiver.

My watch read half eleven.

I heard Eric saying 'Hello' a few times, and then hanging up.

I gave him a questioning look. Eric raised his eyebrows. 'Nothing. Wrong number, I think . . .' Then he grinned at me and gave me a friendly slap on the buttocks. 'Or perhaps it's your boyfriend.'

I mumbled something and turned towards the stove. My blood pressure shot up; my fingers trembled as I reached for a teabag. Michel didn't have our number. It wasn't listed in any telephone book yet.

The only person who had our number, whom I thought capable of ringing us at this late hour, was Peter.

The tiled corridor in the cell block feels claustrophobic. Bright lights, metal doors with bolts at eye level.

I hear someone shouting. The policeman escorting me takes no notice.

Behind us someone is hammering continuously on one of the cell doors.

The corridor ends in a barred door. Another policeman is standing behind it. A gun is dangling on his back.

The panic returns with a vengeance. My heart rate seems to accelerate. My mouth goes dry.

The policeman behind the barred door looks me up and down, exchanges a knowing glance with my warder and opens the door. We enter a brightly lit space with a modular ceiling and pale beige walls. Behind us someone is still hammering steadily on one of the cell doors. The sound dies down when we turn left. A corridor with a lino floor, noticeboards and rotas.

I walked down here yesterday morning – I must have – but I have no memory of it. I put one foot in front of the other. It's almost as if I'm floating, or walking on pillows. My heart is beating uncontrollably behind my ribs.

They're going to interview me. The time has come.

I can smell coffee. I grimace. The smell is disgusting. I retch. The nerves have unbalanced my whole body.

The policeman stops at a door on the right. He opens it and flicks his head commandingly.

I walk past him into the room.

28

Tuesday morning, quarter to twelve. Two dishes of sauer-kraut were crisping in the oven. I'd put a body warmer on over my sweater, but I was shivering with the cold. It was as if the walls were breathing out frost.

Peter was working, upstairs. I could hear his voice above the racket from the tile cutter. His presence was making me extremely nervous. After yesterday's confrontation I could only guess what he had in store today.

My hands had been trembling for days. I snapped at the children and then apologised to them profusely. I could barely eat. I'd lost several pounds.

'Lads, lunch – *manger*!' I called upstairs, when I heard the rattling of the tile cutter subside for a moment.

Shouts of acknowledgement from above, along with white dust particles, which fluttered down into the hall like drizzle.

I took two towels and put the steaming, red-hot dishes on the table. I'd left the plates to warm in a bowl of hot water. I quickly dried them, put them on the table and took another two bottles of water and orange juice out of the fridge. In the meantime I occupied myself by rinsing a few pans. The lads entered the kitchen one by one to wash their hands. Peter was one of the last to come in, with Eric in his wake.

Only when everyone had sat down did I go back into the hall. Peter was sitting next to Eric, the Antoines opposite each other, and there was an empty chair beside Louis.

I waited until everyone had served themselves and scraped a bit of food on to my plate. I didn't dare take any juice. My hands were shaking too badly; I was bound to make a mess.

A dull conversation developed about the progress of the building work. Pierre-Antoine then started telling anecdotes about other houses he and Antoine had worked on last year.

Nothing important came up.

The food was almost finished and I went to the kitchen to make coffee.

When I returned to the table the topic of conversation turned out to have changed. A cold hand grabbed hold of my heart when I heard what they were talking about. Marriages and relationships with large age gaps.

'As a matter of fact I don't know of any marriage in our circle of friends,' said Eric, 'with a large age gap.'

'I do,' said Louis. 'A good friend of mine has a wife who's ten years younger.'

'Does that work?' Pierre-Antoine asked.

Louis put his knife and fork down on his plate and took a crumpled packet of tobacco out of a side pocket of his trousers. 'Does for them. He's always been a bit of an *ado*, never grown up.'

By *ado* he meant adolescent, a word I heard here all the time, which generally referred to young people between the age of twelve and roughly eighteen. And adults who didn't act their age.

'But you often see that,' Antoine remarked, 'men with younger wives. It's not so common the other way round.'

'Madonna always goes for younger men,' said Pierre-Antoine.

'Then again, she doesn't lead a normal life.'

'Do you know anyone with a normal life, then?'

Antoine shrugged. 'No one with that much money, at any rate.'

I couldn't help starting to count. I didn't know how old Michel was. It had never come up and I'd never asked him. I guessed him to be around twenty, making him fourteen years younger than me. Meaning he was born in the year I was allowed to go to my first pop concert unaccompanied and kissed my first boyfriend. Unbelievable.

'How many years' difference are there between you two exactly?' Peter asked Eric all of a sudden. He glanced at me very briefly; no one noticed, but it made me even more alert than I already was.

'Me and Simone? Er . . .' Eric looked at me sheepishly. 'About . . . two years, I believe.'

'Are you the older one?'

'No, Simone is.'

'Ah,' said Peter. He sat back in satisfaction. 'So I thought.'

'What do you mean?' asked Eric.

'That you have a wife who goes for younger men . . . *Boys*, even.'

Eric raised his eyebrows and looked at me cheerfully, with a nod towards Peter, as if to say: 'Do you hear that? He's *crazy!*'

Eric had absolutely no clue what was going on here between me and Peter.

A stable marriage. It plods along, without any hiccups, no problems, never any arguments. So why would he?

Perhaps I should have said something. Cracked a joke to make everyone laugh and then quickly changed the subject. A few well-chosen words in the right order, a face to match. Anyone with even the most basic social skills could have done that without a problem.

Not me. Not now.

I stood up, went to the kitchen and ducked behind the fridge door. Literally hid myself away, and tried to pluck up my courage. Walking off again, like I did last Monday, was no longer an option. Eric would have demanded an explanation afterwards, saying he found it extremely rude of me to leave the table for no reason.

With a coffee pot, cups, milk and sugar I walked back to the table. Shakily I poured out the coffee. Only when I sat down again did I look shyly in Peter's direction. His lips curled in a smile, with a look in his eyes that I could only interpret as demonic.

Louis started talking about his caravan, which had sprung a leak; he was wondering if he could use a piece of tarpaulin from Peter. Antoine sat there yawning, telling us he'd had a late night yesterday – drinks at a friend's house that had got out of hand. So it continued, until it turned two o'clock and the lads stood up of their own accord, like perfectly programmed work machines, and traipsed upstairs.

Peter followed them.

As I was clearing the plates and dishes from the table, I could feel myself growing angry. The rebelliousness slowly started taking over from my fear. This was *my* house, and it was *my* kitchen. Thanks to Peter I no longer felt safe here. I crept through my own house like a frightened rabbit, anxiously peering around.

Was that correct? After the groping and the weird glances, it seemed increasingly plausible. The phone call last night had been from him; that, too, was certain. But what was he trying to achieve? Was it amusement for his twisted mind? Or did his behaviour result from jealousy? He'd found me with Michel after the party. At that moment he'd also looked at me strangely, and not said another word.

Wasn't it typical of men to feel jealous at a moment like that? Did his actions stem from frustration?

It was possible. From now on I wasn't ruling anything out.

The longer I thought about it, the more I couldn't escape the feeling that he had a plan, and that this wasn't simply a consequence of a sick, frustrated mind.

If Peter really was insane, he wouldn't have been able to keep forty loyal employees for so long – even if they did all apparently have criminal records – and win everyone over so easily, including ourselves. That was *logical*.

So there had to be more to it. There was something he wanted from me. It was becoming increasingly clear: I had to take action.

Rue Charles de Gaulle looked deserted. In summer this town was full of life. Now winter was closing in, everyone was evidently indoors, by the warm fire. There wasn't a soul to be seen on the streets, at any rate.

I parked the Volvo in the side street and went into the apartment complex. I didn't come across anyone on the stairs; the corridor was empty too. I knocked on Michel's door three times. Listened. Nothing.

I knocked again, harder this time.

Nothing happened.

Had he seen me driving up and was pretending not to

be home? No. That was impossible: the car was parked too far away.

I looked at my watch. Half eight.

Perhaps he was in a café somewhere, or in Bruno's room. *Or at Peter's house?*

I was startled by a noise. A skinny boy with a ponytail and a dazed look in his eyes darted behind me like a shadow. He opened the door next to Michel's.

'Excuse me,' I said.

The boy waited for a moment and glanced at me. He looked like he was struggling to focus, squinting slightly. Like he was on lots of medication. Or drugs. Or alcohol. Or all three.

'Do you happen to know if Michel is home?' I asked. 'Or . . . will be home, this evening?'

He shook his head indifferently and disappeared into his room without a word.

I went downstairs, outside, crossed the street, where I could get a view of Michel's window. The curtains were closed. The lights were off. What now? Wait till half nine? He might still come.

A biting wind was circulating between the houses, bringing withered autumn leaves and wrappers in its wake. They were tumbling over the tarmac in the wind.

I pulled the lapel of my jacket closer to my skin and shivered then took another look at the dark window on the first floor, and once more at the entrance.

A scooter went sputtering by. A car passed in the opposite direction. I retreated into a doorway. All kinds of thoughts were running through my head. Michel was with friends, or in a café somewhere and wouldn't come home before midnight or so. He had a girlfriend – the girl at the party – and had moved in with her. Michel was asleep and hadn't heard me knocking. Perhaps he'd gone shopping, in which case he could show up at any moment.

I was starting to feel extremely cold now. It was rather desperate to be waiting here on the street. For the millionth time I cursed myself for never asking Michel for his mobile number.

After half an hour I walked back to the car.

29

Every now and then my mother came out with wise words, which I suspected she'd picked up from the psychotherapist she visited once a month — who she undoubtedly told everything she kept from me. Then she'd watch me react furiously to a remark from a friend and suddenly say: 'You can't control what other people do and say. You can only choose your own response. You can only control yourself.'

'Grandma and Granddad called this morning.'

Isabelle and Bastian looked at Eric expectantly. It was Wednesday, the one day they only had school in the morning.

'They're coming to France this week,' Eric continued.

'Awesome!' responded Bastian. 'Are they bringing presents for us as well?'

'I don't know about that,' Eric answered.

'Is your mother completely recovered?' I asked.

'Well enough to feel up to the trip. But they're only coming for the weekend.'

There were frozen pizzas on the dining table. The Antoines and Louis didn't object to the drop in my culinary standards. They cut one slice of pizza after the other from the board.

'How many more sleeps to go?' asked Isabelle.

'Only two.' Eric turned to me. 'They're setting out in the morning so I reckon they'll probably be here by about six. How about you cook something tasty on Friday, then we could perhaps all go out to dinner together on Saturday? It's been ages.'

'Lovely,' I said, softly.

I wondered how I'd be able to combine my in-laws' visit with a solo outing on Friday evening. I wanted to talk to Michel. What's more, I wanted to go and see Peter this weekend. He was due here again on Monday morning, and I wanted to beat him to it.

'I want to go shopping on Friday evening as usual.'

Eric looked at me in annoyance. 'Get that done today. And take the children with you so we can carry on working at the same time.'

'Eric,' I said, as calmly as possible, 'those Friday-evening shopping trips have been my only outings since we moved here.'

'In that case, go tomorrow afternoon, after lunch. It'd be rude to go out when my parents are here, and when they're only here for a few days.'

'You can't be serious,' I said, vehement all of a sudden. 'By the time I'm done with the dishes and clearing up it'll be half two; then I'll get into town at three o'clock and I'll have to head back at four o'clock to be in time for the children.'

Eric angrily chewed down a piece of pizza. 'And you can't put that off just once? My parents are driving hundreds of miles to see us; they're going back on Monday and you simply *have* to go into town by yourself.'

I took a bite of my pizza and wiped some red sauce off Isabelle's chin.

If I went through with this, it would end in an argument.

'Oh well,' I said. 'Maybe you're right . . . We'll see.'

'Which reminds me,' I heard Eric say, calmer already, 'would you ring my mother in a minute? I forgot to ask them to bring satay sauce. And chocolate flakes. I'm really starting to miss those things.'

I mumbled in assent. Enviously I eyed Louis's mobile phone, which was lying on the table next to his plate.

'Can I have a look?' I took it without waiting for the answer and quickly opened the address book.

'It's just an old thing, you know,' Louis remarked.

'But certainly practical,' I mumbled.

Michel's mobile number was stored in it.

'Can I see?' said Bastian.

'Wait a minute.'

I tried to impress the number on my memory. The first two numbers were always the same, so I ignored them. I'd just started working on the first group of three digits when the number slipped away, to be replaced by the name 'Michel'. Then the telephone number popped up on the screen again. 5 3 9 . . . The display went dark.

Damn!

I pressed the menu button to activate the backlight and searched again. 5 3 9 3 5 . . . It disappeared again.

'Since when have you been interested in mobile phones?' I heard Eric say.

'The battery on mine runs down too quickly; I need something simpler, I think.' 5 3 9 3 5 8 . . . The display went dark. What a piece of junk this was.

'And you want one like *that*?'

'Maybe.'

'Louis's is a brick, Simone . . . I don't think they sell those any more.'

I mumbled something and focused on the last two digits. Quickly returned to the main menu.

I put the mobile back down next to Louis, amid loud protests from Bastian. I quickly pushed my chair back and went over to the kitchen, found a pen and grabbed a coffee filter bag. Hurriedly I wrote down the possible combinations of numbers. Out of sight of the lads, the children and Eric, I folded up the filter bag and stuffed it into one of my socks.

I couldn't suppress a smile. It felt like a small victory.

It was almost ten o'clock and I'd just put the children to bed. Eric was running a bath. Everything was working in our brand-new bathroom. The tiles and fixtures glistened at us in the dimmed light of the halogen spots.

The filter bag was still in my sock.

Eric threw his arms around me and stroked my back. 'What do you think? Shall we christen our new bath?'

I kissed him softly on the lips and ducked away from his embrace. 'First I'm going to nip outside . . . I think Bleu needs to pee.' In the doorway I turned round to face Eric. 'Stay where you are; I'll be back.'

Eric blew me a kiss.

My behaviour was simply shocking. Bleu was wagging his tail at the bottom of the stairs.

'Come on, boy, *viens*.'

I opened the door. It was cold and dark outside, but it didn't bother me. I couldn't wait to try out the phone numbers. I wanted to talk to Michel on Friday evening, and before causing a full-blown marriage crisis by sticking to my plan, I wanted to be sure that Michel was actually at home.

Bleu immediately dashed off. He wouldn't be back for half an hour.

I dug my mobile out of my pocket and walked under the archway in the façade towards the side of the shed. If Eric looked outside at all – and the chance was virtually nil – he wouldn't be able to see me anyway.

I bent down to pull the coffee filter bag out of my sock and held the piece of paper close to the dimly lit display.

Besides palpitations, the first possibility yielded the agitated voice of a Frenchman, who wasn't called Michel and didn't know anyone by that name either. The second possibility led to an automated voice, informing me matter-of-factly that the number I had dialled was currently unavailable, and that I could try again later. The third possibility I was able to decipher on the coffee filter bag connected me with a young girl; she sounded young, at any rate. I couldn't help feeling a twinge of jealousy and imagining all kinds of things. As a result, and with a hint of dominance in my voice, I simply said something to the effect of: 'Could I speak to Michel?'

The girl sounded genuinely confused; she definitely didn't know any Michel.

That left the second number. Unavailable. Was this Michel's number? It was possible that he had no signal. It had happened to me often enough. Old houses here had extremely thick walls; some were up to three feet thick, like ours. They were made of fieldstone bricks that had been gathered out of the ground by farmers, brick by brick, and loamed, hundreds of years ago, long before the industrial era. They hadn't been built for modern communications equipment. Barely any signal could pass through.

I tried again, with the same result. After that I entered the number in the address book, under the name 'Michelle'. As a finishing touch I deleted all the recently dialled numbers and calls. No longer traceable. Which reminded me that, whatever happened, I had to intercept the itemised bill from Orange.

I whistled and called Bleu. Eventually his wolf-like contours popped up out of the bushes. We walked back together.

In the yard I could hear the telephone ringing inside. It must have been at least half ten.

I went into the house, closed the front door behind me. In the kitchen I stood still. Hesitating. I picked up the phone.

At that precise moment the line went dead.

30

It was five o'clock, Saturday afternoon and I was ill. At least, that's what I'd pretended to be. No one had questioned it.

Last night I really had been ill. As Eric's parents had turned on to the path, I'd been lying in bed with a burning stomach, feeling as if I might die at any moment. Dizzy, feverish and disorientated. Eric had wanted to call a doctor, but I'd assured him it was nothing serious. I didn't need a doctor at my bedside telling me what I already knew: it had simply all got too much for me. The change of country, language and culture, the numerous new stimuli, the lack of social bearings, the cold, worrying about the children and the total lack of modern comforts; but – to be honest – mainly the tension. I needed to be strong for the children, strong for Eric, all while I was crying and screaming inside. What's more, I hadn't been eating properly over the past few weeks. Last night my body simply said: this can't carry on.

But *I* had to carry on.

I'd already been feeling a lot better this morning, but decided to feign illness.

Listening carefully, my ears picked up the sound of a car starting. Eric, his parents and Isabelle and Bastian were going into town together. They were going to go shopping and stay for dinner, and wouldn't be home before nine o'clock tonight.

I jumped out of bed, ran to the window and looked outside. My in-laws' car was heading towards the path. I gestured gratefully to Heaven.

Within five minutes I was dressed, I'd grabbed the car keys from the worktop and was dashing towards the Volvo.

Peter's car was at the end of the drive, in front of his garage. A white van was parked beside it. I didn't know if Claudia had a car and could therefore only hope that I'd encounter Peter alone.

Oh well, I'd find out soon enough.

I parked next to Peter's Land Rover and got out. Despite my resolve, my hands were trembling.

There was no need to ring the doorbell. Before I'd even reached the steps, Peter appeared in the doorway. He was wearing pleated trousers and a red V-neck sweater.

'I've been expecting you,' he said. 'Come in.'

It was dark inside the house. Our footsteps creaked on the shiny wooden floor. In the living room he showed me to the sofa.

'Take a seat. Do you want anything to drink?'

'No, *merci*.'

He went over to the cabinet and poured himself a glass of whisky. I looked around uneasily. The house looked different from on the night of the party, without all the people, music, candles and Chinese lanterns. The atmosphere was gloomy. Grim, almost. The dark-red velvet of the sofa was worn in places. There was a thin layer of dust on the coffee table, and rings stood out against the varnish. In an alcove in the wall there were wilted flowers in a dry vase caked in limescale.

'How lovely it is here,' I said, to break the ice. At the end of the day, he was the one pulling all the strings, not me.

Peter muttered something to himself and turned to me. I could barely see his face because the ochre-coloured window panes behind him were letting in so little light from outside.

'When I ended up here seven years ago, this house was a ruin. A run-down chateau, with a couple of rotten, dilapidated outbuildings. It was neither use nor ornament. This region was backward. There were no jobs, hardly any shops. Everyone was moving away. I bought it for the price of the land. The money to buy and renovate it was borrowed from a friend of mine, because I literally had nothing. Not a single franc . . . Nothing.' Peter turned towards the window and looked outside.

I held my breath, hardly dared move.

This was leading somewhere. But where? It was becoming abundantly clear that Peter had prepared this conversation better than I had.

'Some people have it easier,' he remarked, taking a sip of whisky. 'They've sold their house in Holland or England at a huge profit. They buy a ruin here with their own money and have it renovated, by people like me. All without a mortgage, as if it costs nothing. Just imagine, how rich you have to be to do that. A lot richer than I was when I came here.'

Peter wasn't generalising. He was talking about us. We'd sold our house in Holland at such a profit we could have paid for our house here in cash. And even then there would have been enough left over for the renovation. It wouldn't even matter if we didn't have any guests for the *chambres d'hôtes* in the first year. How exactly did Peter know that we didn't need a mortgage for the house and the renovation? Had Eric told him? It was possible. At the same time I wondered precisely what we'd told Theo and Betty. Somehow I had an inkling we'd talked about money with them too.

Peter gestured. 'This house, Simone, is my castle, my haven. I want to grow old here. I've done things in my life which . . .' He sighed and pursed his lips pensively, but still didn't look at me. 'Let's say I've had an eventful life, and found peace here. After so many years. I learned the hard way – and I can let that pass – but at a price . . . Yes, I paid a heavy price.'

He paused to take a sip. Swirled the liquid in his glass. My eyes had now adjusted to the dark. Only now did it strike me how tired he looked. He had bags under his eyes and lines on his face that I'd never noticed on him before.

'What are you paying us exactly, for the work we're doing? Fifteen euros per hour?'

I didn't respond. This was a rhetorical question; Peter wasn't expecting an answer. This was a monologue.

'Did you pay the plumbers and handymen the same in Holland as well?'

What was he driving at? Was he now going to start complaining about the hourly wage? I remembered he'd suggested that rate himself.

I shook my head. 'No.'

'And the whores, what did your husband pay the whores he visited? Fifteen euros as well?'

His tone of voice scared me. The way he pronounced the word *whore*, the sudden harshness. Eric had never been to a prostitute. Never.

'Eric's never used whores,' I said, and to my annoyance my voice sounded high-pitched, almost as if I was squeaking.

He cocked his head and laughed. 'Are you sure, Simone? You're leading a nice little double life yourself, aren't you? *Presque Française* . . .'

I locked my hands together in my lap. They were damp.

'Well,' he continued. 'Let me put it like this: whores cost a lot more than fifteen euros an hour. And *male* whores . . . I think the hourly rate for a reasonably good one, one you'd have nothing to complain about, can easily run to two hundred euros. Shortage, a question of supply and demand.' He fixed his gaze on me. 'Big difference, isn't there? Fifteen or two hundred.'

I was gobsmacked.

'He's good, isn't he?' Peter continued, keeping his eyes fixed on me as he sat down in an armchair. 'Our stud?'

I'm falling. Thirty feet, sixty feet, a hundred. There seems to be no end to the devastating whirlpool pulling my hair and clothes and the invisible force sucking me down, faster and deeper, through a black tunnel with no light at the end. Then comes the blow. Bare, pure shame.

'No complaints, then.' Peter knocked back the last drops of whisky in one gulp and put the glass on the table with a bang. 'Good, now down to business.' His eyes sparkled in the half-light. 'You give me two hundred and fifty euros every week. A bargain, if you ask me.'

I was lost for words. I wanted to leave, I wanted to start yelling, I wanted to attack him, scream at him, but I sat there. All the emotions racing through me manifested themselves as shivers that travelled through my whole body.

'Michel won't be seeing you for the time being,' he continued. 'I need him for a while, on another "job".' He used air quotes when uttering the final word.

Peter stood up. 'Come on, time to go, Mother Teresa. Every Monday, till further notice. Two hundred and fifty euros. You're a clever girl, so I don't need to explain what the consequences will be if you don't pay up.'

I stood up and walked bewildered towards the hall, where Peter opened the door for me. As I passed I briefly glanced up at him.

The look in his eyes was steely, completely unfeeling.

On the way home I registered nothing of my surroundings; I drove on autopilot. I stopped the car in a car park as it would have been irresponsible to carry on driving. Vacantly I stared ahead. The tears wouldn't flow. I thought of Isabelle and Bastian, the courage they'd shown, and were still showing, to settle in here. The pride on their faces when they spoke French words like a native, their cautious attempts to accept this country as their new homeland. The way they'd opened up to the workmen, their new social network – 'Daddy's friends', their enthusiasm each time they'd greeted Peter.

But the worst thing was that there was someone else involved. Not only Peter.

I put my head in my hands. I was all on my own. Completely.

I fought against the urge to drive away from here, far away from Peter's monstrous tentacles, back to Holland. All of a sudden the tears came. As I searched through the glove compartment in vain for a tissue to blow my nose, I knew this had to be my aim. It was the only option.

We had to get away from here.

31

In a tourist village by the river, less than twenty minutes' drive from our house, a market was held every Monday morning. Stalls with meat, vegetables, cheese and fish, but also clothes, pottery, jewellery and African masks. They were packed together on the square and the two adjoining streets. I'd discovered an Irish beer brewer and a stall belonging to a bee-keeper selling honey and candles.

It wasn't so hard to imagine constantly bumping into the tourists here in the summer, and having to shuffle inch by inch to join the crowd. Right now it was fairly quiet.

It was a remarkably mild November morning. On a couple of terraces people were sitting drinking coffee with their coats on, unzipped.

I crossed the market diagonally in the direction of a branch of the Crédit Agricole bank and inserted my card into the cash machine. As I entered the PIN, the doubt set in.

Two hundred and fifty euros was a lot of money.

I consoled myself with the knowledge that so much money was disappearing from our account at the moment for mortgage payments and building materials that Eric might not even notice amounts like this. I saw invoices coming through for five hundred euros, eleven hundred, eighteen hundred . . .

Perhaps I should take more out in one go. A regular amount every week would be more noticeable on the monthly statements than various amounts spread over a month.

I withdrew three hundred euros and stuffed the notes into a separate compartment of my purse.

From now I wouldn't be able to spend so much money at the supermarket, or buy the children so many presents, and shopping for myself was totally out of the question. This way the difference wouldn't look as big on paper as it really was.

As I walked back through the market street to the car park, I saw someone I vaguely recognised standing behind a stall. A blond woman, fiftyish. She looked well groomed, tanned and made up, and she was wearing a modern body warmer. As I passed the stall she looked straight at me, with a look of recognition, and suddenly I realised. It was the woman from Amsterdam I'd talked to briefly at the party. I'd forgotten her name, just like practically everybody's name from that evening.

'How lovely!' she cried, immediately coming out from behind her stall to greet me. 'You're Simone, aren't you?'

I nodded sheepishly. Her name still escaped me.

'I'm Lucy, remember? We chatted at Peter and Claudia's house. Do you know who I was just talking to? Rita, she's here somewhere too.' She looked around, trying to spot her over the top of the people's heads. 'I think she's gone for coffee. Jack's here too; you can always find him in Café de Paris, opposite the bank on the market.'

'Jack?' I asked, uncomfortable with the situation.

'My husband.'

'Oh yes, of course.'

'You know what?' Lucy grabbed me by my upper arm, as though afraid I'd run away. She looked round once again, stood on tiptoe to see over the top of the passers-by and started frantically beckoning someone behind a stall on the other side of the street. Then she leaned towards me. 'Let's go and have a nice cup of coffee. Rita might still be there as well. Business is slow today, after all.'

Lucy completely overwhelmed me.

A French woman did the honours for Lucy's Dutch cheese stall, and we walked back to the marketplace where I'd been a moment ago.

Café de Paris was a simply decorated establishment with a tiled floor. A few people, mainly men, were sitting in silence reading the paper – the *Sud Ouest* – and drinking coffee. At the bar I saw two old men drinking something that must have been liquor, pastis. They were wearing knitted sweaters and one of them had a greasy cap on his head. But the clientele consisted mainly of shoppers from the market, sitting around the little tables, deep in conversation. It was warm inside and the hubbub echoed against the bare white walls.

Lucy showed me to a brown table. I recognised Rita straight away. The things I'd remembered about her appearance were her heavily made-up eyes and her jingling gold jewellery. She was still wearing the jewellery now, but the make-up was missing.

Lucy pulled up an extra chair from somewhere and put it at the head of the table. 'Do sit down, love.' In a single breath she rattled off the following to the grey-haired man who was sitting crumbling a piece of cake: 'Jack, this is Simone; Peter's working for her at the moment. You saw her at the party at Peter and Claudia's house, but I don't think I introduced you to each other.'

It had to be said: Lucy had a perfect memory.

I shook Jack's hand. He seemed friendly. He had soft features and fine, almost white hair.

Rita stood up and didn't stop at a handshake. She leaned over the table to kiss me on both cheeks. 'How lovely, and what a coincidence to see you here! Would you like coffee as well? Espresso? Café au lait? I wouldn't go for the cappuccino: they don't understand that here. You get a few drops of cold coffee in a long glass filled with whipped cream.'

'Make it an espresso,' I said flatly.

The fourth person at the table was a man of about forty, balding, with a high forehead, who introduced himself as

Ben, Rita's husband. He was still wearing his jacket. He, too, had adopted the French custom of kissing.

Finally I was able to sit down. The waitress, a skinny girl with a dark-brown ponytail, took the order.

'Do you have a sweet tooth?' asked Lucy.

I nodded.

She ordered something else that I couldn't understand.

'Is the work coming along?' Four pairs of eyes looked at me expectantly.

'We're sleeping in the house now,' I said. 'We have a temporary living room and bathroom, and we've all got our own bedrooms.'

'Now *that's* progress,' Lucy cackled. 'And how did it feel to sleep in your own bed again?'

I attempted a smile. 'The caravan wasn't exactly luxurious.'

'But sometimes that's a good thing, I think,' Ben remarked. 'If you haven't had a proper home to sleep in for a while, no hot water, no heating and so on, then you start appreciating the small things again.'

'For the first few weeks perhaps,' Jack responded, 'but to be fair, you soon get used to it again.'

Lucy took the cups of coffee from the waitress and put a plate with a gigantic meringue down in front of me. 'Meringue,' she said. '*Divine*. I could eat it all day, but my stomach's not so keen. Nor are my scales, for that matter. Have you ever eaten it?'

I shook my head.

'Try it; it's really delicious, very sweet.'

The meringue was indeed cloyingly sweet; it seemed to be a kind of whipped egg white with pure sugar. The pink confection crumbled when I bit into it and it was impossible to eat it without making a mess. My fingers were already sticking together and I felt my tooth enamel cracking.

'Any progress with your heating?' I heard Ben say.

I looked up, but the question wasn't aimed at me.

'One chap came over with solar panels and another with some kind of geothermal heating. It's a good idea: there are practically no running costs, and you don't need to worry about maintenance. But it's simply too expensive. Twenty thousand euros, that's what the one chap from the geothermal heating was asking, and the other one is still working it out. We don't pay tax here, so we won't get a subsidy either. So for the time being we're going to carry on heating with wood and oil.'

'How do you heat your house?' Rita asked me.

'Still with electric heaters for the moment. We have a boiler, but Eric's still working on it.'

'They're expensive, you know, those electric heaters; be careful,' said Rita. 'Last February I was landed with a bill for seven hundred euros . . . for electricity alone.'

'Then again, it was extremely cold,' Lucy added.

'Water's expensive here too,' responded Ben. 'You notice

it on your bill as soon as you've filled your swimming pool.'

'We have a pump with a generator next to the well; that's where we get most of our water from,' said Jack. 'It's practically free that way. Apart from the diesel for the generator, that is.'

I looked at the people around this table. Somehow it felt wonderful to be able to speak my own language, without having to weigh up every word, or wonder whether the noun was feminine, masculine or plural, all while running through the conjugations of the necessary verbs at break-neck speed until I came across the right one. But even at this table I couldn't discuss what really mattered to me. I couldn't discuss that with anyone.

'Are the workmen any good?' Rita asked me.

'Er . . . yes. It's quiet at the moment; only the two Antoines and Louis are working for us now. Peter isn't there any more either. He's got two new jobs.'

'I think I've heard about that,' Rita replied. 'Apparently he's going to restore a country house close to Libourne. And some friends of his – in the Basque Country, I mean – have bought a plot of land. It's said to be very beautiful there.'

Very tentatively I asked her: 'Do you have much contact with Peter these days?'

'Not really. Besides, he's busy, isn't he? He hasn't got time to stay in touch with all his old clients. But you keep bumping into each other here all the same. Everybody knows each other's business. However big and spread-out it may be, it's just like a village. Especially among the foreigners. If you know a few people, you often know all the gossip before the day's out.'

Lucy chimed in and started telling a story about a couple of English immigrants who'd quarrelled with the local mayor, and whose campsite was now up for sale. 'That reminds me: have you done anything about the water yet?' asked Lucy.

'Water?'

'Did you know it contains *thirty* per cent calcium in this region? Haven't you noticed? It's borderline criminal: you pay through the nose for water you can't even drink and which messes up all your appliances. We had some chap come over with a water purification unit, a kind of filter. It works really well. If you want, I'll give you his address. He's reliable.'

'How much did you pay for that?' asked Rita.

'About three thousand euros.'

'So we didn't get such a good deal.' She looked for support from Ben across the table. 'Five? Wasn't it?'

'I can't remember . . . Five, maybe.'

I realised I was in the process of building up a new social network in a foreign country. All four people at the table seemed pretty friendly. They accepted me without hesitation, simply because I was Dutch, like them, and we had a shared history: converting a house in the same region of

France using the same builder. But my head was so full there was no room left to show a genuine interest in their lives. I was being stretched to the limit and I felt like I needed to get away, as otherwise I might start crying, or saying the wrong things.

I stood up abruptly. 'I have to go. It was so nice seeing you all.'

'So soon?' said Rita. 'Love, don't go; you're in France!'

'I have to cook for the workmen.' I glanced hastily at my watch. 'And it's already too late to get lunch on the table by twelve o'clock.'

They understood. Peter had them all well trained.

Rita quickly scribbled something in a small diary she pulled out of her bag, ripped out the sheet of paper and thrust it at me. 'Drop by sometime, whenever you like.'

I put the piece of paper away.

'Will you be back next Monday?' Lucy asked. 'If so, just put a dish in the oven for the lads. Or serve up a couple of pizzas. I did that often enough myself. Don't let Peter's nagging about the food bother you. And you'll have to tell us exactly where you live; I'm beginning to get very curious.'

'Will do,' I said. 'Next time.'

As I drove home along the winding two-lane road, I felt like the cup was full, and it was running over on all sides. Tears were welling up and I made no attempt to fight them back any longer.

I'd done my very best to lock away all my feelings, the raging emotions swirling inside me. Far away, so that no one would understand what was actually going on in my head.

I couldn't do it any more.

Early this morning Eric's parents had left. Under normal circumstances I'd have had all the time in the world for them, looked after them with love and devotion; now all I felt was relief as their car pulled away from our property. And I felt like a traitor, an outsider.

The road in front of me snaked its way through the high hills, along a rock face and a deep valley with a river. I was on my way home, and every Monday morning from now on would be more or less the equivalent of the lions' den. When I got home I'd have to give Peter his hush money unnoticed.

This was my only moment of rest, this moment in the car, alone. I parked the Volvo in a picnic area and stood there crying to myself.

I was entirely at the mercy of Peter's will, someone I hadn't even known existed six months ago. Two-faced Peter, with his cunning games, his intimidation. I wished he was dead; I wished Eric had never met him.

But oddly enough it wasn't Peter who dominated my overwrought emotions.

I hadn't slept a wink last night, but just lain there thinking and running through all the events in my head. And every new piece of the jigsaw I discovered, which fell painfully into place, a perfect fit in the hellish whole, felt like a knife being stabbed into my abdomen, ever deeper, ever nastier, slyer.

Everything had been planned. Everything.

All that time I'd thought Michel was too good to be true that's exactly what he'd been.

The initiative had come from Michel from the start. From the very first meeting, when he held my gaze. Who had come looking for me by the lake? Who had come with me to Biganos because he was 'having trouble with his knees' and then run like the wind through the loose sand along the coastline in Arcachon? And who had lingered at Peter's party, sat there sharp and lucid, acting the supposed innocent among the drug- and drink-addled souls? Damn, they'd simply planned this, Peter and Michel. Every step had been thought out, and I'd walked right into it. No different from any schoolgirl.

What did I know about Michel? He hadn't told me anything himself. Anything at all. The only thing I *thought* I knew was information Peter had whispered into Eric's ear. A pitiful story about a terrible childhood, which had simply made Michel more likeable. More interesting.

Michel hadn't shown up, last week. And why not? He was probably busy seducing another new arrival whose marriage was in a rut. Peter must have been raking in thousands of euros a month this way, while Michel was going at it like a rabbit.

That suited him fine. He seemed born for it.

I threw my head back and stared at the ceiling of the car, while the tears kept flowing, incessantly. My hand stroked the seat beside me. This was where he'd sat. On this seat. Fragments of sights, smells and sounds forced their way into my mind. Michel next to me, in bed in the caravan, while I ran this same hand, which was now stroking the hard seat of the Volvo, over his stomach. Michel on top of me, with an almost solemn concentration in his eyes. Michel opposite me, at Le Pirate, breaking off a piece of bread for me. Beside me on the sofa at the house of Bleu's previous owner, who'd welcomed us so warmly and hospitably. It was evident that she cared for him in some way.

Just like I'd cared for him.

And still did.

I fell forward and placed my arms on the steering wheel. Only now did I grasp the essence of what really hurt me the most, cutting through all the misery.

Thinking about Michel I could only reach for the void he'd left behind. My outstretched hands groped about in the pitch-black darkness, into nothingness.

I simply didn't know what to feel any more, what to think, not to mention what to do.

I couldn't distinguish between the countless thoughts and feelings wildly drifting about in my clouded consciousness.

My life had become one big lie.

★

The door closes behind me. I stand still.

There's a table in the middle of the room. Two men are sitting behind it, looking at me. They're wearing white shirts with a tie. No uniform. One is dark-haired with delicate features and brown eyes that look a little too small for his face. The man to his right is older, pushing sixty, I guess. His hair is grey and his skin pockmarked. He has bags under his eyes, but the blue irises are clear and sharp.

On the table there is a tape recorder, a few sheets of paper, forms or something; I can't see very well.

The older man nods. '*Bonjour, Madame Jansen.*'

'*Bonjour,*' I reply. My voice sounds hoarse with nerves. The nausea is growing.

'Take a seat,' says the blue-eyed man. He has a Flemish accent which makes me shudder. He reminds me of Peter.

I sit down on the empty chair opposite them. Bite my lip.

They suck me in with their eyes, as if they've spent hours studying thick dossiers and are now finally standing face to face with the subject of their study. I feel naked.

'We have a few questions for you, Mrs Jansen,' says the Belgian. 'But let us introduce ourselves first: the man next to me is the murder detective for this department, Philippe Guichard. He's conducting the investigation and this interview. I have been brought in as an interpreter because you are Dutch. My name is Leo van Goethem. We are going to ask you a number of questions. You may answer in Dutch or French, whichever you prefer. Anything said here will be recorded on this tape deck.' He puts his hand on the machine and gives me a penetrating look. 'Do you understand?'

I nod.

'Good. I am required to tell you that you do not have to answer. If you answer, you do so of your own free will. Is that clear?'

'Yes,' I squeak.

'Good. Then let's begin.'

32

'Oh, Mum, please, *one more*.'

'No, Isabelle, it really is time for bed now. It's already nine o'clock; you've got school again in the morning.'

Isabelle opened her adorable blue eyes wide. She had me wrapped around her little finger. 'Oh . . . pretty please?'

'One more, then.' I was unable to resist. Guilt got the upper hand. If it wasn't presents, it was bedtime stories, until Isabelle had fallen asleep halfway through the umpteenth fairy tale, and I could sneak out of her room unseen.

'But after that I really don't want to hear another peep out of you. Deal?'

She nodded and gave her order. 'The one about the duckling.'

I shifted on the bed and opened the book of fairy tales again. Soft light from the bedside lamp fell on the shiny pages. I'd read this story so many times before, I could almost recite it from memory. As I told the tale of a young duckling that was teased terribly by the other ducklings on account of its awkward appearance and grey feathers, my mind wandered.

Sunday had come round again. The week had flown by.

I'd have preferred to stick my head in the sand, completely shut myself off from everything going on around me.

See no evil, hear no evil.

But that wasn't possible.

Last Monday Peter had taken the hush money, entirely in character – silently and out of sight of everyone else – and then stuffed it in his back pocket with a sly smile.

He'd left me there in dismay. Somewhere, very deep inside, I'd still had a spark of hope that it was a joke. A sick joke, granted. But the moment he took the money from me, he put out in one fell swoop that little hopeful glimmer flickering inside me.

As I heard him leave, I'd held on to the worktop and squeezed my eyes shut. I'd hoped, hoped and prayed, that he'd drive over a cliff at dizzying speed, or smash up against a rock in his macho off-roader. One insignificant, fatal moment of inattention.

After that I'd gone outside, to the lake. It had been cold. Trails of mist hung over the still water. The sky above me was monochrome lead grey. After spending an hour in silence, murdering Peter in a hundred different ways in my mind, reality began to sink in again.

Going to the police wasn't an option I'd seriously

considered, that Monday afternoon by the lake. To report blackmail. But the longer I thought about it, the more complicated it became. I had no idea what the consequences would be once I'd set everything in motion. For a start, it was Peter's word against mine. If it went to court, I'd probably have to give evidence, simply because I was the only witness. What's more, it was possible that they would send a *procès-verbal* to our house, or drop by to ask additional questions – and would therefore one day be in our yard, with their police car. This was a spectre that kept haunting me. I didn't want to have to trust the local police to handle the case discreetly. The police were only human.

But the truth was, I didn't dare, because I was too scared I'd set something in motion that would take on a life of its own and I'd lose all control. At the moment, Peter was the only person I had to be wary of. This was more manageable than a whole police force – and who knows what other kinds of authorities.

Perhaps I should turn the tables. The ease with which Peter was blackmailing me, and deceiving his friends, such as Eric, led me to suspect that he was involved in much worse things besides. For all I knew, blackmailing married women might well be routine . . . And possibly not the *worst* thing he'd been responsible for. If I could find something, an activity of Peter's that was highly illegal, then I might be able to report him anonymously, tip off the police. There had to be something, something that could put him behind bars for years. This idea had given me butterflies in my stomach, but nothing more, because I didn't know where to begin. Stand guard at his house? But when? I had to be there for the children, for the workmen, and the only evening I could get away without Eric objecting was Friday. Another possibility was to go and talk to people he'd worked for. Make inquiries. But Rita had said that gossip spread like wildfire here. I wasn't sure where people's loyalties lay, but Peter was evidently very well liked here. So who was I to turn on him?

This had been the sum total of my long afternoon of reflection. In the end, there remained only one solution: we had to leave here. Leave France.

Run away.

'. . . and when the duckling saw its reflection in the water, its heart leapt. It was a real swan.'

Isabelle was asleep. I closed the book, put it on Isabelle's bedside table and turned out the light. Walked quietly out of her room and closed the door behind me.

The cold in the corridor made me shiver and the floorboards creaked under my shoes. I stood there, without turning on the light. Our corridor smelled of paint and wood shavings. I went over to the window. The hills were bathed in soft blue moonlight. My eyes were drawn instinctively to the source, high in the sky. Shifting grey spots seemed to be pulsating in the ochre-coloured ball. I wrapped my arms around me. My breath steamed up the double glazing, clouding my field of vision. I felt just as isolated as the moon overhead, in that empty, silent cosmos.

Eric came upstairs. 'Hello, gorgeous.'

This was a signal; I knew him too well. I wasn't in the mood for sex. I didn't respond, hardly daring to move.

He switched on the bathroom light and I saw myself, a dark silhouette in the reflection of the window, motionless.

'Do you want to join me for a bath? Warm up a bit?' came a voice from the bathroom.

'I want to go back to Holland.'

Muffled speech from the bathroom, running water. 'What did you say?'

I went over to the bathroom and stood in the doorway. 'I want to go back to Holland,' I repeated, with more force in my voice, which quivered with the cold.

He didn't look up. 'At Christmas?'

'Permanently.'

Eric's blond eyebrows shot together. '*What?*'

'I don't want to be here any more. I want to go back.'

His mouth fell open slightly. 'You can't be serious.'

I nodded fiercely. 'I *am* serious. I feel terribly . . . alone.'

He walked towards me, put his arms round me and kissed me on the forehead. 'Alone? Silly thing, where did you get that idea?'

I rubbed myself against him and burst into tears. As I sobbed my heart out, my whole body shook. 'I feel awful, absolutely awful. This whole France business is a big mistake, Eric. I can't settle here, I don't even *want* to settle. I just want to go back, I miss everybody, I miss my own language, the shops, I even miss the old *neighbours* . . . I've never felt so wretched.'

Eric held on to me, looking at me intently. 'Darling, we've only been here four months. What do you expect? It all needs time. You knew it would be at least a year before we'd start to feel at home, didn't you? You *knew* that, didn't you?'

'There's a difference between knowing and feeling,' I sobbed. The words tumbled out of my mouth. 'I . . . I simply can't face it. I feel sorry for Isabelle and Bastian, I've been buying them presents like there's no tomorrow, and I'm at a loose end as to what I can do to soften the blow for them . . . They don't need *presents*, Eric. They need *friends*. Other children to play with, they're getting lonely here.'

Eric exhaled, wheezing slightly. 'Isabelle and Bastian will come round in the end. You saw how well they did in the performance. They'll make friends in due course, once they can speak the language properly. You'll see, I promise.' He tucked a tuft of hair behind my ear. 'Theo's Betty worried for a whole year, and yet their children have gone completely native now, haven't they? Ours are bound to be the same. And then they'll be bilingual and they can grow up in beautiful surroundings, free as birds, without stress and pressure.

You're worried, I understand that, but give it more time. You can't force these things.'

'I'm miserable here,' I continued. 'You're always working, I feel dreadfully alone, and I really don't want to *be* here. My days are filled with cooking, cleaning, looking after the children. The only social contact I have is with the workmen at lunchtime. I have absolutely nothing here. Friday evenings at the supermarket, those are my outings, and even then I'm alone.'

That was untrue. But I wasn't going to stop now. The situation I was painting in utter despair might not have been completely truthful, but the sentiment was. And then some.

'We don't have any opportunities to build up social contacts at the moment, can't you see that? We can't invite people over, not yet. Not *yet*, see?' He sighed. 'I'm too busy with the building work, I'm not in the mood for it. But in six months everything will be different, you'll see. Trust me.' He wiped away a tear from the corner of my eye and gave me a piercing look. 'You know what, when the house is finished, we'll throw a big party for everyone from miles around, a house-warming party, and then we'll actively set about making new friends. Maybe you could join a sports club, or . . .'

Actively set about . . .

Eric saw making friends as a project. He saw every damn *thing* as a project. I suddenly tore myself away from his embrace and looked at him sharply. 'Eric, it makes no difference, I don't want a party, I don't want to join a sports club, I simply don't want to stay here. I want to go home. To Holland. All you think of is this . . . this . . . stupid *house*!' My voice faltered and I stood there waving my arms in the air in bitterness and frustration. I didn't care any more. The lid had been blown off my pent-up emotions and Eric was bearing the full, raging brunt.

He grabbed my wrists. I pulled them away furiously.

'Shush, you'll wake Isabelle.'

'Then *let* her wake up! I couldn't give a damn! You see everything as a project, *everything*: making friends, rebuilding the house, our whole marriage, *for God's sake*!'

Eric was a picture of concern; my reaction alarmed him. He pulled me towards him and ran his hands quickly and nervously through my hair. 'Hey, hey, hey, calm down, now, calm down, Simmy. This is pointless. Calm down now. I don't see you as a project. What gave you that idea? I love you.'

'You *love* me? How am I supposed to know that? You're busy with the house all day, that *fucking house* means everything to you. We're just hanging around on the sidelines, like a dead weight. You're simply ignoring the fact that we're miserable here, you drag your whole family along to this ruin in no man's land and you couldn't care less how it makes us feel. If you . . .'

'I'm rebuilding this house for us. For you, for Isabelle, for Bastian. That's the reason, Simone. I want to get this building work out of the way, I'm sick to death of it as well, believe me. Just like you. That dust, the mess, the noise, my hands are full of splinters, I feel shattered every evening. I'm not used to this either, but I join in anyway, because the quicker it's finished, the sooner we can start building a normal life. *A better* life.'

My voice dropped an octave. 'And what . . . what if then . . . there's no family left to live in that house? You have all the time in the world for Peter and the lads. You discuss everything with them, all you talk about is the building work. You're unapproachable, to me, to Isabelle and Bastian. All the time.'

He looked at me with a mixture of astonishment and concern. 'No time for you? Jesus, Simone . . .'

'You have—'

My words were smothered by a warm kiss that took me by surprise. Intense and affectionate, accompanied by the gentle caress of his fingertips on my neck.

When our lips parted I looked into Eric's eyes and read concern. They exuded an overwhelming love. This gaze, this was what I'd fallen in love with all those years ago. This was how he'd turned my head, when we were still young and carefree and his life had yet to revolve around his job and his busy schedule and bringing up Isabelle and Bastian. It was long before our lives, inexplicably, unexpectedly, from one day to the next, suddenly started running parallel, plodding along, with barely anything significant left in common.

'I love you,' he said, very softly. 'You're my girl, always have been. You and the children are the most important thing in my life. The *most* important thing. I couldn't give a damn about Peter and the lads.' His voice cracked for a moment. 'And . . . if it really is so bad, if you really can't settle here, then it's very simple: we'll go back. End of story. We'll sell the whole thing and just go back.'

I looked at him through a haze of tears. Did he really say that? 'Are you serious?'

'I'm serious.'

Eric started to undress me. Very cautiously, as if I was a delicate mannequin that could break into a thousand pieces at any moment. He put my clothes on the cane chair beside the bed. Kissed every bare patch of skin and mumbled: 'I love you, girl; I love you so much.'

My anger vanished.

He quickly removed his clothes and took me by the hand. He led me to the bath as if I was blind, and I followed him, dipped one foot in the warm water, which made my cold skin tingle. He slipped into the water opposite me, took a sponge from one of the shelves and started lathering me up, lovingly, with circular move-ments. 'I didn't realise that you felt neglected. I always thought you understood, that you were doing your best like me to . . . You're everything to me, I'm doing this for you and the children. You never said anything . . . Besides, it's not always easy for me to read what's on your mind.'

'I've told you so often, but you never listened.'

Without a word, he continued to lather me up. Took the showerhead and started wetting my hair and rubbing in shampoo. I let it wash over me and felt the calm descending on me. The water felt wonderful – foamy and soft, warming my frozen limbs to the bone.

'I love you,' he whispered. 'And I need to know you love me too.'

'I . . . I love you too.' I fought back the tears.

Eric didn't take his eyes off me, held my face in his hands and gave me a searching look. 'We'll pull through together. We've always pulled through together. Including now. The most important thing is that we stay together as a family. You, Isabelle, Bastian and me. The four of us. Nothing else matters.'

The telephone rang downstairs. The shrill ringing screeched and echoed through the hall.

'Leave it,' said Eric, trying to kiss me.

I was now completely warm; my skin was burning slightly.

'We're not going to make any rash decisions,' he whispered. 'It's winter now. It's cold; hardly anything's finished. It's not nice; we have no friends, no social life, not a moment's rest. But it'll pass. I need you, girl. And I promise you: if you still want to go back next year, when the house is finished and the sun is shining, then we'll go back. No questions asked. I promise you.'

33

Monday morning, quarter to eleven. Peter could arrive at any moment, but I wasn't all that nervous.

The conversation I'd had with Eric last night, the love we felt for each other and the bond we had, all in all it had done me a power of good. Enough to face the uncertain future with more faith, at any rate.

I wasn't alone any more.

If everything came to a head, it would be Peter's word against mine, and I was now convinced that my word would be believed. You can't simply wipe out thirteen years of marriage.

To celebrate this I'd made a cheesecake, with blackberries, blueberries and raspberries. I'd found them in the freezer section of the supermarket. I'd been busy in the kitchen more or less all morning. On the menu there was a pasta bake with various kinds of cheese and a salad with Italian ham.

Peter came into the hall at eleven o'clock sharp.

I turned to face him and despite my renewed strength I

felt my stomach contract for a split second. Peter headed for the kitchen, acting like he was king of the castle, like he owned the place, my house, *our* house, and had every right to be here.

I wanted him out of my house, and out of my life.

He stopped in the doorway. No greetings were forthcoming. He looked at me in amusement, with a grin lining both sides of his face up to his eyebrows. His brown eyes twinkled.

He bent down to take a look inside the oven. 'Are you going to poison me today?' he muttered. 'Pasta alla cyanide?'

I crossed my arms. Took a deep breath and said: 'I'm not paying you.'

He straightened up. The pupils narrowed in his eyes and he squinted. 'No?'

'No.'

'Because . . .?'

'It's your word against mine. Eric won't believe you.'

There. He could put that in his pipe and smoke it. Peter could drop dead, literally and metaphorically. I turned round to the sink, turned on the tap and added washing-up liquid. I'd said my piece.

Peter came up close behind me. I could smell it. His aftershave preceded him, like an expanding aura, heavy and, above all, repulsive. When he lowered his face to me, I jerked my head away.

'No more games, Peter,' I said. 'It's over.'

'Don't count on it, Mother Teresa,' he whispered. 'We'll see, soon enough, how tough you really are.'

I'd expected all kinds of reactions, but not this one. Incredulous, I turned round, but he'd already disappeared.

The pasta bake was all finished. I'd managed just in time to save a few pieces of the cake for Isabelle and Bastian this evening. They were in the fridge. I'd hardly eaten anything myself. Peter had been holding eye contact with me for the past hour. Pure intimidation, and it worked, as I felt like a sword was hanging over the table and could fall at any moment.

I pushed this thought aside as best I could. Peter couldn't touch me, I kept reminding myself.

We were sitting drinking coffee and the lads were due to go back to work any minute now. Another ten minutes or so, fifteen, and Peter and Eric would deal with the financial matters for the past week, and then Peter would leave.

Hopefully.

I looked at Eric, who answered my glances with a wink. This helped.

A discussion had broken out at the table between the two Antoines, who evidently disagreed about something to do with cars. Eric sat listening attentively; Louis rolled his third cigarette. Peter played with his mobile phone.

'What on earth do you know about mechanics?' I heard Antoine say. 'I spent three years working in a garage, for

God's sake; I saw more engines then than you have in your entire life.'

'That may be so,' responded Pierre-Antoine, 'but you simply don't have a clue. A Peugeot is a better car than a Renault. End of story. A twelve-year-old knows that.'

I took a last sip of my coffee and refilled everyone's cup. Another five minutes or so.

Antoine threw up his hands as if in surrender. 'OK, have it your way; I can't be bothered to have it out with you.'

Peter tried to make eye contact. I looked down.

Peter's presence was pervasive. It was as if we were the only two people at the table. His eyes were magnetic; he was pinning me down.

I shuddered involuntarily, and got ready to clear the table.

'Ah, here it is . . . Simone, wait a minute; I wanted to show you this.' Peter pressed another key on his mobile phone.

I clenched my jaw and looked at him intently. Most of my confidence had vanished all of a sudden. 'I've been taking some nice photos recently,' he continued. 'This one in particular is really nice.'

He passed me his mobile over the table, with an outstretched arm, not letting go.

The photo had been taken from the side and at an angle, but left nothing to the imagination. Nothing at all. I recognised the wall of Peter's house, the clothes, the curve of Michel's back. My blouse was hanging open, revealing my breasts. Michel's hand under my skirt, his head in my neck. The photo was so sharp you could see I had my eyes closed.

'First we need a few details from you,' says the Flemish interpreter.

I've forgotten his name already; my brain registers everything, but retains nothing.

He recites my date and place of birth, asks me about my family situation, Eric's and my occupations, when we came to France and why.

I answer as best I can. My nerves are betrayed by every word I say.

The detective babbles something in French to the Belgian. The interpreter turns to me again. 'Can you tell us where you were last Friday evening?'

I stare at the old-fashioned tape recorder on the table. The reels are turning; everything is being recorded. 'I went shopping.'

The interpreter leans towards the detective. They speak in rapid French. 'Where did you go?' asks the interpreter all of a sudden.

'Leclerc.'

'What time was that?'

I feel bile rising. The acidic liquid creeps up, seeps upwards through my stomach, into my gullet. I swallow. And again.

'I can't remember exactly. I think . . .'

'What time did you leave home?'

I close my eyes. I can't remember. However hard I try to remember, I really don't know. 'I don't remember,' I say, flatly.

'What time did you return home?'

'I can't remember . . . Sorry.' Friday's events flash through my mind. I don't want to think back to that. Not now. Never again.

Two pairs of eyes catch me and won't let me go. 'Well then,' says the Belgian. 'So you do know that you went shopping at Leclerc last Friday evening, but not what time you left home and came back.'

I shake my head, confused.

The bile has reached my throat. I pull a face and try to swallow.

'Is something troubling you?'

'Yes,' I say; the tears well up in my eyes. 'The coffee smell. It's making me nauseous.'

They look at me impassively and show no intention of removing the coffee cups. 'If you went shopping, as you say, do you have a receipt to prove it? Or did you speak to someone, in or around the supermarket? Someone who can confirm this?'

I try to think. Did I put the receipt in one of the bags? Sometimes I do, sometimes I don't. I find them all over the place. So often you take receipts, without thinking, and sometimes you leave them behind in the trolley. I wonder if detectives are going through our house right now, in search of receipts, evidence. Or searching the car? Every receipt bears the date and time.

Perhaps I'd better keep my mouth shut from now on.

34

The GP was a stocky, dark fellow of about fifty, with tanned skin and arms like a docker. On his desk there was a triangular sign bearing his name, Alain Rodez. There were six hundred people living in our region, and this man was one of no fewer than three GPs practising here whom Eric had been able to find in the phone book. Surgery hours were two till seven, Monday to Friday. No appointment was necessary; it was a question of turning up. It was a stark contrast with the GP system in Holland. This man had and took all the time in the world.

He sat behind his modern desk and first entered all sorts of details into his computer. Name, date of birth, allergies, address, telephone number.

'She's been ill before, over the past few weeks,' I heard Eric say. 'And that's really not like her. I can't remember her ever fainting before, either.' Eric tried to make eye contact with me and squeezed my hand. 'Isn't that right?'

I nodded affirmatively.

The man looked at me. 'What exactly is the problem?'

I shrugged my shoulders. 'It's not so bad; personally I think I'm just run-down.'

'That's certainly possible. You're renovating your house?'

Eric nodded. 'Yes, we've been working on it for nearly four months now.'

The GP typed something into his computer again. '*Bon*. Could you take a seat on the examination table?'

Eric helped me to my feet. I sat down on the hard, adjustable bed covered with a white sheet of paper on the left of the room.

The doctor pushed my hair slightly to one side. I hissed.

'It's not so bad,' I heard him say. 'Superficial wound. I'll disinfect it anyway, since it's dirty.'

The liquid was cold and it stung.

'No further treatment needed,' I heard him say. 'It'll heal by itself. Could you pull up your sweater for a moment? Deep breath. Yes, and breathe out again. A bit harder. Yes, like that. Good.'

He then took a torch and checked my eyes. I had to open my mouth and stick out my tongue. He tested my knee reflexes. Looked inside my ears.

'Could you lie down for a moment? Yes, that's right. Could you tell me if you feel pain?'

I felt no pain. Apart from in my head, but that was easing already.

'Do sit up. Could you roll up your sleeve for a moment? Yes, that's right.'

My blood pressure was high, a lot higher than usual, and this didn't surprise me in the least.

'I'll send somebody round tomorrow to take blood. The blood will be brought to the lab and the results will be delivered to you within a few days. Could you bring them with you next time you visit?'

He sat down behind his desk. 'It's possible you have a light concussion. Try to look after yourself, take some rest. If anything comes up, the dizziness doesn't go away, or you faint again, ring me straight away.'

He then started entering things into his computer again. The printer spat out two sheets of A4.

Using a pen as a pointer he went through the text on the pieces of paper with us. Prescriptions for blood-pressure medicines, something for diarrhoea, a sort of sedative and pills for dizziness – if I wasn't mistaken. I looked at it in amazement. Was I getting all this on the basis of a single fainting fit and slightly raised blood pressure? In Holland I had to get down on my knees and beg the GP for a bottle of ear drops for Isabelle. And even then I didn't get them. This was a parallel universe.

We thanked him for his care and drove to the chemist's. I stayed in the car while Eric went in to collect the prescriptions.

Within ten minutes he was back with a plastic bag full of boxes. 'Now I understand why they call GPs *médecin* here,' he joked, starting the car. 'Blimey, they're complete witch doctors. Are they paid per prescription or something? Christ, we could fill a whole medicine cabinet with these.'

I looked through the boxes in a daze and unfolded the instructions, more to conceal my unease than because I was actually going to use them. I already knew I wasn't going to take any of them.

My ailment couldn't be remedied with medicine.

I resolved, as soon as I was feeling a bit better, to find an internet café. There were bound to be some, in town.

All these powders and pills had given me an idea.

35

Simply typing the Dutch word for 'poison' into the internet search engine yielded twenty thousand hits. As I browsed the pages, my head started spinning. There was too much information to digest in an hour. It became clear at any rate that we lived in a world full of poison. If Peter was walking around with a mouth full of amalgam fillings, then it was only a matter of time before he kicked the bucket, succumbing to a variety of mental and physical illnesses attributed to the element mercury. There might well be botulin in the milk he drank, or one day he might be laid low by the Legionella bacterium that lived in his fountain, or he might use so much aspartame in his coffee and soft drinks that he'd inevitably fall victim to a terrible bout of depression and decide his life was worthless and put an end to it. Even by drinking completely innocent water (gallons at a time, that is) you could suffer from hyponatremia, and become terribly confused and then die.

My concentration was broken by shouting and swearing. I looked up. I was probably the oldest customer in the internet café and certainly the only woman. Around me, in the dark room, which smelled of electronics, with black walls covered in posters, there were mostly boys of secondary-school age, playing games and hurling abuse at each other.

I crossed my legs and typed in the word 'poison' in English this time. The letters on the French keyboard were in different places than on the QWERTY keyboard I was accustomed to, but I slowly got used to it and made fewer and fewer mistakes. Almost ten million hits. I browsed a few websites. They were virtually all from American institutions concerned with preventing children from being poisoned in and around the home.

I returned to the Dutch websites and ended up on an online encyclopedia that had published a handy list of different sorts of poison, complete with explanation.

I shifted in my seat. The leaves of the foxglove, *Digitalis purpurea*, contained digoxin, and a single dose over a quarter of a milligram could stop your heart. Poison that could be picked, just like that, in gardens and, according to the encyclopedia, that also grew in clearings in the woods. One hundred per cent natural.

Atropine was another powerful poison; it was extracted from the berries of the deadly nightshade and was used, among other things, in drop form in eye examinations, to dilate the pupil. Ten to twelve berries were enough to kill someone, or half a gram of the leaves of this plant. I could easily mix it in with the salad. It would probably taste bitter, but that could be masked with a heavy, sweet dressing.

Foxglove and deadly nightshade were far from the only deadly plants and flowers. A world opened up before my eyes. Certain types of poppy were used to make opium and heroin, and the ricin in the beans of the castor-oil plant was fatal in even the tiniest quantities.

I looked outside. November. Little chance of finding berries or flowers now.

The list included cyanide, of course, the only poison I knew by name. It was odourless and colourless, quick and effective. Cyanide affected your breathing and once you'd ingested a small amount your time was numbered. It didn't mention how to get hold of cyanide and in an odd way this was rather reassuring. The idea that potential poisoners could quietly gather lethal information at home behind their computers was slightly alarming.

I typed in the Dutch word for 'cyanide' and let the search engine do its work. Six thousand hits: I was narrowing it down.

Suddenly it proved not to be so very difficult to find out how cyanide was made. You needed ammonia, which had to be exposed to a heated mixture of potash and charcoal, according to one website. This then produced something that resembled sugar, another site informed me. And that was cyanide. Terrorists had barrels full of it, so it said on a third website.

There wasn't much justice in the world.

Potash? I typed the word in. It turned out to be calcium carbonate, a material used by glassmakers. It was obtained from the ash of beech and oak trees and you had to burn down a thousand cubic metres to produce three-quarters of a cubic metre of potash.

I had yet to come across sleeping pills. You didn't need a Master's degree in chemistry, and they were available all year round. My French GP would probably prescribe them, no questions asked. After my visit to him I'd realised he'd give me them by the cartload if I asked.

I logged out, paid the boy with the baseball cap behind the counter four euros and went outside. It was raining and blowing a gale and the wind was carrying leaves and empty wrappers through the street. The Volvo was parked nearby, along the pavement, and I got in.

I sat there for a moment, watching the rain falling on the windscreen, drops flowing into one another, drawing fluid lines.

Then I pulled my mobile out of my coat pocket. It was more out of habit than because I really knew what I wanted to say to Michel, or ask him. In fact I was simply angry. Louis had taught me the most terrible swear words. There was a good chance I'd use them all if I actually got Michel on the line.

He was spared the tirade. I was getting quite familiar

with the automated voice of the lady telling me in a mono-
tone that the number I'd dialled was not available.

I started the car and drove off.

It was only quarter to eleven in the morning, and Michel
was unlikely to be home. Nevertheless I parked the car
directly opposite the apartment complex and got out. The
wind pulled my coat and hair. I crossed the street, went
inside and took the stairs up to his floor. In the corridor I
stopped in front of his room and knocked on the door. And
again.

Silence.

I leaned with my back against the wall and stood there
for at least half an hour, unable to take any action. What
was I doing here? What on earth had come over me? What
had I been doing at the internet café this morning?

Still nothing at all.

I ran my fingers through my damp hair and craved a cigarette. It was eight years since I'd given up, but if someone
offered me a cigarette right now, I'd take it without hesitation.

I jumped when I heard someone coming upstairs. Heavy,
clumpy footsteps in the stairwell.

The young man who came into the corridor had an
angular face, dark-brown dreadlocks held together in a messy
knot on the back of his head. He was wearing an extremely
baggy army jacket and worn-out clodhoppers on his feet,
and he gave me a piercing, almost hostile look when he

passed me. I recognised him. Michel had shaken his hand once.

'*Bonjour,*' I said.

He stopped in his tracks and glanced over his shoulder. Light-green, slightly bulging eyes that looked almost made up, due to the dark skin on his face.

'I'm looking for Michel.'

Without so much as blinking, he put his hands in his pockets and seemed about to carry on walking.

I took a few steps in his direction. 'I can't get hold of him,' I stammered. 'His mobile is switched off. It has been for well over two weeks. Usually I can always get hold of him. I'm scared he's ill or something's happened.'

Just when I began to doubt whether this boy could actually speak, he answered: 'I haven't seen him for a while either.'

My eyes lit up. 'Has he moved by any chance? Or is he on holiday?'

'Not to my knowledge.'

I could feel myself growing uncomfortable under his stare. This reminded me that I was in a part of town that didn't have a very good reputation, to put it mildly, in a completely deserted, windowless corridor, together with a boy who looked like a reclusive drug addict.

His expression changed. He smiled, and this made him no more likeable. 'But *I'm* home. Do you fancy a drink . . . or something?'

I recoiled. 'No, thanks. I have to go.'

I ran out of the long corridor like a bat out of Hell, down the stairs and outside.

In the car I locked the doors. My heart was beating in my mouth. I wasn't sure whether, in my agitated state of mind, I'd placed a sinister filter over my already clouded perception, or whether I'd actually escaped something terrible. One thing was certain: I was never coming back here.

36

The TV screen flickered and bombarded us with commercials. Perfumes, greatest hits compilation CDs and alcohol. Christmas was around the corner.

Isabelle and Bastian were lying in front of the television on cushions they'd taken from the sofa. Isabelle was playing absently with Bunny's tattered ears.

'Do you mind if I nip out this evening?' asked Eric.

It wasn't a question, but a polite announcement.

'Where to?'

'To see Peter.'

Peter? In the evening?

'What for?'

'Yesterday Peter asked me if I'd come over to talk about a particular project.'

'Just you?'

'Did you want to come along, then? I didn't realise you were itching to spend an evening talking about house building and planning permission.'

'No. But what does Peter want from you?'

'He's got plans for a plot of land, which might also be interesting for us.'

I scrutinised Eric. 'I don't have a very good feeling about this, Eric. I mean, I'd rather not go into business with Peter.'

'I won't do anything for the time being. I just want to hear what he's got to say. Either way, it'll be educational. He has contacts, knows his way around here.'

I had to think of something. This new development was not at all to my liking.

Nothing sprang to mind.

Eric stood up. 'Well, I'd better get going. If I want to be back before midnight, that is.'

He kissed me on my forehead, stroked the children's hair and went into the corridor, letting a cold draught into the room.

Three hours later Isabelle and Bastian were fast asleep and I was leafing through bank statements, awaiting Eric's return. The yellow file was balancing on my lap. In the last four weeks I'd withdrawn twelve hundred euros in cash and handed over one thousand to Peter.

Eric had no idea, not yet. It was hard to understand; the figures and data jumped out at me, as if pulsating on the light-green bank paper.

I wondered where the dice would land. Where this would end.

If this would end.

The fact that Eric was now at Peter's house didn't please me one bit. I could only guess what he was after.

I looked up from the file on my lap and stared at the TV screen for a long time. The Englishmen who'd bought a ruin in the Ardèche had had an argument. The Sikh had gone back to London. He thought his friend had lost all grip on reality.

The same could probably be said of me too.

There were two boxes of sleeping pills in the bathroom cabinet. It hadn't been difficult to get hold of them. My blood test results had come back normal, so GP Rodez's conclusion had been simply: exhaustion. Perfectly normal for people trying to build a new life in a foreign country in spartan circumstances. My half-hearted explanation that I was having trouble sleeping led, as expected, to him prescribing me enough sleeping pills to fell a horse.

I'd carried them out of the chemist's as if they were ammunition, with a thumping heart. The boxes had been burning a hole in my coat pocket. When I got home I couldn't put them away fast enough, hidden from the children on the top shelf of the bathroom wall cabinet, in a plastic bag behind the bottles of suntan lotion and tubes of face scrub and mudpacks.

School broke up in a week and a half. The holidays lasted from 18 December until 3 January. I wanted to go to Holland with the children. Isabelle and Bastian could probably stay with Eric's parents and Erica might be able to put me up. I hadn't called them yet, but I was certain they'd welcome us with open arms. I might be able to persuade Eric to come. In his view, he couldn't afford to take two weeks off. He couldn't allow himself even to consider taking a holiday before the house was finished. On the other hand, he probably wouldn't want to be on his own at Christmas.

I'd suggest it tomorrow. But whatever he said, I was going anyway. The idea of being able to spend two weeks with friends and family, in my own country, away from this misery, away from Peter, was stopping me from flipping out completely.

In fact it was a miracle I was managing to function.

Evidently I was stronger than I thought.

Bleu was whining and barking. His claws tapped and grated on the wooden floor. Eric was home, judging by Bleu's reaction. I brushed my hair out of my face and lifted my head from the pillow. Two o'clock in the morning.

Two o'clock?!

Bumping on the stairs. My heart missed a beat.

They've been drinking together, far too much, and Peter's told him. That's why it's got so late . . . Eric is angry with me.

The bathroom door opened. Running water. Eric was brushing his teeth.

I lowered my head back on the pillow.

Peter hasn't said anything. Eric would never calmly start brushing his teeth if he'd found out his wife was cheating on him.

More bumping. The toilet flushing. Footsteps in the corridor.

I lay there stock-still.

He did his best to open the door quietly and close it again. The floorboards creaked beneath his feet. He undressed and slipped into bed beside me.

I still hadn't moved.

The next moment his hand slid under my T-shirt, and I felt a not overly convincing erection against my back.

I didn't respond.

His hand followed the slope of my ribs to my waist and stopped at my hip. I could smell peppermint on his breath, mixed with alcohol. Whisky.

'Goodnight,' he mumbled, and turned away from me.

37

Cows are colour-blind. To us the grass is green, but to a cow it's grey and if a cow could argue it would tell us condescendingly that we were simply imagining all that green.

Differences in perception can't always be explained by anatomy. When reconstructing an event no eyewitness account is the same. The perceived colours differ, the facial expressions, what was said, the intonation, the locations, the distances, the time and the sounds. All eyewitnesses resolutely defend their conflicting statements – just like a cow (if it could speak).

'What did Peter want yesterday?' I asked.

The lads were gone, we'd had dinner and the children were in bed. A day like any other, with the difference that this question had been on the tip of my tongue the whole time. We'd been together in the same house practically all day and only now, at ten o'clock at night, did we have the chance to speak together in peace.

Eric was sitting beside me in the living room, playing with a calculator. 'Peter has a piece of woodland, eight acres. He's been trying to get a CU for years and—'

'CU?'

'Something-or-other *Urbanisation* . . . Planning permission, shall we say. And that's come through now. So he can start building. He wants to put up twelve cottages, wooden chalets, scattered through the woods. For the first ten years he wants to rent them out, and then start selling them off individually as second homes to foreigners or Parisians.'

'Why rent them out first?'

'Because if you sell them straight away you have to hand over a large part of the profit to the taxman. That percentage falls after a number of years. So if you rent the cottages out for a while first, you kill two birds with one stone: it brings in money straight away that you pay little or no tax on, and you don't have to pay so much tax when you sell them. Peter sees the chalets as a retirement fund. According to him they wouldn't cost much more than twenty thousand to build per cottage, possibly even less. He already has the land and the plans have already been drawn up too. He's shown me everything: the designs, a floor plan and the costings, and it looks really good. It's just a case of getting started. He estimates the cottages to be worth a hundred or a hundred and fifty thousand euros in around ten years' time. A hefty profit, then, and in the meantime you rake in the rental income. So those cottages end up costing you practically nothing until you sell them.'

'And what did he want from you, then?'

'Two things. He was wondering if I could take on some of the rentals. That didn't seem to be a problem. And he needs money.'

I shifted position on the sofa. My expression hardened. 'Money?'

'Yes. It came as a surprise to me too; I always thought Peter was pretty well off, but it would appear otherwise. It just goes to show, you can't judge a book by its cover. Expensive house, nice car . . . That party he threw, that must have cost a bob or two as well, if you ask me. But you can turn Peter on his head and you won't get a cent out of him. That's why he wants to do this together with me.'

I did my very best to stay calm. Peter had no money? I wasn't buying that.

'But . . .' I began, '. . . Peter has forty people working for him. He's always telling us he's never short of work. So how can he afford his people's wages, and his materials?'

'He says he gets only a percentage of the hours the lads work. He deducts a lot of money for insurance and income tax. What's left is enough for him to get by on, but no more. There's a reason he joins in with the work himself. And his work isn't even done when he gets home in the evening.'

I was starting to get nervous. 'So Peter has the same plan that you had when we came here . . . Are you not reversing the roles now? You could build cottages without him. Surely you don't need Peter at all?'

'But I do. I've learned a lot on the job about building and things like that, over the last few months, but I can't touch the knowledge that Peter has. He's got experience, equipment, contacts with suppliers who give him discounts *and* he doesn't have a huge wage bill. So I don't think it's such a bad idea at all to enter into this together, as a matter of fact . . .' Eric probably saw my agitation growing, so to placate me he added: 'But don't worry about it for the moment; I want to get this house finished first. We'll cross that bridge when we come to it.'

He'd probably already agreed to it; all the signs were there.

This made me angry. Angry and afraid at the same time.

I shook my head. 'I won't have it. Eric, I just won't have it.'

Eric held my hand. 'Listen, Simone. This is a fantastic arrangement. Peter will supply the men, labour, shall we say, he has the land and the plans and the CU, I only have to pay for the building work and in exchange I rake in half the rent and in ten years' time half the proceeds from the sale of the cottages. We're talking twenty-four to thirty thousand euros per year in rental income, and in ten years' time seventy-five thousand euros or even more will be released every year, for twelve years. I don't think we should pass this up. It's a lot of money, Simone, an awful lot of money. And all I have to do is invest around two hundred thousand euros so we can build the things.'

It was decided. A done deal. All the signs were there, his whole demeanour and the way he spoke. I couldn't believe he hadn't discussed something so important, so major, with me.

I felt like my stomach and bowels were twisting around each other and winding ever more tightly together. My vocal chords seemed paralysed. Finally I found my voice: 'We don't even *have* two hundred thousand euros, Eric. Even if we put in the rest of our savings, we'll still have to borrow more. And then we won't have any money left to live on. No safety net, just debts.'

I struggled to stave off a panic attack. My breathing was rapid and I started shaking. This was a nightmare, a total nightmare.

'That's why I only wanted to do this when the house is finished and the *chambres d'hôtes* are up and running,' said Eric, soothingly. 'Then we'll be getting the income from them. If we start in, say, May, then the first cottages will ready by the autumn and we can start renting them out straight away. I could, for example, make a website advertising both the *chambres d'hôtes* and the cottages, killing two birds with one stone. And anyway, in the winter months Peter was planning to rent the cottages out to lads like Louis, who don't want to spend the winter in a caravan. That won't bring in so much money, a few hundred euros per month, but it's better than them standing empty . . . I think it's a brilliant idea, to be honest.'

I said nothing and looked at Eric. How on earth should I respond? I didn't believe it would turn out as Peter had described it to Eric. I couldn't believe it.

Not with Peter.

Peter had me in his pocket, but at the moment it was still a matter of two hundred and fifty euros a week. We could still afford that – thank God.

But if I let this go ahead, we'd go bankrupt in under six months. I just knew it. Then that rat would have not only me, but my whole family in his clutches. Then he'd have sucked us all dry, taken everything he could fleece us for, and more besides, because Eric was prepared to get into debt for that juicy, non-existent carrot Peter had held out to him.

Eric didn't know Peter like I knew him.

And Peter understood all too well that I could never tell Eric what I knew.

Peter was much more dangerous than I could have imagined.

'Cat got your tongue?'

I looked up. Took a deep breath. And another. I was still shaking. 'I . . . I just don't think it will work, Eric. Of course, I can see that we could earn a lot of money, but I don't trust Peter.'

Eric frowned. 'What makes you think that?'

I gulped. 'Peter might well be friendly now, but surely you know how it works? You see it all the time with people who go into business together. In a year's time you could have an argument, or he could go crazy and then all our money's tied up in it. It makes us dependent on Peter. And I don't want that.'

'Oh, Simone, we aren't doing this on the basis of trust; hopefully you understand that, don't you? I wasn't born yesterday. Peter and I will establish a separate s.a.r.l. for this, a French limited company. We'll get everything registered by a notary.'

Who's probably also in Peter's pocket.

I shook my head. 'I just don't want this. End of story. Not with somebody else, not with so much money. Why don't you buy a plot of land yourself? Then the lads can build houses on it and we'll pay them by the hour, like we're doing now. There's absolutely no need to go into business with Peter.'

A shadow passed over Eric's face. 'In that case the houses will cost double. I'm really disappointed in you, Simone. I mean it. You're paranoid; you're not being realistic. Peter—'

I jumped up and raised my voice. '*Peter, Peter, Peter!* Not so long ago you were telling me that the children and I were the most important thing to you, and that you couldn't give a damn about Peter and the lads. *Yesterday* you said before you left that you'd be back before midnight, and you come in in the middle of the night, *hammered*, and now you're telling me you're going to set up a business with the same Peter you couldn't give a damn about and hand over two hundred thousand euros. While your wife who means *everything* to you is *dead* against it!'

Eric narrowed his eyes to slits. 'So you *were* awake, last night? When I came home? Then why did you pretend to be asleep? What's all that about?'

'I was trying to sleep, I was exhausted and I was angry with you.'

'And now you're taking it out on me? That's what it looks like.'

Eric got up from the armchair in anger and went into the corridor. The door slammed shut with a bang.

Dammit!

I rushed to the door and ran after him towards the stairs. My voice boomed through the hall. 'You're not doing it. If you do, I'm going back to Holland by myself, *with* the children. Do you hear me, *goddammit*? I don't *want* this, you hear, I don't *want* this.'

Halfway down the stairs he turned to me. 'Have I ever made an error of judgement? Never . . . And now I need to get away for a while before I say things I regret.'

Eric headed for the front door. Bleu pattered cheerfully around him and ran through his legs, slipping outside with him. Eric closed the door behind him.

I collapsed on the stairs.

This was a nightmare; there was no other word to describe it.

I couldn't believe this was happening.

Eric would come back later and say he was sorry, that he'd lost control. I stared at the closed front door and sat there as if in a daze. Completely numb.

As time went by and the cold seeped into my clothes, through my skin, lodged itself in my flesh and finally reached my bones, I saw Eric and me, our marriage, our family, circling in the air, like a bubble, swirling in the wind, until the inevitable end came. *Pop*.

The telephone rang. The sound was piercing and roused me from my lethargic state.

I was still sitting on the stairs; my limbs were frozen and I was shivering uncontrollably. I stood up. My legs were asleep. I more or less dragged myself down the stairs to the kitchen. If it was Peter – and I was convinced it was – he'd feel the sharp end of my tongue. I wasn't going to hold back any more; I'd call him every name under the sun.

My hand hovered over the receiver in the kitchen.

Should I really speak to him in this state of mind? Was that really wise? I was too emotional now, not lucid. I'd . . .

Rrrring.

What should I say? I thought of the sleeping pills, of my visit to the internet café. If I wanted . . . really wanted to do something to Peter, then I couldn't do it openly. Never. He'd win every time. So . . .

Rrrring.

Peter was bound to know that this new trick of his would infuriate me. He was *bound* to know that I'd do everything in my power to put Eric off.

Rrrring.

'Hello.'

Crackling on the other end of the line. A man's voice, nervous, and with a French accent. I struggled to understand it.

'*Comment?*' I asked.

'It's me.'

'*Me?*'

Peter, speaking French?

I frowned. Who was this? I quickly glanced at my watch, half ten.

'Are you alone?'

Oh God . . . that voice . . . Michel!

My heartbeat quickened and sent the blood through my veins like a filter pump gone haywire.

I gripped the receiver with two hands.

My voice trembled. 'Er . . . yes.'

My emotions were on a rollercoaster, lurching from apathetic to dazed to angry, to . . . to what?

Michel.

All kinds of thoughts crashed through my mind. I should be angry with him, ask him where he was, tell him that I . . . or . . .? Tears pricked behind my eyes.

'Simone? Are you still there?'

'Y-yes.'

'I'm in . . .'

He said something I couldn't fully make out. It sounded like *Pays-Bas*, Holland. The torrent of words on the other end of the line continued unabated. Why was he talking so fast? My brain wouldn't play ball; I tried to concentrate on what he said, but it was more difficult without being able to see him.

It was impossible. I didn't catch a word of it.

'*Arrête de* – stop . . .' I began. I didn't get the chance to finish the sentence.

The front door swung open. Eric. Bleu ran in ahead of him from the hall. Clouds of condensation escaped from his snout as he cheerfully sauntered up to me.

I threw down the receiver in a reflex, just before Eric could see me.

I stared at Eric wildly. And I burst into tears. Not holding back, but with screaming howls, completely uncontrolled.

I saw Eric approach me as if in slow motion. His face was rosy from the cold. He put his arms around me and pulled me close to him.

'Sorry,' I heard him say. 'I shouldn't have done that. I . . . We've got too much on our minds at the moment. Far too much. Sorry, darling. We won't mention it any more, OK? We're going to finish this first, together. OK? I'm getting ahead of myself.'

He kissed my forehead and wiped away my tears with his thumb, but they kept on coming. 'Come on, we're going upstairs; you're completely frozen.'

38

'You never call!'

Miranda. The last time she rang me was a few months ago. Back then the lads had just started work. The sun had been shining and it had been warm.

It seemed like ages ago, scenes from another era.

Now I was standing here cooking with my winter coat on. 'I never get round to ringing.'

'Out of sight, out of mind? Simone, I'm fed up with it, you know? We all miss you. Hannah was asking after you only yesterday. She's back with Fred again. And we've made plans to come and see you in the spring. Will the guest rooms be ready by then?'

'I don't think so.' Miranda was the last person I wanted to talk to; she was a voice from a past life. A life where Miranda had slotted into place.

'Oh. Well, we'll see. Maybe we'll come over next summer . . . Are you coping there? How far along are you exactly?'

'The bedrooms are finished, as is the bathroom, but those

are in the guest quarters. They're now working on the house itself.'

'*Jesus*, is it turning into a ten-year plan? Like on *No Going Back* or something? Do you know that programme? Or do you only watch French TV now?'

'No, we have a dish and I haven't had time to check out the French channels yet. We don't watch much TV, anyway.'

'How are the children doing? Aren't they having an awful time at school? I bet they stand out, with that blond hair, among all those dark children?'

'There are just as many blond children at the school here as in Holland,' I replied. 'Isabelle's teacher is even fairer than Eric.' I wanted to leave it at that.

I pictured Miranda and the group of mothers at school, shaking their heads over that irresponsible couple who'd casually taken their children away from civilisation and dumped them among the great unwashed in the deep, backward South of France.

It didn't bear thinking about.

No matter how awful and out of place I was feeling, I couldn't stand it when people criticised our decision to move to France. The more Miranda persisted with her imaginary preconceptions, the more pressure I felt to tell her how *wonderful* it was here.

'Is everything available there? Can you get hold of peanut butter and things like that, for example? Or is it mainly local produce?'

Local produce.

I had to end this conversation as soon as possible, otherwise I'd just get even more defensive.

Besides, I'd promised to take Isabelle and Bastian into town to choose a present. Then I could withdraw money at the same time. For Peter.

'Oh, Miranda, look at the time: I have to pick the children up from school.'

I put the phone down without waiting for her answer.

It was very strange, but only now did I truly realise that my friendship with Miranda was over, simply because we now lived in two different worlds. I hadn't told her I was coming to Holland soon. My friendship with Erica had survived. I was eager to see Erica, and Eric's family, but not Miranda.

Eric was coming to Holland with us. He'd promised me, when we made up after our argument last night. Our first proper argument in years. In fact it was a miracle the bomb hadn't gone off sooner.

As I tried to find a parking space outside Leclerc it dawned on me that I'd been thinking of Michel nearly all morning. Not only that. I'd lain awake till four a.m. in the total darkness. With Eric's deep, steady breathing right beside me, I'd tried to remember exactly what Michel had said during that confusing phone call. The only thing that had stuck in my mind was him asking if I was alone. Other than that, he'd spoken so fast that I literally hadn't caught a word of it. I wasn't sure if he'd said he was in Holland, but the longer I thought about it, the more puzzling it became. I really couldn't remember. In all likelihood the miscommunication wasn't only a result of the language barrier. Yesterday I was bordering on hysterical. I couldn't even remember how long I'd been sitting on the stairs and how I'd got to the kitchen.

Now I felt calmer, but that was all because of Eric, who'd assured me he wouldn't go into business with Peter. Not if I didn't want him to. This gave me breathing space.

'Kids, we're here.'

I got out and opened the rear door for the children. We went into the shopping centre, which was buzzing with activity. There were stalls with cakes and sweets, and ceramic vases and dishes, and I heard a voice coming from a loudspeaker. Music. A fashion show was in progress. There was a long queue of people waiting at the cash machine in the bank, so I decided to go and buy presents first.

The toy shop was possibly even busier. Christmas shopping was in full swing.

'Bastian, we're going to choose a present for Isabelle first, and then for you. You really must stay with us, because it's extremely busy here and I don't want to lose you.'

'I can speak French now, you know,' came his laconic reply. 'If I lose you then I'll just tell them who I am and where I live. And what you look like, that kind of thing.'

I pulled his stubborn body towards me and cuddled him. 'I know that, darling, but not everyone is going bring you back to your mother. You know that, don't you? Mummy's told you often enough.'

Bastian looked round defiantly. 'All the people here are parents; there aren't any scary men. And I'm not a baby any more.'

'Stay with me anyway.'

I guided them to an aisle where pink was the dominant colour and where Isabelle's eyes popped out of her head. Bastian stayed by my side, still uncooperative.

The lads were sure to know where Michel was. The only reason I hadn't dared ask them was because I was afraid I'd give myself away; if anyone so much as made a humorous innuendo, my face would betray me. But perhaps, I now wondered, it would attract attention precisely if I didn't ask after him. After all, some of the workmen were missing. It would be completely acceptable for me to ask where they were working now.

I could bury my question, the same way people in video shops sandwich a blue movie between two family films. Discreetly hidden among all sorts of other, trivial questions.

I could also use this tactic on both Rita and Betty. Rita seemed to be the most willing of everyone to answer questions about Peter and his motives, and Betty would possibly also be more talkative if Theo wasn't around.

Betty and Rita. I'd ring them later and, like a typical Dutchwoman, try to invite myself round for coffee with them this week.

'I didn't speak to anyone,' I say.

The detective and the Belgian interpreter watch me impassively.

'And . . . and I can't remember if I kept the receipt.'

The interpreter leans across the table. 'I want to ask you once more to think hard about what time you left the supermarket, and what time you returned home.'

I shake my head. 'I don't know, I really don't.'

'Ten o'clock?'

I look up in confusion. 'Maybe. Ten o'clock . . . Yes, ten o'clock I think.'

'Who else was in the house, at that time?'

'My husband Eric, and Bastian and Isabelle.'

'What did you do that evening, after you came home?'

I can't remember exactly. After telling Eric I was ill, I fled straight upstairs. I sat staring into space on the bed, completely paralysed, terrified, worried sick.

'I went to bed.'

'Do you usually go to bed so early?'

'Yes.'

The interpreter pulls a face and plays with his coffee cup. He gives me a piercing look.

I feel the nausea growing, growing all the time. This

room has no window. The strip light dances before my eyes and that sugary, sickening smell of coffee is blocking my windpipe.

'When did you last see your purse?'

An iron claw squeezes my windpipe.

39

Louis and the Antoines didn't know what Bruno and Michel were up to and nor did they care. I'd asked after them, taking a proper look at Louis's crippled hand for the first time while he washed his hands, and then shamefacedly launched into putting the finishing touches to the salad, thinking my stare might appear rude.

Not only did they have no idea where Bruno and Michel were, our decimated team of workmen referred to Bruno and Michel as a pair of arrogant brats they preferred not to work with and had little or no contact with in their free time. They didn't say so in so many words, but their expressions and their snorts required no further explanation.

'They're probably on another job,' Louis had muttered.

'Or in gaol,' Antoine had added.

I was about to ask why when Eric came in and my unspoken question shattered into a nervous cough.

We were sitting in Betty's kitchen, with a dish of sweets and two cups of liqueur coffee with whipped cream between us. So far the topic of conversation had been the *chambres d'hôtes*. Her glasses had been replaced by a pair with touches of black, red and brown, no less striking against Betty's pale face than its bright blue predecessor. She was wearing a tiger-print sweater and her thin brown hair hung in rats' tails on the back of her head from a wide hairclip with a tiger motif.

'I'll give you the numbers for those people.' She stood up to get a pen and paper from a sideboard. 'They'll advertise for you on their website. They charge fifteen per cent of everything booked via them.'

'Do they also take care of the payments and things like that?'

'No, you have to do that yourself. All they do is match supply and demand. The advantage of this company is that they advertise more than ten thousand *chambres d'hôtes*, so logically it's the first port of call for many holidaymakers. They give very basic information, but you can also create a link to your own website.'

She put down the piece of paper in front of me. I put it away in my bag, knowing I wouldn't need it. As soon as the house was finished I'd make every effort to go back to Holland.

Every effort.

Betty sat down opposite me and pushed the dish of sweets towards me across the green tablecloth. 'Have some more of these. Theo's on a diet; I can't palm them off on to him any more. How's the building work going, by the way? Everything on schedule?'

Renovating a house is remarkably similar to being pregnant. Somehow I couldn't escape the comparison. When you're pregnant everyone asks how it's going – how are you feeling, do you know what it is yet, is the baby's room finished yet? It's not so very different with a renovation.

I was starting to sound like a broken record.

'It's going fine. Peter only works on Mondays now and Louis, Antoine and Pierre-Antoine are with us the rest of the week.' I ran my hand through my hair. I had to keep going now, before Betty took over the conversation again. 'Now that I'm here . . . The last time we came over you said that the lads have criminal records. I talked about it with Eric afterwards, because to be honest it gave me a shock. I mean . . . the lads are with us all day; they eat with us; we have two young children . . . Do you understand? Before you told me, I had no idea; I thought it was a normal construction company.'

Betty sipped her coffee, sizing me up. 'Peter didn't tell you?'

I shook my head.

Betty took a sweet from the dish, looked at it and put it back again. 'Theo doesn't like me passing this on. It doesn't feel right to speak ill of Peter and the workmen after everything he's done for us. And they're not doing anything wrong, not any more.' She took an agonisingly slow sip of her coffee.

'Eric and I both really like Peter too,' I lied, to reassure Betty. 'But you can't blame me for being curious about what's going on, can you?'

'Are you having difficulties with Peter?'

'No.' I gestured as if swatting away an annoying insect. 'Oh, never mind. I don't want to cause you trouble. The thing is, since you told me, I've kept wondering what sort of things the lads got up to, and that affects the way I act around them. I hate it, really. Because we're so happy with them. And they seem so friendly.'

Betty shifted in her seat and wound a loose wisp of hair between her thumb and forefinger. 'You know . . . this area is vast; there are people living here from all over the world. Some, like you and me, came here to realise their dreams. Others to escape from their nightmares.'

I stared hard at her. I was unable say anything, not even to encourage her. But there was evidently no need.

'Peter had an international haulage business back in Belgium. He had a load of regular clients, but there were some who used him to transport things which . . . well, let's say, illegal goods. He confided this to Theo one evening. Those jobs, they were very lucrative.'

'Did Peter also say what kind of things they were?'

'He often drove to the Basque Country and northern Spain, for people connected to ETA, so . . . well. Drugs and weapons, Theo thinks.'

'So Peter transported drugs and weapons for ETA?' I

could hardly say the words. I only knew ETA from the television news and the papers. Bomb attacks, misery, innocent victims, terrorism. What kind of man was Peter? It was far worse than I thought.

Betty remained remarkably calm. For her this was clearly old news. 'More or less. Peter earned an enormous amount of money from it, but it did go wrong sometimes. People found out which of the lorries contained this stuff, and these lorries were raided in the middle of the night . . . So eventually their own men, from ETA or wherever, accompanied them on those journeys. For protection, shall we say. They also sent men to "work" at Peter's company, because they thought one of Peter's employees was tipping off the other side. Then a member of staff disappeared one day . . . Six months later the remains were found. In Germany.'

I knew that my mouth was hanging open slightly, but I no longer cared. 'And Peter knew about this?'

'Of course he knew. And he was scared by then. Because those men who were on the loose in his company, they weren't going away. They snooped into his computer files, knew all about his clients, the routes and so on. And he couldn't do anything about it.'

'This sounds . . . very serious.' I didn't know what else to say.

Betty grabbed my hand across the table. 'Peter wanted nothing more than to sell his business. But he couldn't get rid of it, because those Basques, they wanted Peter to remain the owner. In fact they'd pretty much taken over his business.'

'How . . . how did Peter end up here, then?'

'Eventually one of the lorries was raided and some people were shot dead. Peter was scared he'd be next. He fled in a panic and left everything behind. His business, but also his wife and children.'

'Oh God . . .'

'After a year or so he met Claudia here and set up that construction business.'

'Why didn't he go to the police? I mean . . . leaving your wife and children behind?'

Betty cast me an almost stern glance. She raised her blue, arched eyebrows. Perhaps they'd been tattooed on. 'In that case he'd also have had to tell the police why he'd fled.'

'Accessory to terrorism,' I thought aloud.

Betty stood up. 'Jesus, Simone. I'm serious: it really doesn't feel right to tell you this. It's gossiping. I don't see why I'm telling you this either. Peter's back on the straight and narrow; he's trying so hard to build a new life. He's actually a victim in a way . . . Everyone has skeletons in their closet. Without a doubt. Almost everybody's got a story, certainly in this area. You're bound to discover that when you get to know people better. Not all as serious as Peter's, but still . . . People have a right to a second chance: that's what I believe. Peter as much as the next person.'

'So Peter's actually on the run still? And those . . . those people on his tail, they're still looking for him?'

'I don't know. I assume not. Otherwise they'd have found him long ago. And I think we'd notice if they did.'

Silence fell. Betty stood up and sat down again. This was now the second time she'd tried to distract me. As if she didn't want to be here, as if her body was urging her to run away from me, but something was holding her back. She was feeling extremely uncomfortable. I was scared she wasn't going tell me anything else, that she'd clam up and show me the door.

And I still had more questions. 'So what did the lads do?'

'I really don't want to go into that.'

'Bad things?'

She looked up. There was a dazed look in her pale eyes. 'That depends what you mean by bad.'

I put my hand on my neck. 'I'm not sure what I mean by bad . . . Violence, I think.'

Betty still said nothing. My mouth was getting dry.

'I don't know exactly what they did anyway,' she said softly. 'But I do know they're back on track now. They work hard. No other employer would have them. There's not much work here, in this region, so nobody's going to employ someone with a criminal record. But Peter did, to give them a fresh start. I think that's only to be applauded.'

'But what did they do then?'

Betty threw up her hands. 'Car theft, armed robbery, drugs, that sort of thing.'

Armed robbery . . . I felt all the blood drain from my face. Could Michel . . .? No.

'Robberies . . . that sounds pretty serious.' My voice was strangely distorted. 'Is anyone working . . . or has anyone worked on our house who's done something like that? To your knowledge?'

She shook her head. 'All I know is that nearly all the lads have been in prison, so I don't know exactly who did what. Peter put them back on the rails. They work their socks off now, honest work. Can you now see why I have misgivings about telling you this? I could kick myself for bringing this up, especially now I see your reaction. Peter is trying to make amends for what he did wrong earlier in his life . . . isn't that . . . simply wonderful?' Her voice betrayed regret. 'Now that you know this you're going to view them differently, aren't you?'

'This . . . Well . . . Yes.'

She lowered her eyes. 'I should have kept my mouth shut.'

'I'm glad you told me. Now I kind of know where I stand.' I attempted to look at her as sincerely as possible. 'I really won't take advantage of this, Betty. Don't worry.'

Peter the victim: I wasn't going to fall for that idea. And certainly not for Peter as a sort of saint – a one-man rehabilitation clinic.

A criminal who'd had links to the underworld. *Terrorists*. He'd participated in arms supply and drug smuggling. Who knows how many people had died partly as a result of Peter's greed for money? *Murdered*.

I held a new trump card. When Eric heard that he was making friends with a serious criminal, it would spell the end of the budding friendship.

40

Cognitive dissonance is a term mainly familiar from the world of marketing. It means that consumers (want to) see their own purchase as the best choice, often against their better judgement.

Even when, with hindsight, something proves beyond doubt to be a poor buy (for example, because that expensive widescreen television gets slated in Which? *Magazine), the internal dialogue nevertheless tries to put a brave face on the purchase ('I don't care if it uses so much electricity, at least the picture is sharper than on those other models') — and it is often fiercely defended to the outside world.*

Cognitive dissonance does not by definition have to be applied to consumer products, but can equally be observed in choices and decisions in daily life.

No one likes to admit they made the wrong decision.

'Peter's a criminal.'

Eric looked at me over the rim of his wineglass. 'A criminal?'

'I went for coffee at Betty's house today, and she told me how Peter ended up here.'

'What were you doing at Betty's? I didn't get the impression you clicked very well.'

'I don't have much choice here, do I? We don't know that many people. I went over to ask her how she goes about running her *chambres d'hôtes*. She gave me the number and address of a company that liaises between individual *chambres d'hôtes* and holidaymakers. It's aimed mainly at the English market. She gets nearly all her guests via that company.'

'What's Peter got to do with this?'

'Betty asked me in confidence if Peter had talked about his past. I said he hadn't and then she told me about it. I nearly jumped out of my skin.'

Eric put his wine down on the sofa table beside him, but didn't appear particularly alarmed. 'What did she say, then?'

'That Peter fled from Belgium. He transported drugs and weapons for ETA.'

Eric was still looking at me impassively.

I decided to lay it on thick: 'Then someone at his company, a haulage company, was murdered by those people because they thought he was tipping off other criminals. And that wasn't the only murder. Peter is on the run.'

'Did Betty say that?'

I nodded.

'Betty should cut the crap.' Eric picked up his glass of wine and took a sip.

I shifted on my chair. Eric's impassive demeanour confused

me. 'Eric! He's on the run from ETA! The man doing up our house is on the run from a terrorist organisation and the lads working for us all have criminal records. Do you think that's normal or something?'

'I think Betty's exaggerating everything.'

'I don't think so. You don't make up something like that, do you?'

Silence fell. Eric seemed to be thinking. Finally he started speaking. 'Peter's told me a few things about his past . . . But Betty's dramatising it.'

I shot upright. 'You *knew*, and you didn't say anything to me?'

'No.'

'Why not?'

'Because you'd only start worrying. Peter has a past, but that's behind him now.'

'Did you know that some of the lads working for him have committed armed robbery?'

'Is that what Betty said?'

I nodded.

Eric snorted. 'A few of them did indeed do that. A long time ago, under the influence of drugs, gone astray, away from home, hopeless future. Wild oats.'

'*Wild oats?* Christ, Eric . . .' It was as if I was talking to a stranger here. I'd never witnessed Eric like this. It didn't seem to bother him at all. 'Do you also know who committed those robberies? People who've worked for us?'

He shook his head. 'No, I don't know. And I don't care, to be honest.'

'You don't *care*?'

'You know, Simone, I think you should put it into perspective. Since we moved here, I've seen that some people have a very different way of life from the one we've always had. They've all escaped the rat race; they've made different choices than most of us would. They live differently. More freely. They don't worry about mortgages; they don't wash their cars at the weekend. They live for the day, and they might have done things they shouldn't. But have you noticed that they seem happy, despite having to work hard? The solidarity here is infinitely greater than I ever experienced in all those years I worked in Holland. If someone's short of money for fuel oil, there's always someone willing to help out. If someone has an empty fridge, they can always pull up a chair somewhere else. It's down to earth. More human. That attitude really appeals to me . . .'

At this point my mouth fell open. I gulped. Was this Eric? 'So you don't mind that Peter's a criminal and that we've brought a group of criminals into our house to do it up?'

'They were criminals. Not any more. And besides, that's only a word, a term. Peter was down and out when he accepted the offer from those guys. And it's still doubtful whether it really was ETA. If that's true, do you really think Peter would still be going about his business here, two hours' drive from the Basque Country, and would be able to run an entire company? Of course not. Betty was grossly exaggerating. I'm incredibly glad that Peter and the lads are helping us out for relatively little money. You've learnt a lot of French from Antoine at lunchtime, and you still are . . . They've shown us the way to various agencies. You're forgetting, Simmy, that without them we'd still be stuck in the caravan now. Those lads may well have made mistakes in their lives, but whatever they were, it's history.'

'Aren't you scared they'll do it again? That they'll . . . reoffend?'

He shook his head. 'I don't see why. You can earn a lot more money from crime with less effort. So the fact that they're doing this work tells me all I need to know. And it should do the same for you too.'

'I don't get it, Eric. You're . . . You'd have reacted very differently in Holland. You always said they should hand out harsher punishments, that they should lock people up for longer and things like that.'

'In Holland I didn't know anyone like Peter and the lads. It's easier to judge when you're standing on the sidelines. I've started to take a different view now, perhaps also because I really like Peter, and the same goes for the lads. You can't keep judging people for what they did in the past in a different situation. I see things as they are now. A bunch of hard-working lads, having a lot of fun together, helping each other out, without backbiting and jealousy. One person doesn't have to have a flashier car than the other; they don't chase after each other's women. People aren't judged on their possessions. Have you noticed how everyone respects Louis? The lad's no oil painting, and he lives in a leaky caravan somewhere at the back of Peter's property, but he matters all the same. Try finding that in our old social circle. All that counts there is your job, your house and your car. If we'd parked a car on our drive like Pierre-Antoine's, the neighbours would have been up in arms and the council would have come and towed it away. There's more to people than their possessions or their jobs. To judge solely on that basis is as hypocritical as it gets. People are more honest here. More authentic. Everyone's unique, rich or poor. They make mistakes, like everyone does, and they try to make the best of things. I'm not going to blame Peter, in any case. And I hope you're not going to either.'

41

It was so cold I'd had to scrape the windscreen and was regularly warming my hands in the dishwater in the kitchen sink while cooking. The lads were wearing several layers of outer clothing with thick coats on top. They donned gloves and balaclavas while they worked. There wasn't much laughing and joking any more. They looked stern, with their faces contorted by the cold. Altogether, anyone would have thought we had a bunch of bank robbers working for us.

Maybe we really did.

Everyone kept their coats on over lunch. Eric had put an electric heater near the table, but it made little difference.

I'd given everyone their own individual plate of salad. Pieces of tomato and cucumber, prunes and sea salt in a dressing of olive oil with lemon juice and frozen parsley. Yesterday I'd stopped preparing one big dish from which everybody could help themselves.

An individual dish for everyone.

Peter had cleaned his plate. I'd sat there staring at him, and briefly, for a fraction of a second, he'd glanced at me vacantly. For a moment I was afraid that I'd given myself away. That he could read my mind.

There was nothing harmful in the salad.

Not yet.

After everyone had gone back to work, I'd paid Peter. He'd lingered in the kitchen for a while, giving the impression he wanted to talk to me. Clearly he'd picked up on the change in my demeanour. I'd turned away from him and started doing the dishes. After that he'd disappeared into the right wing to help the lads.

Peter might think he had everything under control, but as long as he dutifully polished off my salads, any Monday afternoon could be his last. It made me feel it was me, not him, who was pulling the strings. This was heartening.

And more frightening besides.

I didn't know whether I actually had the power, the courage. Whether I was desperate enough to be able to sit by as Peter ate a salad that would prove fatal to him. And whether afterwards, when the contents of his stomach were examined in a laboratory, I could really act the innocent when doubts were cast on his last meal, consumed at Simone Jansen's house.

I was becoming increasingly preoccupied with this. Almost every day now, I watched *The FBI Files* on the Discovery Channel, and similar documentaries. I soaked them up like textbooks. The investigations, the autopsies, the interrogations. And the more preoccupied I became, the more I ran through the steps one by one in my head, the more anxious I grew. I wondered whether I was making a fool of myself. Whether the thoughts churning through my mind and dominating my days really were based on everyday reality. I probably wasn't thinking clearly any more, but I didn't know what to do to get a grip. I was living mainly in my inner world now, where there was no sounding board, no one to rap my knuckles or take issue with me. It was just terribly quiet and lonely.

And there was fear in the air.

I kept going round in circles, and there seemed to be no way out.

More than once this gave me the urge to come clean with Eric. What stopped me was the knowledge that my confession would crush him. He trusted me, us, implicitly. I couldn't hurt him. And I didn't want to lose him. I didn't want to lose my life with the children and Eric.

And I would lose them.

The knowledge that I'd cheated on him, in his own car, in his own bed, would have blown a hole in his trust, and destroyed everything he believed in and held dear. My words would eat away at our family like an inflamed wound, ever further and deeper, until, after a long, painful process, there was absolutely nothing left.

The telephone rang. The sound cut right through my clouded head and triggered the automatic response of picking up the receiver.

It took a while for it to dawn on me that I had a Frenchman on the line, from some company, asking for Eric.

'One moment,' I said, and headed to the right wing. I hardly ever came to this part of the house. A corridor with various rooms. There was a narrow spiral staircase at the end leading to the tower. Soft light fell on the dark wood floor from the small window in the tower. Dust swirled slowly round in the chink of light. The floor was strewn with lagging, sawdust, shrink-wrap and empty plastic water bottles that had probably been left there since last summer. It was dusky.

Someone was hammering in the distance. A little closer I could hear Eric talking. I stopped in my tracks.

'I don't know if it'll happen. Simone's got it into her head that she doesn't want to stay here. Maybe she'll change her mind when the winter's over, but I've got my hands full with her at the moment. I seriously have to consider that she really will want to go back. And if we have to go back, then I badly need every cent to be able to buy a place in Holland; I have no illusions about selling this house. It could take a year or more.'

Silence.

I stood motionless in the corridor. My heart was beating in my mouth.

'Shall I have a word with her?'

Peter's voice.

'There's absolutely no point,' I heard Eric answer. 'But thanks for offering.'

I waited, but could hear only hammering and sawing. The conversation was over. I coughed before entering the room and looked at Eric, then Peter, and back again. They both acted as if nothing had happened. Peter smiled amiably.

They were shutting me out.

'There's someone on the telephone for you. Monsieur Gaudon, or something.'

'Ah, I was just going to call him. The boiler man.'

Eric slipped out of the room and I followed on his heels.

'When did you last see your purse?' repeats the interpreter.

I hold my arms in front of my stomach and pull a pained face.

My purse . . . that's it. The proof. The link. A futile moment of carelessness.

Yet there's no way I could have known it at the time . . .

'I don't know,' I respond. 'I think . . . Friday, I think.'

'When you went shopping, on Friday evening, at Leclerc?'

I remember. I paid with Eric's card, because mine got damaged and doesn't always work. I was in a rush on Friday, a huge rush to leave the shops. I didn't want to wait and see if my card would work or not and waste time. That's why I'd handed the checkout girl Eric's card from the start. Eric had given it to me before I went shopping. I'd put it on the kitchen table at home before I went to bed.

'No,' I say. 'I paid with my husband's card.'

'It wasn't in your purse?'

'No. In my coat pocket. My own card doesn't always work. I took my husband's card and paid with that.'

'And your purse?'

'I think . . . I don't know. I . . . I didn't have it with me in any case.'

'Because you'd lost it?'

'I can't remember. I don't think I took it with me.'

'It's important for us to know when you last saw your purse.'

I swallow. A shiver runs down my spine. 'Friday, I think. Or Thursday.'

'Where do you leave your purse when you're at home? In a cupboard? A drawer?'

'All over the place,' I say. 'Usually I just leave it on the worktop, sometimes on the table; occasionally I also put it in my coat pocket. Or I leave it in the car.'

'Could someone have taken your purse from your house?'

A glimmer of hope flickers inside me. 'Yes, that's possible.'

'Does the name Peter Vandamme mean anything to you?'

I close my eyes. 'I feel really sick,' I squeak. 'I need to vomit.'

Suddenly I collapse forwards. The bile gushes from my mouth on to the floor.

No one reacts.

'Is it true that Peter Vandamme renovated your house?'

I hold my head between my knees and stare at the puddle of mucus in front of my feet. 'Yes,' I say, and another shiver travels through me. 'That's right.'

His tone of voice changes all of a sudden. 'Do you know that this man, your builder, was murdered, last Friday evening, at approximately half past ten?'

I look up. 'Yes. The policemen who arrested me yesterday told me.'

42

Sleeping pills were not a good method of poisoning people. Antidepressants were. In fact, they were particularly well suited to it. These, too, would be pretty easy to get hold of from Rodez, the village witch doctor, but if residues were found in Peter's body I'd be top of the list of suspects. I assumed that Rodez made a note of what he prescribed his patients and that records were kept at the chemist's.

Of course, the internet was a wonderful medium; I could order a few boxes from America just in case, from one of those semi-legal or perhaps even illegal laboratories, but where was I going to have these tablets or pills delivered, and how was I going to pay for them without leaving tracks? I abandoned the plan to poison Peter with drugs.

Plants still seemed the best option. The castor-oil plant, the foxglove, that kind of deadly greenery. After spending three-quarters of an hour surfing the web in an internet café, reading up on all the poisonous plants and their constituent parts, I typed Peter's name into a search engine. Only one Peter Vandamme popped up, in the whole world. And it wasn't our Peter. But if he was indeed on the run, he'd be pretty stupid to do so under his own name.

Peter wasn't stupid.

So there was no point to what I was doing now. I was well aware of this. Perhaps I was here simply to convince myself I could regain some control over my own life.

I logged out, paid the man behind the counter and went outside. I pulled the lapels of my coat together and walked with my head bowed and my eyes half shut through the rain to the car. Out of the corner of my eye I could see an off-roader parked behind our Volvo. Dark colour. There was someone inside.

My heart leaped into my mouth. Peter.

He got out and made a beeline for me. Raindrops were falling on his hair and running down his ashen face. 'I need to speak to you.'

I looked at him. Water was getting in under my lapels and under my clothes. I shivered. 'Why?'

'Come with me to the car; it's more comfortable in there.'

I shook my head. There was no way I was getting into Peter's car. My hand was clasped tightly around my bunch of keys.

At that precise moment he grabbed my arm and dragged me along. I resisted and almost fell over.

'Simone, I mean you no harm. I . . .'

I stood looking at him, panting.

'Wait . . .' he said.

Keeping hold of my arm, he reached into his back pocket and pulled out fifty- and hundred-euro notes. A whole bundle of money. He stuffed them into my damp hand and folded my fingers around it, like a rich uncle secretly slipping his favourite child some money.

I looked at it in bewilderment. This was an awful lot of money.

'Stash it away,' he said. 'It's yours . . . Both of yours. I want . . . I need to speak to you for a minute. Please.'

I looked at him in astonishment and tried to swallow, but my heart was still blocking my throat. It expanded, then shrank again, expanded and shrank. My ears were ringing. 'I don't . . . I don't get it.'

Peter looked at me with an expression that under normal circumstances I'd describe as desperate, but I wasn't sure about anything any more, not now.

What I *was* sure about was that I wasn't going to get into his car. It was too risky. Next he'd carry me off, strangle me and dump my lifeless body somewhere in one of the numerous, uninhabited acres of woodland in the surrounding area. Throw it into a ravine. Hide it in one of the thousands of caves.

He'd blackmailed me. He was a criminal with links to terrorists. He'd assaulted me, not so long ago. And he'd followed me, this morning. He must have been waiting outside here for at least an hour.

Or had he seen our car by chance? No. He'd given me

my money back. This encounter had been planned.

I felt like his prey, unable to flee or fight, paralysed and wide-eyed, waiting for what was to come.

Peter pressed his lips together and looked down. He spoke loudly to make himself heard above the natural disaster raging around us. 'Simone, love . . . Sorry. I went too far. It dawned on me yesterday, when I was driving home. I want to apologise.'

A gust of wind pulled at my coat and my hair.

His eyes flitted in all directions. 'There: a café. Would you be comfortable with that? Would you be comfortable going to a café with me? I mean you no harm. Honestly.'

I followed his gaze. There was a small café across the road. A curtain of rain was pelting the tarmac pavement from the protruding red awning.

'All right,' I said, hesitantly.

He let go of my arm. We crossed the road. Peter opened the door for me.

It was warm and dry inside, and there was a parquet floor and a dozen rectangular tables. Shiny deep-red ashtrays and little vases with artificial flowers on the thin dark-veneer table tops. An electronic dartboard was hanging on the wall near the bar. We were the only customers. Peter guided me to a table far away from the window, as if he didn't want us to be seen together.

Ill at ease, I sat down on a wooden chair. *Peter's given me back all the money I've paid him over the past few weeks.*

A man of around fifty appeared, wearing a white shirt and a knitted spencer.

'Tea? Coffee? Something stronger?' asked Peter.

'Tea, please.'

I heard him order tea, and a cup of coffee and a whisky for himself. I briefly glanced at my watch. It was ten to twelve.

It wasn't long till the lads would be sitting down to lunch. There was a dish of potato gratin with cheese, broccoli and mince ready in the oven. Eric just needed to heat it up.

'Count it again.' Peter nodded towards the bundle of money in my coat pocket. 'It's everything you gave me.'

Shaking my head, I stuffed the banknotes deeper into the lined pocket. I believed him all right. I took off my coat and hung it over the chair to dry. Peter laid his brown leather jacket on the chair beside him.

He sighed deeply. 'Sorry,' he said, softly. 'What I did . . . I shouldn't have done that. I want you to know I'm sorry. I went too far. I was angry with you. At least that's what I thought, but actually I was angry with someone else.'

With Michel?

'Before Claudia, I had a girlfriend. I met her here, shortly after I came to live here. I was on my own, as was she, and I moved in with her. She was everything to me.' He rubbed his face. 'I bought the house where I'm living now. We did it up together . . .'

The man came back with our order and put two well-thumbed menus on the table.

'Do you want anything to eat?'

'No.'

Peter took a quick look at the menu and ordered an omelette with salad. Then he looked at me again. 'And one day I found out that she was having an affair with a guy who was working for me. A young lad. At least ten years younger than me. It was more than a little painful. I nearly drank myself to death when she left with him to open a café in Spain. From one day to the next I was on my own. I was in pieces. I had a tough time. I came very close to topping myself. I'd been through a few things and this was the last straw.'

I didn't dare say anything.

'You look a lot like her. When I first saw you, it gave me a fright. I was keen to work on your house myself, in the beginning, and spend time with you both. None of that is your fault. You're not her; it was all in my head. I thought about you a lot. When I saw you and Michel, that morning, it reawakened the memories. Not right away, in fact. It came later and I kept on brooding and fretting. The anger returned. Things I'd suppressed long ago resurfaced and I became increasingly angry. With Michel. With you. And with myself . . . But it wasn't about that. Not really. I want you to know that it wasn't about you. I wanted to punish you, but in reality I wanted to punish Véronique.'

Hot steam rose from the tea glass. It didn't occur to me to dunk the teabag in it. I wasn't thirsty.

'You know,' Peter continued. The words came out of his mouth in fits and starts, and I was straining to follow him. 'Eric's a great guy. I've grown fond of him. His family means everything to him. And the guy is only doing his best. When I saw that you and Michel . . .' Peter looked away from me. 'Anyway, it's about time this stopped. This way I'm essentially stealing from Eric too, and I don't want to do that. My money's run out. Simple as that. Things aren't easy for me at the moment. But that's my problem. And nobody else's.'

Silence fell. I wasn't sure what to say.

When he tried to touch my hand across the table I pulled it away. A shadow passed over his face. 'There's no need to be scared of me any more. I'll leave you alone. It's a good life here, honestly. Maybe I've blown it for you . . . I hope you'll reconsider. See my side of the story. I'm sorry. I'm really sorry.' Peter looked at me so sincerely it was almost painful. 'Eric told me you want to go back to Holland. I'm afraid that it's my fault. I think if you stay here a while longer, and you can start enjoying the weather and your new house, you'll . . . Give it some more thought.' He took a big gulp of his whisky. 'Go on: drink something.'

I looked at the tea glass and dropped the bag into it. 'Did you only do it because of your ex-girlfriend?'

He nodded. 'Yes . . . It had nothing to do with you or

Michel or Eric. Well . . . it did a bit. I was jealous too. I pulled that kid out of the gutter, for Christ's sake. He was good for nothing. He's been in young offenders' institutions, snorted cocaine, smoked cannabis, smashed everything in sight to pieces . . . he was on a path of self-destruction. He'd stopped caring. I was fond of him, but I'd never seen him as a rival.' Peter grinned sheepishly and ran his hand nervously through his hair. 'That's nonsense, of course.'

I could feel myself beginning to calm down already.

'I'm such an idiot. I'm sorry. I needed money as well. I don't know what came over me. I hope you can let bygones be bygones. Can you?'

'I don't know what to think any more,' I said, truthfully. 'Sorry.'

Why was I apologising? Was I now feeling sorry for Peter all of a sudden?

His story sounded plausible. It made him more human. It was also in keeping with his demeanour. He seemed confused, ashamed, nervous.

'So Michel's got nothing to do with it?'

'With what?'

'With that . . . hush money of yours. I thought you and Michel . . .'

'Sorry I gave that impression. He's got no idea.'

'Where is Michel?'

'I've kicked him upstairs. He's near Arnéguy, in the Basque Country. Near the Spanish border. It's very remote, high mountains. He's there with a team building a summerhouse for friends of mine. I simply packed him off, into the snow. He didn't even know about it in advance himself. I rang him one Saturday morning, when the bus was already on its way to his house.'

When I heard the words Basque Country everything began to fall into place.

Mobile phones didn't work in remote mountainous areas. So that's why I hadn't been able to get through to Michel. I'd arranged to meet him on a Sunday, in that little park with the caravans. Michel hadn't turned up, simply because he'd been picked up and sent to work the day before. I'd been mistaken when Michel had rung me; I thought he said he was in *Pays-Bas*, Holland. He'd said *Pays basque*. The Basque Country.

Hadn't Rita mentioned this too? That Peter was working on two new projects, including one in the Basque Country?

Why hadn't I thought of this before?

I took a sip of the tea. It was lukewarm now. Then I looked at Peter. He was stabbing at the omelette and taking large bites. His glass of whisky was empty.

'Have you ever called me?' I asked. 'I mean, late at night?'

He looked up from his plate in surprise. A shred of lettuce was hanging from the corner of his mouth. 'Called you? Why?'

I bit my bottom lip. It had been Michel. Michel had been trying to ring me. 'When is Michel coming back?'

Peter stared hard at me all of a sudden. So intensely it gave me a fright. 'He'll be out of the picture for the time being. But . . . is that important to you?'

I nodded.

He shook his head. His expression softened again. 'Simone, love . . . It feels awful to say it . . . but you're better off staying away from him. He'll – *excusez le mot* – fuck anything that moves. You're not the first. And certainly not the last. Somehow I wasn't surprised when I found you with Michel. Do you understand? He has a reputation. It's not the first time he's screwed a married woman. It's a trophy for a boy like that. A kick. A challenge.'

I felt all the blood drain from my face.

'Pardon my French,' Peter continued, 'but I can't sugar-coat it. I care about that boy, but he can't keep his dick in his trousers.' Peter coughed. 'He's not worth it. Stay with your family. That's the only piece of advice I can give you. You have something that an awful lot of people want and can't have: a loving husband, two wonderful children. A stable foundation. Eric really is a good guy; he wants to give his family a better future, and he's working hard to achieve that. And he's right; he's doing the right thing. Besides, life is better here than in northern Europe. There's more space; people don't keep themselves to themselves. No traffic, no haste, no stress and no red tape. You're incredibly lucky, Simone. A hell of a lot of people would love to be in your shoes. Don't jeopardise all that for a boy like Michel. If you do, you'll be on your own one day. I really mean it, from the bottom of my heart. See it as fatherly advice.'

Part II

43

The swallows were back again.

A few of them tried to fly inside. They smashed into the double glazing, lay dazed in the courtyard while they came round, and fluttered onwards, disorientated.

'They're used to brooding here,' said Eric. 'Last autumn I had to scrape at least five nests off the roof beams. This house has been empty for so long. They don't know any better.'

The poor creatures. They flew here all the way from Africa; they were born and bred here, just like their ancestors, and now we'd made their nesting place inaccessible. Perhaps they'd go into exile in the sheds. We had enough of them and weren't planning to do them up for the time being. I resolved there and then to ask Eric to leave at least one of them untouched, so that the birds could keep one nesting place, whatever happened.

A swallow swooped in through the doorway, dived elegantly through our hall, landed on the balustrade and then flew gracefully back outside.

'Shall I stick newspaper over the windows or something?' I asked Eric. 'One of them is going to end up dead before long.'

'I'll take care of it.'

I went outside, towards the lake. The trees were in bloom. Here and there the delicate red petals of poppies were sticking out above the grass.

Bleu was by my side. His fur was covered with thick tufts of undercoat like pieces of felt. I pulled a few of them out, but it was a hopeless task. He was panting loudly. Our husky cross clearly wasn't built for walks in the blazing sun. The winter had suited him better.

Halfway to the lake I looked round at our house. It had turned out beautifully. The ugly grey stucco was gone. The authentic yellow-red bricks were now visible. The pointing between the higgledy-piggledy lumps had been repointed shallowly with yellow cement. There were window boxes with geraniums in colours that were almost painful to the naked eye, so brightly did the flowers reflect the sunlight.

The house was finished.

All that remained to do was the outside. Level the yard, dig trenches for the electricity and water so that we could connect exterior lighting, fountains and outside taps.

Mountains had been moved over the past eight months.

Strangely enough, I'd started to feel increasingly at home here. The visit to Holland, in December, hadn't worked out as I'd expected. Or hoped. Almost without thinking, I'd assumed that I'd burst into tears at the sight of the windmills, the flat meadows with Friesian cows, the ditches, our old village. The rivers.

It had been cold – cold and bleak – and the wipers swished continuously to and fro to keep the windscreen of the Volvo clear. Traffic lights everywhere, one-way streets, seemingly endless traffic jams, thousands of lights, hoardings, hubbub, roaring engines. Stifling suburban streets that all looked the same. A visit to one of Eric's old colleagues in Amsterdam was punished with a wheel clamp, meaning we had to search for a whole hour in the pouring rain, dragging the reluctant children along through the teeming crowd, honking horns and zigzagging scooters, for the office of the parking authority, where Eric had to pay several hundred euros to an uninterested and downright unfriendly official. Erica – I'd been looking forward to seeing her again enormously – was ill at home and looked grey and weary. She was keen to come to France, she'd told me, in the spring. It wasn't possible to take time off any sooner. Work was piling up at the office and she couldn't afford to go away for a week before then. A few of her colleagues had already been fired owing to disappointing trading results.

I couldn't sleep, in Eric's parents' house. I shot up in bed at every sound. The neighbours flushing the toilet. Someone honking their horn somewhere in the neighbourhood. A siren in the distance that seemed to be approaching and then died away again. A bang sent me to the window in alarm, where I spotted someone bent over in the twilight, putting out a wheelie bin.

All those sounds, people, houses, cars, the lack of daylight in the dark days before Christmas, the hours spent looking for a parking space: it was suffocating.

Eric's parents had gone to an awful lot of trouble to give us a good time. There was a Christmas tree with silver and white baubles, and chocolates hanging on it for the children. We ate turkey, which was a little on the dry side. Salad bathed in oily salad dressing; the lettuce sliced far too thinly, meaning it wilted at the edges.

I missed olive oil. The vinegar. Basil. Louis, the Antoines. The peace and quiet and the space, the winding lanes where nobody ever came. The Limousin cattle in the hilly landscape. My view.

I missed France.

That week in Holland brought home to me that I'd rather be stuck in a half-finished house in the middle of nowhere, speaking broken French, than in this overpopulated chaos, among all the people who were so dear to my heart. Or had been. Still, it had been my home for thirty-four years. I'd been happy there. Six months in France had stripped me of my roots forever.

★

I sat down by the lake and watched the insects buzzing around each other just above the surface of the water. I laid my head in the grass and turned my eyes to the sky. It was clear blue, with the odd patch of cloud. A sparkling dot was speeding through the air, leaving a straight white line in its wake, that slowly expanded and then faded into the infinite blue as the aeroplane progressed on its journey. I could hear crickets chirping, still rather tentatively, but they were back.

And I felt the calm descend on me.

This was the life.

Peter had kept his word. Over the past few months there'd been cautious advances. He and Claudia had invited us round a few times, and we'd had a lovely evening every time. I'd started to see Peter more as a person. He'd made mistakes and was trying to make amends. Although I could and would never again trust him completely, my fear of him had been pushed into the background.

Eric hadn't breathed a word about the cottage project and had thrown himself into making a website for the *chambres d'hôtes* instead. He'd bought a digital camera and I'd used it to take photos of the rooms and the picturesque local villages. We'd got in touch with various internet companies that ran holiday sites and matched supply and demand. In a couple of weeks or so the courtyard would also be finished and the final photos could be taken. Hopefully we'd be able to receive a few guests in high season and start earning our first money.

Perhaps it had been a good thing, my fling with Michel. I now knew how lucky I was. Eric was reliable, kind and caring. Entertaining. Our French adventure had driven us apart at first and then brought us much closer together. Wasn't it true that all good relationships go through a very bad patch at some point? I could remember reading something like that once. Every relationship is put to the test eventually. If it lacks a solid foundation, then a crisis like that is the point where people divorce. Others come out of it stronger and closer than ever.

I considered myself lucky that Eric and I belonged to the latter group.

The sex still wasn't mind-blowing, but after all the strong emotions I'd experienced I couldn't even regret that. There was more to life than just sex. It felt safe and familiar, lying in Eric's arms.

I hadn't seen Michel since November, but he'd been on my mind the whole time. Fond memories that washed over me were mercilessly alternated with intense feelings of shame. How could I have been so stupid?

I couldn't forget Peter's words.

I'd been a trophy. A challenge.

The fact remained: I couldn't understand why Michel had gone to so much trouble to ring his *trophy*. If he was staying in an inhospitable region near the Spanish border, that couldn't have been easy. I imagined him in some café, vainly dialling our number time after time on a pre-war telephone, only to have to drive twenty miles along a windy road back to the building site.

But perhaps I'd got it wrong and he'd bagged himself a Basque beauty. Or a whole flock of them. All the residents of the village between the ages of fourteen and forty, for example.

It shouldn't bother me any more. The shame was too great, as was the relief that it was all over. Michel was history, as far as I was concerned. I truly believed that.

I'd find out soon enough if that really was the case. Michel, Bruno and Arnaud were through with their mountain adventure. As of tomorrow they were coming to do our court-yard.

44

Michel jumped out of one of Peter's battered vans.

He looked irresistible. Far better than I remembered.

I clenched my teeth and stood in the yard, with an empty watering can in my arms as a barrier.

My heart was pounding behind my ribs.

His lithe movements. Tanned arms sticking out of a sleeveless T-shirt.

Bleu made a beeline for him and jumped up at him, wagging his tail. Michel larked about with him as if nothing was the matter. As if nothing had happened. As if it wasn't nearly five months ago but only yesterday that he'd been here last.

He looked in my direction and our eyes met. A scorching look, causing my system to short-circuit even at a distance. Everything faded to vague background noise. The cold winter months, the confusion, the loneliness fell away. Everything fell away.

I pressed the watering can tighter against me.

I should hate him. But the traitor that was my body

called out to him and all the hormones in my body were chanting his name.

With all the willpower I had in me, I turned my back to everyone and went inside. To hell with French etiquette. Kiss Michel? That was out of the question. I simply couldn't do it.

I ran upstairs and, like a coward, locked myself in the guest bathroom. For at least half an hour I sat there against the wall with my eyes closed. Shaking violently and cursing myself.

Lunch was a disaster. I was so flustered that the onions, which were supposed to add flavour to the potatoes, had been burned to a crisp.

Michel was sitting diagonally opposite me, unabashed and stripped to the waist.

I did my best to ignore him. My very best.

Peter turned to Eric. 'Have you heard that story about John and Patricia? The English couple?'

I heard Eric mumbling that he hadn't.

'Disaster. They bought a house last winter, similar to yours. But not *so* bad. The roof was OK in any case. I put a team of workmen on the job and we managed to finish it off last week. John came round last night. It turns out they're in quite a bit of trouble. They bought that house with their own money and financed the renovation, and now it's done the money's run out. Patricia went to the bank to apply for a mortgage, but was turned down.'

'Why?' I heard Eric ask.

I looked cautiously in Michel's direction. He gave me a grin that would have quickened the dead, and made a compliment in French dialect about my completely botched soup-kitchen meal.

'*Merci*,' I said softly, staring at my plate. I could feel my heartbeat, the blood being pumped round. My breathing.

'They don't grant mortgages retrospectively here,' Peter's deep voice penetrated my inner world.

'How do you mean? No second mortgages?'

'Yes, simple as that. You can only get a mortgage here when you buy a house. If you're renovating you might be able to get a kind of building loan. But when everything's finished you won't get another cent.'

I looked up again. Only briefly. The intensity with which Michel held my gaze effortlessly blew holes in the shaky defensive wall I'd put up around me.

I looked down.

Ten working days.

Right now ten minutes seemed too much to ask.

'John has a house worth at least half a million on the open market,' Peter continued. 'But they can barely afford to eat. Now they've managed to rent out their own house and they're living in one of the *gîtes*. John's going to England next week to work. They're flat broke. A complete disaster.'

I looked at the people around the table. Bruno had an earphone in one ear and was nodding his head rhythmically.

Arnaud and the Antoines were eating in silence. Louis was giving Bleu a potato.

'So,' I heard Eric say, 'what it boils down to is that if you've run out of money, you can't remortgage your house, but have to sell it?'

Peter took a bite of his potatoes and hummed in assent. 'That's what it boils down to, yes. Stupid rule. Do you know how many people fall into that trap every year? Who fall head over heels in love with a house, throw themselves into renovating it and only make enquiries afterwards, when it's too late? I'm telling you, it's a disaster.'

Michel tried to touch my feet under the table. I choked on my orange juice and anxiously pulled my feet under me. Kept them crossed under my chair.

Why, it suddenly occurred to me, had Peter picked Michel for these last two weeks, out of all his forty employees? I didn't believe it was coincidence, let alone thoughtlessness or a strange sense of humour. There had to be a reason . . . Money? Since our conversation in the café in December, I hadn't heard Peter mention that building project of his. This surprised me, because I could imagine that if he'd found a backer, he'd surely have been getting on with it right now, instead of digging trenches at our house for fifteen euros an hour. I rubbed my hair nervously. I thought it was over. That I could get on with my life, which had turned out better than I could have imagined only last winter. Now Michel was back, and Peter was suddenly starting up a conversation out of nowhere about people who were flat broke.

I was fiddling about in the kitchen. After finishing the washing-up I'd started compulsively clearing out the fridge. I looked at all the best-before dates, threw away the odd half-empty pot or tin with indefinable contents and scrubbed the inside of the fridge clean. Then moved on to the microwave, the oven. I kept scrubbing, removed shelves from the cupboards. Under no circumstances did I want to go outside where everyone was at work in the brilliant sun. The radio was on, but I couldn't tell if it was speech or music. I could hear the machines rattling and whirring. The diesel fumes were penetrating as far as the kitchen.

Michel appeared to be standing there all of a sudden. He brought with him the smell of sun, air, fresh sweat. His smell. Feeling awkward, I crossed my arms.

He closed the door behind him. 'I've come to get water.'

I nodded towards the fridge. He took two large bottles out of the door, put them down on the worktop and stood there. 'Simone, I . . . I've missed you so much.'

I wanted to say 'I've missed you too' but the words remained unsaid. The silence that hung between us was broken by shouting from outside. Someone was calling his name. It sounded urgent.

He briefly glanced outside and then looked at me darkly, rubbing his upper arm. 'Simone . . . That time I rang you

. . . What did you mean by "stop"? Stop ringing? Is it over?'

I had no idea what he was talking about. Thankfully, I nodded. Only then did vague fragments unfold in my head of the brief phone call the night that Eric and I had had that flaming row. I'd wanted to say 'Don't talk so fast', but the sentence had remained unfinished because Eric had come into the hall and I'd slammed the phone down in panic. Michel had interpreted it as a rejection.

Someone was calling his name again. Michel ignored it. He kept looking at me, searchingly. After an almost tangible silence that hung between us, he said softly: 'Because of the children?'

I struggled to keep my voice under control. 'That too.'

'Eric?'

'Yes.'

He sniffed. Then looked nervously out of the window towards the yard. The sound of the heavy machinery continued unabated outside.

He started nodding, bit his bottom lip. 'OK. OK.' Then rubbed his hair and muttered: '*Putain*.'

Not so long ago Louis had filled me in on the French expressions you didn't find in a standard dictionary. *Putain* means whore, among other things, but is used as a swear-word in France. If you're pissed off with something, if your hammer lands on your thumb, if you're at your wits' end: *putain*.

'Michel!'

Michel looked up. He grabbed the bottles from the worktop. They were heavy, but he held them by the neck, seemingly effortlessly clasped between his fingers in one hand.

He stopped in the doorway. 'Are you sure?'

I nodded and looked at the ground. It was impossible to look at him. 'Sorry.'

45

Michel wasn't here today. Over lunch it emerged why not.

Bruno ate my tagliatelle with bacon with his mouth open and, gesticulating wildly, gave me a blow-by-blow account of how Michel had completely lost it last night. In the evening they'd gone for a drink in a café at Michel's request. Michel had hit the bottle and had then gone deliberately looking for trouble. He'd spent the night in a police cell.

Bruno was beaming; he found it extremely funny.

Peter shifted in his seat. 'Has he been charged?'

'No,' said Bruno. 'The bloke he punched in the face was pretty worked up himself . . . Hilarious.'

Eric tried to make eye contact with me across the table. I didn't know how to respond.

'Is he at home now?' asked Peter.

'Yes. He called me at seven o'clock to tell me he'd been released. So I went to pick him up and took him home.'

Peter put some authority into his voice. 'Michel called in sick.'

'Yes, he *is* sick. Man, he looked completely grey, alcohol poisoning or something, I swear. Hilarious.'

Peter ignored Bruno's giggling and took his mobile phone out of his pocket. He pressed a few keys and went outside with the mobile phone to his ear.

'How is he?' asked Eric when Peter returned to the table.

'It'll pass. He'll be back tomorrow.'

'Is there anything wrong with the lad? Has he got problems?'

'Problems . . . who hasn't,' said Peter, dropping the subject.

We continued eating in silence.

Bastian and Isabelle were in the back of the car. They were talking nineteen to the dozen about everything that had happened at school. I did my best to show an interest, but by the time we arrived home I couldn't even remember the gist of it.

Michel had lost it and spent the night in a cell.

Was it because of me? Or had it happened before: Michel drinking and then becoming aggressive? I found this almost impossible to imagine. Yet Peter had told me a different story: before Michel started working for Peter, his life had apparently gone pretty badly off the rails.

Who was I to believe now? Peter, or my clouded perception that didn't want to hear a bad word said about Michel?

Perhaps the truth lay somewhere in the middle.

Bastian looked astonished when he saw the enormous piles of sand in our courtyard. It looked like a war zone. There wasn't a single blade of grass left standing. Louis was sitting on a small trencher with a roll-up in his mouth, digging a trench straight across the yard. The others were standing there with shovels and pickaxes. It was only April, but the sun was beating down on their sweaty skin.

'Wow!' cried Bastian. 'Mummy, can I ride on that? With Louis?'

'No, I'd rather you two stayed inside. It's dangerous.'

Bastian looked at me condescendingly. 'You always think everything's dangerous. I'm not a baby any more, you know.'

'I just want you two to stay inside.'

Isabelle sided with her brother: 'But, *Mummy* . . . it's gorgeous weather! We've been inside all day.'

'I'll make you some fruit. And you can have a lolly. I'll put the TV on, and later, when the lads are gone, you can play outside.'

Isabelle rolled her eyes and groaned. 'That'll be ages . . .'

She was absolutely right. How glad I'd be when the renovation was over and the children could run around the grounds to their hearts' content. During the first few months of the renovation I'd constantly had to keep them away from the house, and now we were entering a stage when, conversely, they weren't allowed to play outside. I felt sorry for them. Rules at school during the day, ditto at home.

'Do you know what we're going to do this weekend?' I said, with forced cheerfulness, as I took Isabelle by the hand and manoeuvred the children around the piles of sand towards the front door.

'Looking at fireplaces . . . choosing curtains . . .' Bastian responded. 'Going to stupid shops.'

I could hear the resignation in his voice. He wasn't being cheeky; he'd just had enough. These two weeks were the home straight, not only for me and Eric.

'No, we're going canoeing.'

'Canoeing? What's that?'

'Paddling down a fast-flowing river in a narrow little boat, like the Indians. Along the rocks.'

'Cool!'

46

Michel didn't look at me.

He hadn't even greeted me.

He was totally ignoring me.

There was a swollen, purple patch near his left eyebrow, forcing his eye partly closed. A line of black stitches disfigured the skin of his left cheek. Deep, dark-red scratches ran down the back of his right hand and his nose was slightly swollen. He shovelled down his food mechanically. Questions from the lads about his stay in the cell and the fight were fended off with Yes and No. Michel wasn't in the mood to socialise. He was here to work, full stop.

There was a dull ache in his eyes. My heart went out to him and I couldn't do anything, give anything away.

It was now clear – painfully clear – that Michel was angry with me. Angry, disappointed.

It was because of me.

Which would mean that Peter hadn't been telling the truth when he'd informed me so charmingly that Michel 'couldn't keep his dick in his trousers', and, therefore, that

Michel had serious feelings for me. Or perhaps I'd simply hurt Michel's male pride, by rejecting him.

There was no way I could ask him outright. It was impossible to isolate him from the others. Michel had been avoiding me like the plague all morning. I could, of course, visit his room on Friday evening after going shopping. I could do that.

And then?

Talking would inevitably lead to something very different. That's what my body was telling me. It was all ready, poised to pounce on him, lick his wounds and ease his pain.

Calling on Michel at home was asking for trouble.

I looked at Eric, then at Isabelle and Bastian, who were at home as always on a Wednesday afternoon and were therefore joining us for lunch. I looked at Peter, who seemed alarmed by Michel's surly behaviour and was keeping an anxious eye on him. And I knew what I had to do: stay strong. For a little while longer, and I'd never see him again.

'Eric,' I heard Peter say. 'Are you doing anything this evening?'

'Nothing special . . . why?'

'A few business associates of mine are coming over. It's about those chalets. It's starting to take shape now. The plans have been approved . . . I was wondering if you wanted to join us as well.'

Eric sipped his water. 'OK. Eightish?'

'Great.'

I felt the blood draining from my face. My eyes shot towards Eric in panic. He ignored me.

'Eric, I'd rather you stayed at home,' I blurted out. My voice didn't sound half as tense as I felt.

Eric gave me a withering look. 'We'll talk about it later.'

'But—'

He almost spat the word out: '*Later.*'

I gritted my teeth.

The conversation continued in French. I listened to Peter explaining something to the lads, telling them he had a big job – *un boulot* – coming up, for which he might need a few extra people. That they had a meeting with a few business partners this evening and that Eric might be joining them.

Over my dead body. Our whole future was at stake. If Peter yet managed to persuade Eric to invest two hundred thousand euros in his plan for the houses, then in a year's time we'd be living next door to Louis in the woods, in an identical leaky caravan. There was no way Eric was going to Peter's house tonight. I'd make that crystal clear to him, as soon as the lads had gone.

'You're overreacting, Simone,' said Eric, coolly. 'It makes no sense at all.'

The children were sitting in front of the television in our new living room and I was clearing the table.

'I don't want you to go and see Peter,' I said, as calmly as possible.

'I told you at Christmas that we'd drop it for a while, until the house was finished. Now, it *is* finished, and the website is done. You can start your side of the business; now it's time for me to carry out my plans.'

'But not with Peter.'

'Don't start this again.'

'We can't afford two hundred thousand!'

'Who says it's two hundred thousand?'

'Isn't that what you said in December? Two hundred thousand euros: more money than we have.'

Eric looked at me in annoyance. 'There's no way I'm going to invest two hundred thousand, Simone. I'm not stupid.'

'You were more than happy to do that last year.'

He gestured with irritation.

I almost threw the dishes into the dishwasher. I'd have liked nothing better than to throw them at Eric's head. With almost superhuman effort, I controlled myself. My voice trembled. 'Why are you going to see Peter then?'

'Because I want to hear what he's got to say.'

'The only thing Peter wants from you is money. You don't need to go and see him tonight to find that out. You can take it from me.'

'There's no point talking like this.'

The last plate bit the dust. It broke in my hand and fell to pieces on the open dishwasher door. Shards hit the stone floor and flew in all directions.

'Bingo!' cried Bastian from the living room.

I didn't react. I was jumping up and down with the adrenalin.

'Jesus, Simone, what on earth's wrong with you?'

'I don't want you to go and see Peter tonight,' I said sharply. 'I don't want anything to do with Peter. Do you hear me, goddammit? *I don't want this!*'

Eric looked at me darkly. 'I'm not going to let you dictate what I can and can't do; have you gone completely nuts? Stop being so highly strung. If I want to go and see Peter tonight, that's what I'll do, end of story! What's the matter with you? What have you got against Peter? You don't mention it for months and now you're starting again.' Eric crossed his arms stiffly. 'Is there something I don't know about perhaps?'

I stood there as if frozen, a piece of the broken plate still in my hand. What was I supposed to say?

'Eric, I completely agree with you, about the plan to build the holiday homes. You know that; we've established that. But to do it with—'

'Am I going to have to do it *by myself*, then? *How?* Tell me *how*!' Eric threw up his hands in a helpless gesture. 'I need other people, don't I, Simone? Jesus . . .' He turned his head away and jerked it back to look at me again. 'Are you going to start giving me this bullshit again? You just don't want me to, do you? You just don't *want* me to do anything for myself.'

'I do, but—'

'No, Simone. Something's not right. Something's just not right. Is there anything I should know?'

I said nothing.

Eric leaned towards me. He was very angry. Angrier than I'd ever seen him.

I tried to stay calm. 'Eric . . . I don't trust Peter. It's a feeling—'

He snorted. 'A feeling.'

'Yes.'

'Well, I'll tell you what you can do with your feeling,' he said, pointing at me aggressively. 'You can shove it. I've been pushed to the limit for months. I knew you were having a hard time; we've all been having a hard time. I've spared you as much as I could. But it has to stop some time. I want to go ahead with this, Simone. I get on well with Peter. I'm learning all the time. Peter has good ideas; he's an expert, with contacts, with . . .' Suddenly he threw his hands up. Frustration was written all over his face. 'For God's sake, I've said this so many times. I can't take this any more, Simone. I really can't.'

I looked at him in silence.

'I'm doing this for *us*,' he said. 'Don't you understand that? If you give in to your fear, you'll never make any real money. You'll only ever be fiddling around. There's always some risk involved with business. And I'll limit the risks I'm taking as much as possible by getting everything registered by a notary.'

I shook my head. 'But I don't want to take any risks at all.'

'Are you two arguing?'

I looked up. Isabelle and Bastian were standing timidly in the doorway. Isabelle was holding Bunny by the ears, looking at us, wide-eyed.

'A little,' I replied, trying to sound as reassuring as I could. 'Go back and watch television. I'll be with you in a minute.'

Eric looked at his watch. 'I'm leaving. I want to look those business partners of his in the eye. We'll talk about it tomorrow, when there's something concrete to discuss.'

He walked towards Isabelle and Bastian and gave them both a kiss on the forehead. 'Be good for Mummy. And bed in half an hour.'

I'd tucked Bastian and Isabelle in. The shower I'd taken after that hadn't really freshened me up. With my hair still damp, I sat staring at the TV.

I had to take action. Peter was forcing me to. I no longer had a choice.

Was this how it worked? Were murderers not born, but made by circumstances? The very idea sent my heart racing.

For the tenth time in half an hour an anxious little voice was telling me to come clean with Eric. I could leave out the details, the voice told me. That would soften the blow for him as much as possible. I'd say I hadn't *really* gone to bed with Michel . . . Just a bit of cuddling, nothing serious. Just on that one evening, when I'd had too much to drink. I could try to engineer it so that Eric's anger would be directed towards Peter.

No.

Eric would flip out. He'd go and confront Peter. Then track Michel down and . . .

Bleu was barking. Loud and shrill.

I looked at my watch. It was half nine. Was Eric back so soon? Had the meeting been cancelled?

I got up out of the armchair, went over to the window and held the curtain to one side. It took a moment for my eyes to adapt to the dark.

Eric's car wasn't there. I couldn't see anything unusual.

Bleu was barking again. There was someone there after all. Or something.

A cat?

I held my hands to either side of my face like blinkers to shut out the light from the room and peered into the twilight.

My heart missed a beat.

There was someone under the archway, at the entrance to the courtyard.

'Do you have any idea who could have murdered Peter Vandamme?'

The interpreter is gazing at me intently. The detective

beside him can't understand a word of what we're saying, but he's leering at me like a crow, with dark beady eyes.

I shake my head and avoid their gaze. 'I don't know,' I squeak. 'I . . . I feel ill.'

'Have you, or your husband, ever had any problems with Peter Vandamme, by any chance?'

The interpreter's voice suddenly sounds very far away. I'd like to faint so I don't have to be here any more, so I'll be taken back to my cell, where I'll be alone. That's not going to happen. My body never does what I instruct it to. It leads a life of its own and doesn't take the slightest notice of me. It's never taken the slightest notice of me.

Perhaps I should just say nothing from now on. Nothing at all, until someone assigns me a lawyer.

I hear the chairs on the other side of the table being pushed back, but I sit still.

'We have no more questions for now,' says the interpreter. 'Thank you for your cooperation. You will be taken back to your cell.'

At the same time, as if pre-arranged, a uniformed officer enters.

'Take *madame* back,' I hear the detective say.

47

I ran to the hall and opened the door. Bleu squeezed past me and dashed into the dark yard.

Michel emerged from the black shadow of the archway. He was wearing jeans, a T-shirt and a dark cotton jacket. The strained muscles in his neck betrayed his uncertainty, the tension. His dark glance, more penetrating now that one of his eyes was being partly forced closed by the swelling near his eyebrow, took my breath away.

'What are you doing here?' I whispered.

He didn't answer, but cast a brief glance at the house. 'Is Eric away?'

'Yes.'

'Are the children asleep?'

I nodded.

He ran his hand through his hair, looked at me darkly. The tension, tangible like static electricity, sparked off him.

And off me.

It was impossible to say who took the first step. Perhaps we did it simultaneously. His lips touched mine, his mouth half open, directly followed by his tongue, pushing, caressing. A moan escaped from his throat as my hands disappeared under his T-shirt and felt his skin, the muscles, the warmth radiating from him. That fantastic groove marking his spine, which hid the muscles in his back and ran down to below his waistband.

I heard a car approaching in the distance.

Eric?

The thought sobered me up. I turned my head away and looked anxiously towards the driveway. 'Where is your motorbike?' I whispered.

'In the bushes. It can't be seen from the path.'

I heard the sound of the car die away. Just someone on the main road.

I looked nervously at the house. Bastian's room, diagonally below the tower, looked out over the courtyard. If Bastian had been woken by Bleu's barking, he could be watching us now. Michel followed my gaze.

There was no movement behind the window. Everything appeared utterly peaceful.

I felt Michel's hand around mine.

'Come with me,' he whispered.

For a moment I stood there motionless. 'Where to?'

He didn't notice my hesitation and dragged me along. We passed under the archway, turned right and walked up the hill, through the tall grass. It rustled under my bare feet. High above us the firmament was turning a deep, dark blue.

Thousands of stars were visible between the racing clouds, whose movements were casting irregular shadows on the blue landscape. Everything smelt of grass, flowers, spring. Of Michel, who was walking beside me and hadn't let go of my hand for a single second, as if afraid I'd run away if he did.

We stopped near the lake. He sat down and pulled me beside him in the grass. We sat there in silence, captivated by the darkness and the sounds of the night. Almost everything had faded into the background now apart from his body, so close to mine, his smell, which drew me towards him. I wanted to wallow in it and cuddle up against that body. Forget everything. Just live for the moment, like there was no tomorrow.

No.

He turned his head towards me, still holding my hand. 'I missed you so much in *Basque*. I thought of you every night. After I finally got through to you and you slammed the phone down, I thought I'd go crazy.'

I didn't dare look at him now. If I did, it was all over; I'd no longer be able to think, only feel. I'd fall backwards and beg him to give me everything he had.

He'd give it to me.

I closed my eyes to calm myself down, to clear my head. Michel was here now, I had to talk to him, there were still so many things left unsaid. It was impossible. There was something in my throat stopping me from speaking. When

I opened my eyes, I stared across the water surface, which was reflecting the light from the crescent moon.

'Look at me.'

I shook my head.

He grasped my face and forced me to look at him.

I could feel myself weakening, as if my bones were no longer made of calcium, but rubber. Elastic.

'Leave Eric,' he said, softly.

I wrenched my head away. 'No, Michel.' I was shocked by the sad, but firm tone my voice had adopted.

'Why not?'

I squeezed my eyes shut to fight back the gathering tears. 'Because I don't want to.'

'You *do*,' he said, now defensive. 'I can see you do!'

'I don't want to lose my family.' It sounded so weak and so unbelievably pathetic, but it was true. I couldn't be any more honest. I could maybe abandon Eric. But not Isabelle and Bastian. Never.

His hand let go of mine and slipped to my neck. His fingers caressed and massaged my skin.

'But I can *feel* it,' he whispered, giving me a light kiss on the lips, then on my nose, on both cheeks, my forehead. 'So can you.'

I turned my head away, pulled my knees up and put my arms tightly around my legs. It seemed a pointless gesture. Michel knew every inch of skin on my body. Every lump and bump. Every nerve ending.

Everything.

'I'm sorry,' I whispered.

He stood up abruptly. 'I don't believe you.'

I looked up in confusion. He towered high above me, then turned round and took a few steps away from me. I saw him picking things up off the ground. Pebbles. He took one out of a packed fist and threw it forcefully into the water. His whole body swung with it. Young, strong, everything in perfect balance. The pebble ricocheted over the surface of the water. Three, four times. Then sank.

'Michel . . .' I said, weakly.

He took out another, then another. Examined the pebbles in his hand. Moved his fingers, forcing the stones to glance off each other and making a tapping noise. He transferred them to his right hand, made a fist and threw them into the water in a powerful arc. A fountain of water droplets sprang up in the moonlight. Silver rings in the water, expanding, merging into one another. Then he threw his head back and rubbed his face with his hands. He mumbled something I couldn't understand.

'Michel . . .' I whispered again.

He looked down at me. Pain and reproach in his eyes.

With a jolt I realised that what I felt was more than animal attraction.

I was totally and utterly in love with Michel.

And he with me.

The final nail in the coffin.

Neither of us said anything.

It was unspoken, but that was fine.

We both knew how things stood.

Michel sat down beside me again. He leaned over me. Four fingers of his right hand ran up the inside of my thigh. I trembled.

'No.' I pushed him away. 'I want to . . . talk. I want to know more about you.'

'Why?'

'Because . . . I want to get to know you better. I don't know you. Not properly.'

'What am I supposed to do? You don't want to see me any more; you want to get to know me. What on earth do you want from me?'

I shook my head. 'No. No . . . I . . .'

He had a point. What *did* I want?

'I am who I am,' he said. 'Nothing more.' His gaze was fixed on the water.

'There's always more. Where do you come from? What kind of education have you had? Do you have parents? That type of thing.'

He looked at me sideways; irritation came through in his voice. 'Of course I have parents.'

'Do you still see them sometimes?'

'No.'

'What kind of people are they?'

He rubbed his face. 'I don't feel like talking about it.'

'I do.'

He rolled on to his back and put his arms behind his head. There was a long silence. I saw his chest rising and falling with his breathing. 'My mother was a competitive swimmer. My father a scientist or a marketing man or something. I'm not sure. He worked in Silicon Valley.'

'In America?'

'Yes.'

'Is your mother American?'

He shook his head. 'No, she comes from Bordeaux.'

'And your father?'

He shrugged his shoulder. 'American, Canadian, Mexican, French: I don't know. All I know is he worked there. I don't even know his name. I don't care either.'

'How did they meet?'

'My mother moved to America to swim for the American team. The company this guy worked for was sponsoring the team.'

I had to make a real effort to understand him. He was speaking indistinctly and very quietly.

'You don't know your father?' I asked.

He answered, but I couldn't understand him. He was probably speaking in dialect.

'What did you say, just now?'

'A philanderer, charmer . . . that's what my mother said sometimes. And that I looked like him. She hated me for it. She'd fallen pregnant; this guy was married and didn't want to know.'

'Where were you born?'

'In hospital, Bordeaux. Caesarean. My mother had trouble walking afterwards. She was in a wheelchair for a long time . . .' He jerked his head round. 'Hey, listen: I really don't feel like talking about this, OK?'

'I really want to know.'

I really did. It was the first time he'd told me anything of real consequence. About himself. The first time it had come from his own mouth, not on the grapevine.

He ran his fingers along his nose and still didn't look at me. 'So my mother was in a wheelchair, and that was because of me. When she could walk again she had a baby to look after, and her whole career was down the drain. She couldn't swim any more. Swimming was her life, her whole world. She could barely make ends meet. She got fat; she almost ate herself to death. She got a new boyfriend, some junkie who got her hooked on heroin. I think she just wanted to die.'

Cautiously I edged up to him and turned on to my side. It was wonderful to hear him speak. To be with him. Listen to his voice. Look at him. I wanted to lie against him, but didn't for fear he'd clam up.

'So actually, I pretty much had to look out for myself,' he continued. 'When I was twelve, I was taken away from my mother and put in a children's home. I did bad things; I couldn't care less any more.'

An owl flew past in front of us, in a horizontal, silent flight.

'What kind of things?'

He shrugged his shoulder. 'Just stuff. Bordeaux is a big city.'

I thought back to the conversation with Betty. 'Armed robbery?'

His eyes sought mine. 'Actually I wasn't far off . . . I fought, stole, smoked dope, burgled houses, drank, shot up, everything. I was angry with my mother, my mother's boyfriend, I was angry with the whole damn world . . . Still am sometimes.'

'How did you end up here? How did you meet Peter?'

'Through Bruno, who I met in the detention centre. After that he moved into rooms in Libourne. When I got out I looked him up. I had nowhere to go. Bruno was already working for Peter then. I went along one time, to work; I had to do something. Earn money. Start doing something useful.'

'Where's your mother now?'

'I don't know, and I don't care. Maybe she's dead. That was what she wanted.'

'Don't you have any other family?'

He turned to me. 'Hey, listen: those people have never been in the picture, OK? When my mother was in the shit, everyone washed their hands of her and me. I have no family as far as I'm concerned, apart from Peter and Bruno.'

I was speechless. The story of Michel's background was probably the saddest I'd ever heard. I thought of my mother, who despite her numerous shortcomings had wanted the best for me. Sundays in the park, feeding the ducklings, watching television on Saturday evening. A warm, comfortable home. Compared with what Michel had experienced I'd been thoroughly spoilt. I was almost embarrassed at prising this out of him.

Michel sat up, leaning on one hand. He rubbed his hair impatiently and looked at me gloomily. 'Well. That's that. My wonderful background. Who I am. Now you know. My mother a drug addict, my father an unfaithful bastard . . . So what does that say about me? I never finished school, do a job everyone looks down on because no one else will employ me. A criminal record doesn't look good on a job application. I'm no good at anything. That's how it is; it won't change . . . *Putain!* Was that what you wanted to know?'

His words cut through me. As I looked at Michel and was struck once again by the pain in his eyes, I realised how young he was. Michel wasn't some streetwise big shot in his thirties or forties, master of his own destiny, giving women the run-around. The age gap fell away when we ended up in bed together, but he wasn't so strong when it came to verbal communication, and to be honest, neither was I. I had to concentrate to get my meaning across, to avoid saying the wrong thing. Right now it was particularly important that what I said came across as intended. 'You're you,' I said, sensing this was what I should say, because perhaps no one else ever said it to him. Or could say it. 'You're good-looking, healthy, intelligent, strong. You've got nothing to do with your parents, apart from the fact that they brought you into the world. Their choices were their choices. You can make different ones.'

He gave me a sidelong glance and snorted. 'Girls my own age are superficial bitches, in my experience, so I fell in love with a happily married woman with two children.' His face broke out in a sneer. 'Fantastic choices I make. Just like that fucking father of mine. No, even worse.'

I looked at him in confusion, feeling drunk. Tears were streaming down my face. I couldn't help it; there was no stopping them.

'*Putain*, Simone . . .' His voice sounded an octave lower. He leaned over me and kissed me on the neck. I shuddered, I wanted him, I wanted to ease his pain, stroke him, caress him, make him forget everything.

'I don't want it to end this way,' he said softly. 'Not like this.'

My hands strayed across his face, I kissed him gently on the mouth, licked his lips, all while the tears kept flowing, and salty liquid stung my cheeks.

He pulled the middle of my thong to one side, I felt the knuckles of his hand and fell backwards. Threw my head back and stared at the treetops, gently swaying to and fro.

At the heavens, the clouds racing along high above us in the dark-blue sky. The moon, the stars. I felt his mouth caressing the inside of my thighbone, his hands slowly driving me wild. I sank into a state of bliss, pressed myself closer against him, wallowed in his smell, came alive under his touch and when I looked up, his eyes devoured me.

His eyes twinkled in the twilight. 'I want to fuck you.'

A sigh escaped from my mouth. 'Come here.'

I tugged at his jeans, pulled the garment down over that wonderful, tight bum of his. Put my hand between his legs and could only groan. My breathing quickened as he raised himself up and took off my thong, pulled my vest up impatiently. A cool wind blew over my hot body and dried my tears. I couldn't stop shivering and took his coat off. As he kissed me, deep and slow, I spread my legs and urged him on. I thrust my hips up, clawed at his back, squeezed my fingertips in his buttocks.

He whispered in my ear, half-finished words, unintelligible. 'Say it,' he moaned. 'Say it.'

Desire had completely taken over. '*Baise-moi*,' I whispered. I would have screamed it out loud if he'd asked.

As he entered me and started thrusting, lightning bolts shot through me, thickening my blood to lava, flowing steadily through my veins. I closed my eyes, opened them again, to absorb the dark glint in his eyes.

'I've missed you so much,' he moaned, burying his face in my hair, as he raised the tempo and I automatically followed suit, putting my arms around him and leaving deep scratches down his back.

I'd never believed in coming together. That was a myth, it only happened in films and books, but now it was happening again, not for the first time, I was there, Michel was there – when the release overwhelmed us, sending shock-waves to all the nerve endings, which contracted and then relaxed, until our overheated bodies were clinging to each other, dazed and sweaty, and we sank into a hazy stupor.

I nestled my face in the hollow where his neck met his shoulder and where I felt his carotid artery beating against my lips. His heartbeat, slow and strong, against my chest. Gradually my hands came back to life, they felt his body, the muscles, his skin that was beginning to cool down, as was mine, and I wanted this moment to last forever.

If the world ended right now, I wouldn't mind. Michel and me, by the lake, with the moon as our witness, that was all that mattered now.

I started shaking. It was really cold now, the grass was damp with dew and a cool wind was brushing over us. Trails of mist were forming over the water surface, stretching towards us, swallowing us up.

'Are you cold?' he whispered.

'Yes.'

'Shall I warm you up again?'

He started moving again, slowly, gradually, I felt him expanding inside me, filling me once more, and thought I was going crazy. Christ, he simply *kept going*, with a break of a few minutes at the most. He lifted himself on to two hands and lowered his face, licked my lips, as he raised the tempo and my legs started shaking uncontrollably. My God, how wonderful this was. All I could do now was groan, surrender, put my hands against his chest.

A grin in the twilight. 'Are you warming up now?'

'Yes,' I whispered, 'don't stop, please don't stop.'

It sounded desperate and this was how I felt. I wanted to prolong this moment, for as long as possible, I didn't want him to go home, this was the last time, the very idea terrified me. As if everything would stop after Michel, as if my life from now on would consist only of daily routine and a dull emptiness that no one else could fill.

Life after Michel.

I wanted more, much more than this, I wanted to taste him, indulge him, hear him moan and watch him close his eyes.

I drew back, keeping my hands on his chest, and sat on my knees in front of him, caressed his chest with my lips, slowly towards his stomach, which he was holding in, the same as his breath, after which I sank down even further, with my mouth open, and finally tasted myself deep in my throat.

He got up on to his knees and grabbed me by the hair, and with the flat of his hand he rubbed along my cheek, my mouth, so he could feel what I was doing. He carried on running his fingers through my hair, caressed my jaw, my face, and whispered words I didn't know but understood perfectly. I carried on, looked up at him, lost myself in him, used my hands, my tongue, curved my back and tried to make eye contact, but he was somewhere else, his mouth open, his eyes closed, speechless, surrounded by the night.

'*Je jouis*,' he whispered. A warning. Polite.

I kept going, nothing else mattered.

I drank him.

Out of the corner of my eye I saw a beam of light flashing across the valley before dying out. I heard the faint sound of a car, an engine being switched off. Michel heard and saw it too. He sat up and looked up at the hilltop, with his mouth half open, still dazed like me.

'Eric,' I whispered, my heart missing a beat. 'Eric's home. Oh my God . . . What time is it?'

Michel pressed the side of his watch. 'Half eleven.'

I jumped up and started gathering up my clothes. I couldn't find my thong anywhere, until Michel passed it to me. I put on my skirt, my vest, ran my fingers through my hair.

I stood there as if paralysed, looking at the hilltop, and heard Bleu whining in the distance. When Eric didn't find me inside, he'd go looking for me. And come here.

How can I explain why I'm outside in the dark at half eleven at night?

I had to get back to the house. Fast.

Michel came up behind me and pressed his cheek against my temple. Kissed me.

'Good luck,' he whispered. 'With everything.'

He wasn't referring to the situation I'd find myself in tonight with Eric.

He was saying goodbye.

'You too,' I whispered, and started climbing the hill.

48

Eric came running up to me. Bleu got there first. I was scared the dog would betray Michel's presence, so I held him by the collar as I approached Eric.

All I really wanted to do now was go to bed. Sleep, or try to at least.

Have a good cry and start afresh.

I was exhausted. Mentally and physically shattered. I couldn't remember ever feeling so empty. So hollow.

Eric looked at me, wide-eyed. Concerned, he increased his pace. His shirt was open at the collar, and I could gather from the way he moved that he'd had too much to drink.

Drinking and driving, on the perilous windy lanes along cliff faces and ravines. Fantastic. Peter drank like there was no tomorrow and infected everyone who hung out with him.

I clenched my teeth.

No confrontations now, please.

'Jesus, Simone, what are you doing outside? The front door was open, and when I didn't find you in bed I went through the whole house.'

I didn't stop, but carried on walking. I wanted to keep Bleu and Eric as far away from the lake as possible.

Eric watched in surprise as I walked past him towards the courtyard. He sauntered beside me. 'Simone? What's going on?'

'You're drunk,' I said.

'What the hell are you doing outside?'

I didn't respond. When we entered the hall and I closed the door behind Eric and Bleu, I turned to Eric.

He stood there looking at me in silence and clearly had no idea how to handle the situation.

'I'm going to bed,' I said. 'I need some time to myself.'

After that I walked past him into the corridor and up the spiral staircase. Once upstairs, I went to Bastian's room. He was breathing steadily, sound asleep. I pulled the curtain to one side and looked towards the path.

No sign of Michel. I couldn't hear anything.

I woke up at five o'clock. I could barely open my eyes. They were swollen, even though I couldn't remember crying last night. But I had. By the lake. More than once. I felt a pang in my belly, a spasm, for a split second.

The bed was empty on Eric's side. Eric had never been an early bird. I always had to drag him out of bed in the morning.

I sat down on the edge of the bed and rubbed my face, squeezed my eyes shut and opened them wide again. My vision was still blurred.

Eric was downstairs. He was sitting at the kitchen table in a T-shirt and underpants. His hair was in a mess. There were copies of floor plans on the table in front of him. Beside him, a notepad with costings. A calculator. A cup of coffee.

He looked up when he heard me come in. 'Are you feeling any better yet?'

I ignored his question, went over to the fridge, took a carton of pineapple juice and rinsed out a coffee cup that was still in the kitchen sink. Filled it and emptied it in a few gulps.

Then I looked at Eric and, pointedly, at the floor plans. 'No, I'm not feeling any better.'

Eric made a vague gesture over the sheets of paper and said: 'I can't pass this up, Simone. It truly is a brilliant plan. One-off investment, a guaranteed income for the next ten years, and then our pension taken care of in one fell swoop, at a huge profit. I've gone through the figures over and over again. It all adds up. Even assuming we get only half the rental income, and discounting the rise in house prices, we're on to a good thing.'

I stood motionless. This had to stop. I couldn't take much more. It was all about to come crashing down. I didn't have the energy to stand up to him, to start yet another row or appease him. I was completely empty. Worn out.

'Eric,' I said softly. 'The day you invest our money in Peter's project is the day I leave.'

I meant it; it was no empty threat. Perhaps that's why I said it so calmly, so assertively. I meant every word.

Eric looked at me feverishly. '*What?*'

I turned round and went to the bedroom, flopped on to the bed and burst into silent tears.

49

The courtyard had turned out beautifully. Limestone steps linked the two levels. There was a fountain, and Eric had put little trees in colossal, blue-glazed pots. The lads were finishing off smoothing the gravel, which was beige, but now looked white in the bright sunshine. It was almost painful to the eye.

I stood in Bastian's room looking outside.

It was Friday. The final work day.

I leaned against the window frame and watched Michel rolling up cables and lugging away barrels of waste, putting them down outside the courtyard on the grass near the archway. I absorbed every movement. Every facial expression. His smile when someone made a joke. The shrug with one shoulder in a moment of confusion or awkwardness.

The endless stream of strong emotions – the move, Peter, Michel, money – there seemed to be no end to them. They'd left me completely exhausted.

Eric had spared me one of my worries at least. Last night he'd gone to Peter's house and come home at around ten. I'd been watching television and not even greeted him when he came in. For the past few days I'd been avoiding him as much as possible.

Eric had stood beside me, cautiously pulling at the back of the chair. 'I'll probably never understand what's come over you,' he'd said. 'But you and the children are more precious to me than anyone or anything. I've told Peter to count me out. Now, and also in any future project.'

I'd stood up, put my arms around him and we'd stood there like that for minutes on end.

We could get on with our new life. Peter had been here for the last time yesterday. Today was the lads' final day on the job. Our holiday started tomorrow. Eric had declared he wanted to do nothing for the time being other than reading, and laying out a small vegetable garden at his leisure. The break might end up lasting weeks, months perhaps, as long as it took for the dust and cement to disappear from his pores.

My wounds needed to heal too, but they weren't on the outside. This house had been built partly by Michel. He'd held the bricks in his hands, the tools. Everything here reminded me of him. But then again, perhaps that was a good thing. I didn't want to suppress the memories of him. Slowly, they'd have to find their rightful place.

I went down the spiral staircase, to the living room. Every day the space, the luxury and the ambience struck me anew.

It was the most beautiful house we'd ever lived in. A few years ago I'd never have thought a house like this lay within our reach. I felt proud that I was able to live here, and could soon start welcoming guests.

Erica was coming to visit soon. She was staying for a week, and I was looking forward to it. I wanted to cook for her and Gerard, spoil them with tasty food and good wine, so they'd start feeling better and go back to work refreshed. If it stayed as warm as it was now we'd be able to eat and drink in the courtyard deep into the night. Which reminded me that I wanted to buy two braziers. Perhaps I should take Isabelle and Bastian into town with me, straight after picking them up from school. In that case I wouldn't have to say goodbye to the lads either. I'd given them all a case of wine yesterday as a parting gift, and Peter a box of whisky. As a thank you for the work, for their presence, the company, the French lessons, their stories.

Michel's attitude had changed since our parting. He acted as normally as possible, didn't make things difficult for the two of us. A switch had evidently been flicked somewhere in his head.

I heard the door open and turned round, half expecting it to be Eric coming to fetch water.

It was Michel. Despite the heat, he was wearing a T-shirt and jeans. The shirt was sticking to his chest. He stood there in the kitchen.

'Sorry to walk in like this, but . . .' He rubbed his upper arm hesitantly and looked at me awkwardly from under his eyelashes. 'I need money.'

I frowned. 'You need money? What for?'

He stood there, bobbing from one foot to the other. 'Eric didn't pay me last week. And I badly need the money to pay the rent, otherwise the landlord will throw me out. He's coming to collect it tonight. And I don't have anything. Same for Bruno. Peter doesn't have a single cent either. I've got nowhere else to go.' He gestured helplessly. 'Sorry,' he said once more. 'I really don't want to ask you, but . . . I don't know where else . . .'

I stared hard at him. 'You haven't been paid?'

With my own eyes I'd watched Eric, when the lads had gone home last Monday, counting out fifty- and hundred-euro notes on the table in the hall. Peter writing out an invoice, for last week and this final week of work at the same time. I'd be damned if I hadn't seen Peter stashing the money away himself and signing the invoice.

I was still staring at Michel.

He raised an eyebrow. 'It's happened before,' he said. 'Eric not paying us. It's not the first time . . . A lot of clients do that.' Then he said something I couldn't understand.

'I've got no money here.' That was entirely true. Fifty euros perhaps, no more.

He came closer. Looked at me now. 'Simone, I—'

'I'll . . . I'll write you a cheque. OK? Then you can show

it to that landlord, and then take it to the bank this evening, or tomorrow morning, or . . .'

'I'll leave early,' he said.

He followed me over to the writing desk and I opened the drawer. Removed the chequebook, flipped it open and grabbed a pen.

'How much?'

'Two hundred. That's a month's rent.'

I wrote out a cheque for two hundred and twelve euros and thirty cents, signed it, wrote his address on it, his first name. My pen stopped in its tracks. 'Come to think of it, what's your surname?'

'Martin.'

I wrote the name on the cheque. Tore out the sheet of paper and gave it to him. He looked at it in surprise. 'It's too much.'

'Two hundred is a round figure; it'll stand out. I can't explain that to Eric. This way it looks like shopping or something. The bank statement only gives the cheque number and the amount, not the recipient.'

Thanks to Peter, I thought wryly, I'd become an expert in financial trickery.

'You're an angel,' he said, and walked away.

I put the chequebook back in the drawer. I had a bad feeling about this.

I turned round. 'Michel?'

He came back out of the hall and held on to the doorpost.

'Michel . . . Eric paid the money. I saw him do it. He paid your boss, on Monday. For two weeks in one go.'

He frowned. 'Are you sure?'

'Yes. A hundred per cent sure.'

Michel nodded briefly, muttering something. With a brief '*Salut*' he disappeared outside via the corridor.

I didn't move from the writing desk. You could blame Eric for all sorts of things, but not for failing to meet his commitments.

It could only mean that Peter wasn't paying his people. At least not always, not every week. And shifted the blame to the clients.

'Simone?'

I looked up. Eric in the doorway. If he'd been there just a moment earlier, he'd have witnessed me paying Michel.

'I've come to tell you I'm nipping out to fetch those two pictures and the garden seat. I'm giving Michel a lift: he needs to pop into the bank and then I'll drop him at home. Will you keep an eye on the time?'

He was referring to the children. It was half two.

'OK,' I said.

Eric didn't move. 'Strange to think, isn't it, the last work day?'

I nodded. 'I think I'm going to have to get used to the silence again. It won't be long before I start missing them.'

'We're going to have a fantastic few weeks, Simone. We're really going to live well. Maybe we could go to Arcachon this weekend, with the children. It's going to be eighty-two degrees, great beach weather.'

'Yes, lovely,' I said, absently.

'OK then, see you later.'

In no time at all Bastian's room had been transformed into a mini war zone. The cables from his PlayStation were strewn across the floor, together with games, loose CDs, dozens of open comic books, toy soldiers and dirty clothes. I started tidying the books and putting them on his book-case, arranging them by colour, sorting the games and placing them upright next to his small television. I got down on my knees to pull the washing out from under the bed and threw it in the plastic wash basket.

A car pulled up in the yard. I heard it stop near the archway, but took no notice. It was probably a courier with a package and the lads were now accustomed to signing for parcels.

It was nice and cool, here inside the house. Someone once told me that they used to make the walls so thick because it was great insulation; it kept the heat out in summer and, conversely, inside in winter.

I was about to enter the corridor with the washing basket pressed against me, on my way to Isabelle's room, when I heard someone coming up the stairs. It didn't sound like Eric's footsteps. They sounded heavier. And hurried.

I went over to the stairwell, the wash basket still in my

arms, and came face to face with Peter. He stared at me like a madman. I jumped and automatically recoiled until my back was literally against the wall.

'What are you doing here?' I tried to put some authority into my voice, but I was shaking too badly.

'What the fuck am I *doing* here?' He grabbed at the wash basket and tore it out of my arms with a single forceful moment. The basket bounced on to the floor and the washing scattered across the corridor and the stairs.

In a blind panic I took to my heels in the direction of the bathroom. Peter had caught up with me before I'd even reached halfway, and with his fist clasped around my upper arm he hurled me at the wall. I smashed into the stucco and doubled up in pain. He had almost dislocated my arm.

'You, bitch!' he hissed. 'You fucking bitch! You've blown it, for everybody. Stupid cow!'

He was squeezing my arm so hard that it was cutting off the circulation and I was afraid he'd break my bones.

'Now you listen very carefully for a moment,' he said, almost pressing his face against mine, and I could smell his whisky breath. 'I'm not going to let you make a fool of me. You're messing with the wrong man.'

At the same time he pressed me against the wall and shifted his grip to my throat. 'I need every cent. And if you don't tell Eric soon that it's OK for him to give them to me, I'll make your life hell . . . I'll completely destroy you. The whole caboodle.'

His hand was in an iron grip around my throat and his forehead was almost resting against mine. I opened my mouth wide in a desperate bid to get some air. A rasping noise escaped from my throat.

'I should have done this a lot fucking sooner.' He tore open my blouse. The fabric ripped. 'Try explaining this to your toy boy, to Eric, go ahead and tell him, what I've done to you, just tell him. I'll destroy everything, mark my words. You, Eric, that whole fucking family of yours. You'll never sleep through the night again, ever.'

He tugged my bra up and looked at me pointedly as he squeezed my breasts hard. I closed my eyes, I didn't want to see him any more, I wanted to step outside myself, but the rancid whisky smell wafted over my face and I started to retch. Peter let go of my throat. Gratefully I sucked in air, but he immediately grabbed my hair and pushed my face hard against the wall. I froze when I heard the sound of a zip and tried to tear myself loose, but he pulled my head further up so that now I was barely touching the ground and hanging against the wall as if paralysed.

Peter brought his face next to mine. A hand pulled my trousers down roughly.

Tears welled up in my eyes. I tried to tell myself it wasn't real, it was a bad dream, not real. Peter had lost his head, he was disturbed, a dangerous lunatic. And there was nothing I could do.

Aren't any of the lads outside who can hear this?

'This is what you want, isn't it?' he whispered. 'Say it. Bitch. Is this what you want?'

I tried to shake my head, to say 'No', but the ball of his hand was now pressing on my larynx and his fingers were gripping my jaw and squeezing my cheeks against my back teeth. I could taste blood.

Suddenly he let go of me and pushed me away from him. I hit the ground with a bump, automatically pulled my knees up and shielded my breasts with my arms and hands.

Peter looked down at me, zipped up his trousers and sneered. 'I'll give you a week. Next Friday that hubby of yours is going to come and tell me he's going to invest. If not, I'll be back. To finish the job . . . in all sorts of enjoyable ways. The choice is yours.'

I stood under the shower for almost an hour. Wiped my body, washed it again and again, with trembling hands. Lathered myself up, checked my bruises, stood under the spray with my mouth open to wash the blood away.

I had to go and pick the children up. It was already gone four. I couldn't keep standing here. I had to make myself presentable, dry off, get dressed, go outside, put on a brave face. Throw my torn blouse away, in such a way that no one would notice. But I stood there till the boiler was empty and the cold spray drove me out of the shower cubicle. I cried silently, because I knew that Peter would carry out his threat. If Eric didn't invest, Peter would come back.

He'd pick up from where he'd left off just now, and then tell Eric everything, finally show him the photo. Peter would go to prison, but my family wouldn't come out of it intact. Peter could destroy everything. Everything. And if Eric *did* give him the money, we'd go bankrupt and be forced to move penniless into a caravan in a field.

I couldn't stop snivelling. The tears had run dry.

'I'm going shopping,' I said. 'As soon as I get back I'll cook something delicious.'

Eric looked at me in amazement. 'Aren't we going to have a nice evening out together? To celebrate the first night of our holiday? Perhaps we could go for dinner?'

Bastian looked up at Eric expectantly. 'Yes, to *McDo*!'

'No, not to McDonald's,' I heard him say. 'To a proper restaurant.'

'Oh . . .' replied Bastian. '*Boring* . . .'

I cleared my throat. It was still sore. 'I . . . actually I don't really feel like going to a restaurant.'

Eric raised his eyebrows. 'Why not?'

'I think I'm coming down with something. I feel shattered.'

'In that case, shall I go shopping with the kids? Then you can relax at home.'

'No, I've been stuck here all day. I'd like to get out for a while . . . Alone.' I could barely look Eric in the eye.

'What's wrong with you?'

'Just give me time,' I said. 'It'll pass . . . OK? It's nerves, I think. All these . . . changes.' I bit my bottom lip. 'Is there anything in particular I need to bring back?'

Eric shook his head. 'Not for me. Don't buy too much. We don't have any extra mouths to feed now, for the time being.'

'I know.'

I hear the cell door swing to behind me. I sit down on the bed, stare at the slogans on the wall and look at the small window. Raindrops are pattering against the glass. Somewhere in the distance I hear someone shouting and swearing.

What am I doing here? I don't belong here. What am I doing in France anyway? Eric's plan. Two children? Eric's plan. All the important decisions, my whole life long, have been made for me. Before I got married it was my mother who made the decisions for me. Even when I married Eric, I was basically carrying out her instructions to the letter. Eric was exactly the type of man that she had in mind for me; he was an almost perfect fit for the mould she'd cast for my potential husband. Except she didn't understand that Eric was still at the beginning of his career at that time. He had his sights set high, had his feet firmly planted on the first few rungs up the ladder, but she couldn't see it. All she could see was his earring and his student loan. Only a year before we got married did the fog lift. I can still remember vividly how her approval meant everything to me.

After we got married Eric took over the brainwork seamlessly from her. He had the ideas and I carried them out. He turned left, I followed; if he stopped, I was right beside him. If he went full speed ahead, I ran after him, stumbling in a bid to keep pace with him. Was it a lack of character? Cowardice? I don't know.

Michel was the first time I strayed from the path. I did it for myself, in the knowledge that no one, absolutely no one, would give their approval.

And look where it's got me.

50

Michel opened the door. The surprise was written all over his face. Bruno was sitting on the settee in front of the television. He looked guilty, like a child that had been caught out for something. And there was a girl. She was sitting on Michel's bed, about eighteen years old; she was gorgeous, with long dark hair and an enviably slim waist and taut skin.

'It's OK,' Michel reassured Bruno. 'Nothing fazes her . . . being Dutch.'

Only then did I understand what he was talking about. Bruno changed position and, with an apologetic grin, pulled out a flat white packet from the space between the cushion and the back of the settee, and stuffed it in his trouser pocket.

I looked at Michel's eyes. No dilated pupils.

'What do you want?' Michel seemed irritated, abrupt. Evidently the switch in his head had been flicked quite drastically. I wasn't supposed to be here; it didn't fit the picture. We'd said goodbye, and now I was going back on my word.

'I need . . . I want to talk to you.' I looked at Bruno once more. 'It's . . . it's important.'

A brief nod from Michel was sufficient to send Bruno out of the room. On his way out he chuckled and winked at me. The girl looked at me with undisguised hostility and followed him.

I quickly slipped inside. Michel closed the door. He studied me, kept looking at me, darkly, rubbed his upper arm. 'Has Eric found out?'

'No. It's about Peter . . .'

'What about Peter?'

I squeezed my eyes shut and fought back tears.

Michel took a step forwards and was about to put his arms round me, but I waved him away. I sat down on the bed and tried to think straight.

Where should I begin? With the photo Peter had taken? With the assault this afternoon? It would have been hard enough to tell him in my own language, never mind in French.

'Peter blackmailed me.' I'd already found this word in the dictionary months ago. I looked up at him. 'Remember, that party at Peter's house? How we were outside in the morning and Peter saw us?'

He nodded. His eyes flashed searchingly across my face.

I took a deep breath. 'Peter approached me afterwards. He made me give him money. Two hundred and fifty euros a week. Otherwise he'd tell Eric.'

Michel stuck his chin out and barked: '*What?*'

'He'd . . . he'd taken a photo, with his mobile phone.' I picked at the duvet. Looked at him again. 'He said he'd show it to Eric if I didn't pay up.'

'You gave him the money?'

'Every week.'

'*Putain, Simone . . . Tu déconnes!*'

'No, I'm not joking, honestly.' I cleared my throat. It still felt sore. My cheeks were cut up and swollen on the inside. You couldn't tell by looking at my face. Peter had known exactly what he was doing. 'Later he gave me all the money back. He said he was sorry. It was to do with his ex-girlfriend, who looked like me; he was jealous. He'd wanted to be you.'

Michel shot forwards and his eyes flashed over my body, as if looking for marks. 'Did he touch you?'

I put my head in my hands.

'*What*, what did he do?'

I shook my head. 'Listen, Michel, I—'

Michel grabbed hold of my face, but I hissed and pulled it away. His eyes were boring straight through me. 'What did he do?'

'Please, listen . . . Peter is working on a project, a building project, and needs money. A lot of money. Eric wanted to give it to him, but I stopped him. I don't want to get involved, because I don't think we'll get the money back.'

I kept on talking, there was no stopping me now, I poured

everything out, including how Peter had felt me up, last year, in the kitchen, and what he'd said, how scared I'd been. How lonely I'd felt when Michel was in the Basque Country, how I'd thought it had been intentional, that Michel had seduced me for the money, how this was more or less what Peter had insinuated, how he'd called him his stud – *étalon*, and had later told me he'd made this up, but that even so, Michel 'couldn't keep his dick in his trousers' and I should stay well away from him.

I fumbled for words. I muddled up verbs, *être* and *avoir*, past tense, present tense, I stumbled over the inflections and searched frenetically for nouns which usually rolled off my tongue. Michel listened carefully. Helped me find words, responded invariably with '*putain*' and stronger swear words when he understood what I was trying to say, rubbed his nose, his upper arm, paced up and down the room. I told him I suspected Peter of withholding money, because Eric had paid him every week.

I ended my muddled monologue by telling him how Peter had dropped by this afternoon, come upstairs and threatened me.

And almost raped me.

Michel snorted. He put one hand over his mouth, then ran it through his hair and let it rest on his neck, turned his back to me, looked out of the window, and then back at me again. The sinews stood out in his neck, he clenched his fists. There was a glint in his eyes that made me shudder.

Silent rage.

The next moment Bruno entered. The girl wasn't with him.

Michel started talking to Bruno, super-fast and partly in slang, I could only catch a few words. Swear words, Peter, money. Bruno was becoming increasingly worked up, as was Michel.

I grew frightened and stood up. 'I didn't want to cause you any trouble. But I didn't know what else to do. I can't get help from Eric. I'm . . . I just don't know any more.'

Bruno seemed to have completely stopped listening. He didn't even see me any more and stood there jumping up and down with adrenalin, maybe from the cocaine or whatever it was he'd taken, and was now just effing and blinding. Suddenly, without warning, Bruno dashed towards the door and shouted that he was going to see Peter to get his money. He sprinkled his intention with yet more swear words.

'You stay here,' I heard Michel say.

Bruno was already gone.

Michel rushed after Bruno. I grabbed my coat from the bed, ran after him into the corridor, and saw Michel catch up with Bruno, grasp him none too gently and start having words with him. Bruno wrenched himself away and started shouting, at me, at Michel.

Michel grasped him again and dragged him back to the room. I couldn't understand half of what he was saying to Bruno. They were talking over each other, and I stood by the door, silently, not knowing what I could do to calm Bruno down.

Michel was far from calm himself.

I had the feeling I should go, for just a moment, and leave them alone, so I went into the corridor, to the toilet. I stood there, and could hear Michel and Bruno's muffled voices as I looked in the mirror and tried not to panic.

I was scared. Bruno was in a frenzy. Michel was keeping his emotions under far better control, but he, too, was seething. I was unable to calm down and went back into the corridor, where I almost bumped into Bruno, who was hurrying downstairs. At the same time Michel emerged, locking the door behind him.

'I'm going with Bruno,' he said, dashing towards the stairwell. 'Otherwise it'll end in tears.'

I rushed after them.

'Please be careful, Peter is very dangerous,' I cried.

Michel didn't answer, but kept looking at me as he went outside and crossed the street, where Bruno started the car impatiently and revved the engine. With my arms clasped around me I watched Bruno's car head to the end of the Rue Charles de Gaulle and, just before the traffic light at the junction changed to red, turn left.

Ten minutes later I was still standing on the pavement, staring at the junction as if paralysed. Time had ceased to exist. The world, any form of reality. It was as if I was dazed, incapable of movement, as if I found myself in another dimension.

Slowly it began to dawn on me what I'd set in motion. It had been a mistake to come here. What was going to happen now?

What have I *done*?

Trembling, I walked back to my car and tried to find my car keys. As my fingers rummaged in my coat pocket, it felt strangely light and empty. I tried my other coat pocket. Empty. The keys were in the inside pocket.

But my purse was gone.

The sunlight falling through the small window of my cell tells me it's morning. It's my third day here. Last night I didn't get a wink of sleep, but just lay there listening to my own breathing.

I still feel ill and weak, but my brain is working again. I'm starting to feel calmer, resigned.

Peter has been murdered. He's dead. What happened? How? Who? The uncertainty is eating away at me. Bruno was worked up, but Michel was . . . seething.

I shouldn't have told Michel anything. I should have held my tongue. Or perhaps I should have gone with them, not let them leave without me. Then things might have been different . . .

Could I have done anything to prevent it?

I sit up with my arms around my knees and focus on the

rectangular window abutting the ceiling. The warmth from the sun can't be felt in here, but it can be seen, a long, narrow strip illuminating part of my cell and bed.

The detective questioned me about the purse – *my* purse – at length yesterday; they kept going on about it, as if it was really important. Evidence. Did they search Michel's room and find my purse there? In that case Michel must be a suspect. Do they think I assisted him? What do they know? What kind of things did they find?

If they searched Michel's room, they probably also turned Peter's house upside down. His paperwork, his computer, his mobile phone . . .

I run my fingers through my hair, which is full of knots and feels dry and brittle.

They found the photo. The photo of Michel and me. That's their link. My purse in Michel's room, a photo of Michel and me on Peter's mobile phone.

But why haven't they said anything about Michel? Anything at all? So was I mistaken in thinking I heard Michel shouting, the first night in this cell? *Dis rien . . .* Don't say anything. I could have sworn it was Michel's voice. But I don't know for sure.

I'm scared.

My life is over. I'm an accessory to murder.

Eric will find out I had an affair. Or maybe he already knows.

I'm on my own. Completely on my own.

The strange thing is, I'm not even that worried about myself. Only Isabelle and Bastian. My children, my everything, my entire world.

And Michel. My God, please, let it have been Bruno. Not Michel.

The cell door opens. I look up. A policeman I've never seen before is standing in the doorway. '*Madame Jansen?*'

I get up off the bed stiffly. Another interview? Has he come to tell me I can call a lawyer?

'You're free to go.'

I look at him in disbelief.

Eric is standing in the foyer of the police station. He runs up to me, almost knocking me over. 'Simone, what a muddle.' His voice is steeped with emotion. 'I've been trying to reach you for three days now, nobody would let me see you . . .'

He pushes me away and takes a good look at me. 'Darling, how are you? Did they treat you well?'

'Oh yes, only . . . I was so scared.'

'Come on, we're going, away from here.'

Eric holds on to me, one arm around me; he squeezes my waist, presses me against him and leads me outside. The dazzling sunlight on the sandstone walls is almost painful to the eye.

'How are the children?' I ask.

'Fine. I told them you'd gone to Holland.' He looks me straight in the eye. 'I didn't want to . . .'

'I understand. Eric . . . Did they . . . What sort of things did they ask you?'

'Who?'

'The police.'

'They came over twice, a man, what's his name . . . Philippe Guichard. One of those dark chaps, a typical Frog.'

'What did he want to know?'

Eric shakes his head as if he'd rather forget all about it. 'Everything. What I knew about Peter, how long he'd been working for us, about the payments . . .'

We've reached the car. Eric's eyes are watery, I notice now; the whites of his eyes are bloodshot and his skin looks grey. He's hardly slept. Same as me.

'Simone . . . I'm so sorry about everything I did. That business with Peter. Look where it's got us . . .'

As I look into Eric's eyes, I can see he has no idea.

None at all.

How is that possible? The photo, my purse.

I say nothing.

Eric opens the door for me and I get in. Automatically fasten my seatbelt and lay my head against the headrest.

Eric slips in next to me and looks at me. 'It's so unreal, Simone.'

I nod, but I'm not sure which part of this crazy emotional rollercoaster he's found to be surreal. 'What happened, Eric, I mean . . .'

'You don't know?'

I shake my head. 'They . . . they didn't tell me anything.'

Eric clasps his hands around the steering wheel and stares vacantly into space. 'Claudia told me that when she came home, Bruno and Michel ran past her and drove off in Bruno's car. She found Peter inside. Stone dead. She called the police and they managed to force Michel and Bruno off the road just before they reached Bordeaux. They were on their way to Spain, to the mountains . . . The poor woman. You wouldn't wish that on anyone . . . Michel beat him to death in cold blood.' He raises his hands to emphasise his words. '*Beat him to death*, Simone.'

I sit there as if paralysed and focus on my breathing.

'Bruno also took things from the house,' Eric continues. 'And they smashed stuff up. His television and DVD player, mobile phone, his computer and laptop, according to Claudia, they'd more or less torn the place apart. It was a battleground in there. When you read about that kind of thing in the newspaper you think: who on earth would *do* something like that? And I'll be damned, those lads who did it . . . I *know* them. And well. So I thought.'

I can't look at Eric. Everything is falling into place.

Mobile phone smashed up. Computer, laptop: every possible back-up.

I clench my teeth but I can't control myself; I need to know. 'How . . . how do they know Michel did it?'

'He confessed yesterday.'

I close my eyes. 'Why, Eric?' My voice sounds oddly quiet, frightened.

'Money. Did you know that Peter didn't pay those lads half the time? The invoices he made out to us don't even appear among his paperwork. None of those lads is insured; most of them just work cash in hand. Peter had debts with people in the Basque Country, criminals. It would appear this has been going on for a long time; they already had him in their sights. I'm so embarrassed, Simone. I should have listened to you when you said you had a bad feeling about him. I got carried away with everything.'

Eric puts his arms around me and kisses me gently on the forehead. 'Hopefully we'll be able to laugh about this next year. About you being banged up.' A smile on his face, which disappears instantly. 'Claudia won't be able to laugh any more. She's lost her husband.' His hand feels for my thigh. 'Darling, you've no idea how happy I am to see you again, to have you with me. I still can't get over the fact that we had a gang of criminals in the house. Peter with his fraud. It puts a different complexion on Betty's story, doesn't it? And Bruno and Michel. Especially Michel. He was such a nice lad.'

'What . . . what's happening to them now?'

Eric takes the car keys out of his pocket and puts them in the ignition. 'Michel and Bruno?'

I nod.

'They've been questioned; they've been held here at the

station, like you, and they were taken to prison this morning awaiting trial. Things aren't looking very good for them. And *rightly so*.'

'When will that be, the trial?'

Eric looks at me, frowning. Then shrugs and starts the car. 'It could be six months or so,' he says, looking in the wing mirror and turning on to the street. 'It all seems to be rather complicated. Bruno's being charged with assault and battery, vandalism, unlawful entry and theft. It's Michel who's really carrying the can. He's being charged with the same, plus manslaughter. He can expect five to eight years, according to that Guichard.'

I don't look at Eric. His words hurtle through my head like an express train. Every word hits me.

Five to eight years . . .

I swallow and rub my hands over my face.

'It could be a mitigating circumstance,' Eric continues, 'the fact that those lads got screwed over by Peter. He kept them dangling for years, it seems.'

The Volvo races through the streets. I still can't get over the fact that I'm free, really free. I can move, I can go out when I want, go home, turn the light on and off myself. Watch television. Take Bleu for a walk.

I don't have to be scared of Peter any more.

'Is that why they . . . I mean . . . How did they know . . . How did they find out that Peter was withholding money?'

'Don't you know?'

I look at him in amazement. 'No.'

Eric changes up to fourth gear. The hills are getting higher, the buildings scarcer. 'Michel called me, Friday night. I already told you when you came home, but you were feeling ill, remember? Perhaps that's why you've forgotten. He called me to ask if I'd paid Peter, and obviously I told him I had. He said that Peter had told the lads we were having money problems, and that's why he hadn't been paid.'

'Friday night?'

'Yes. Michel rang only a quarter of an hour or so before you came back from your shopping trip. It sounded to me like he was in a car.'

We're almost home. The wheels race over the tarmac. The unbelievably blue sky stands out against the green of the woods and the meadows. Beige cows are clustered under trees in the shade.

'What did they do? What did they ask you?' says Eric, all of a sudden.

'It was about my purse. I don't know why they kept going on about it, I . . . I couldn't understand it.' My breath catches in my throat. I can't say anything more. I need to hear it from Eric.

'That man, the detective,' says Eric, 'apologised at least thirty times for arresting and detaining you. They'd found your purse, right next to Peter's body, with Peter's blood on it. With Michel's jacket. That was there as well.'

I put my hands over my mouth. 'What?'

'With Michel's fingerprints,' he continues. 'And that bastard admitted during questioning that he pinched your purse, in the afternoon, on the last work day. Because he had no money. *Pinched* your purse! And then the cheek to call me that very evening. Unbelievable! The lad's been coming and going for months and then he suddenly does something like this.'

I collapse. Michel must have put my purse in his pocket. I'm almost certain that it fell out of my pocket on to his bed when I was in his room. Maybe Michel was scared I'd forget to take it with me and have to explain myself when I got home . . .

I close my eyes and see Bruno before me, raging, in his car. Michel looking at me and hurrying to the car.

He put it in his pocket and forgot all about it.

A knife stabs into my belly. It twists and it turns and it cuts and it's more painful than all the pain I've ever felt.

Michel has cleared me. Completely.

He's taken all the blame.

Epilogue

Eric and the children are swimming in the lake. Isabelle is wearing colourful Mickey Mouse armbands; Bastian is lying on a bright-pink Lilo and is squeezing the edges. They squeak. They laugh.

Eric's pretending to be a shark. Dramatically, he swims towards them, pulls scary faces, dives underwater and pushes Bastian's Lilo into the air. Bastian shrieks with pleasure.

'Are you coming in?' Eric calls to me. 'The water's lovely!'

I shake my head. 'I'm going to get something to drink.'

I turn round and start walking, up the hill.

At the highest point I stop. My eyes are met by rolling hills, like waves in an ocean, in blue, grey and violet. High above me aeroplanes are traversing the cloudless sky. Swallows nose-dive and then rise again; I hear the crickets chirping.

I take a deep breath and wrap my arms around my upper body.

It's summer.

Last year we bought this house.

This is what we came for. To burn all our bridges. A new life, in another country. It forged a bond. The kind of pact celebrated in songs.

But everything is so much more beautiful in a song, a book or a film. Magnified. The truth is seldom as extraordinary as the story would lead us to suspect. We close our eyes to everyday reality and take photos of the prettiest places we visit and the special moments in our lives, which are so rare a camera doesn't feel out of place; we show them to friends and acquaintances, hang them on the wall and paste them into albums, thereby creating our own coloured, censored history.

But there's always a parallel history. One that can't be grasped, can't be seen. Only felt.

And sometimes it's a story that can never be told. However beautiful, however dramatic, however overwhelming and intense it may have been.

Never.

As I watch Eric and the children, down there in the lake, my hands reach instinctively for my stomach. Slight rumbling, like whirling air bubbles. I know this feeling.

I'm no longer alone in this body.

> *Me gustan los aviones, me gustas tú*
> *Me gusta viajar, me gustas tú*
> *Me gusta la mañana, me gustas tú*
> *Me gusta el viento, me gustas tú*

Me gusta soñar, me gustas tú
Me gusta la mar, me gustas tú

Que voy a hacer, je ne sais pas
Que voy a hacer, je ne sais plus
Que voy a hacer, je suis perdu
Que horas son, mi corazón

Manu Chao, 'Me gustas tú'
Proxima Estacion Esperanza

Acknowledgements

During the writing process I've had to lean on a few people from time to time, especially Annelies, who provided constant support and motivation. Thanks to Thierry, for the practical solution to a tricky plot problem and for his sympathy. To Peter, for his comforting words and constructive criticism, and of course to Wanda and Renate, for their unparalleled cooperation. Many thanks also to N., who was able to describe to me in detail the inner workings of a French prison. I would also like to thank anyone I might now be forgetting for their reading and sympathy.

Last but not least, thanks to my parents, who have always supported me in my ambition to be a writer, and above all to B., who after twenty years still manages to surprise and inspire me every day.